MW01172485

RISE OF THE EAGLE

Also by J.E. Ribbey

The Last Patriots Series
American post-apocalyptic thrillers
Archangel
For You, My Dove
Rise of the Eagle
Operation Gray Owl

Young American Adventures
Middle grade historical fiction
The Innocent Rebel
Defiant Retreat
Under the Wing of the Storm
Deceptive Victory

RISE

OF THE

EAGLE

J.E. RIBBEY

Soraya Jubilee PRESS

SORAYA JUBILEE PRESS
An imprint of The Jubilee Homestead LLC,
Stanchfield, Minnesota

Copyright © 2023 Joel and Esther Ribbey

Visit the author's website at JERibbey.com
All rights reserved. No parts of this publication may be reproduced, stored in a retrieval
system, or transmitted in any form or by any means, electronic, mechanical,
photocopying, recording, or otherwise, without the prior written permission of the
copyright owner.

Printed in the United States of America

Library of Congress Control Number: 2023907876

Print ISBN: 979-8-9875823-4-3
eBook ISBN: 979-8-9875823-5-0

Editing and Cover Design by Esther Ribbey

This is a work of fiction. Any similarity between the characters and situations within its
pages and places or persons, living or dead, is unintentional and coincidental.

To our four incredible children,
whose hearts are woven into every page of these stories.

Prologue

AHHH!" shrieked Caleb, sitting bolt upright in the dark, gasping for air.

A gentle arm slipped around him, pulling him close.

"Another nightmare?" Sara asked.

"It's nothing," he hissed, removing her arm. Wiping the sweat off his forehead with the back of his hand, he climbed out of bed. "You wouldn't understand."

"Caleb, we've all been though things—seen things. If you'll just talk to me, I think it would help. I pray for you every day, that—"

"You should stop," he said coldly. "It's been ten years, if God was going to rescue me from my demons, he would've done it a long time ago. Just give it up . . . I have," Caleb replied, pulling on a t-shirt. "The God you believe in doesn't exist, and if He does, He isn't interested in me."

"Caleb, we don't always understand—"

"Save it, Mom!" he said. Buckling his pistol belt, he stormed out of the room.

Tromping down the stairs, he moved through the kitchen and out the back door. The night air felt fresh in his lungs. How could she possibly understand what he'd been through? An eleven-year-old kid, abandoned by his family, tortured daily by a Chinese narcissist who only found pleasure in pain, only to have his best friend killed in a botched rescue attempt that had taken his family painful weeks to plan. All while God looked on and did nothing. No, if the nightmare was to end and his demons silenced, he'd have to kill Li. Only then would he find peace.

His brother, Aaron's, infuriatingly slow planning only added to his anxiety. Since the Americans came together nine years ago, first taking the port city of Duluth before pushing the Chinese south, Caleb had only picked up bits and pieces of intel on Li's whereabouts. The captain, now a major, was always one step ahead of them.

Years of training had molded Caleb into the best. He lived for the next fight. He was cold, fearless, driven. He'd proven himself in countless battles, earning him a reputation. He was a terror, his unorthodox fighting methods were renowned by fighters on both sides of the conflict, but it was never enough.

Currently, they were tied up in Tennessee, continuing the slow push south. Everything to the northeast had been liberated over the last decade. No one knew how things fared on the other side of the Mississippi; rumor had it the Americans in the southwest were giving the Russians a good go of it, though no one knew for sure.

The truth is, the Americans would probably have wiped themselves out in the civil war if the Chinese and Russians hadn't shown up. Caleb was so young when it started, he couldn't even remember what they'd been fighting about. He could only remember losing his father when the Chinese attacked their farm, and then being taken captive. Everything after that was war.

Chapter 1

*Some sicknesses can be isolated, controlled, cured. Others must
be cut out. A sacrifice of the lesser for the sake of the greater.
But when the sickness lies in the heart, in the soul, the result of
an unhealable wound, the cure, like the sickness, is often found
in the places the eye cannot see and the mind fails to comprehend.*

Feeding rounds into his pistol magazine, Caleb brooded over
the mission ahead. His older brother had spent the better part
of a week preparing the American troops to hit the airfield outside
Jackson, Tennessee prior to their assault on Jackson itself. He
hated planning. He and his team could take that airfield in less
than an hour on any given day, but would Aaron give them a
chance? No. In fact, his team had been grounded due to "rogue
activities" a few nights earlier when they dismantled a checkpoint
with "unnecessary brutality."

His team, made up of guys he selected himself, was the most
proficient Chinese killing machine east of the Mississippi, possibly
the entire country. They were all skilled fighters, men who had
nothing to lose, no moral code when it came to the Chinese, men
who lived for the hunt. They were better in every way than the
Chinese parasites infesting their land. And he would prove it if he
had to wipe out every last one.

He'd trained for a decade with every skilled fighter they'd come across. He could best anyone in hand-to-hand combat, knives, and pistols. He could clear a room by himself better than most teams. He was surgical. The battlefield was his clay, and he could shape it any way he saw fit. He understood his enemy, not just their tactics, he understood their minds, their fears, the way they clung to life. He exploited their weaknesses, took them apart, then moved to the next. In every battle he sought a competitor, someone who could challenge him, and every battle was a disappointment.

He'd come to hate everyone: Chinese and American. They were all cowards, weak, unable to do what needed to be done. Fear halted the American advance, the incessant need for plans that negated all sacrifice. It betrayed them, emboldened their enemies, cheated their momentum. They quibbled over what to do with the squatters rather than treating them like any other enemy. There were no Chinese civilians.

"I hear we're sitting this one out," Darrian said from behind him.

"That's our orders," Caleb said.

"But . . ." Darrian prompted.

Caleb turned from a small desk strewn with pistol rounds and magazines and smirked. "But I'm done taking his orders."

"So, we're not sitting this one out?"

Sighing, Caleb finished loading the magazine he was holding. "The team is. I'm not getting you hemmed up on my account, but there's no way I'm sitting this one out."

"And what happens to us if you get hemmed up?" Darrian asked, folding his arms across his chest.

"I'm the Eagle. Not much Aaron can do about it."

"Maybe you should just listen this time, and then we can—"

"We can what?" Caleb interrupted. "We'll never catch up to Li at this rate. They're retreating, eventually they'll give up. When they do, they'll all go home, and if that happens before I get a chance to settle the score with that peacock of a Chinese animal, he'll be gone! If you want out, then get out now. I'm going to take that entire airfield by myself tomorrow."

"Alright, man, if that is the way you see it. I'll tell the team to stand down and let you handle this one on your own. We'll be ready if you need us," Darrian offered.

"Good. Load up but keep it quiet," Caleb said.

At the door, Darrian gave a short nod to a tall, bearded man before he disappeared down the hall.

"What are you up to, little brother?" Seth asked, walking over to the desk.

"Oh, you know, preparing to stand down tomorrow while you guys take the airfield," Caleb replied, turning away and grabbing another magazine.

"You have a funny way of standing down," Seth said. Picking up one of the empty magazines, he began filling it with rounds.

"You and I both know my team could have taken that airfield a week ago," Caleb said.

"Maybe, but probably not without alerting the rest of the PLA or getting some of your guys torn up."

"There's no 'maybe' about it. And my team may get torn up, but that's because we do most of the tearing up," Caleb replied. "We've excepted the cost of war."

"Caleb," Seth tried to reason. "Aaron has led us to more victories than anyone could have imagined ten years ago. If the entire army fought like your team, there wouldn't be enough of us left to mount any sort of resistance. Your team is the best, hands down, and it has its purpose, but so does Aaron."

"You're just like him," Caleb scoffed, "Afraid to get your hands dirty."

"You don't really believe that," Seth sighed. "We've all got jobs to do, and Aaron's is the hardest of all."

Rolling his eyes, Caleb jammed in another round.

"You only have to worry about your team and yourself. Aaron worries about all the teams, about all of us. You only worry about the next mission. Aaron has to see how each mission fits into our goals for the war. You only worry about the enemies in front of you, Aaron has to worry about all of them," Seth tried again.

"There wouldn't be so many to worry about if he'd just quit grounding my team!" Caleb fumed.

"What you're talking about is mutiny, and if we're divided, the Chinese will get the upper hand again. He can't afford that, not even for you," Seth replied.

"Is that why you left me in that camp for so long? Was I in the way of the 'greater plan'?"

"Caleb, that was ten years ago! We got you out as soon as we could. We were all just kids back then, and we did get you back."

"You killed Sam! We had a plan, we were going to escape, and you showed up and got him killed. Does Aaron count that loss?!"

"He counts them all . . ." Seth said quietly, setting down the loaded magazine.

Patting Caleb on the back, he turned and left the room.

Double checking Seth's magazine, Caleb slid it into his gun belt. Sitting down on the bed, he looked around the room. The house the Reddings were set up in had once been occupied by squatters who fled the American advance. The room was painted pale pink with white trim around the windows. Two pink pillows lay on a wrinkled pink comforter covering the twin sized bed. He hadn't considered its color when he chose it. He liked the view from the second story windows, and it was the most isolated room in the house.

The rest of the army was spread out throughout the town. Out his window, Caleb saw troops moving around. Everywhere they went, every battle they won, they added to their numbers. First, they were merely squads, then platoons, then companies, and now entire battalions. His brother Aaron and a few other strategists had been more or less elected to command, while those who had experience and leadership abilities were placed where needed. There were thousands of them now.

They had captured vehicles, armor, artillery, radio communications, body armor, night vision, medical supplies, and more from the Chinese. Any instructions or controls were translated by his brother-in-law, Wu, and other Chinese defectors who had joined the American resistance. A few years ago, the Canadians had finally offered their air support as the Americans began to gain the upper hand. The Chinese were now being squeezed between the American advance and the southern coast.

The fighting was getting more and more desperate. The Chinese empire wasn't ready to face the shame of losing their half of the US on the world stage. Caleb could feel the tension. The more they fought to hold on, the more pleasure it gave him to take it away. In the end, he'd make sure they all knew the helplessness he'd felt, they would all know shame, they would all die for nothing. Just like Sam.

Below him, Aaron had gathered with all the team leaders to go over the airfield mission. Sliding his window open a crack, Caleb leaned in to listen.

"Command will be Blue Team. Red Team will make the main assault, with Blue providing flanking support. I'll be going in on this one. Our main objective is to disable the airfield and any aircraft present at the time of the assault. Our secondary objective is to retrieve any intelligence we can find that will give us an edge when taking Jackson.

"Blue Team sniper, Red Team sniper, and Archangel will head out at 0400 and take up positions here, here, and here," he said, pointing to three points overlooking the airfield on his tablet. "You will provide overwatch for your individual teams but take orders from Archangel.

"Red Team, you will set up here in this ditch about two hundred yards east of the wire and wait for the sun to break the horizon behind you, then you go. Blue Team will move into position on the northwest corner and wait for you to engage before moving in and flanking the airfield. We'll meet at the traffic control tower in the middle. Remember, all teams stay in communication and follow orders, we don't want to lose anyone on account of friendly fire.

"We'll have the Canadians on the line for air support, but it'd be better if we didn't need them. So, let's pull this off quick and quiet, and get out of there. Taking out this airfield will save a lot of lives when we hit Jackson. Any questions?" Aaron concluded.

Carefully sliding his window closed, Caleb checked his watch. Snipers are heading out at 0400. He'd need to be in position before then. Pulling out his notebook, he scratched out a rough drawing of the airfield, marking the positions of the teams and snipers. The direction both sides would least expect him from was the south. It was further behind enemy lines, near the barracks, and had very little cover. All the more reason to go alone. The most important thing was to get to that traffic control tower first. Satisfied, he set the notebook down. No more planning necessary. Now the waiting part.

By 0330 the following morning, Caleb was already in position. His charcoal ripstop pants were black with dew from crawling the last hundred yards. Pulling off his shooting gloves, he hung them on a barbed wire fence to dry and leaned against the steep bank of a drainage ditch. Gazing through the tall grass at the top, he had a clear view of his target. Crickets chirped from a nearby rotting stump; a small stream of water rippled near his feet. His Harley Davidson jacket was a bit overkill in the mild air, but he loved the effect it had on the PLA.

Checking his watch, he sighed. A little over two hours until sunrise. Someone was sure to notice his absence before the mission kicked off, but Aaron would have no choice, the show must go on. He watched the PLA under the intense lighting of the airfield. Two pairs of soldiers patrolled the perimeter opposite each other. The guards in the towers chatted quietly, pausing occasionally to scan the darkness beyond them before returning to their conversations. A few civilians sat huddled in an open bay under the glow of security lights, probably squatter refugees fleeing the American advance.

The airfield was only five miles behind the front lines, a few miles outside of Jackson. The main airbase for the area was in Memphis, where most of the aircraft had already retreated to, but this airfield would become a vital refueling station during the battle for Jackson. After the Americans took it, the PLA would be forced to return to Memphis to refuel, costing them vital airtime.

It was a dance; taking the advantage from the enemy and gaining it for yourself. And the side with the most advantages wins. Most of their battles were won before they began, it was only a matter of time and lives before the inevitable became reality. Caleb knew Aaron was key to their successes, but he took all the fun out of it. Caleb fed on the competition, the challenge, he preferred to play his battle of wits face to face.

Grinning in the darkness, he imagined Aaron's face when he raided the traffic control tower and found Caleb waiting inside. If he ran into any trouble, his mom would have his back, no one was a better shot than Sara. Sure, she'd give him a severe tongue lashing, but in the end, he was still her baby.

As the morning crept ever closer, the darkness slowly gave way to gray, transitioning to pinks and oranges. Tensing in the ditch, Caleb waited for the opening shot. His toes pawed the damp ground in anticipation. The crickets in the stump grew quiet. He eyed his first targets, one of the patrol teams deep in conversation strolling past him on the other side of the fence. He could feel it, the hunger, the lust for the conflict ahead, it beckoned him. Fire spread through him, awakening all his senses, bringing him to life. It was intoxicating.

A beam of sunlight shot across the airfield, a rifle sounded, a lone Eagle rose from the ditch, guns drawn.

Chapter 2

I've got eyes on Red Two Six. He just entered the compound; may God have mercy on their souls. Red One Six out."

"Aaron, sounds like your brother decided to take matters into his own hands . . . again. Get in there before he gets himself killed. I'll cover you. Archangel out!"

Chambering a round, Sara began engaging targets from her nest on the hillside. Her radio crackled with chatter from the pine needles beside her.

"Archangel, this is Angel One. Caleb just exited the first barracks and appears to be moving to the second. Blue Team is through the wire and is currently stacked against the HQ. Angel One out."

"Red Two Six, this is Blue Six. What do you think you're doing? Over!"

Silence.

"Caleb!"

"It's no use, Aaron! Push on! Archangel out."

Sweeping into the small hanger, Aaron's team cleared two bays of hostiles and converged on the small air traffic control tower. With a grunt, Aaron's heavy gunner dropped to his knees, holding his arm. Aaron immediately heard Angel One's rifle and a PLA sniper fell from a catwalk to the south. Three shots rang out inside the tower followed by the echoing of boots coming down the service stairway. Aaron motioned to his team, holding up three fingers, then two. Kicking in the door, he held his rifle on a lone American in a Harley jacket, grinning with satisfaction.

"You're late . . ."

"What did you think you were doing out there?!" Aaron shouted, slamming Caleb up against the wall.

"Liberating the country, big brother," Caleb answered coldly.

"This isn't a game, Caleb. People's lives are on the line, we have a responsibility to each other! You could've been killed, possibly by one of us! Follow orders or stay out of the fight." Aaron pushed away in frustration.

"Me, get killed? I came out of this better than Schmidt there." Caleb straightened his jacket with a shrug of his shoulders.

"We had to rush because of your stupidity. That's my point: you put everyone at risk!"

"You may fear the Chinese, Aaron, but the Chinese fear me!"

"Give me a break!"

"That last officer I clipped just kept saying 'Ying' over and over. It means Eagle."

"I know what it means," Aaron chuffed. "Can't you see this vengeance thing is going too far. It's been ten years since they killed Dad, he'd never have wanted this."

"I'm not doing it for Dad."

"Blue Six, this is Archangel. Better sabotage those birds and get out of there, trouble is sure to be on its way, Archangel out."

"Is it true you're pulling the Eagle out of the field, Aaron?"

"I have to, Darrian. He won't follow orders and that's dangerous. And don't call him 'the Eagle.' He's not a hero."

"Apparently not to you," Caleb said from the doorway. "In case you missed it, I just took out half that airstrip on my own with only these." He held up his twin Chinese QSZ-92 pistols.

"You're forgetting all the guys mom dropped trying to make sure her youngest son didn't get himself killed!"

"With respect, Aaron, this family spat could go on all night. All I know is I'm not going out there without Caleb, he's my team leader and the best we have," Darrian said, leaving the room without waiting for a reply.

Caleb smirked.

"I'm not changing my mind, Caleb. You've got to stop believing you're above everything and choose to be part of it. We're a team, a family. We work together."

"You're not my dad, Aaron."

"Maybe not, but I do outrank you."

"Says you! No one gave you that rank but yourself. Apparently not everyone feels you're the 'best we have.'"

"I may not be the best fighter, but I'm the best at keeping our people from getting killed," Aaron fired back.

"Tell that to Sam!" Caleb shouted, stepping further into the room, fists clenched.

"It always comes back to that." Aaron waved his arm in exasperation. "Why couldn't you have just jumped off that train like the rest of us!"

Without warning, Caleb thew a solid right hook, knocking his brother against the wall. Aaron threw his arms up in defense as Caleb pressed forward. With a swift swing, he knocked Caleb off balance and tackled him to the ground. Aaron fought to hold Caleb's arms to his sides as his brother writhed under him. Grunting, they rolled across the floor, each fighting for control.

"Boys!" Sara yelled, rushing into the room.

The struggle stopped and they slowly got to their feet, never taking their eyes off each other.

"You're not going back out there, Caleb, and that's final!" Aaron said, spitting blood on the floor.

"Then I'll go on my own," Caleb muttered. Shoving Aaron aside, he stormed out.

Without looking at Sara, Aaron retreated through the back door and sat on the step. He needed air. He'd been leading missions for ten years now, organizing, planning, managing, and strategizing. Their victories far outweighed their losses, though the losses were always difficult to bear. No one questioned him. No one except Caleb. After their dad was killed, Aaron had thought rescuing his little brother would be the most difficult test he would ever have to endure, now it was clear the most difficult test would be Caleb himself.

It was true that Caleb was the best combat fighter they had, he'd spent every waking minute of the last several years training with anyone who would teach him: ex-military, MMA fighters, wrestlers. Seth was a close second, but ten times the team player. Caleb preferred to write his own script and had made a name for himself doing it. Thanks to today's performance, Aaron had a potential mutiny on his hands.

He shook his head. This is the thanks I get for getting you out of that place . . .

"Aaron?"

"Over here," Aaron mumbled.

"Well, I just had a talk with Caleb," Sara said, joining him on the step. "He informed me that you are an egomaniacal control freak who doesn't appreciate his talents and so he's going to win this war on his own."

"He said that?" Aaron scoffed, tearing the blade of grass in his fingers and throwing the pieces to the side.

"More or less."

"I did what I had to do, Mom. He's going to get somebody killed."

"I didn't come here to challenge you, Aaron. After I talked to Caleb, I knew you would be harder on yourself than he was."

"He blames me for everything; for Dad, Sam, for taking so long to get him out. I know that's why he does it, why he takes on every fight by himself in total disregard for his life or anyone else's.

Just to prove it could be done faster or better. He's doing it to punish me . . ." Aaron said, hanging his head.

Sara turned towards him and gently raised his chin. "He may believe that, but his belief will never make it true."

"Do you think he's serious about taking off?"

"I don't know. Sometimes I like to think he's still the same little boy he was before they took him, but that's just a mother's wishful thinking. We rescued his body, but his heart is still lost. Grief, pain, and hate are his captors now and they have more sway than I do. All we can do is wait and see. And pray. God won't give up on him, Aaron, don't you."

Squeezing his hand gently, Sara left him to himself.

Chapter 3

Caleb woke early. In truth, he'd hardly slept. His mind seethed over Aaron's rebuke. Vengeance? What about justice? Didn't any of them want to see Li pay for what he'd done to him, to all of them? Every battle since they'd taken Duluth had been a bitter disappointment. The only information he had gleaned on Major Li was his promotion and transfer further south. How much further remained a mystery.

If the rumors were true, the Russians were struggling in the western states and even European nations had finally tired of China and Russia's bullying and declared war in Europe and Asia. While the rest of the militia rejoiced at these reports, Caleb's desperation only deepened. If Major Li was transferred back to China, Caleb's chance at justice would disappear with him. His mind was made up, it was time for the Eagle to fly the coop.

Strapping on his plate carrier, Caleb looked over his gear. One assault pack filled with essentials, his pistols, extra magazines, and boots. It was enough. He threw on his leather Harley jacket and instinctively reached for his radio before thinking better of it. No radio, no strings. He crept down the stairs and out the back door in his socks. If he woke Aaron, he would wake Sara and the whole thing would be off.

The door creaked behind him as he slid on his boots. Busted. Caleb froze, bracing himself for the berating he was about to receive. Straightening slowly, he turned.

"Can't let you wander off on your own, somebody's got to watch your back," Darrian said, grinning. His loaded pack and sniper rifle hung over his shoulder.

Caleb growled as he grabbed his other boot, "You nearly gave me a heart attack!"

"Everybody knows the Eagle is only as good as the angel on his shoulder."

"Well, if that's true, I'd better wake my mom," Caleb jested.

"Ouch. She may be a slightly better shot, but I don't have any qualms when it comes to the squatters. If we leave the weeds, they'll just grow back. Aaron's too soft, they're living in our homes for Pete's sake," Darrian said, throwing out his arm.

"You all set, then?" Caleb asked, finishing with his boots.

"Good to go."

"Leave your radio, we're going dark."

Smirking, Darrian set his radio on the step. "You really are moving out of your parent's basement."

Rolling his eyes, Caleb shouldered his pack and set off down the road towards the south end of town. They'd soon encounter a squad of Americans on the last leg of their night watch once they reached the southern edge of their perimeter. At first, he'd worried about coming up with an excuse for leaving, but then again, he was the Eagle. Who was going to stop him?

"Halt!"

Caleb and Darrian stopped as an armed guard materialized from a dilapidated home. They'd arrived at the outskirts of town.

"Where are you headed so early in the morning, Caleb?"

Caleb's heart sank as he recognized the voice, it could only be his sister-in-law.

"Soraya?" He cringed.

She approached him with her QBZ-95 slung over her shoulder. "Does Aaron know you're moving out?"

"No." Caleb scowled. "And I'd like to keep it that way."

"You know I can't do that. Fortunately for you, he had a hunch you were serious this time and gave orders to let you pass."

"He what?" Caleb reeled in disbelief.

"He doesn't want to fight you, Caleb, he just wants you to be happy. No one is forced to fight with us, not even you. It's no accident I'm on guard. If you left, he wanted you to know he loves you and he's sorry for all the disappointments. He knew you wouldn't hear it from him, so he asked me."

Running his hand over his shaggy hair, Caleb sighed and then looked at her. This scenario was not amongst those he had rehearsed in his mind during the long night. His emotions ran from cold to hot and back again.

"Are we leaving or what?" Darrian muttered from behind him.

He glanced quickly over his shoulder then back to Soraya. Finally, he nodded. "We're leaving."

Caleb trudged past Soraya. She'd become more than his sister-in-law; she was his friend. The compassion on her face shook his resolve but he couldn't turn back now. There were too many questions that needed answering, he had to find Major Li, and deep down he knew he needed to find himself.

Their company had spent the night in Humboldt and would push on with the rest of the battalion to initiate the battle for Jackson in the morning. Every city was a battle and, though he hated to admit it, Aaron's meticulous planning, while painfully slow, had kept the American casualties to a minimum. Caleb knew Li was too high profile to leave in the direct path of the American tsunami. To catch him, Caleb would have to beat the wave as well.

Darrian was a seasoned vet. Ten years Caleb's senior, he had been with the Reddings since they first arrived in Elysium, their original hideout in northern Minnesota. He had the instincts of a wolf, able to feel danger as much as he could see or hear it. Darrian had been Caleb's overwatch since he joined the fray, and next to Sara, was the most dangerous American Caleb knew.

Caleb and Darrian pushed hard all morning circumnavigating Jackson. Caleb knew Li was further south and, for his part, this city was a waste of time. The areas surrounding the city were all but deserted. It seemed most of the outlying Chinese had been pulled into Jackson to defend against the Americans. The lack of resistance allowed Caleb and Darrian to make good time, by half past noon they were already south of the city.

Huffing from their rapid pace, Caleb prepared to sprint across another abandoned corn field. "I'm glad you volunteered to join me."

"You're the closest thing I have to family, brother. I've got no wife or kids. Looking out for you is the only thing I've ever been good at," Darrian replied.

"Let's hope we don't break that streak," Caleb said, exploding into a sprint towards the overgrown fence line on the far side of the field.

The feeling was intoxicating. Adrenaline heightened all his senses, his nerves spread beyond him, into the environment itself. He could feel its pulse. Fear and ferocity. The sum of predator and prey all at once. He lived for it. More than a rush, it was an awakening. Mission after mission his need for it had grown. An unsatisfiable hunger to settle the score for Sam, for his father, for his innocence.

Dropping to a knee as he hit the fence, a feeling of disappointment mingled with relief washed over him. Surely there had to be a few Chinese soldiers maintaining strategic positions, intent on slowing the already crawling American advance. Peering through the fence, Caleb scanned the next field and the farmstead beyond.

A familiar hum buzzed over his head and sent up a spray of dirt only feet behind him. There it was, his faithful friend. Adrenaline surged again into his bloodstream; the game was on.

Looking back to where Darrian was positioned, he signaled contact from the direction of the farmstead. Darrian signed back as another round ripped through the dry grass just above Caleb's head. He lived for this, the struggle, life and death. It was as simple as that.

It was the ultimate high stakes game and Caleb was all in. Where there should have been fear and caution, there was only fury.

I am a storm.

He signaled to Darrian to be ready, then, gathering his legs beneath him, he tensed all his muscles. Three, two, one. . . . Springing over the fence, he drew his pistols and raced towards the old farmhouse. Dirt flew behind him with each stride as he poured round after round into the house.

The report of Darrian's rifle brought a smile to his face as he dove behind the septic mound. He caught his breath for a moment before bursting over the mound firing even more rounds blindly into the house as he ran for an abandoned tractor at the edge of the yard. A lone rifle returned fire from an upper window, a few rounds even clinked off the tractor, but Caleb knew that the battle was already over. The enemy fire went silent and a moment later, the final report of Darrian's rifle concluded their victory.

Caleb signaled for Darrian to join him and together they cleared the remaining buildings. The sniper and his spotter were the only Chinese assigned to this position. Searching the soldiers turned up nothing of significance. Caleb grabbed a few more magazines for his pistols and a couple of field rations.

"His wife is hot!" exclaimed Darrian, holding a family photo from one of the dead soldiers. "Too bad." He tossed the picture on the floor and walked out of the house.

Caleb studied the fallen photo. A smiling young woman sat on a bench with two small girls in school uniforms leaning against her. As he turned away to follow Darrian, something halted him.

He wasn't sure why, but he picked up the photo and tucked it back into the soldier's pocket. "You should've never left home."

"You freak me out when you do that," said Darrian, as Caleb joined him outside.

"Do what?"

"Leave your position and go running straight at them."

"I've got you looking out for me."

"No one's one hundred percent. Do you wanna die?"

Caleb sighed, "Some days I do. The fight is the only thing left that makes me feel alive. It's the only time I feel anything."

"What are you gonna do after we catch him?"

Caleb sighed again, "Who knows, maybe we'll just finish each other off and that'll be the end of it."

"Wow, man, you need to find a hobby or something."

"Who has time for a hobby?" Caleb said, picking up his pack. "Let's get going, I'd like to see if we can make Henderson by dark."

The terrain flanking the highway that led to Henderson was rugged and wooded. The team fought their way up sharp hills and down steep valleys. Caleb pressed on relentlessly with Darrian fighting to keep up. They would have walked right down the highway if it wasn't for the military traffic running to and from Jackson.

"Looks like your brother's gonna have his hands full," panted Darrian when they paused just long enough for a few gulps from their canteens.

"It won't matter, Aaron and the rest of them will outsmart them one way or another, even if it takes them a month," replied Caleb. "You good?"

Darrian's expression was less than convincing, but he nodded anyway. Caleb smirked and tore off down another ravine.

By nightfall, the two were sitting atop a hill overlooking Henderson. They watched for an hour as light, but constant, traffic trickled north to shore up Jackson. Caleb wanted to move on and just leave it be, but he knew his family could use every edge they could get. He just needed to get Darrian on board.

"I see a handful of Americans loading trucks at what looks like a motor pool," Darrian said, glassing the town through his scope. "Most of the Chinese seem to be either on guard towers or working that supply line to Jackson that's crawling through town."

"Maybe we could recruit a couple of those prisoners, if we can get to them."

"You wanna go in there?" Darrian balked, then rolled his eyes. "Of course you do."

Studying the town, Caleb noticed it wasn't overly fortified. They'd been in plenty worse. There was a fence topped with concertina wire, a variety of concrete obstacles choking the main roads with less significant roads blocked completely. Guard towers dotted the perimeter every hundred yards or so, with a pair of light armored vehicles patrolling just outside the wire. The real hurdle was the several hundred soldiers in full battle rattle, many of them in vehicles headed north, with many more in support on the ground.

"I don't know, man. That's a lot of trouble. These guys aren't sleeping soundly in the barracks, they're armed and ready to go," Darrian argued.

"We'll burn it," Caleb said, still studying the town. "We'll burn the whole thing down. The wind is from the south. If we can get enough houses lit, the fire will travel north towards the convoy. The Chinese will have to react and try to put it out or they'll lose everything. In the confusion, I'll see if I can get to the prisoners. If I can't, at least we slowed them down a bit."

"Ok, I smell what you're stepping in," Darrian said, swinging his scope to the guard towers on the south side of the compound. "The guards in the towers are spending more time looking at the convoy than the perimeter, shouldn't be too difficult to slip past them, just watch out for that armored patrol."

Together, they drew up a plan. Caleb would set several houses on fire one block in from the perimeter while Darrian provided overwatch. When Caleb finished and gave the signal, Darrian would cause a distraction which would hopefully create an opportunity for Caleb to get to the prisoners and, if nothing went horribly wrong, get them out.

"We can't possibly take them all," Darrian said.

"I know. Most of them would be better to stay with the Chinese until the rest of the Americans get here anyway. But if we could pick up a couple capable guys, it couldn't hurt."

"They'll need gear."

"We'll get it on the way, there's bound to be a few check points not far from here," Caleb concluded, dropping his assault pack. "You've got to make them think the whole of the American army is knocking on their door. Once they've bought your distraction, move to the rendezvous point and I'll meet you there with whoever I can dig up."

"And if they're no good to us?"

"We'll cut 'em loose," Caleb answered. "I'm all set, give me your lighter, just in case."

Taking the lighter, Caleb gave Darrian a fist bump and was gone, disappearing in the darkness down the hillside.

Chapter 4

Caleb hunched patiently at the edge of the trees. Thirty yards of open ground and the patrol road lay between him and the perimeter of Henderson. He chose a spot between two guard towers; when he hit the fence, they would be fifty yards on either side of him. The armored patrol took roughly twenty minutes to make a full round, more than enough time. The night air was filled with the sound of diesel engines, creaky suspension, and barked orders. Nothing to it.

Feeling for the oversized wire cutters at his hip, he exhaled slowly. The armored patrol vehicle rolled past, he waited for it to round the corner. Springing from the tree line, Caleb sprinted to the fence, and in seconds, was cutting his way through. This is where the bulk of the large cutters made up for its weight; the wire put up little resistance.

Once inside, Caleb ran to a stack of pallets between two houses and paused, setting up the next phase. In the darkness, he took in everything; every sound, every sight, every smell, his mind calculating odds, mulling over options, overcoming obstacles. All his senses were on fire, he felt alive again. The streets were deserted except for the main highway. All he needed to do was advance one block further into town and start setting houses on fire.

The evening was repressively warm and humid for May, or at least it felt that way under the circumstances. Sweat dripped off Caleb's nose as he prepared to sprint to the shadowy entryway of an abandoned home thirty feet away. In a series of quick bursts, he darted to the single-story home that would be the first of his victims that night. Grabbing the doorknob as he took one last glance behind him, he twisted. Locked.

Crap!

Circling to the side, he found smashed out windows from looters. Bingo. Inside, the house was musty, rodents and critters had left their sign everywhere. The floor sagged under his weight. Considering the termite damage, it was impressive the home was still standing. He found a shredded queen-sized bed and lit the edge of it on fire. He had long since learned mattresses burn amazingly well once you get them going.

The timer had started; he had to hit several more houses before the first was discovered. Jumping out the window, he jogged to the next house, always keeping to the shadows. Immediately, he realized this home had a worse infestation. Squatters. Signs of the Chinese citizens imported to colonize the U.S. were everywhere: the out of place well-kept yard, a few children's toys, and the house was in pretty good shape given the last ten years. This was not part of the plan. He loathed them. If it weren't for the mission, he would have driven them from the house at the very least, but tonight they would get a pass. If he was successful, the whole city would burn anyway.

Spitting on the house, he trotted to the next. He was running out of time. This house was vacant, the door hung ajar from a single hinge, the rotting ranch-style porch was missing its steps and had more gaping holes than boards. The trick to this house would be getting inside.

Caleb ducked under the porch to where a hole in the deck opened in front of the door. Placing his palms on the threshold, he vaulted into the house. This house resembled the first in many ways, the smells and decay, but there was something extra, a more potent smell . . . death.

He had been around death for as long as he could remember, but he never felt comfortable spending time with it, especially when he had no idea where it was exactly. With an involuntary shudder, he moved to the bedroom. The door creaked as it swung open. Instantly, the full force of the putrid odor hit him like a wave, and his stomach revolted. The corpse of a uniformed Chinese soldier hung from an exposed beam, a bedsheet around his neck. He slammed the door without thinking. Spinning away, he gasped for air. Stumbling over to a rat-infested sofa, he held the lighter to the fabric until it ignited and leapt out the door, still heaving.

He was out of time. Scrambling out from under the deck, he ran to the next house. Why don't things ever go according to plan?! Without hesitation, he kicked in the door and set both the couch and a bed on fire. Dashing back outside, he looked down the street. Sure enough, he could see leaping orange flames in the windows of the first house. It would only be a matter of minutes before clouds of smoke erupted form the home signaling to all the Chinese that they were under attack.

He jogged to the end of the block. Finding the place where he was to signal Darrian, he waved his arms three times and then ducked into the shadows. A sharp muzzle flash from the hillside confirmed the message's receipt. A moment later, the deafening wail of a siren reverberated throughout the compound, and the place erupted in gunfire. The dashed strings of tracer rounds lit up the night as the Chinese probed the surrounding hillsides for enemies.

Suddenly the flames in the first house breached the walls, sending the fire's glow into the night. The brilliant show of fire superiority was reduced to chaos as the soldiers bought the lie: the Americans were inside the wire.

Caleb grinned as he waited patiently for his chance to rendezvous with the American prisoners. Fear and chaos were his favorite weapons. As long as the threat was outside the perimeter, everyone felt safe and could follow their training. Once the threat was inside . . . well, fear is a difficult beast to control. As the next house erupted, it was clear the Chinese were reeling. Lights from the guard towers swung wildly from the fence to the hillsides, to the burning houses, and back again.

As the first squads of soldiers began clearing houses near the first engulfed home, Caleb moved one block further north. Then he cut sideways through several yards, arriving at the edge of the city park where they had dug the mortar pits. On the other side of the pits was the motor pool. The prisoners were all lying face down on the ground guarded by two soldiers near the far side of the park, pushing sixty yards from his position. The mortarmen were busily laying down a continuous barrage of fire from all three tubes onto the hillside Darrian had just been shooting from. Everyone's eyes were fixed on the show to the south.

Caleb did the math: nine mortarmen plus a sergeant and the two guards, twelve. The mortarmen weren't carrying their weapons, and the sergeant only had the side arm at his hip within reach as far as he could tell. The two guards, while distracted, were holding QBZ-95's at the low ready. Noise wouldn't be an issue, no one would know the difference in the current din. He was good, and fast. Clearing the mortar pit would be easy. Plus, he was sure Darrian would appreciate a respite. The two guards were the real threat, how to take them out before they got him, without hitting a prisoner?

Now he wished he had a radio, or a rifle for that matter. Looks like it's going to be the ol' straight at 'em surprise technique again. While this was his signature move, it was usually the result of impatience and a general lack of planning that forced him to adopt it so often. His body bore the scars of more than one close call. He gave his options one more go around before gritting his teeth and accepting he had no other options. Darrian couldn't hold out forever.

Three, two, one . . . release the monster. Flying from his cover, Caleb sprinted towards the pits. He held his fire until he was at point blank range. The mortarmen in the first pit never saw him coming, the others didn't even have a chance to yell. He dropped the sergeant and dove into the third pit, its lifeless occupants lay next to the tube, one still gripping an unused mortar round. Sand rained down on him as the two guards opened up on the pits. Holstering his pistols, he picked up one of the QBZ-95's leaning against the pit wall and charged it.

Please be dialed in . . .

He switched on the red dot and waited. There was a break in the suppressive fire as the guards reloaded, it was an unfortunate error on their part. Popping up from the hole, Caleb picked his targets and fired. Breathing a sigh of relief, Caleb looked down at the men laying at his feet. The rifle was zeroed enough to do the job.

"Thank you," he said genuinely.

There was no time to take it all in, there never was. The PLA would soon realize the mortar tubes were quiet. Hopping out of the pit, he dashed over to the prisoners. Several of them were already sitting up, eyeing him with confused apprehension as he approached.

"It's alright, I'm an American," he said.

"Is this a rescue?" an older man asked.

"Not exactly, my partner and I are, umm, an advance party. The rest of the Americans are battling up in Jackson right now, but they're working this way."

"You *are* here to save us though, right?" asked the man again.

The rest of the prisoners leaned in to hear his response over the ruckus of gunfire still searching for Darrian.

"We can't take all of you now, we'd be hunted down for sure. We could use a couple of guys willing and able to fight to join us as we keep pushing south. The rest of you have a better chance of surviving if you endure the Chinese for a little while longer and get liberated by the main army."

The expressions on the prisoners' faces were beyond pathetic, some began to cry, others started arguing over who would go with them.

"Look," Caleb said, sighing. "All that gunfire is raining down on my buddy right now and that will be you if you come with us. I need fighters. Help is on the way, and it will be here soon, but that's not my mission."

"Why are you here then?" pressed the old man.

"To slow down that column of reinforcements. They're heading up to Jackson to build up defenses against the American advance—your rescuers." His answer was partly true.

"I figured if we were already at it, why not see if a couple of you would join us? I know this is difficult, but we don't have time to discuss this, we'll all die if I stay here. Last call."

"We'll come with you."

A sturdy looking young man, somewhere in his early twenties, with disheveled sandy blond hair and dim green eyes met his gaze. Beside him crouched a young stocky Hispanic man, his eyes ever shifting, watching the shadows. Caleb looked them over quickly.

"Any injuries?"

"We're good," said the blond-haired man. "We ain't got no family either."

"Good enough," said Caleb. "Collect some gear, we're moving."

Departing through the mortar pits, collecting gear along the way, Caleb could hear the soft sobs of prisoners they left behind. War was cruel, ugly, and unforgiving. Leaving them behind was the best decision, though he knew the Chinese would not be kind when they discovered what happened. If it wasn't for the need of laborers, they would probably all be executed.

It made him feel like an animal, leaving them to the wolves because he didn't have the means to save them all. He hated the Chinese, but he also hated Americans. He hated the sobs, crying never solved anything and, as Sam had pointed out, it gave the Chinese great satisfaction. He hated the fear that made them slaves, the cowardice that kept them from fighting back. Was living so precious that slavery was better than death? The illusion that living was the same thing as life, clinging to the hope that God would send someone less cowardly to rescue them, disgusted him. If you want freedom, then fight for it. Find a way or stop all the crying and accept what is.

"Let's go!" he hissed back to the two men trying to keep up.

Slinking through the shadows to the northeast, they were nearly to the wire when the shooting stopped. Halting, Caleb motioned to get low. Is Darrian dead, or simply on the move? Regardless, they had to get out. He had chosen this spot from the hill. Pallets piled high with supplies were packed tightly near the wire, a tactical error in the compound's layout. Darrian's attack had drawn most of the attention to the south for the moment, but Caleb knew they were still looking for the Americans responsible for the fires.

The three of them crept to the wire.

Chapter 5

Neither prisoner spoke as the thick trees swallowed the base behind them. Caleb had been part of many prisoner rescues over the years and one thing he knew for sure, people were unpredictable. Some would make a run for it as soon as they were free, others would break down crying or start thanking God. Others, who had been captive for too long and were broken in the head, would actually try to get back into their prison.

Then there were the vengeance types. They came in two forms: the crazy ones who would just start pummeling every Chinese person they could find, living or dead; and the professionals who were intelligent enough to control their emotions and join the fight. It wouldn't take long, and he would know.

The men slipped down one of the overgrown roads that had been cut off from the town. Weeds and a few small trees managed to carve out an existence in the cracked asphalt, slowing their progress as they worked around them in the darkness. Caleb, who hadn't intended to drag Darrian into his personal quest, found himself in knots wondering if his friend had managed to endure the bombardment. He missed having a radio.

"This is why I was going alone," Caleb muttered.

"What's that?" whispered the Hispanic.

"Nothing. Another hundred yards and we'll be at the rendezvous point, we'll meet with my buddy there," Caleb said.

"So, what do they call you, anyway?" asked the blond-haired man. "I'm Lance, and this here's Eddy, or at least that's what he goes by, his real name's kinda long and hard to remember."

"Caleb."

"That was some fine shooting back there, you been at it a while?"

"All my life."

"Us too, us too. Eddy and I used to have a great time with them squatters. Eddy's awfully handy with a knife, he likes to make a statement, used to cut 'em up real good. I'm more like you, I prefer a little fire power when I go into a place. Shoot, them squatter gals sure know how to put up a terrible ruckus when a fella's just looking for a little bit of fun. We were making a pretty good go of it for a while, then one night we kicked in the door of this one house, and it wasn't squatters, it was some sort of army unit. We were on the floor and hog tied before we knew what was happenin'. That must have been, oh, three months ago."

"Six," corrected Eddy, his voice cold and calculating.

"Right, six months."

So, Eddy's the brains of the outfit. It was apparent these guys weren't fighters, they were thugs; ruthless, unprincipled thugs. But they hated the Chinese, and were young and strong, if they could follow orders, it might give them an edge in a fight. Darrian's going to love these guys. He thought sarcastically.

Reaching the rendezvous point, Caleb halted and listened intently. Toads chirped, crickets sang, vehicles hummed in the distance.

"What is it?" asked Lance.

"He isn't here," whispered Caleb.

"Says who?" replied a familiar voice.

Caleb let out a sigh of relief. "I thought they'd really gotten you this time."

"If you'd taken any longer on those mortars, they might have."

"You're right, I wanted to take the mortars sooner, but even if I had, things wouldn't have gone according to plan, and it would've turned out the same anyway."

Darrian snorted, "That's a fact."

Lance cleared his throat from behind Caleb.

"Right." Caleb threw his thumb over his shoulder. "Darrian, this is Lance and Eddy. This is Darrian, our overwatch."

"My, you're a big fella," said Lance. "Must be nearly seven feet tall, aye, Eddy?"

Eddy said nothing.

"Six-six," replied Darrian.

"That's a big guy, a big guy. I suppose the squatter ladies really go wild when you come at 'em," he said with a laugh.

Even in the darkness, Caleb could make out Darrian's amused expression.

"Well, now that we're all acquainted, we'd better push a little further down the road and cross the creek up ahead before we set up camp for the night," Caleb said, slapping Darrian on the back as he pushed past him.

It was two in the morning before they made camp, everyone was exhausted including Lance, who had finally run out of things to say. Caleb was convinced Eddy had developed some special ability to tune him out, there was no other explanation for how he could've endured him for so long. On the road, they learned that Lance's father left his mother before the civil war had begun and he hadn't seen or heard from him since. His mother died of disease a couple of years into the war which left Lance on his own.

He'd met Eddy roughly five years ago by chance when they had both decided to loot the same house. Lance also told Eddy's story, though Caleb couldn't figure out how he'd gleaned all that information based on how few words Eddy had spoken so far.

Eddy grew up in the country where his family survived the civil war and even the invasion by living off their small farm. For a few years they bought their independence from the Chinese by supplying the local garrison with food, but eventually their supply couldn't keep up. Eddy's father tried to explain their desperate position with a squad of soldiers that showed up to collect. That's when they shot him and took all the livestock they had left. The soldiers took his mother into the barn and Eddy, hidden under the deck, listened for an hour as she screamed. Then came a shot followed by silence, and the soldiers left. When Eddy went to the barn, he found his mother's bare body in the dirt, a hole in her head.

As Caleb lay against his pack later that night, he shook his head at the ugliness of it all. He'd heard so many stories over the years and witnessed so many tears. Where was God while Eddy's mom cried out? Where was God in any of this? He knew his mom would have some response; she always did. If there was a God, he had certainly abandoned America.

It was midmorning when Darrian, who had taken last watch, roused the small band. Breakfast was Chinese field rations, eaten cold. The night had done everyone good; Lance immediately began talking about the lovely morning, a rock he'd slept on that his shoulder wouldn't forget anytime soon, and his favorite combinations of Chinese ration sauces to mix together. Eddy even said thanks when Darrian handed him his ration.

Their goal for the day was to find an obscure checkpoint, make quick work of it, and gather supplies to finish outfitting Lance and Eddy. It would also give Caleb a chance to see what they were made of.

Caleb hadn't noticed Eddy's height in the darkness, he was a stocky five foot nothing. Caleb felt like a giant standing next to him, though he was only five-ten. Two scars cut across his face. A long thin line running parallel to his left eyebrow just below the hairline and another, still a deep purple, across his cheek. The ends of three more scars protruded out the neck of his shirt. Caleb knew those stripes; Eddy had taken a beating during his time with the Chinese. Though he said nothing, Eddy's posture communicated volumes; he was not a man to be trifled with, and he wasn't looking for friendship or attachments. Eddy would be taking care of Eddy.

The only thing about Eddy that puzzled Caleb was Lance . . . what is he doing with that guy? There had to be more to the story than just happening upon one another and deciding to stick together, but what was it?

Caleb reached into his assault pack for his own Chinese ration, but it wasn't there. Feeling around, his pulse quickened. It was gone. One of their new companions was about to wish he'd never left the Chinese outpost. The dirt, fine sand really, near his pack was wet and soft. He studied it, whoever took his breakfast was sure to have left a track, but which one of them was it? Then he saw it, a faint depression in the sand, the outline of a worn-out sole. Curiously, the track did not lead into their camp but rather came from the outside, besides, it was much too short and narrow to be a man's track, even Eddy's.

"What is it?" asked Darrian.

Caleb lifted his finger to his lips and pointed to the tracks and the direction they pointed. Darrian nodded and grabbed his rifle. Caleb motioned for Darrian to head up the hill and around while he continued to follow the tracks. Forty yards down the creek bed the trees opened, allowing Caleb to see an old bridge not too far off. Signaling up the hill, Caleb watched Darrian assume his sniper position overlooking the bridge.

"You think he's in there?" asked Lance with a sinister grin.

Caleb jumped. He had forgotten all about them.

"You two wait here, I'm going to check it out, if I get into trouble, come running."

"How will we know if you get into trouble?" asked Lance.

"Oh, you'll know," Caleb said, unholstering his pistols.

Creeping along the eroded creek edge, he welcomed the extra sense of excitement of the unknown, the imagination's playground. He reached the place where the natural edge of the creek gave way to recycled concrete piled on either side when the bridge was built to prevent erosion. He signaled to Darrian. Darrian motioned that he was blind to what was under the bridge. Caleb nodded. Looking back to where Eddy and Lance hunkered near a fallen tree, he motioned for them to be ready. Lance nodded; Eddy rolled his eyes.

Caleb rose from his position slowly, eyes scanning the nooks and crannies of the cement slabs. The sound of water flowing over rocks echoed under the bridge creating a static that frustrated his keen ears. He crept slowly up the embankment towards the crevice where the bridge met solid ground. He could sense it, a presence. Something shifted in the shadows, pulled itself tight against the concrete piling. Caleb froze, two wrappers from his stolen ration lay near the edge of the shadow. This is a bad spot . . .

He knew Darrian couldn't see him from where he was, and Lance and Eddy, if they were still waiting, would be no help at all. This is a bad spot. Leveling both pistols in the shadow, he called out.

"Come out now with your hands in the air or I swear I will let these guns eat!"

He waited a moment, but nothing moved, nothing spoke, nothing shot back. He tried again in broken Mandarin. Still nothing. As his eyes adjusted to the blackness, panic swept over him; the shadow was empty. Then he felt it again, the presence; but it was too late. Pain shot through the back of his head, and he was driven to the ground. Catching himself on one knee, he rolled as a second blow rained down on him. He dropped his right-hand pistol in time to catch the tree branch and jerk his assailant from the shadows.

A filthy, moppy-haired, ninety-pound boy, wearing baggy overalls and a large plaid button up shirt with sleeves nearly rolled up to the armpits, fell from his perch atop a concrete slab right onto Caleb. Caleb instinctively shoved him off and rolled back to his knees. Holstering his other pistol, he twisted the boy's arm behind his back and held him to the ground.

"Get off me, you thievin' trash!" yelled the boy.

Caleb couldn't believe the nerve, and with blood trickling down the back of his neck, the fire of his temper soared.

"Listen, you little wretch, that's my breakfast you stole this morning, and if you don't stop squawking, every Chinese soldier within five miles of here is going to descend on this place and we'll both be done for," Caleb growled through clenched teeth. "I ought to beat you within an inch of your life."

"Go ahead! You wouldn't be the first!" the boy challenged, writhing under Caleb's weight.

"Hold still, or so help me I will drum the life out of you right here and now!" Caleb said, twisting the boy's arm until he let out a shriek.

The boy quit moving.

"Alright . . . I was just hungry, ok?" he said, more civil this time.

"How did you find us?" asked Caleb.

"I followed you out of the outpost when you got Lance and Eddy, I was a slave there too."

"I said no kids," Caleb said, smashing the boy further into the dirt with his weight.

"I know," grunted the boy. "That's why I followed you instead of volunteering. I couldn't stay there."

Caleb growled. Jerking the boy to his feet, he collected his other pistol and holstered it.

"Did you leave me any breakfast?" he asked.

Wincing, the boy confessed, "I haven't eaten in two days."

Caleb didn't reply. Half dragging, half carrying the boy, he walked out from under the bridge and into the light. He had only seconds to figure out how he was going to explain how a ninety-pound brat got the jump on him . . . some Eagle.

As Lance and Eddy appeared, Caleb could already see a satisfied grin on Eddy's face. That was nothing compared to Darrian's throaty laughter as he ruffled the boy's hair.

"Nice job, kid, you're the first human being to put a scratch on the Eagle in some time," said Darrian, giving Caleb a playful shove.

"Alright, alright . . ." Caleb said. "He says he was a prisoner with you guys."

Lance nodded, "Yeah, I remember him; feisty kid, probably the only one who could match the number of stripes Eddy got."

"What are we gonna do with him?" asked Darrian.

"I ain't feeding it," declared Lance.

"That's ok, somebody already did," quipped Eddy.

Caleb glared at him.

"This isn't a charity mission; we're never going to catch Major Li if we keep this up," Darrian added.

"I won't slow you down! I'm good at sneaking into places, and I'm stronger than I look," said the boy.

"No one asked you!" Caleb snapped.

"We weren't any older than that when we started, aye Eddy?" Lance said.

Eddy didn't reply.

"Neither was I," Caleb sighed.

Darrian groaned. "And now we're babysitters."

"Does it have a name?" asked Caleb, running his hand down his face in exasperation.

"My name is . . ."

Caleb's hand flew to the boy's mouth.

"I didn't ask you," he growled.

"His name's Rice," offered Lance.

"Rice?" Caleb asked, raising an eyebrow, finally willing to address the boy.

Rice pushed his hand away, rolling his eyes. "I've been a slave all my life, my mom died in the compound when I was one, she never gave me a name. Rice is the first word I learned to say in English, I had to beg the other Americans for food, the slaves kept me alive. Since rice was the only word I knew, everyone just started calling me that."

"Wow, that's—" Darrian began to say.

"Life," finished Caleb. "If you're coming with us, you're going to have to suck it up. No pouting where we're going. This is enemy territory, weakness and hesitation will get you killed."

Rice nodded.

"Go wash up in the creek, you're a mess. If you get sick, we're leaving you behind," Caleb said.

Again, Rice nodded.

"Speaking of sick, you'd better let me have a look at that head," said Darrian. "He split you wide open."

Caleb followed Darrian over to a large cement slab near the water's edge. Darrian pulled a rag out of his pack, wet it in the water, and gently dabbed away the blood.

"I can see your skull, it's gonna need some thread."

Caleb tensed; he hated needles.

Darrian pulled out a needle and a small travel-size dental floss he'd picked up somewhere. "Ah, mint flavor."

He heated the needle with his lighter and threaded the floss through the eye. "You ready?"

Caleb nodded.

"Ahh, that burns!" Caleb growled.

"Oh, don't be a baby, the mint is probably good for it," Darrian said, forcing Caleb's head back around.

Caleb grit his teeth as the floss drew his flesh back together. It really did burn, though the pain of mint in the wound distracted from the needle's fresh pokes. At last, a snip of the scissors meant the process was over.

"There, give it a few days and it'll just be another battle scar," Darrian said.

"Thanks."

"I wouldn't go around fighting any more kids for a few days," Darrian teased.

"Yeah," Caleb had to laugh at himself.

Thanks to the morning's escapades the day was well behind schedule. Rice had returned from washing and looked like a human at least, his fine form looked as though the wind would blow him over at any minute, but Caleb had already learned that the scrawny insect was more than capable of dishing it out. His stomach groaned as he looked the boy over . . . *Rice*.

Caleb pulled out the weathered map of Tennessee he'd found in a gas station, and everyone huddled around.

"We're here, just south of Henderson." He pointed to the small dot on the map. "Based on what we've experienced, there should be a checkpoint here on the highway, about a mile south of Selmer. They're using this highway, and towns like this are usually set up as regional garrisons; they like to check any traffic on the roads about a mile before it gets to town. We'll get there around midafternoon, barring any more unforeseen situations, and hit them just as the sun's going down. We should be able to get enough gear to outfit the rest of you well enough then we'll press on and find a place to stay for the night," Caleb said.

"What exactly is our intended mission out here?" asked Lance.

Darrian shot Caleb a quick glance.

"Our mission . . ." Caleb paused and thought for a moment. "Our mission is to kill a high priority target, Major Li. He's a naval transport officer responsible for many atrocities against America and is vital to their supply chain. He's stationed somewhere south of here; our job is to find him and take him out."

Darrian gave him an approving nod.

"Ahh, so if we take him out, it disrupts the supply chain," said Lance.

"And sends a message," added Caleb.

"Simple enough," replied Lance.

Caleb folded up the map, and the five of them moved out along the creek.

Chapter 6

Caleb low-crawled to the top of a sparsely wooded hill just south of the town of Selmer. The setting sun behind him cast the hill's long shadow to within fifty yards of the highway. He scanned for the checkpoint and found it exactly where he expected it. Predictable. He continued to scan for available cover with disappointment. These guys had cleared the trees and brush way back, the nearest shrub was a good hundred and fifty yards from the half-dozen soldiers manning the small shed and concrete barriers which made up the checkpoint. His only advantage would be the blinding light of the setting sun hitting them directly in the eyes.

Shimmying back down the hill, he reported the situation to his squad. Darrian would have to work fast; they'd all have to work fast. No matter what happened, they would meet at the fork in Oxford Creek a couple miles down the road. If the plan was going to work, it had to start now.

Darrian took Rice to keep him away from any trouble and set up at the crest of the hill, Lance and Eddy crawled their way through the grass and weeds to the closest remaining shrub. Caleb worked his way a couple hundred yards further south down the ravine before cresting the hill and getting into position. Any second now. . . .

BOOM!

Caleb watched from his hideout as a Chinese soldier lighting up a cigarette was flung into a concrete barrier and then slumped to the ground. The shrub at the bottom of the hill opened up as Lance and Eddy laid down suppressive fire from the QBZ-95's they took from the dead mortarmen. The Chinese soldiers dove for cover. Good, at least they can follow a plan. Caleb waited until the cowering soldiers were all hidden behind the barriers before charging across the open field towards the shack. My turn.

As the Chinese soldiers collected themselves, they began returning fire. Caleb closed the distance with ravenous speed. He was only a few strides away when he drew his pistols and, leaping onto one of the barriers, poured both magazines into the remaining soldiers hunkering on the other side. Then it was over. The emptiness of death always swallowing the high of battle.

With his lungs still burning, he waved all clear and signaled Darrian to keep watch up the road. Motioning for Lance and Eddy to join him, he walked into the empty shack; the radio chattered endlessly. On a shelf he found what he was looking for, a case of rations, he nearly tore it open and ate right there, but there was no time. Lance and Eddy arrived as he began filling a pack.

"Grab all the gear you need, body armor, weapons, ammo, and food." He tossed an empty pack at their feet. "You've got three minutes."

"Why three minutes?" asked Lance.

"Because the Chinese will be here in ten with vehicles and dogs, and I, for one, have no intention of making it easy to find us."

The two men went to work stripping the soldiers, Caleb grabbed a couple replacement magazines. He found some cordage, a new lighter, and three grenades. After stuffing in as many loose rations and bottles of water as would fit, they shouldered their packs.

"All set?"

The two men nodded. Caleb signaled for Darrian to move out, then he walked into the shack and picked up the radio. In broken Mandarin, he delivered a message, then smashed the radio on the floor.

"Let's go!"

Sprinting across the field, the three made their way up over the hill and down into the creek. They paused only for a moment as they hit the cool water before pushing further downstream towards the fork.

"Where did you learn to speak Chinese?" asked Lance.

"My sister is married to one," Caleb huffed.

"She what?!"

"He's a good one, I guess, I don't know, you can't choose your family, right?" Caleb replied.

"I guess not! That's got to be a kick in the gut," Lance said in disbelief.

"Well, you don't see her with me, do ya?!"

"What did you say back there, anyway?" Lance asked.

"I told them it's too late for them, the Eagle has descended."

Lance let out a long whistle as they trudged down the creek. "They'll put a price on your head if you keep that up."

"I've already got one."

Caleb held up his hand, halting midstride. Something's wrong. His hair stood on end. "Oh no . . ." he whispered.

"What?"

"Culvert, now!" he yelled, dashing for the large metal cylinder draining water into the creek. The three of them crammed themselves into the two-foot diameter pipe as a rocket exploded in the creek. Rocks and water sprayed Lance's back as the distant hum of a drone reverberated in the culvert.

"They'll burry us alive in here!" shrieked Lance.

"Shut up!" Eddy barked, elbowing him in the dark.

Another rocket thudded in the ground somewhere above them, sending a shower of dirt into the water. The culvert was holding its own.

They waited patiently in the darkness, frigid water running down the length of their bodies cramping their already cramped muscles. Caleb could feel Eddy shuddering below him; they couldn't stay here. Either they would be found by patrols already looking for them or they would all get sick from the wet and cold.

"We've got to move," Caleb said as calmly as he could.

"Ok, ok," Lance said, sliding down to the opening.

Once they were all outside, Caleb listened intently. Nothing.

"It must have returned to refuel, that or the culvert hid our heat signatures and they lost us. Either way, we need to move fast," Caleb said.

Collecting their scattered gear, they took off at a jog down the creek. The fork was approximately two miles ahead. While their wet clothes were slow to dry without the sun's warmth, the quick pace helped drive the chill from their bones.

"We'll need to find a bridge or something to camp under tonight, something that will block our heat signatures in case they keep looking for us," Caleb said, thinking out loud.

"I guess they got your message," Eddy said with a grin.

It was the first affirmative thing Eddy had said since meeting him.

Relief spread over Caleb as they reached the fork, Darrian and Rice were already waiting for them.

"I thought that thing got you!" Darrian said in relief. "We were about to hit the trail in case they came back."

"You couldn't have just left him out there?" Caleb asked dryly, nodding towards Rice who was sitting up on the bank.

"I tried, he's faster than he looks," replied Darrian with shrug.

"We hit 'em pretty good, got some grub and gear. We need to ditch this creek and find a place to hide for tonight. We're in their playground; no noise, no talking, keep some distance between each other. Keep your eyes and ears peeled. I'll take point, followed by Lance, Rice in the middle, then Eddy, and Darrian. If you hear or see anything, quietly relay it up and we'll halt and check it out, if we get into contact, get some cover and look to Darrian or me for instructions. We've been in a lot of scrapes, and it's worked out so far."

He looked intently around the group. "Everyone understand?"

"Where's my gun?" asked Rice.

"You've got to earn it," said Caleb. "Let's go."

Chapter 7

Y ou've been marchin' us for three days straight without hardly a word. Are you plannin' on tellin' us sometime soon where it is we're headed?" complained Lance. "Why, we done skirted nearly twenty check points and twice as many squatters—I thought the goal was to get rid of the Chinese?"

"Our mission," replied Caleb evenly, "is to kill Major Li, who happens to be a transportation officer. There's an awful lot of traffic heading to and from the front, and it all leads to Memphis. Memphis just so happens to sit on the Mississippi River, the perfect place for a naval transportation officer to be located, especially considering the circumstances."

"And what if he ain't there?" snapped Lance.

"Then hopefully we can grab someone who can point us in the right direction," replied Caleb.

"Does that really work?" asked Lance.

"It's got us this far," replied Caleb.

"If the guy was telling the truth," added Darrian.

"Perfect," muttered Eddy.

Caleb shot Darrian a glance, which was met with a casual shrug and a grin. Darrian always seemed to get a kick out of getting Caleb's dander up.

Cresting a tall ridge, Caleb held up his hand and halted the column. "We'll take a breather here."

"I didn't think you'd ever stop," Lance complained.

The band dropped their packs and sprawled out, resting against the tree trunks. Caleb dug out his binoculars and scanned the changing landscape in front of him. For days they'd been hiking through steep tree-covered ridges and deep ravines filled with a spider web of small boulder-filled creeks and rivers. What lay in front of them was old ag fields and farmsteads, a few hills and tree-lined creek beds, then the flatter lands of the Mississippi River valley, and in the distance, Memphis.

"You really think he could be there?" asked Darrian, plopping down beside him.

"It's my best guess . . ."

"There could be thousands of PLA in there."

"Uh huh . . .," said Caleb, still glassing.

"Got to admit, I'm starting to miss our old unit," he sighed.

"What? I'm not enough company for you?" Caleb jested.

"Not against that." Darrian nodded towards the distant city.

Setting down the binoculars, Caleb eyed him. "You're actually worried?"

"We're alone out here, if we get into a scrape with these guys, there's no help coming. Based on those reinforcements, Aaron is at least a month behind us, maybe more. And honestly, our "team" isn't the caliber of what we're used to."

Caleb looked back towards Memphis.

"It's not that I'm afraid of dying, I'm afraid of dying for nothing," finished Darrian.

Caleb studied him; they'd been through a lot together. Darrian felt more like an older brother than Aaron did. They'd come so far, survived so much; this was the closest he'd been to getting his life back.

"Give me one more chance to find him in Memphis, if he isn't here, we'll turn back," Caleb sighed.

Darrian took the binoculars and glassed the city off in the distance. "Alright, but none of your usual storm the castle nonsense. We go in quiet, get the intel we need, and get out."

"Awe," Caleb protested. "I feel like we can take 'em."

"I'm serious, we've never been in a spot like this before. If we're discovered, we won't escape."

"Sounds like you boys are fixin' to decide our fates for us," interrupted Lance, causing them both to flinch. "That's not how Eddy and I roll. We don't risk unless there's no other option."

"If that's so, then how did you manage to get caught?" asked Darrian.

"They set a trap," growled Eddy.

"I guess I should have just left you boys there if you're too afraid to do your job," replied Caleb. "I asked if there were any fighters . . . not cowards."

Eddy was on his feet in a flash, already reaching for his knife, but Darrian's big hand grabbed his shoulder and forced him back down.

"Look, everyone's got their own reasons for doing what they do. Let's just finish this mission and after that you boys can decide whether or not you wanna stay," Darrian said.

Eddy glared at Caleb. "After this, we owe you nothin'; we're done."

"Perfect!" exclaimed Caleb sarcastically.

Pulling out his map, Caleb motioned for everyone to huddle around. "Our best shot at finding the target or his whereabouts is to get close to the docks. If we can grab a transport solder, it's possible they've at least heard of Li or, best-case scenario, we get eyes on Li himself. He was a bit of a peacock in the past, enjoys parading himself in front of his prisoners."

"How do you plan on getting near those docks?" asked Rice, craning his neck to see over everyone's shoulders.

"We'll use that wooded ridge north of the city as a base camp and do our glassing from there. If we need to infiltrate and extract a prisoner, I think our best shot would be to use the river. Float down near dusk, grab one, and boat back up."

"Why not just wait till dark?" asked Lance.

"Because they have night vision, and we'd light up like fireflies," replied Darrian in his best teacher voice. "Fortunately, they're cumbersome, and the Chinese don't like to put them on until they absolutely have to, making dusk an opportune time to strike."

"It helps that we're so far behind enemy lines, these soldiers are likely pretty complacent, and complacency kills," added Caleb. "The trick is going to be getting to that hill unnoticed, there are a lot of fields and farms between here and there, some are bound to be occupied by squatters."

"Slow and easy?" suggested Darrian.

"Slow and easy," agreed Caleb.

The band grabbed their gear and descended the ridge. Giving up their forest cover had them all on edge, even Caleb. Memphis was big and hummed with military and civilian traffic going in and out. Helicopters came and went delivering men and supplies. The base was supported by a battery of eight artillery pieces, not including mortars, and a well-stocked airfield. Only God knew how many soldiers were garrisoned there.

A three-and-a-half-mile maze of overgrown field fences stood between them and the hill. Scrubby trees covered them overhead, while wild vines ensured their slow and steady pace, especially with Lance declaring everything poison ivy. Halting at an intersection of two fence rows, Caleb waved Darrian forward.

"What is it?"

"The field's tilled." Caleb pointed to the overturned clumps of dirt and then a farmhouse a hundred yards from their corner. "What do you think?"

Darrian checked the farm with his scope. "They're home . . ." he replied.

Caleb scanned their surroundings, "Fencerow's pretty thick, I don't think they'd see us if we kept low."

"Yeah . . . should be ok," replied Darrian, scanning the farm again.

Caleb waved the rest of them forward. "Here's the situation, we've got squatters at the farm and the field's been tilled. We need to cross to the next field; it's got to be at least two hundred yards. Everyone keep low and absolutely no noise; sound carries a long way out here."

"Why not just let Eddy and I have at 'em, we're what you might call experts in their kind," Lance said with a sinister grin.

"Because if we 'have at 'em' and they're discovered, we'll be discovered and never mind the mission, we'll be lucky to make it out of here alive," replied Darrian, obviously annoyed.

"Let's move out," Caleb cut in. "We've only got a couple hours before dark and we need to make that hill."

Caleb led the way through the fence, crawling along the berm formed between two fields, always keeping an eye on the farm. The smell of fresh earth reminded him of his family and their farm in Minnesota, of his dad. Thanks to the Chinese, it was all gone. Gritting his teeth, he pushed on.

They were only fifty yards from the end of the field when a tractor growled to life at the farmstead. Caleb halted as a large John Deere tractor drove out onto the tilled ground dragging a disk harrow. Moving quickly up the far edge of the field while decimating the overturned earth behind it, the tractor turned at the end of its row and plowed towards them. Motioning everyone tight to the berm, Caleb pulled dry grass over himself and prayed the others followed suit. He lay motionless, holding his breath, as the tractor rolled past, brushing his boot with a disc. Breathing a sigh of relief as the tractor rounded the corner, he motioned slowly with his hand, and they were on their way again, in a slow-motion race to make the field edge before the tractor's second pass.

* * *

Arriving at the hill just before dusk, Caleb and Darrian set up a crude shelter with mylar blankets spread over an a-frame with a camouflage tarp cover. Their tent was tucked neatly under a thick oak canopy only thirty feet from a ledge that dropped seventy-five feet to the river below.

"What's the point of these if you have the tarp for a cover?" asked Rice, pointing to the mylar layer.

"It blocks our heat signatures from the drones during the cool night, otherwise there's a good chance they'd spot us up here. During the day everything absorbs the sun's heat and it's much harder to pick us out," Darrian responded.

A shocked expression filled his face. "They can see our heat?!"

"If they happen to look in the right place . . . yeah," replied Darrian. "The trick is, they don't know they ought to be looking for us, and with all the squatters fleeing the American advance, it's got to be getting pretty difficult to decide which heat signatures are friend or foe."

"Alright, that's enough tactical lessons for one night. I'll take first watch, the rest of you get something to eat and hit the sack," Caleb said, digging his binoculars out of his pack.

Sitting in the doorway of their humble dwelling thirty minutes later, Caleb could hear the others jockeying behind him for enough room to stretch out. The occasional grunt or curse assured him that taking first watch was the right choice: people were easier to push out of the way when they were asleep.

Northwest Memphis spread out below him. To his right, the Mississippi River flowed south to the docks. Just like in Duluth, there were cranes and railway lines paralleling the river. The docks were all lit up as bright as day as crews moved around on forklifts and trucks loading and unloading the ships. He shook his head as memories of his captivity in Duluth played in his mind. A large cargo vessel was being unloaded at the nearest dock. He could see rows of armored personnel carriers, several light armored tanks, and an assortment of ammo and fuel trucks waiting for their turn to drive onto American soil.

He focused on the control tower, but the distance was too far to make out more than basic human silhouettes. Armed security towers dotted the river's edge the full length of the compound, their search lights danced from shore to shore. Pairs of soldiers with a dog paced each dock on a continuous loop. There were soldiers and cameras everywhere. This place was on a whole new level.

Caleb set down the binoculars, his eyes burning from the bright lights. What would Aaron do? The suggestion hit him so loudly he straightened and looked around to make sure Darrian hadn't heard it. He picked up the binoculars again.

What would Aaron do?

The following morning, Caleb cleared a four-foot square area of ground. Using twigs, he made an arrow in one corner with the letter N above it. Gathering everyone around, he laid out phase one.

"This will be our sand table; we'll work up a model of the docks and north edge of the compound. As we fill in the details, we'll have a better chance of coming up with a successful plan. We'll take turns watching the compound day and night." He held up a notebook. "In this book, we'll write down all the intel on the changing of the guard, mealtimes, officer schedules, prisoner routines, patrol routes, and any other details beneficial to the mission. What we're looking for is a chink in the armor, an opportunity to infiltrate, grab a prisoner, and get out."

"So, uhh . . . how long's something like this supposed to take?" asked Lance, gesturing towards the square with disgust.

"Let me guess, planning isn't really your and Eddy's style?" Caleb quipped. "We're not going anywhere near those docks without a plan, a plan that gives us a shot at pulling this off without all of us winding up dead. If you want to finish this mission so you can go off on your own, we need those details, and you're on first watch," Caleb huffed, tossing Lance the binoculars and notebook.

Lance walked over to a log overlooking the base and plopped down, muttering.

"And what if he can't write?" Eddy said, sneering at Caleb.

"Then you can write it for him," Caleb said.

Darrian and Rice joined Caleb in creating the sand table.

"So, when did planning become your style, Aaron—I mean, Caleb?" jested Darrian.

"Stow it!"

"Hey, man, I'm just—"

"We're here to kill him, whatever it takes!" Caleb seethed. "I know he's here . . . it's like, I can feel him."

"And then what?" Rice asked.

His young voice shook Caleb. Rice had taken quite a beating too, according to Lance. "Then we'll hunt down every last one of these animals."

"I want to help," Rice spoke firmly. "I'm tired of being treated like a pet, even the Americans in the camp treated me that way. I'm a person, and I'm strong enough. I want a life too."

Raising an eyebrow, Caleb looked at Darrian and back to Rice. "Alright, but you have to follow orders. We don't have time to teach you everything, so pay attention and teach yourself. That's how I learned. You have to get hard, no more tears. Accept the pain, absorb it, let it fuel you, and when the time comes, return it without mercy." Caleb's eyes burned into Rice's. "Learn from what you fear and become it. Embrace the pulse of the battle, let it sharpen your senses, let your inner victim die, become a predator until there's no longer reservation, no hesitation, only execution. You only preserve your life because without it you cannot take theirs. And maybe, when this is all over and they're all gone, we'll have earned the right to live."

Rice, eyes wide, finally blinked and nodded his head.

"Good, now go get me some sticks and pebbles for the sand table," Caleb said, turning back to the project at hand.

Rice jumped up and headed for the woods.

"He's just a kid, Caleb."

"There are no kids, only victims and those who refuse to be."

Shaking his head, Darrian slung his rifle over his shoulder and strode off after Rice.

It was late afternoon by the time Darrian and Caleb put the finishing touches on the model. Lance and Eddy stayed on watch most of the day to avoid getting roped into helping. Darrian was reaching to adjust a thin strip of bark that represented the dock when his head shot up, his eyes searching the woods.

"What is it?" whispered Caleb.

He held his finger to his lips, pointing down the hill behind their camp. Glancing back at Caleb and Rice, he motioned for them to get down. Creeping to where he had left his rifle resting on an oak, he took it and scanned the woods with his scope.

Turning to the lookout position, Caleb's temper flared; there was no one there.

"Where are those goons?"

"I didn't notice them leave," replied Darrian, without taking his eye from the scope.

Rice shook his head.

"Perfect."

Caleb unholstered his pistols. "You got anything yet?"

"Not yet, but it's headed this way," Darrian said.

Caleb darted to a log about twenty yards to Darrian's right to get another angle on whatever was moving up the hill. It was getting close. Game time.

Chapter 8

Caleb slid his fingers to both triggers as Eddy exploded from the bushes dragging along a squirming Chinese soldier. Lance followed behind them, grinning proudly. A mixture and rage and relief collided in Caleb's mind, and it took everything in him not to shoot all three of them.

Jumping up, he stormed towards the men, fingers still on the triggers. "Give me one good reason why I shouldn't kill you both."

"I'll give you two," Eddy sneered. "One, I got your freaking informant while you were busy playing sticks and stones with the other kids, and two, just because we owe you doesn't mean we work for you." He slammed the terrified soldier to the ground.

"What happened to his ear?!" Rice blurted.

"He didn't need two of 'em," jeered Eddy darkly.

Caleb didn't know Darrian could move that fast, but before he finished raising his pistols to destroy everyone in front of him, he was pinned in Darrian's arms.

"Don't do it. You don't have to like it, but don't do it. You're gonna get us all killed. You aren't gonna tame that guy and you know it. He messed up, and it could've been bad, but it wasn't. Let's just take what we can and finish this. Then we can be rid of them," Darrian finished through grit teeth.

Caleb finally relaxed and holstered his pistols shakily, adrenaline still coursing through his veins.

"Are you boys done hugging? I knew you'd be excited, but I had no idea," Eddy laughed.

Caleb tensed and Darrian tightened his hold.

"I'm fine," Caleb said through clenched teeth.

Darrian released his grip. "Just cause I'm holding him back doesn't mean I don't agree with him," he said, slinging his rifle over his shoulder.

"Whatever," replied Eddy. "Just ask this guy if your target is around so Lance and I know how much longer we have to live in this dump."

"Where did you get him?" asked Caleb.

"It was easy, I was watching the guys working the docks. When they quit for the day, this guy left the compound and biked to a house at the edge of town. Lance and I snuck to the house, made sure no one else lived there and snatched him," Eddy explained, cracking his knuckles.

"No one saw you? And you're sure no one else was in the house?" Caleb asked.

"He's telling the truth, alright? He was alone!" Lance spit out. "I think you're just jealous we pulled this off without all your fancy planning."

"I'm not jealous, I'm furious. You left your position without telling anyone, exposing all of us," Caleb replied.

"Want us to take him back, boss?" Eddy's feigned remorse was even more infuriating.

Caleb walked over to his pack and pulled out his med kit. Holding it up, he motioned to the soldier's ear.

"I'll bandage it."

The man nodded hesitantly. Caleb bandaged his missing ear and then sat back staring at the soldier.

"Do you know who I am?" Caleb asked, removing the man's gag.

The soldier shook his head.

Caleb pointed to his Harley jacket hanging on a tree branch. "I'm the Eagle."

The man just shrugged his shoulders.

"Have you heard of me?"

The man shook his head again.

Caleb felt his face flush as Darrian snickered.

"You have two options," he continued. "Either you cooperate when I ask you questions, or I'll let him ask the questions." He gestured to Eddy.

The man nodded that he understood.

"Good. Do you know a Major Li?"

The man furrowed his brow before answering. "There are many Li's in the PLA."

"He would be a transportation officer; he was stationed up in Duluth a few years back."

The soldier just looked at the ground.

"He likes looking over the prisoners who work the docks, and he's really fond of his cane."

The soldier still didn't answer.

"Hey! I can have him ask you," Caleb said, pointing at Eddy.

Eddy pulled his knife, grinning.

Reluctantly, he nodded his head.

"You do know him?"

The man sighed and nodded again.

"Is he here?"

Without warning, Eddy burst in and grabbed the soldier, holding his knife to his remaining ear.

The soldier shrieked, "He's here, he's here!"

"Do I have to do everything?" huffed Eddy. "It's too bad for him we're gonna cut him up when this is all over."

Caleb glared at him.

"Well, we ain't keepin' him, and we ain't givin' him back," Lance added.

Caleb stood the soldier up and half drug him over to their sand model. "Where's Li?" he demanded.

The soldier studied the model for a moment and then pointed to a pinecone that stood for a large control tower near the docks.

"Where does he live?"

The soldier looked at Caleb, his eyes pleading.

"Where does he live?" Caleb repeated through grit teeth.

Reluctantly, he stooped over and made a dimple in the dirt a short way outside their model.

"He lives in town," Caleb said.

He had Rice fetch a handful of pebbles and he laid them out like the houses in the area the soldier had indicated. "Which one?"

The soldier studied the grid and then pointed to a pebble halfway up the second block overlooking the crooked stick river. Caleb looked at Darrian.

"You finally found him," Darrian affirmed.

"It seems Lance and I will be working with you a bit longer," sighed Eddy. "But first, let's take out the trash." He grabbed the now writhing soldier and retied his hands behind his back while Lance gagged him.

The thought of what was about to happen turned Caleb's stomach. He believed in pest control, but not torture. But what could he do? Lance was right, they couldn't keep him, not that Caleb wanted him to live, but he couldn't shoot the soldier or the whole Chinese army would know they were there.

"What are you gonna do?" asked Rice.

"We're gonna carve him up a bit before we feed him to the coyotes," sneered Lance.

"Why would you do that?" asked Rice, sounding more concerned.

"Because they're animals and it's what they deserve," replied Eddy.

"You're the one's acting like animals!" Rice's eyes were wide with disbelief now. He looked to Caleb, who looked to Darrian.

"Hey, he's their catch," Darrian said, holding up his hands.

All at once, the soldier dropped to the ground, freeing himself from Lance's grasp, and rolled to his feet. A couple of quick strides later, he leapt off the ledge and out of sight. A muted splash permeated the stunned silence.

"Fool, his hands are still tied," Lance shrugged.

"You're the fool," Eddy said, cuffing Lance over the head. "He wasn't trying to escape."

Caleb sighed in relief. Though something still gnawed at him in the pit of his stomach, he pushed it away. It was definitely better this way.

"If that guy washes up near the docks, we'll be in for it," Darrian said. "I'll keep watch on the compound."

"Good, hopefully he'll get hung up in that log jam. The rest of us will pack up camp," Caleb said. "If we're caught, we need to be ready to move, and if not, we'll hit the house tonight, accomplish our objective, and get out of here."

As the band set into motion, Caleb noticed Rice still standing watching the bluff where the soldier had jumped.

"You alright?" asked Caleb.

"I don't understand."

"He thought it was better than what Eddy had planned for him," Caleb said.

"But why didn't he just try to escape?"

"Are you feeling bad for him? Look what they've done to you, to all of us," Caleb retorted.

"They're not all bad," Rice whispered.

"What's that supposed to mean?"

"Back in the camp, when my mom died, it was a guard, not the other prisoners, who kept me alive. I couldn't tell anyone, or he would be punished. He was gentle and . . . and sad. He used to put medicine on my back when I got beat. He taught me Mandarin. He didn't know much English, but one word he said a lot was 'sorry.' He treated me more like a human than anyone ever did. A couple years ago he got sent someplace else, but I don't know where."

Caleb's mind drifted to the Chinese man who had married his sister. He could picture Wu risking his life for an American child. He'd deserted the Chinese army, and therefore his entire homeland, to avoid being part of its atrocities. Caleb shook his head. One or two anomalies didn't change anything.

Chapter 9

Hours had passed since the soldier leapt from the ledge, but no alarm rose from the city. Caleb tugged on his lip as he watched the control tower on the dock; anxiety and anticipation slugged it out in his stomach. He'd yet to lay eyes on Li, but he was sure he was there. Without confirmation they couldn't carry out the mission and time was ticking; in another hour the sun would set.

"Still nothing?" Darrian asked, sliding next to him on the log. Caleb shook his head.

"I know you're itching to go, so am I, but all the work over all these years will be for nothing if we mess this up." Darrian sighed. "Even if we spot him, I think we should wait until tomorrow, so we have plenty of time to come up with a good plan. We dodged a bullet with that soldier . . . let's not waste it."

Caleb set down the binoculars. After a moment he nodded. "I know this is our only shot, everyone needs to be ready and do their job. We won't live to try it again."

Darrian held out his hand and Caleb handed him the binoculars.

"But if we don't go soon, I'm likely to slip off during the night and do something stupid," Caleb said, only half jokingly.

"Wouldn't be the first time, that's what got us into this mess," Darrian said, elbowing him in the ribs.

"You have any regrets about following me?" asked Caleb.

"Naw. I love the adventure. Aaron's a smart guy, and his way is the only way we're gonna really win this war, but it's too slow for me. All I've got in this world is me; gotta live while l can."

The distant hum of helicopter rotors drew their attention to the sky where a tiny black dot began to grow to the south. As it drew closer, Caleb noticed it was one of the larger transport helicopters flanked on either side by attack helos. It circled the base, flying right over them as they hunkered next to the log. Finally, it made its approach and landed on the airfield. Caleb took the binoculars back and jabbed his finger at Darrian's scope.

The handful of soldiers waiting on the tarmac saluted as four men in uniform exited the large helicopter. One of them returned their salute, holding a thin cane in his hand. Caleb's heart raced as he focused on the rigid figure.

"It's him," he whispered.

"Which one?" Darrian squinted into his scope.

Caleb handed him the binoculars. "The one in the middle, with the stick."

"You're right; he does walk like a peacock."

"He never goes anywhere without that cane."

Li was escorted into a military vehicle which promptly left the compound. Following the river road, they came to a stop on an elaborate stone circle driveway before an enormous stucco mansion with four Tuscan pillars reaching two stories to the arch above. It was the house their captured soldier had pointed out. A soldier quickly jumped out and opened the back door of the vehicle. Li stepped into view and, flanked by two of his men, climbed the great stone steps to his front door. The two soldiers stood guard outside and the vehicle pulled away.

"Looks like he wasn't lying about the house," Darrian said.

"Yeah ... Didn't expect him to have a guard detachment though, maybe he's as important as I was making him out to be."

"He thinks he is, at least," Darrian said.

"Well, if he is, maybe this really will help our side somehow."

"Now, all we need is a plan," Darrian said.

Caleb let out a deep breath getting to his feet. "Let's go tell the others."

Back at the tent, Caleb put Rice on guard so the four of them could work. He wasn't looking forward to this part. Thanks to Eddy's hostilities, he was already sleeping with one eye open. He purposely lingered outside, pretending to give Rice instructions, allowing Darrian plenty of time to break the news to Lance and Eddy and get through the initial barrage of unwanted advice and questioning. Finally, guilt for leaving Darrian to deal with the mess alone sent him under the flap.

"So where are we?" he asked as he sat down.

"Turns out that animal was telling the truth," Lance sneered. "You oughta thank us, we caught you a good one."

Caleb chose to swallow his pride for the sake of progress. "Thank you. You've saved us considerable time and effort."

"You hear that, Eddy? Ol' Colonel Got-To-Do-It-My-Way here just thanked us."

Eddy remained unaltered.

"We've caught a break with Li living outside the wire. He's not alone on that block though, there are several other officers who live there; some with guards. There's also an armored patrol that does a circuit of the neighborhood. On top of that, they're only a couple of blocks from the compound housing thousands of soldiers, vehicles, and aircraft. All that being said, this time we do need a plan." Caleb braced for the rebuttal he knew was coming.

The silence lasted longer than he expected when Eddy finally spoke. "Why not just let Hawkeye here knock him off with the long gun?" he asked, gesturing to Darrian.

"It may come to that," replied Darrian. "But this is a no fail mission, meaning he needs to be confirmed dead. I can take a shot, sure, but unless I hit him in the head, there's no way of being sure he's actually dead. Based on the cover in that area and where

I would need to be to cover you, I won't be close enough to be comfortable taking a headshot. Lastly, my rifle doesn't have a suppressor so when I start shooting, it's gonna touch off a war and we're just a little bit out gunned here."

"So, is this just a suicide mission or somethin'?" asked Lance.

"Only if it has to be," Caleb replied coldly.

It took the better part of four hours for the four men to agree on a plan. They would strike at dusk. Darrian would take up position halfway up the hill with Rice and provide overwatch. Lance and Eddy would knife the guards and stand as their replacements. Caleb would infiltrate the house and execute the target. If anything went wrong, Lance and Eddy were free to go. If the mission succeeded, they were free to go. Regardless, this would be their last night together.

Late into the night, Caleb lay awake, staring at the ceiling of their makeshift tent. Hours had passed since he tried to fall asleep, but who was he kidding? He had trained and prepared for this mission for ten years. He played it out over and over in his head. Rehearsed what he would say to a surprised and terrified Li right before he pulled the trigger. He'd show him, just as Sam had said, that he was better, that all of them were better.

Reaching deep into his pack, Caleb pulled out a small cloth covered bundle and set it on his blanket. He'd been saving these for emergencies. Carefully, he unfolded the cloth in the dim moonlight. Two dark cylinders lay neatly in the center. Reaching for his pistols, he took one and carefully screwed a cylinder on to the end of the barrel. He took the second pistol and repeated the process, laying the two pistols on the cloth when he was finished. They looked unnatural with their elongated barrels, the balance would be off as well, but he'd practiced; for years he'd practiced.

Going suppressed really wasn't his style, but desperate times. . . . Without the suppressors, there was very little hope he would make it out alive. Even with them, there was a significant chance he wouldn't make it, but he had accepted that possibility a long time ago. Li would receive what he had coming, after that . . . he'd never seen anything beyond that. Caleb lifted his eyes to the sky. *I hope you're watching, Sam.*

"Caleb . . . Caleb."

Caleb woke with a start, someone had him by the shoulders. Rolling away, he wrenched his attacker's arm behind him.

"Easy, easy, it's me," Darrian cried out.

Caleb released him, catching his breath. "Sorry."

"It's ok, man," Darrian said, rubbing his shoulder. "I'm surprised you slept at all."

"That makes two of us," Caleb rubbed his eyes. As he adjusted to the light, he saw Rice hunched up against a tree outside the tent. "What's wrong with him?" he asked Darrian.

"Nerves, probably," Darrian shrugged. "Maybe you should go talk to him."

"Why me?"

"'Cause you're the one who let him join us. Besides, he looks up to you. You still aren't afraid of him, are you?

"Alright, alright!" Rolling his eyes, Caleb climbed out of the tent, walked over to the tree, and squatted next to the boy.

"Nervous about tonight?" he asked.

Rice's big eyes met his briefly, then quickly looked away. "I'm fine."

"Look, I'm not gonna sugarcoat it. I told you life wouldn't be easy when you joined us. I don't know how tonight's gonna go. We have a good plan, but things don't always go my way. If anything happens, stick with Darrian; he's a good guy and he's been at this a long time."

"And what about you?" Rice asked.

"What about me?"

"What if something happens to you?"

"Just run, and don't look back," Caleb said, getting up. He patted Rice on the back and walked away.

The hours passed murderously slow as they checked and rechecked their gear in nervous anticipation. Even Lance seemed to be lost for words as Eddy went over their own escape route for the third time. For their team, Darrian selected a secluded creek about a mile away as a rendezvous point if all went well. There would be no goodbyes, no reunions. Once Caleb completed the mission, the two groups would go their separate ways.

Caleb studied the house, the yard, and the neighborhood. He studied the patrol routes, the distance from the compound to the house. Calculated the time it would take soldiers from the compound to arrive, helicopters and drones to get in the air. He planned his exit route carefully. He could outmaneuver dogs and soldiers, but the drones—drones were on another level. His one hope was that the significant population of non-combatant Chinese would make him hard to identify as he made his way through neighborhoods and out of town.

As he pondered the drones, an idea struck him. He pulled out his Chinese camouflage poncho, one of the mylar blankets, and his roll of dental floss. Taking a needle from his sewing kit, he carefully stitched the mylar onto the backside of the poncho, making sure to include the hood. Finishing, he held it up. The poncho hid the mylar well.

"Genius!" Rice said. "They won't see your heat."

Caleb glanced up with a satisfied grin.

"Can't believe I didn't think of that . . ." Darrian said.

"Right?!" replied Caleb.

"I'm making one," declared Darrian, already moving to his pack.

Rice glanced at him, a pleading expression on his face.

"Grab your poncho." Darrian surrendered with a sigh.

As the sun sank into the western sky, Caleb holstered his pistols and donned his poncho. He knew Aaron would do some sort of pep talk to ease everyone's anxiety, but he couldn't find the words.

"Well, this is it. Everyone do your job, and we should come out of this ok. If anything goes wrong, don't hesitate, just run. There's nothing to it. As soon as that car leaves the compound, we move." When he finished, he headed to the observation log.

"Why does he do that?" asked Lance.

"Do what?" asked Darrian.

"Why don't he ever act afraid? Too tough?"

"He's a ghost," answered Darrian dryly.

"A ghost?" chuffed Lance.

"The PLA ground the life right out of him, took everything he loved until the light just went out. He feels nothing, loves nothing, fears nothing. I've known him for ten years, the only time you see any life in those eyes is right before he's about to go straight at 'em. Numbers don't matter, danger doesn't matter, when it's all over it's usually just a big disappointment and he's already searching for the next fight. He lost someone, and he blames himself, he was just a kid, and he hates himself for being afraid. Living made him afraid, so he let himself die. He became the reaper. To the Chinese who've heard of him, he's the America they fear. If he can't escape his hell, neither will they—a ghost."

"So, like you, Eddy," Lance replied.

"No, not like Eddy. Eddy preys on the weak, Eddy still wants to live. Caleb hunts the ones who think they're strong, where they think they're strong. And then he resents them when their strength isn't enough," Darrian said.

"They've just pulled a vehicle around," called Caleb. "Yeah, it's him, he's climbing in now! Let's move!"

Chapter 10

Caleb placed his hand on the ground, the intensifying vibrations of the armored patrol heralded its coming. He stood in the shadow of a marble lion directly across the street from Li's mansion. Somewhere, he hoped in the shadows of Li's home, were Lance and Eddy, poised to take out the guards as soon as the patrol rounded out of sight. Nervously, he felt for his pistols. Of course, he knew they were there, but it calmed his nerves as he ran his fingers over the cool metal of the slides.

The patrol rounded the corner and rolled up the street. As it approached, Caleb saw the soldiers deep in conversation, laughing as they passed. Complacency kills. Taking a deep breath, he prepared to sprint for the door. His heart pounded in his chest with a painful ferocity. The serge of adrenaline set his limbs on fire as the wave of heat washed over him. Sweat seeped into his clothes under the stifling poncho. Suddenly, he was eleven again and about to confront his tormentor. He placed a hand on the lion, steadying himself as nausea overtook him and he vomited.

Wiping his mouth with the back of his hand, he tensed as the patrol rounded the bend out of sight, setting him off like a rocket. The guards had only a moment to take it all in before Lance and Eddy hauled them into the bushes flanking the house. So far so good. . . .

Hitting the door, he wrenched on the handle, and, to his surprise, it turned. His momentum carried him into a large, vaulted entryway. His eyes winced in the bright lights. To his left an astonished Major Li spun around in a leather armchair, a glass of gin still in his hand. Drawing a pistol, Caleb leveled it on Li's face. He held a finger to his lips as he quickly strode over to the chair. Li pressed his back into the chair wide-eyed, the ice in his glass trembling.

Sliding his hood off his head, Caleb asked in practiced Mandarin, "Do you remember me?"

Li shook his head nervously.

"I'm the boy who escaped from Duluth, I worked with the old man cleaning ships," he spoke coldly. "The old man who died the day I escaped."

Li furrowed his brow, then slowly nodded.

"You used to beat us every d—"

Out of nowhere, Caleb was knocked to the floor, his pistol clattered across the polished tiles and bounced off the wall.

Rolling to his back, Caleb already had his other pistol drawn and pointed at his assailant. A fine-boned woman wearing white loungewear was picking herself up off the floor. Caleb froze. Behind her, Li dove for the fallen pistol. Caleb shook himself, rolling to his right as Li reached the gun. Caleb leveled his sights on Li as the woman launched herself at him again.

Li rolled over, firing three times. Caleb felt fire in his thigh as the woman went limp in his arms. Flinging her to the side, Caleb returned fire, striking Li in the chest, knocking him off balance. Caleb steadied his aim, firing twice more. Li slumped to the floor and remained motionless.

Panting, Caleb holstered his pistol and felt his wounded leg. There was no exit wound, his thigh oozed bright red blood.

A shriek sounded from the dining room as a young woman rushed in, collapsing next to the first woman. Agonizing sobs filled the room. Caleb's head spun, a mixture of pain and confusion. It didn't feel right, nothing felt right. He looked back where Li lay on the floor, blood soaking his shirt and he felt . . . nothing.

No wave of relief washed over him, no darkness rushed out of him, no satisfaction filled him. Just emptiness. It was over.

The woman's sobs raked his ears. Cradling the fallen woman's head, her body convulsed uncontrollably with her wails. Blood from the woman stained her clothes. Looking up at him, she shook her head, tears and mucus stringing from her lips.

He fell back against the wall. Her eyes judged him, her pain joining his own in witness against him. It was all wrong.

The door flung open behind him.

"We're all gonna get it if you don't shut her up!" cried Lance.

"Eddy trotted over to Li, picked up Caleb's pistol, and pointed it at the sobbing woman.

"Don't!" Caleb heard himself say.

Eddy only looked at him through narrowed eyes and put the barrel on her head.

Instinctively, Caleb drew his pistol, shooting at the same time. Eddy's pistol flew from his hand and skidded across the floor.

"I said don't." Caleb slowly stood up.

Eddy glared at him and swore, holding his bleeding hand. Tearing the sleeve off the dead woman's blouse he gagged the sobbing girl. Lance pulled a string from Li's boots and tied her hands behind her back. Eddy motioned to the door and Lance hoisted the girl onto his shoulder.

"Spoils of war," he cackled.

As Lance turned, her eyes met Caleb's. Where he expected to see hate, he saw pleading. He'd seen those eyes before. . . . Where? Then he knew; she was the girl from that day in the rain, the little girl in the white dress who'd looked at him with pity as he shivered in the cold Duluth mist.

"Leave her," he commanded.

"I'm done taking orders from you!" snarled Eddy over his shoulder, "You got what you wanted."

Without hesitation, Caleb bolted between them and the door. "Put her down, Lance!" he growled, leveling his pistol at Lance's face.

Out of the corner of his eye, he saw Eddy's slight nod.

In a single move, Lance dropped his shoulder and launched the woman into Caleb's arms, then pounced on him like a wild dog. Caleb's wounded leg gave way and he fell backwards, flinging the woman clear of the fray as Eddy lunged at him with his knife. The hard tile floor ground against his spine and dug his pistol belt into his back as he fought to free himself from Lance's grasp while kicking Eddy away. Scoring a boot to Eddy's midsection, he leaned forward, grabbed Lance's ear between his teeth and bit down hard. With a howl, Lance rolled away, giving Caleb enough room to raise his pistol.

Both men dove behind a sofa as Caleb cut loose. He rolled to his second pistol just as he emptied the first. Time was running out. He slid over to the girl, trembling on the floor, trying to hide her head behind her knees. Pulling her to her feet, he emptied his second magazine into the wall just above the sofa and raced for the door, half dragging the woman behind him.

He had no way of knowing where the armored patrol was, and there was no doubt in his mind that someone had heard the commotion. Running through the neighborhood with a hostage on his shoulder would be suicide. He burst from the doorway and signaled to Darrian, who he knew would be watching, to cover him. Throwing his poncho over the woman, he hefted her onto his shoulder and took off for the thick undergrowth of the forest that separated the neighborhood from the river.

Within seconds, he heard the familiar sound of Darrian's rifle and then the night exploded with the wail of sirens as the compound began laying down fire on the hillside. He didn't look back; he couldn't look back.

Thorny branches tore at the poncho as he ran, slashing his face and hands. As he hit the river's edge, he found what he was looking for, a game trail. He paused, panting. His clothes clung to him, soaked with sweat and dew. And blood. His leg throbbed and his heart drummed in his ears as he strained to listen. The confused din of the compound rattled on behind him, but no one followed. Under the poncho, he could feel the woman's body rise with each breath. What was he going to do with her?

A snapping twig sent him running again. Somewhere about quarter mile ahead was the mouth of the creek, and a mile and a half up the creek he would rendezvous with Darrian and Rice. That is, if they made it off that hill alive.

The bubbling sound of water rolling over pebbles quickened his stride; the creek was near. Just ahead, the trail dropped down a steep bank and he could see it pick up on the other side. As he reached the ledge, he slid down the bank to the cool waters below. The woman under the poncho squirmed and let out a squeal as the cold water hit her legs. Caleb pulled off the poncho and set her down gently on a sand bank before dunking his head under the water.

He shook the water from his eyes as he straightened and then studied her. Long sleek hair clung to her pale skin. She trembled, staring through him, eyes unblinking. Shock. He'd seen it a hundred times over the years.

"I'm sorry about the poncho," he said in his best Mandarin. "The drones will see me if I don't use it."

She didn't move, blink, nothing.

What did he expect? Sorry the poncho is hot, please accept my apology, I did just murder your family. Stupid.

He moved to her side and untied the gag. Wrapping the sleeve around his leg, he cinched it down tight, groaning as the pressure squeezed the slug in his thigh. Then he cut the boot laces from her hands. Her arms drooped lifelessly to her sides.

"We can't stay here. Can you walk?" he asked tentatively.

There was no answer, he didn't expect any. It was his turn to look on her with pity. His stomach churned. He had meant to punish Li, he'd finally gotten even, gotten justice for Sam and all the others. But the truth was, Li wasn't feeling anything now, only this woman was. Only she was left to carry the weight of her father's sins, only she was broken and empty sitting on this beach. The only one who'd ever looked at him with pity. Caleb shook his head, clearing it. No, Li got what he deserved—she shouldn't have been there. None of them should even be here. They brought this on themselves. An eye for an eye.

He should've left her, would've left her. But his conscience wouldn't rest knowing what Lance and Eddy had planned for her. That wasn't justice or even revenge . . . it was . . . darkness.

Donning the poncho, he bent over and scooped her up in his arms. Her tiny frame felt almost weightless, a hundred pounds tops. That's what it feels like, to have it all taken away, that's what your people did, to me, to all of us. You took everything!

Caleb trudged bitterly forward; she was ruining his revenge.

Chapter 11

After another quarter mile, Caleb was forced to stop and rest. His leg quivered now, the bandage red with blood. The compound had gone quiet, all except for the helicopters hovering along the river's edge, their search lights flashing here and there. He set the woman down on a log, half expecting her to tip over, but she managed to hold herself upright. Crawling to the creek's edge he found a spot where the water bubbled over a long stretch of pebbles. He bent over and sucked up the water, swallowing large gulps until he was full.

"You want some?" he asked.

Nothing.

Perhaps letting Eddy shoot her would have been more merciful than this. Now he was stuck dealing with this dead weight.

Rolling his eyes, he cupped water in his hands and brought it to her mouth. At first, she just stared through him as the water slowly dripped between his fingers. But then she moved her head ever so slightly and sucked up what was left.

"Want more?"

Nothing.

Sighing, he sat back against the log. His thigh quivered through his soaked pants.

"Look," he said in English, "I know this is a bad situation, but those guys back there were really bad guys who would do really bad things to you." He sighed again; she probably had no idea what he was saying anyway. "I would have left you there if they hadn't shown up, but things didn't really go my way."

Still nothing.

He tried his broken Mandarin again, this time with supporting hand motions. "We have under a mile to go, and my leg would really appreciate it if I didn't have to carry you."

Nothing.

"Honestly, I'd love to just leave you here, I'm not sure if they're following us, but if not, you could just follow the creek to the river and back home. The only problem is, I'm not going to make it far on this leg and if you pointed them in the right direction, I'd be in big trouble. So, at least for a little while, we're stuck together. The last option would be to just shoot you." He paused, looking for a reaction, his hand in the shape of a pistol pointing at her head.

Nothing.

Huffing, he dropped his hand and said, "But I think we both know I won't do that—which brings us back to would you pleeeease be willing to walk?"

To his surprise, she stood from the log.

"Thank you."

Hesitantly, he took her by the hand. It remained limp, but she didn't refuse. Together they stumbled their way down the shallow creek. Every step was painful now; the adrenaline was gone. Stopping near some deadwood, Caleb found a long, forked branch. He held it up to his side for size and then broke off about a foot. Placing the forked end under his armpit, he took a hopping step—the branch held.

"It'll have to do."

The girl sat quietly waiting on a small sandy island, the color had returned to her face. He wasn't sure if this was a good thing or a bad thing. She was easy to handle in shock, not very helpful, but manageable. If she got her wits about her, in his current state, that could be a problem. It was unlikely she could do him harm, but if she ran, he'd never catch her. He looked at her feet, he could hobble her with the bit of boot lace he had stuffed in his pocket after freeing her. Wait, she's in socks!

He nearly facepalmed at the revelation. She'd been walking for over a quarter mile on a cold rocky creek bed in only her socks. He balanced uneasily on the crutch; this is not how he had pictured the night going. This girl was ruining everything, and now she has no shoes?!

"Sorry about your feet," he managed to say.

She rubbed them together in the sand as though it was the first time she'd thought about them.

"We've got another half mile or so, then we can rest."

She stood quietly and turned up the creek ahead of him.

So far so good. . . .

As they neared the bend in the creek that defined the rendezvous, Caleb let out a low whistle. The woman froze in her tracks in front of him.

"I'm checking to see if my friends are here," he whispered. "Looks like we got here first." He tried to sound confident, but he had no idea of knowing if anyone else had even survived.

"Let's hunker down on that sandbar, I'll stretch the poncho over that willow. Should give us enough cover."

He watched her trudge over to the sandbar and plop down on the ground. Stringing the poncho out over her head, he studied her. She was petite, with sleek hair that reached halfway down her back. She was wearing gray heather sweatpants that stopped at her calves and a simple teal t-shirt. Three toes stuck out the tattered end of her left sock, a rusty stain slowly crept across her heel on the right. Under normal circumstances, she'd probably have a fit right about now over her looks, but she just sat staring back down the creek.

His leg throbbed, sitting seemed worse. He limped back and forth, waiting nervously for any sign of Darrian. Not only was he a friend, but without Darrian, he'd have no supplies, no extra ammo, no med kit, no food, no water . . . nothing. As the pain in his leg grew, so did his anxiety. Waves of nausea and dizziness washed over him with each pulse of his heart until he found himself sitting midstream.

The cool water tempered his fever, enabling him to think again. He glanced over to his prisoner. She was watching him, or through him, he couldn't be sure. They were in a bad spot, and unfortunately, they couldn't stay long. It was possible Lance and Eddy would be captured and, given their current relationship, they'd be sure to give the PLA the location of their rendezvous. *Where are you, brother?*

At last, the distant splashing of footsteps revealed someone's approach. Straining his ears, he could only make out a couple distinct footfalls. He drew his pistol all the same, waiting. . . . At last, a familiar low whistle echoed around the bend. Caleb answered. Two poncho clad figures trotted into sight.

"Dude? What are you doing in the middle of the stream?!" asked Darrian.

"I'm hit, and I didn't have my kit. The pain was beginning to compromise the situation, so I put some ice on it," Caleb winced as he pushed himself out of the water.

"How bad?" asked Darrian.

"It'll heal, once I get the slug out," Caleb assured him.

"Who got you?" Darrian asked, setting down Caleb's pack.

Caleb didn't answer.

"Who's this?!" asked Rice, taking a step back.

Darrian swung his head in her direction.

"What on earth?!" Darrian exclaimed.

"She was there, there was nothing I could do. Lance and Eddy were going to take her," answered Caleb, putting his hands up.

"So? Then let 'em take her! Since when do you give a hoot about a dirty Chinese chick? They would've done us a favor. Is that what the "cover me" was all about? Miss Chinatown over there?" Darrian hissed.

"It's his daughter, I think . . ." replied Caleb.

"His daughter? What on earth do you want his daughter for? Have you lost your freaking mind?!"

"Look, I don't know what came over me, ok? I just couldn't let them take her. You know what they would do."

"Oh, you couldn't, huh? Did she see the whole thing?" Darrian asked.

"I don't know, probably!"

"Then don't you think the first thing she's gonna do is kill you when she gets the chance, maybe us too?" Darrian kicked water in his face. "You're a fool, Caleb! You deserved to get shot! Give me your pistol, I'm gonna take care of this right now!"

"I can't," Caleb whispered.

"Yes, you can, and you're gonna!" Darrian demanded, storming over to him.

"She was there."

"I know, that's why we're gonna do something about it!"

"No, she was in Duluth."

Darrian paused. "Duluth?"

"Yeah." Caleb looked over to where she was huddled up, as if awaiting her sentence. "She showed up on a boat with her mom one day. It was cold and raining but Li made us all stand in formation to welcome them. He paraded them around in their white dresses and umbrellas while we froze. For some reason, they stopped by us, and I remember her looking at me. I don't know, it was different than anyone else. She felt sorry for me. I never saw her again."

He looked up at Darrian. "I used to hate her. But when I saw her over Lance's shoulder, having just lost everything, something in me just—I couldn't let her endure what they would take from her too." His head hung in defeat.

"So let me get this straight. I've watched you live like a zombie for the last ten years because of this girl's dad, and then the first thing you actually feel when it's all over is an overwhelming need to protect her? For the love of—" Darrian turned around and stomped back to the beach leaving Caleb in his wake.

Rice squatted down next to the girl. Digging in his pack he pulled out a pair of boots. "We picked these up a couple of days ago, it's the smallest size we've found, so when I found a second pair I grabbed 'em. They're still a little big, but they've got to be better than just running around in socks." He held them out to the girl.

Nothing.

"She's been like that the whole time," Caleb said.

Rice slid over to her feet and loosened the laces on the boots.

"You, too?" groaned Darrian. Glaring at Caleb, he said, "Get over here before you bleed to death."

Limping to the beach, Caleb flopped down on his back. Darrian rummaged around in his pack and pulled out a med kit. He lifted out the iodine, tweezers, and a scalpel. Laying them on the lid of the tin, he opened a fresh gauze bandage.

"We need to be quick," Caleb gasped. "Those two goons will turn us in if they get captured."

"They didn't get captured, I watched them escape, that's why we're a little late," Darrian said, pouring iodine on the wound. "Rice, get over here and hold the lighter so I can see what I'm doing!"

Rice hurried over and plopped down beside Darrian. "Have you done this before?"

"Thanks to this idiot, I've had the pleasure a few times."

Darrian prodded around the wound with his finger. With a groan, Caleb's head fell back and he stared, unseeing, up at the stars. Grabbing a nearby twig, Darrian rinsed it in the creek and placed it between Caleb's teeth.

"It's deep," he said. "I can't get the tweezers open wide enough to grab the bullet—I'm gonna have to use the knife."

Taking a deep breath, Caleb clenched his fists and nodded.

As the knife entered his flesh, Caleb went stiff, his teeth dug into the twig.

"I'm gonna be sick . . ." cried Rice.

"Don't you even think about runnin', I need that light. If you've got to hurl, do it to the side, but don't you leave me in the dark!" Darrian said, pulling the knife from the wound. "Let's see if that did it," he said, inserting the tweezers into the opening.

Caleb's world spun; white heat exploded in his head. He groaned.

"I think I've got it!" Darrian said. He looked over to Rice. "This is the worst part. Get ready to hold him down if I need you to."

"What about the light?"

"I've already got a hold of it. If I need you to, drop the lighter and lay across his chest. Don't let his hands get down here."

The lighter in Rice's hand trembled.

"Ok, brother, I need you to be a big boy. Don't. Reach. For. Me."

Caleb nodded, grabbing fistfuls of sand. The twig was already in splinters between his teeth.

"One, two . . ."

Waves of pain enveloped him, clenching his fistfuls of sand, he fought to hang on. His body tensed and he resisted the urge to fight back as Darrian jerked the slug free. Then a blanket of darkness folded over him, his world stopped spinning, and he was lost to the black.

Chapter 12

Y ou don't need to be afraid of those two, they won't hurt you. I know Darrian talks tough, but I don't think he could have done it if he'd wanted to. And Caleb over there, to me he seems . . . I don't know, he makes me sad. He's the most driven hopeless person I've ever met. He doesn't want to live, but he won't just lie down and be killed either. For him there isn't a tomorrow, or an *after all this* like the rest of us talk about. He really is a ghost, a terrifying and pitiful ghost, but he's an honest ghost. You'll be fine."

Caleb cracked his eyelids. He was looking straight up into the pail glow of a cloudy night sky. He shifted his weight slightly and was punished with a flash of searing pain. Groaning, he carefully relaxed again.

"You're awake!" cried Rice, jumping up from his seat next to the prisoner and coming to his side. "Darrian said to give you these if you woke up before he got back."

He held out two large white pills and a tin cup of water.

"Can you sit up?"

"I don't know," Caleb managed.

"Well, we're going to have to give it a try," Rice said encouragingly.

Rice moved to his head and wedged his hands under Caleb's armpits. "On three, ok?"

Caleb nodded, digging his elbows into the sand.

"One, two, three!"

Rice pulled up as Caleb lifted. Using his good leg, he pushed his rear back.

As the pain rose to punish him again, he ground his teeth together, breathing heavy out his nose. They managed to get him sitting well enough. Taking a few moments to collect himself, he nodded that he was ready.

"They'll help with the pain, according to Darrian," Rice said as Caleb popped the pills in his mouth. "Darrian said it was real deep, and that it may have clipped the bone. You bled a lot . . ." he glanced away for a moment. "More than I've ever seen a living person bleed."

Caleb thought he saw him blink away tears.

"Darrian was worried too, he said we'd have to wait and see if you'd wake up. I think that's the real reason he went out to find stuff for your stretcher. I knew you'd pull through, you're the fiercest person I've ever known, your story couldn't end like that," he said, giving Caleb a half smile.

Everything felt as though it were in slow motion, he felt weak, it was uncomfortable. His eyes wandered over to the prisoner. As they did, her eyes rose to meet his. There it was again, pity, pity for him, pity for her, pity for the whole awful mess. His grand accomplishment, all wrongs righted, everything made even—it was pitiful. She was right, he was pitiful.

He looked down at his tightly wrapped leg, a mound of gauze protruding over the hole. Chuckling to himself, he shook his head. Li might still get the last laugh . . . pitiful.

Darrian returned with two long poles and dropped them on the beach.

"Ahh, so the Eagle lives again," he said, giving Caleb a warm pat on the back. "Doesn't look like you'll be walking anytime soon so we're just going to have to carry you."

It took Darrian only minutes to make a stretcher using a poncho and the poles. With Darrian at the head and Rice at the rear, they were moving again. The prisoner walked behind Darrian next to the stretcher. They continued up the creek, putting more distance between themselves and Memphis.

The travel was brutal by moonlight. The team of litter bearers staggered and slipped over rocks and debris, dropping every now and again into a deeper pool. Each jostle sent fresh reminders of Caleb's wound clawing through his nervous system, yet that wasn't his greatest discomfort. She was always there, every time he opened his eyes, she loomed over him. Her empty eyes, expressionless face. The reaper had to have more life in him than she did.

After a couple of miles Darrian halted the group where the creek bed widened into a sandbar at the base of a tall, eroded cliff. Several twisted willows with exposed roots had blown over creating a tangled lean-to along the bank.

"This look ok to you?" he asked Caleb.

"It's perfect," Caleb whispered weakly.

Warm light glowed through Caleb's eyelids. He ran his tongue over dried flaking lips and strained to open his eyes. A fly picked its way across his face and, reaching up, he managed to brush it away. At last, his eyes opened in slits; watering as powerful daylight flooded in. From nearby he heard Rice acknowledge his movements.

"Sleep well?"

"How long have I been out?"

"At least a day and a half," he said. "You've had a pretty good fever."

"I need water."

Filling a tin cup from a canteen, Rice brought it over.

As he drank it, Darrian appeared.

"Hey, I'm glad you're up. We've got a situation . . . well, several. Can you sit up?"

Caleb forced himself up, his leg was stiff, but the pain was manageable.

"Good," Darrian said. He pulled out a map of Tennessee and laid it on Caleb's lap. "Remember how odd it seemed that the docks at Memphis were unloading military hardware, not loading it, like you'd expect in a normal retreat?"

Caleb nodded.

"Well, I've been doing a little reconnaissance, and something is up. They appear to be pulling back all across this area from Henderson to Brownsville, maybe further, but I've been watching the traffic and they're redistributing troops, tanks, APCs, both north and south, in force. Not only that, but fresh troops are arriving up the river every day." His finger traced the routes. "I think it's a trap. They know we don't have the best intel, and they've been on the retreat for a while. I think they're faking this retreat and setting up massive flanking counter attacks. If the Americans take the bait, they'll be completely surrounded before they figure out what's what. It's perfect."

"It's desperate." Caleb looked up at him. "Aaron is so focused on what's in front of him that, as long as they're retreating, he'll keep pushing. He wants this war over."

Darrian sighed, nodding his agreement.

"If you're right, then we have to do something." Caleb thought for a moment. "You'll have to leave me here and warn them."

"Leave you?! What, with a kid, and a Chinc who wants you dead? Are you hearing yourself? You've been out for almost two days with a fever, your leg is probably infected, and we're surrounded by thousands of Chinese." Darrian scowled at him.

"Hey, we've been in worse."

"No, we haven't!" Darrian challenged.

"Ok, ok, maybe not, but we're not leaving my family—America—to be destroyed on account of my bum leg."

"I can do it," Rice interjected.

"Do what?" Darrian mumbled.

"I can take care of him. I'm strong, and brave when I need to be, I've watched you change his dressings. Xiuying can help me carry him."

"Xiuying?" asked Darrian with a raised eyebrow.

"Yes, that's her name. She has one of those, you know."

"And why would Xiuying be of any assistance?"

"I don't know, because she has nothing else to do?" Rice shrugged.

Standing, Darrian threw up his hands.

"We have to warn them," Caleb said. "And you know you're the only one who can. Traveling on your own you could make the trip in four or five days, maybe faster depending on the advance. They have to be warned before they hit the bottom of the trap, while they're still able to retreat."

"Caleb, the only scenario that's a sure thing if I go, is this girl running off and turning you in the first time Rice falls asleep. He can't stay awake forever, and you would be powerless to catch her. You've ruled out putting her down . . ." He hesitated, as if giving Caleb a chance to change his mind. Sighing, he continued. "Aaron is a slow mover, if the PLA retreat too fast, he'll catch on. We've got a couple weeks, maybe a month, before the trap will be ready to spring; let's just see how far we can get. If it gets down to the wire . . . I'll go," Darrian replied.

Rice jumped up and stomped his way up the bank.

"Where you going?" called Darrian.

"To relive myself!"

"Kids got some fire," chuckled Caleb.

"Yeah, he's just hot because I didn't think he could—"

Darrian lurched and fell over as a rifle report tore through the calm morning.

Flinging himself off his stretcher, Caleb bear-crawled his way over to Xiuying, hauling her behind the fallen trees. Panting, he saw Darrian through the branches, lying face down in the sand and pebbles where he'd fallen.

"I bet you thought we'd forgot about you!" hollered a familiar voice.

"Lance . . ." Caleb muttered under his breath.

Another rifle round blew through the branches above his head.

"You shoulda let us take the girl. Everything would've been fine, but your boy over there nearly shot Eddy's ear clean off, tried to kill him. And now he's lying in the dirt. Eddy doesn't forgive and forget."

Another round slammed into the log in front of them.

"You give us the girl, we'll call it even, whad'ya say?"

Caleb watched Darrian; he didn't move. He was gone. No time for grief. . . .

Drawing his pistols, he looked at Xiuying. Her small frame clung tightly to the log in front of her. She was afraid, and she wanted to live; good. He studied the opposite bank; they were there somewhere. There, a shuddering twig, a flash of movement, a dark shadow. Crawling along the logjam, Caleb sprang up to his knees firing into the shadow before dropping back down.

"Hey, Ghost, not bad, you actually clipped me," laughed Lance, sending several more rounds into the log.

"Where's Eddy, where's Eddy," Caleb whispered to himself, searching the trees and shrubs. "Where's Rice?"

The creek erupted as a drone rocketed the willows they'd been calling home. Splinters rained from the sky. Caleb's ringing ears muffled Xiuying's screams beside him. Another rocket sent up a spray of water, mud, and splinters from the logjam that had concealed Lance's position. Caleb collected himself and hauled his pack from the debris. He caught Xiuying by the hand, peeling her from the log.

"We have to go!" he shouted over the ringing in his ears.

Leaving the creek, they plowed their way northeast through the understory and deeper into the woods. They were only a couple miles out of Memphis. For all he knew, the whole Chinese army could be converging on them. Beside him, Xiuying stumbled and clawed her way forward, holding his hand like a vice. The forest erupted as the first artillery blast flung them mercilessly to the ground, showering them in debris.

Chapter 13

The trees shook and shuddered under the merciless artillery bombardment. Opening his eyes, Caleb saw Xiuying trembling beside him. Her hands covered her head, and she shook violently with every explosion. A large tree several yards to their right had sustained a direct hit and lay with its roots reaching for the sky. Grabbing her by the arms, he drug her to the new crater and rolled her in. Slipping down beside her, he covered her with his Harley jacket and buried his head in his arms.

The bombardment ended as dramatically as it had begun. The silence was stunning. With his head aching, Caleb peered out of the hole. The entire hillside looked as though a tornado had swept through. Trees lay in every direction; the ones still standing were peppered with shrapnel and wrapped in twisted limbs. The drone would be back soon to look for survivors.

He tried to pull his jacket off Xiuying, but her hands fought him as he slid it from her face.

"It's ok, it's over, but we have to keep moving! If they send that drone again, we'll be finished!"

She writhed in the dirt, wedging herself further under the roots. He'd let her keep his jacket. Kneeling, he slipped an arm around her, and with his other arm under her legs, he lifted her out of the hole. The motion sent fresh waves of pain through his leg, and he let out an involuntary groan. Scanning their surroundings, he saw no one. So far so good.

He walked as briskly as his leg would carry him, over the hill, down a valley, another creek. He didn't know where they were, which direction they were going, there wasn't a plan. Darrian was gone, Lance and Eddy could be gone, might not be, and Rice . . . he had no way of knowing. The Chinese knew where they were now, had certainly connected them to the hit on Li, making them high priority targets. Aaron and the rest of his family were with the Americans currently battling their way into a trap. And here was the mighty Eagle, terror of the Chinese, lost in the woods carrying the daughter of his nemesis, who would probably be the death of him.

Grief tore at him, fear drove him, compassion slowed him. It was madness. He had no where, no why, no how. He trudged on, whether towards danger or away from it, he had no way of knowing.

Stumbling upon an old gravel road, he followed it. It had clearly been abandoned since the war as much of the less arterial infrastructure had been. Small trees and shrubs had carved out an existence in the hard packed surface. Caleb scanned the woods on either side hoping to come across an old home, something empty but still habitable in an emergency.

After an hour of steady walking Caleb felt his leg beginning to give out. He'd passed several homes that were more dangerous on the inside than the woods on the outside. The sunlight was beginning to wane when the road crossed a trickling stream over an old concrete bridge. Sliding gently off the road, he looked underneath. He thanked God when he saw a flattened sandy ledge where someone had taken the time to make a place to sleep. The telltale black creosote on the wall where a small fire had once burned gave it the final homey touch.

Gingerly carrying her over the chunks of rock and cement piled up to prevent erosion, he set Xiuying on the ledge leaning her back against the concrete wall of the bridge. Her eyes fluttered open, and she held his jacket tight while taking in her surroundings.

"You've been sleeping for quite a bit," Caleb stated the obvious, trying to fill the awkward silence. He slipped off his pack and found his canteen. After dipping it in the stream, he handed it to her. "It should be clean enough."

She reached out and took it, taking a large gulp before handing it back to Caleb. He took a swallow and set it down on a rock.

"I'm gonna go find some stuff to make a fire," he said, scratching his head.

She just looked at him.

"Right."

He walked out into the fading evening light. As he collected twigs and branches, part of him hoped she'd run off. He couldn't catch her, but she was likely just as lost as he was, and he doubted she'd ever finished Girl Scouts. He looked down at his leg, the bandage was bright red and blood had seeped into his pants. It hurt. He knew he was running desperately low in his med kit.

You're in a bad way, Caleb.

As if in agreement, a large fox squirrel began chattering angrily overhead. Caleb felt for his pistol; it still had the silencer on it. Slowly setting down his bundle of sticks, he chambered a round. Taking aim, he dropped the fluffy rodent in a single shot.

"Got any friends?" he asked, picking up the squirrel.

After a short hunt that failed to turn up anything else, he returned to the bridge. It was dark under there, really dark. He kicked himself for leaving Xiuying without any light. He could hear her breath quivering as he stumbled his way across the stones.

"It's just me," he said, trying to sound reassuring.

He found the area where he'd left his pack and felt around inside. Finding his container of matches, he pulled it out and struck one. He held the match in one hand while situating a small handful of twigs near the burn mark on the wall. As the flame reached his fingers, he threw the match in the stream and lit another. He held the half-spent match near the base of his pile and the flame leapt up the dry sticks, flickering wildly as it consumed them. Breaking several larger branches over his knee, he fed them into the fire. The light filled their tiny cave, making the shadows dance on the walls.

He pulled his knife from its sheath and proceeded to skin the squirrel.

"I doubt you've ever tried one of these before, but they're quite good," he said. "I can't actually remember a time in my life when we didn't eat them. It would have to have been before you people showed up . . ." He let his words trail off, replacing them with another awkward silence.

He rinsed the squirrel in the stream and slid it onto a narrow stick. He balanced it across a couple of rocks, leaving the squirrel suspended six inches above the fire. Taking out his knife, he cut his bandages off, gasping as the pressure released. After rinsing his wound with water from the canteen, he studied it through the rip in his pants. Blood oozed up and out of the hole, running around his thigh. He fumbled around his pack and pulled out his med kit; setting it down, he reached over and flipped the squirrel.

Returning to the med kit, he could feel her watching him. He glanced up just in time to catch her look away. Popping open the kit, he studied its meager contents. His gauze was all used up, the tube of antiseptic was all but empty, two alcohol wipes, and a few Band-Aids. He felt the urge to panic creeping up. He closed his eyes. Pull it together, Caleb!

Blood rolled off his thigh dripping on the underside of his pants. What had he learned, what had he heard over the years? What would Sam do? He caught the firelight glinting off his knife. Burn it. That's right, he'd heard of guys burning their wounds to stop the bleeding. His wound was a hole, a deep hole. How do you burn a hole? He looked at his knife, it wouldn't do. He closed his eyes, processing his options. A hole, a hole, how do you burn a hole? Then he saw it, a baseball sized piece of concrete with a six-inch length of thick rebar protruding from it. He pictured inserting the glowing rod into his wound.

"After the squirrel," he gasped. Looking over at Xiuying, he caught her glancing away again.

"Time to eat," he said, taking the squirrel off the fire. Twisting off a leg, he held it out. "It'll help take the edge off."

She took the squirrel without misgivings and peeled a bit of meat off with her teeth, chewing slowly. He tore off a leg for himself and went after it like a starving man. Twisting off another, he handed it to Xiuying as she threw the bone from the first into the fire. He took the last leg and worked off every last shred of meat. He glanced over at Xiuying who was trying to do the same.

"Here," he said, handing her the stick with the squirrel on it. "You can have the rest."

Throwing more wood on the fire, Caleb slid off the ledge and collected the rebar. Kneeling near the water, he washed the rusted metal as best as he could manage. The wound throbbed and oozed as he scrubbed. He limped back to the fire under Xiuying's questioning gaze.

After placing the metal rod in the fire, he added a few more branches and gave her an uneasy smile. She looked from his leg to the fire and then to his face, her eyes growing wide as she connected the dots.

"I've got to stop the bleeding . . ." he said, doing his best to sound confident.

She shook her head, sliding further back on the ledge.

Taking the rock end in his hand, he held the tip of the rod over the wound. The heat curled the hairs on his leg. Then he remembered the water. Setting the rod back in the flames, he collected his canteen and filled it from the cool stream. Sliding back up on the ledge, he set the open canteen next to his leg. Reaching out, he took the rock again in his hand. He took a deep breath to settle his nerves. It didn't seem to help. Spreading the wound open, he held the dancing rod tip over the open hole.

"I know it probably won't mean anything but, I'm sorry," he said, slamming the rod into the wound.

Lights flashed in his mind. Colors, vivid and grand, swarmed him. Voices danced through his head like the menacing cackles of madmen languishing in forgotten places. Everything spun in different directions and yet he was still. Layers of darkness washed over the decadent spectacle until everything was lost to the loneliness of the dark. Leaving only a little boy sitting on a stack of cardboard, shivering in the dark, longing for a familiar flicker of light.

Sam . . .

Chapter 14

Mandarin voices permeated his dreams. Sometimes speaking in hushed tones, other times the voices were intense and clear. The smell of alcohol, rubber, and breath. The clanking of metal, swishing water, and shuffling feet. Flashes of light followed by darkness. He drifted on a slow currant, somewhere between the living and the dead. He saw Darrian, Sam, his father. He saw Li and his wife, and countless other soldiers, faceless, nameless, only a uniform. He fought through endless days of war, filled with loss, void of purpose or hope. If only he could quiet the voices.

He hunted the far corners of his mind, fought to extinguish every last one, but there was no end. At last, he collapsed, exhausted and empty, in the frost laden tundra of his mindscape. They surrounded him, the faceless uniforms of a thousand soldiers. Voices humming and murmuring, like the angry chorus of a colony of bees. Drawing his pistol, he held it to his head and pulled the trigger.

Gasping, Caleb sat bolt upright in his bed. Bed? Plastic tubes were taped to his hand, a bag of clear liquid hung next to his head. He was in a small room with two narrow windows. Judging by the length of the shadows, it was either midmorning or midafternoon. A large portrait of the Chinese President hung on the wall dwarfing a small desk. Shelves full of medical equipment and supplies occupied the remaining space in the room except for a small chair in the corner with a familiar body curled up under a gray wool blanket.

So, she had turned him in. Lifting his arms, he was surprised not to find any cuffs. Other than the plastic tubes, there was nothing tying him to anything. There was a shuffle of feet outside the door, the knob turned, and in walked a bald, middle-aged man wearing thick rimmed glasses and a lab coat. The man jumped when he saw Caleb sitting up and rushed the bed, whispering harshly in Mandarin at Xiuying who had already flung the blanket to the floor and was on her way to the bed. Caleb fought franticly to keep the man's hands off him.

"It is ok!" Xiuying whispered in English. "He is helping you."

Caleb looked at her and back to the man. The man rattled off several expressive sentences, nodding back at the door.

"He says if you do not calm down, the soldiers will hear you and we will all die," Xiuying interpreted.

Caleb stopped fighting. Xiuying nodded affirmingly at him. "He needs to check your pulse," she whispered holding out her wrist and tapping it.

The man in glasses looked at Xiuying and then to Caleb nodding his head with a gentile smile.

Caleb slowly extended his wrist. The man gently placed his fingers on Caleb and watched the clock. After about thirty seconds, the man shook his head and spoke to Xiuying.

"He says you got too excited, your heart rate is elevated and that is not good for your recovery."

The man looked at Caleb and held his finger to his lips. After checking the bandages on Caleb's leg, he gave him a pat on the shoulder and headed out the door.

Xiuying returned to her chair. As she sat, he noticed his Harley jacket hanging from the back of it. An unexpected sense of relief washed over him, like the return of an old friend.

"Where are we?" he asked.

She looked up holding her finger to her lips. She'd cleaned up; her hair hung straight, and her face had found a glow he hadn't noticed before. Her eyes were red and tired, the tiredness of tears, but they looked on him with pity all the same.

"We are back where you found me," she replied softly.

"Memphis?!"

She held her finger to her lips again, but this time there was fire in her eyes.

"Did you turn me over to them?" he hissed, quieter this time.

"No," she replied, looking at the floor.

"What does that mean? Then how'd I get here? And when did you start speaking English?"

"You are going to get your heart rate up again! Dr. Kim said to rest," she chided.

The chopping sound of rotor blades drew his attention to the window. Two attack helicopters flew low over the building, causing the portrait on the wall to shudder. They banked hard and proceeded on towards the horizon.

"The airfield is a couple miles from here, they fly day and night. You will get used to it," Xiuying explained.

"How'd I get here?" Caleb asked again.

"When you pulled a Rambo, as Dr. Kim called it, you went down with that thing still sticking out of your leg. I did not know what to do so I pulled it out. The smell was so terrible, I could not hold down the rodent you fed me." She seemed to search for words. "You did not wake up. I just looked at you laying there by the fire . . . your face kept changing . . . you groaned . . . like an animal."

"Why didn't you just kill me?" Caleb asked.

She studied the floor, never glancing up. "I wanted to. I saw your guns, the guns that killed my parents, and I wanted to. I thought about it, I pictured your gun in my hand, I saw my mother lying on the floor next to my father, and I saw you." She swiped a tear off her cheek. "I heard a voice inside ask me where does it end?

"I know who you are," she said, finally looking up. "You are the boy in the rain from the day I arrived in New Chi— I mean, America. It is your eyes . . ." she said, wiping another tear. "I know who my father was, I know what he did to your people, to you. I know you have lost—no, that you were robbed of your world, of your people, and my father did that. So . . ." she sighed. "You searched, turned the world upside down, until you found him. Then, you took everything, and in the place of your emptiness you created more emptiness." She fiddled with a locket that hung from her neck.

"I knew I could kill you. If I hated you enough, I could kill you, but all I would be doing is adding more emptiness, more hurt, more revenge. I saw it in your eyes that day in the rain, the hate. I knew there would never be a place for me in your world, and never a place for you in mine. When I heard that you escaped that night, I knew you would be back, I think my father did too.

"Sometimes he would come home after a long day with new stories of someone known as the Eagle who was looking for him. My mother and I heard the tales of your exploits as he wrung his cane and drank himself to sleep. He called you The Demon."

"He made the demon," Caleb whispered through clenched teeth.

"We choose who we become," she replied evenly.

Caleb met her gaze with contempt.

"Or you would be dead," she whispered, her eyes filling with tears.

She got up and, walking to the door, she whispered, "Rest." Closing the door behind her, she left him alone in the room.

Caleb laid back against the pillow. Choice? What choice did he have? What option had life left him? Kill or be killed, that was the only choice left for someone who refused to be a slave, wasn't it? And she still hadn't explained how he got there or how it was that he wasn't turned over to the Chinese . . . yet. Why was she helping him? Was she helping him?

Sweat began to bead on his forehead, his empty stomach churned, his heart was indeed racing. Closing his eyes, he tried to take deep breaths. He missed that familiarity of the battlefield, the control, the focus of the mission. He felt more fear here in this warm bed with its clean sheets than he had in years. There was nothing familiar here, no escape, no guns, no control, and honestly, he needed to use the bathroom.

The door creaked and Xiuying reentered the small room carrying a steaming bowl of rice with chopsticks. Her eyes were still red, but dry. He sat up and she placed the bowl on his lap.

"Um, I uhh, need to use the restroom," he said.

She nodded and set the bowl off to the side then held out her hand to help him up. Reluctantly, he took her hand and slowly slid himself out from under the blankets and off the bed. He blushed, realizing he was only wearing a gown.

"I—where's my clothes?"

"One of the nurses offered to mend and clean them. I suggested they burn them."

"What?!"

"Here." She opened a tiny door behind a shelf of supplies.

Inside was a tiny toilet facing a sink hardly bigger than a dog bowl. Above the sink, a stained mirror revealed an unshaven, disheveled face that someone had given a half-hearted effort to clean. After squeezing in the tiny room with the IV stand, he was just able to close the door. When he was finished, he washed his hands and gave his face a more thorough cleaning before he met Xiuying on the other side of the door.

"Rice," she reminded him, helping him back to bed. After securing him under the covers, she held a bite up to his mouth.

"I can feed myself," he said, roughly taking the chopsticks.

She gave them up with a shrug.

The rice was warm and soft. He tried to savor it, but his hunger won out and he wolfed down the whole bowl, hardly taking a breath.

"Sorry," he said, handing her back the bowl.

"I will get you more."

"Wait," he said, catching her by the arm. "I'll eat more later. You still haven't told me where I am, or how I got here. Or how it is I'm not being executed by a squad of PLA soldiers."

"You are in my uncle's hospital. He is the doctor who was here earlier. After you blacked out, I wandered down the road we were on until it crossed a paved road. I was able to catch a ride with a couple of local people heading into Memphis. I borrowed a phone and called my uncle who met me and listened to the situation. We drove back as close as we could to that old bridge and carried you to his car. Once we got here, he cleared this space in this secondary supply room and we . . ." She searched for the word. "Snuck? You inside," she finished.

"Why?"

"Because . . . I had to prove to myself, my mother, God, that I was not you. That I could choose to be different, that I could love my enemies, even if it did not make any sense."

She turned to leave.

"And your uncle? Why's he helping me?"

She didn't turn around. "He and my mother ran an underground church. They started it in China, and it came to America with them. Most of the staff here are members, they have as much to fear if they are discovered as you do."

"He's your mom's brother?"

"Yes."

"You didn't tell him?"

"I told him before I asked him to help you," she whispered, walking out the door.

Caleb leaned back against the wall. God? What is this? He hadn't talked to God since 'Sam had been killed. His god was himself. When he needed something, Caleb made a way. When he needed rescue, Caleb got himself out. He didn't need anyone's permission to live however he wanted to live. God had left him feeling powerless and alone in that camp; Sam had gotten him through. Li was probably rolling over in his grave watching his brother-in-law take care of the man who put him down.

His head ached as two more helicopters buzzed past the hospital, probably still looking for him. Here he was, back in Memphis, surrounded by thousands of Chinese soldiers, with more arriving every day. He was hiding in their midst, being cared for by the daughter and brother of a man he had hunted for over a decade and had brutally gunned down in his own living room. Oh, and the ones caring for him just so happened to be closet Christians also living in fear of their own government. His mom would have a thing or two to say about this situation. His mom!

He had to find a way to warn them. Pressing down on his wound with increasing pressure he found it didn't take much to make sweat beads form. That was only part of the problem, he was virtually naked, and a quick scan of the room assured him his pack and guns were nowhere to be seen.

The clock said it was a little after five when Xiuying and Dr. Kim returned to the room. Dr. Kim walked over to Caleb's side and muttered something apologetically. Caleb was able to decipher some of the words, something about his dressings and infection. He looked at Xiuying with a confused expression.

"It is time to change your bandages," she said.

Dr. Kim pulled out a small syringe and patted Caleb on the shoulder.

"For pain," he said, injecting the liquid into the IV.

"Oh, it can't be that bad," said Caleb. "I've hardly even noticed any pain today."

Dr. Kim looked up at Xiuying, who translated for him. Chuckling, he shook his scissors at Caleb and muttered under his breath. He cut away the gauze wrap, revealing a nasty looking hole surrounded by raw, burnt flesh.

"Ready, John Wayne?" he said with a smile.

"Ready for what, and whoooo'sssss oooowwww!"

Xiuying clamped her hand firmly over his mouth as Dr. Kim pulled the gauze stuffing out of the hole. As the gauze was lifted away, he relaxed a little and she lifted her hand, allowing him to breathe. The doctor scolded him as he soaked a cotton ball pinched in a pair of forceps, in iodine.

"He says the hole could have been much smaller if you would not have burned all the healing tissues. He was forced to cut out all the burned flesh, making the wound much larger," Xiuying interpreted.

Caleb winced as the doctor dabbed the iodine on all the surfaces of the wound. He tried to watch but eventually the cotton ball disappeared into his leg entirely.

"Why?" Caleb gasped, trying not to think about what was happening inside his leg. "Why'd he call me John Wayne?"

"You do not know who John Wayne is?" asked Xiuying in surprise.

Caleb shook his head.

"He is a famous American actor, my uncle's favorite. A cowboy, soldier, very manly, very heroic. He is in so many American movies." She stared at him in disbelief. "You know what a movie is, right?"

"I know what a movie is . . . I just can't remember ever seeing one," Caleb grunted as the doctor did another pass.

"All done," Dr. Kim said.

"Good," Caleb said, laying back on his pillow, panting in relief.

Grabbing some gauze off one of the shelves, the doctor said in Mandarin, "Now we have to pack it again."

Caleb shot up, Xiuying looking at him in surprise. "I heard what he said!"

"You speak our language?"

"Enough," Caleb said. "You invaded my world when I was little, remember?"

The doctor looked at Xiuying for interpretation, but she just shook her head.

Looking at Caleb, the doctor asked his question again, "Ready, John Wayne?"

"I wish Chinese pain killers worked better," Caleb groaned.

"They do, he just gave you a small dose because you look like a tough guy," Xiuying replied with a smile.

Caleb grasped the edges of his mattress as the doctor packed the wound with clean gauze. When he finished, he wrapped the wound and patted Caleb on the shoulder.

"He says you are a tough guy," Xiuying said.

"How often does this tough guy have to endure this?" Caleb asked.

"Twice a day until the wound closes up."

"Twice a day?!"

"If it gets infected, you will lose your leg entirely," Xiuying said, matter-of-factly.

The doctor nodded to Xiuying and hurried out of the room, leaving the two of them in an awkward silence.

"You don't have to babysit me," Caleb said.

"I am responsible for you."

Caleb scoffed. "I can take care of myself."

"No, if you are discovered, my uncle and his staff will be punished, probably killed. My job is to keep them safe by keeping you hidden."

"I still don't understand why you're helping me . . ."

Getting up from her chair, Xiuying walked to the door. "I am going to see if I can help my uncle, he is the only family I have left. Please, just rest, and do not do anything to raise alarm."

Caleb watched her go. In the silence he felt alone, alone with himself. The only family she had left? He wondered if she had taken the time to morn her parents, if she'd been able to attend their funeral, had she wept for them as he had for his dad, for Sam? Did she feel the same way when she saw him as he did when he saw Li?

What was wrong with him?

Shaking his head, he remembered, or reasoned rather, that if they had never come, his dad would be alive, he would have never met Sam, there would be no Li, he couldn't have killed anyone, she would still have her family. It was their fault, they invaded, they killed first, this is what war does to people. If they had never come, he wouldn't be here now, they wouldn't need to hide him, he wouldn't need their pity.

His blood ran hot. This whole mess was their fault. Why should he lie here feeling sorry for any of them? He was nothing more than the reaping they had sown. An eye for an eye.

He caught a glimpse of his jacket still hanging from her chair. He needed to get out of here. The Americans needed to be warned and the war needed to go on. Until the end, until they were all gone. Where were his things?

When Xiuying returned later that evening, she was wearing mint-colored scrubs and carried a steaming bowl of soup in her hands.

"My uncle hired me as a nursing assis—"

"Where are my things?" Caleb interrupted coldly.

Xiuying stopped.

"Where are my clothes, my pack, and my guns?" he asked again.

"You do not need them here," she replied.

"I'm leaving."

"You cannot leave yet," she said softly.

"And you can't keep me a prisoner!" he shouted.

Xiuying ran to his bed, setting down the soup, and clamped her hand over his mouth.

He grabbed her wrist and twisted it forcefully spinning her around.

"This is all your fault!" he hissed at her. "If your people had never come here, my family would still be alive, your family would be alive, and I wouldn't be here. You destroyed everything by coming here!" He pushed her away, sending the soup bowl clattering to the floor. "Now, get me my things or turn me over to your Chinese friends and let's get this over with!" he shouted.

The door flew open, and Dr. Kim ran to the bedside holding a syringe. Caleb moved to grab his hands but Xiuying dove on his chest, pinning his arms down. Caleb struggled to lift her as the doctor squeezed the syringe into his IV. In seconds things went from fuzzy to black. Everything faded to the sound of Xiuying panting in his ear.

When Caleb awoke, his room had changed. He moved to sit up but found himself unable to. Lifting his head, he noticed the thick Velcro straps holding his hands to the frame of the bed. He wiggled his feet and found them to be bound as well. He slammed his head back against the pillow.

Above him, a fan spun lazily under a textured ceiling. The large room was well lit with windows, the walls were painted a light shade of gray, with white trim. A piano sat in one corner flanked by family portraits. Next to him stood the IV stand with a steady drip conveying fluids into his system. An itch between his shoulder blades signaled the beginning of madness as he fought to ignore it.

A plain white door to his left opened and in stepped a Chinese officer carrying a coffee mug.

Chapter 15

I'm not telling you anything," Caleb said, fighting his restraints. The officer eyed him from his studded leather chair, taking a sip of coffee. "Does this look like an interrogation room to you?" he asked casually. His Chinese accent was light, and his English refined.

Caleb didn't respond.

"Your friends at the hospital—" the officer began.

"I don't have any friends!" snarled Caleb. "Least of all Chinese scumbags."

The officer took another sip of coffee. "Do you always shoot first before you understand the situation?"

"Chinese are Chinese, there's nothing more to understand."

"Then why did you rescue Li Xiuying?"

"Rescue? I took her prisoner!" snapped Caleb.

"I see," he said, taking another sip. "So, you shot at your own men who wanted to take Li Xiuying, carried her to safety on a severely injured leg, and protected her during an artillery bombardment because that is how you treat your prisoners?"

"I killed her parents too, or did she fail to mention that?" Caleb fired back.

Oddly, the officer's face reflected remorse instead of anger or surprise.

"She said you killed her father, but her father is the one who shot and killed her mother, which is when you were shot."

Caleb blinked. Had she really witnessed the whole thing?

"She also said her father had made you a slave and treated you terribly when you were only a boy, and when you escaped, your dear friend was killed."

"Why would she tell you that? Aren't you just going to kill her too?"

The officer took another sip of coffee. Then he got up and walked over to a large box sitting in a corner. Bending over, he lifted out a Harley Davidson jacket with an eagle across the shoulders.

"You're the one they call the Eagle, aren't you?" he said, walking back to his chair with the jacket.

Caleb didn't respond.

"I've known you for a couple years now. A surveillance video, a traumatized survivor, a glimpse on a bit of drone footage." The officer took another sip of coffee.

"Guess that makes me quite the catch," snapped Caleb.

The officer sighed, uncrossing his leg. He studied Caleb carefully as if considering which way to direct the conversation.

Finally, he leaned back in his chair. "What does Xiuying see in you?" he muttered in Mandarin.

"A dragon," replied Caleb, also in Mandarin.

The officer eyed him uncomfortably. Apparently, Xiuying had forgotten to mention that he spoke their language, well sorta spoke their language.

The officer shook his head. "Look," he said. "To the Chinese government, I am Col. Chen, Army Intelligence Officer, but to Xiuying and Dr. Kim, I am Pastor Chen."

"Right," said Caleb, "and I'm Santa."

Col. Chen looked offended, like only one can who has just divulged a great secret only to be ridiculed in return.

"Oh, and will Xiuying and Dr. Kim be joining us for communion, Pastor, or will they be too busy with the firing squad to make it?" Caleb asked sarcastically. "I should have realized; this isn't an interrogation, it's a confessional. Lord, have mercy!" He broke out in laughter. "I'm sorry, Colonel, but you're going to have to do better than that!"

Col. Chen stood up, obviously flustered, and marched out the white door he'd entered, Caleb's laughter following him all the way.

Outside, Caleb heard a vehicle fire up and drive away. Alone again. Caleb-1, Col. Chen-0. He felt his body relax; he'd failed to realize how intense the exchange had gotten. His stomach growled with intense hunger, and he regretted not eating the bowl of soup Xiuying had brought him. Tugging at his restraints availed nothing. He was hungry, he needed to use the bathroom, and that itch between his shoulder blades had returned.

He looked up at the IV drip, the bag was over half empty, watching the steady drip made his eyes hurt and he looked away. Perhaps the hospital wasn't so bad. His situation had clearly not improved, though he had noticed a familiar pack sticking out of the large box in the corner and could only assume the rest of his belongings were also there.

Helicopters hummed in the distance, but they didn't fly over his new location. He also noticed that very few vehicles drove within hearing distance. Wherever he was, it was out of the way of the main travel routes. He heard birds: woodpeckers, finches, and the occasional robin. Perhaps they'd moved him to the edge of town, or maybe onto the compound near the river, though he'd probably have heard boats if that was the case. Maybe he wasn't even in Memphis at all. He'd have to find a way of drawing that information out of the colonel before making his escape.

He was near to bursting when the sound of a vehicle outside brought him some hope. Either he'd be permitted to use the bathroom or be shot by the firing squad; either would bring relief from his current predicament.

His muscles tensed as footsteps walked up the back stairs and into the house. The screen door slammed. Feet shuffled in the room beyond the white door before it swung slowly open. He prepared to meet the colonel with an amused smile and snarky remark when a tired Dr. Kim appeared.

"Doctor?" Caleb said in surprise.

Behind him came Xiuying carrying a tray of medical supplies, still dressed in her mint green scrubs.

Caleb looked them over from head to toe for signs of abuse and restraint. Other than the bags under their eyes, they seemed to be fine.

"Time to change your bandages," said the doctor.

Xiuying's eyes never lifted to meet his. A twinge of guilt dug at his gut. He knew he'd hurt her when he wrenched her arm. Apart from being Chinese, she'd done nothing to deserve his hostility.

"May I use the restroom first?" Caleb asked.

The doctor looked at Xiuying with a nervous expression.

Caleb ground his teeth; they were afraid of him. He'd behaved like an animal and bit the hand.

"I really need to go."

The doctor mumbled in Mandarin.

"No!" Caleb said before Xiuying could interpret. "I don't need a catheter. I'll behave myself and come right back, I promise."

Xiuying interpreted without looking at him.

The doctor shook his finger in Caleb's face and then motioned to Xiuying.

"I know, I messed up. I'm sorry I hurt you. Look, I'm a prisoner, ok? I don't know what's going on, I don't understand why you're helping me or if you're really helping me. I don't know where I am, all my friends are dead and I . . ." He stopped short of revealing his knowledge of the Chinese trap. "I'm going to wet the bed!" he finished.

Xiuying moved to the side of the bed, her jaw set. "We are all prisoners," she said, removing the Velcro restraint.

The doctor protested but didn't stop her from setting him free. Xiuying helped him off the bed and lead him down a hall to the bathroom. He tested his leg as they went, it carried only a little weight before the pain caused him to back off. The bathroom was clean and well lit. A large square mirror covered the wall above a moderate marble vanity. A white towel hung on a simple chrome hook on the wall next to a lone outlet. This was no military facility bathroom; this was someone's home.

When he'd finished in the bathroom, he opened the door to find Col. Chen waiting for him in the hallway. The officer grabbed his IV stand, guiding it out into the hall while Caleb followed along reluctantly. When they returned to the living room, the officer helped him back in his bed. His gentle demeanor unnerved Caleb. *What is going on?*

With his bed now flanked on either side by Xiuying and Dr. Kim, and Col. Chen at the foot, he felt claustrophobic. *Were they all in on it? What was their aim? What did she mean they were all prisoners?*

Dr. Kim reached for the restraint on his side of the bed, but Xiuying shook her head. Col. Chen and Caleb looked at her in surprise. She looked at Caleb for the first time and held out her hand until he hesitantly took it. Lifting him to a sitting position she reached up and untied the top of his gown. Caleb stiffened as she slid the fabric to the edge of his shoulders. Col. Chen and the Doctor moved to the head of the bed to see what she was doing. Gently she traced the scars on his back. Her fingers felt cool sliding across his skin.

"My father did this to him. We did this to him. To him, to his country, his family. . . . Would we behave differently?"

A strange emotion washed over him. He felt embarrassed, like a little boy again, exposed, but not because of the gown. Her touch went deeper than his skin, revealing the still bleeding wounds of his soul. He slid the fabric back together and she tied it in place. Why wouldn't she just hate him? What about her, what about her parents? Why did she keep sticking up for him?

Gently, she helped him lay back down and picked up the tray of medical supplies. Dr. Kim followed her lead and moved to his wounded leg, leaving Col. Chen standing at his head. The doctor cut the wrap from his leg and with a warm grin said, "Ready, John Wayne?"

Caleb sighed mournfully. "Ready, Doc."

He gripped the edge of the mattress as the process began. "Is he really a pastor?" he grunted to Xiuying, trying to take his mind off his leg.

She nodded.

"But he's a soldier, an officer?"

"Like I said, we are all prisoners."

"What does she mean by that?" he asked Col. Chen.

"She means that we all belong to the State. None of us wanted to be here. We all had lives in China, but the State does not ask, it commands. Xiuying and her mother were forced to come here because of her father. I was forced to join the military, and because of my education I was made an officer. The doctor's hospital was forced to immigrate to be part of the New China settlement. Most of the colonists are poor working people chosen by draft to leave their homes and families to populate and settle New China. None of us wanted to be here, none of us wanted to invade your world, none of us came by choice. To refuse is imprisonment, maybe death, people disappear and are never heard from again. We've all lost people."

Caleb winced as Dr. Kim began the iodine process. The colonel pulled a handkerchief from his pocket and dabbed Caleb's forehead.

"We have been persecuted since before your time. If we are discovered, none of us will survive, it is the choice we all make for our faith. In truth, we want to be free like you do. Free to live how we choose to live, free to believe what we believe without fear," Col. Chen continued.

"Sounds like the old America," Caleb said.

"Yes, we want to live like America," the colonel said.

"You could fight back." Caleb gasped as the cotton ball disappeared into his leg.

"How? Only the military has weapons. The drones watch us more than they do Americans. There are secret police everywhere, suspected traitors are prosecuted without a fair trial and executed."

"Aren't you in the military?" Caleb asked.

"I am only one man," Col. Chen sighed.

"I'm only one man," Caleb replied.

Clearing his throat, the doctor spoke in Mandarin.

"He says that the wound is healing well, but we still need to pack it today," Xiuying interpreted.

"Bring it on," Caleb said through grit teeth.

The doctor nodded emphatically. "Yes, John Wayne," he said, flexing his muscles.

The doctor packed the wound and wrapped it carefully. When he finished, he nodded his respects and left. Col. Chen also had to report for night duty, leaving Xiuying and Caleb alone in the house. She changed into a pair of jeans and t-shirt and sat in Col. Chen's leather chair with a cup of tea.

Caleb watched her for a moment. Her thin, almost fragile, frame curled neatly between the arms of the chair. Her fine facial features looked more tired than ever in the pale light of the single corner lamp. Her eyes stared off into another world as she sipped her tea. Col. Chen's words repeated in his mind. They never wanted to be a part of the invasion. They were slaves of their own nation, forced into service, forced to colonize, forced to leave their homes and families to complete the Chinese conquest of the eastern United States. They lived in fear just like the Americans did. They were not at all like Major Li. He shook his head as he processed.

Looking up from his thoughts, he saw her watching him. She managed a small smile.

"Want to watch a movie?" she asked.

He raised his eyebrows. "Sure."

Getting up, she walked over to a wall mounted flat screen TV and unzipped a large black canvas case filled with discs.

"These are contraband, but everyone has them, so the police turn a blind eye. Even my father had his own collection hidden in his dresser drawer." A wide smile spread across her face as she slid out a disc with a dozen titles printed on it. "Oh, this is going to be a treat," she said, sliding the disc into a slit on a thin rectangular machine. She picked up a remote and slid her chair next to the bed facing the TV.

The screen flickered to life and several small pictures appeared. She selected the first one and in moments a movie began to play. The title flashed up on the screen, *McLintock,* followed by the name John Wayne. She turned to him with a wide grin and raised her eyebrows. Caleb's heart raced with anticipation. Was he really about to watch a movie?

Hours passed as they watched movie after movie starring John Wayne, only pausing long enough for Xiuying to make noodles for dinner. Caleb found himself hungering for the next story as soon as each movie ended. Tales full of courageous defenses, charges, sacrifices, love, and selfless heroism. A good guy who stood up to the bad guys when no one else would.

As they finished *The Alamo*, Caleb turned to Xiuying. Her head rested against her knees still curled in the chair. Her eyes were closed, and her hair danced away from her face with each breath. Glancing at the clock, Caleb's burning eyes strained to read: 3:23 a.m.

He felt funny, but good, a strange feeling of being full, not a food full, but something different. It had a warmth to it, and he felt himself smiling. It felt foolish, but what did it matter, no one could see him anyway. It was such a strange and unfamiliar feeling that he felt awkward, out of balance, like when Dr. Kim had given him the medication to sedate him. He held his head between his hands steadying himself.

Looking back at Xiuying curled in her chair, he was aware of another feeling. Vulnerable. Not her, but him. What she'd done earlier, tracing his scars with her fingers, unfolding his past like she'd known him her whole life. Even with his gown tied, buried in his blankets, he felt exposed. She knew him, not the John Wayne Dr. Kim saw, but the little boy huddling in the darkness. The little boy who was still afraid.

Reaching up, he closed the hose on his IV and disconnected it from his hand. He slid quietly out of bed and walked around to the chair. Balancing his weight on his good leg, he bent over and scooped her up. She moaned quietly as he lifted her, but her eyes remained closed. Limping over to the couch, he laid her down, placing her head on a shammed pillow. He took a folded afghan from atop a large chest and spread it over her. Satisfied, he limped to the lamp and turned it off.

Grabbing the remote, he climbed back into bed. The night was still young. . . .

Chapter 16

Caleb awoke to the gentle shaking of Dr. Kim. His head ached, and his eyes burned in the bright daylight. His arm itched and tingled where the remote had left its dimpled marks. He squinted at the clock, 8:30. Groaning, he rolled over and pulled the pillow over his head. He felt the doctor fiddle with his IV and connect the tube back to his hand. Someone tugged at his blankets, and he fought to hang on to them.

"We need to change your bandages," Dr. Kim pleaded.

"Come back later," Caleb moaned.

The doctor muttered as he fought for the blankets.

"He says he cannot come back later, but maybe today he will not have to pack your wound," came Xiuying's voice.

Caleb quit struggling. Rolling over, he lifted the pillow from his face. Xiuying held out a glass of water and a couple white pills.

"You should not stay up all night. You are still recovering," she said.

Caleb took the pills and tossed them in his mouth, chasing them down with the water.

"You didn't stop me," he said, handing back the glass.

Dr. Kim flipped back the blankets, revealing the bandages, and began cutting them away.

"Where's Col. Chen?" Caleb asked.

"Sleeping. His night duty ended an hour ago," Xiuying answered.

"Ready, John Wayne?"

"I've gotta be honest, Doc, I don't feel much like John Wayne this morninnnnng."

Doctor Kim looked up with a smile, holding the gauze in his forceps.

"I'm starting to think you like that part," Caleb groaned.

After a thorough examination that consisted of more pain than seemed necessary, Dr. Kim nodded in satisfaction and wrapped the wound, forgoing the gauze packing.

"You need to start moving your leg a few times a day every day. Bend it, walk on it, massage it. It is likely that you will have a permanent limp, but the more you are able to move it as it heals, the less severe the permanent damage will be. I will bring you a cane after I finish my shift today," Xiuying interpreted for the doctor.

Caleb nodded his thanks, and the doctor nodded in return before grabbing his things and heading out the door.

"Are you hungry?" asked Xiuying.

"Starving."

"Me too," she said, heading into the kitchen.

She appeared fifteen minutes later with two steaming bowls of congee with eggs. Caleb swung his legs off the bed, letting them dangle, and dug in ravenously before noticing Xiuying's head bowed and eyes closed. He paused, if for no other reason than to be polite. His whole family prayed, which was fine with him, he just never saw a use for it. Why interrupt what God had going on if he could take care of it himself? She finished after a moment, and he began eating again.

"Thank you for breakfast, and the movies last night," he said between bites.

She nodded.

"It got me thinking. How bad do you want it?"

She looked at him with a puzzled expression.

"Freedom," he continued. "You say you're all slaves or prisoners, and you want to live free in America like the John Wayne movies show but you all live your lives in hiding, in fear."

Her chewing slowed but she didn't look up at him.

"America was only free because they fought for it, just like in the movies. Out gunned, surrounded by bad guys, with little hope of victory, but Americans fought."

"You are still fighting," she said.

"Yes, exactly! But even if we win, and you all go back home, you still won't be free."

"We have existed this way for a long time."

"Is existing the same thing as living?"

"Is that what you are doing? Living? Your life is nothing but war and killing. Vengeance, without ever counting the cost or considering the outcome of your logic. What world is left when we have all killed each other for our own just cause?"

He could sense the trembling in her voice.

"You should get some rest," she said. Collecting his dishes, she disappeared into the kitchen.

He wanted to argue, but his burning eyes and aching head compelled him to take her advice.

Caleb opened his eyes, the room was dark and cold, and quiet. He was alone. Sitting up, he felt exposed, vulnerable. Something was off, a gnawing fear rose from his gut. Where was everyone?"

Dragging footsteps outside moved towards the front entry. No one had used that door since his arrival. His pulse quickened as he strained to calculate his situation. Looking around frantically, he failed to find a suitable defensive weapon within reach. The doorknob rattled and his eyes flashed back to the entry.

"Dr. Kim?" he called out. "Xiuying?"

Nothing.

He looked back down the hallway to Xiuying's room; surely, she'd heard him call her name.

A warm liquid dripped onto his hand. Spinning around, he found himself face to face with Major Li. Jumping back, he nearly fell out of bed. Blood oozed from the corners of his attacker's mouth and stained his uniform. Caleb fought to put distance between them as the major, sneering, pulled up a pistol and leveled it on Caleb's forehead.

In a moment, frozen in time, the gun went off.

Exploding from his sheets, Caleb gasped. The world spun around him, its bright light piercing his eyes. Someone restrained him, not forcefully, but securely. Gently, pulling him back.

Straining against her, he gasped for air, flailing to free himself from the tubes entangling his arms. He felt her climb onto the bed behind him, wrapping her arms around him. In the chaos her voice caught him, arrested his panic, her lips beside his ear calling him out of the darkness.

"Shhh, Caleb, you are ok. You are ok. You are safe now," Xiuying said softly, guiding him backward until his head lay in her lap. Carefully, she wiped the sweat from his brow with a cool cloth, all the while whispering, "It was just a dream, only a dream . . ."

His world ceased spinning, the fear melting away as he remembered where he was. His pulse slowed, and his muscles relaxed. He didn't fight it. Closing his eyes, he let her peace restore him.

After a few minutes, she slid out from under his head, placing it on a pillow. "I will get you a glass of water," she said.

He watched her go. Her graceful form seemed to float as she moved across the room. She was so unlike him; gentle, smooth, graceful, peaceful, kind. She glowed with a warmth and life he had never known. She was so out of place in his cold and unforgiving world. His mind couldn't make sense of her, but his heart longed for her light.

She returned with the glass of water and placed it on the stand next to his bed.

"I was wrong about you . . ." he whispered. "I was wrong about all of you. I thought . . . I thought you were all a plague. A horde of vultures who saw an opportunity in my crippled country and decided to come pick our bones clean. I thought you were all the same, murderers, rapists, slavers, and thieves. You destroyed my home, killed my dad, took me as a slave, beat the life out of me, killed my friends, and ravaged my country. You weren't human anymore. I didn't want to know your story, I didn't care how you got here or why, I just knew that as long as you were here, I'd never get my life back."

He sat up, it was too late to stop it. Xiuying lowered herself onto the chair next to the bed, her dark eyes never leaving his.

"You're right, I wasn't living. I let myself become everything I hated, and it hollowed me out. I surrounded myself with people like me, hurt and angry, and convinced myself that my cause was just, whatever the cost. But then I saw you, that look in your eyes, even as you knelt over your mom. It grabbed me, like it did that day you got off the boat in Duluth. It called out my cowardice, exposed my wounds, my cheap selfish existence. I knew there was more life and courage in you than I could ever pretend to have. I'm both drawn to it and hate it, that light in you. It compelled me to rescue you when it made absolutely no sense. I couldn't let that light be destroyed. Not before I understood it.

"Even now, I look in your eyes, those eyes that see right through me, and where I should see hate, I see compassion. When you should leave me to die, you rescue me; when you should lock me up, you set me free; when you could starve me, you feed me; when I'm in torment, you comfort me; and it freaks me out!"

Trembling tears overflowed his eyes as he looked up at her.

"Why can't you just hate me . . . like I hate myself?!" He crumpled off the bed and onto the floor, sobbing beside her feet.

Softly a hand lay on his back as she knelt beside him.

"I forgive you, and my mother would forgive you too," she whispered as warm tears fell on his neck.

"Why?"

"Jesus."

All the pain poured out of him as forgiveness washed over him. The injustice of her forgiveness shook him like an earthquake. He'd spent the last ten years running from a God who had abandoned him in that shipping container only to find He'd never left him for a moment. Here, of all places, hovering over the shattered remains of his heart was the undeniable, unescapable, unfair, love and forgiveness of God. And it was too much. He let it all go and fell into the arms of the One who'd chased after him for so long.

"Jesus," he wept.

In the end, he lay on the floor trembling and exhausted. He'd cycled through pain and sorrow, joy and laughter, healing and forgiveness, and back again as the life and love of God worked to put the pieces back together. He let go of Sam and his father, let go of his childhood that was stolen, let go of his anger, fear, and the emptiness he'd called home. Through it all, Xiuying never left his side. He didn't even notice when Col. Chen entered, awoken by the commotion in his living room. He knelt beside Caleb and prayed over him, kissing him on the head.

The two of them helped him to his feet and back into bed. Xiuying's eyes were red and swollen but she smiled at him warmly. The weight of a lifetime of darkness dissolved as he felt life rushing into him. He felt . . . new. He breathed differently, his heart danced joyfully in his chest, his eyes filled with light. He was exhausted but wanted to run, shout, laugh. For the first time, he wanted to live.

Caleb sat the rest of the evening eagerly listening as Col. Chen explained the story of God's love and salvation to him. Caleb had heard the stories all his life, his mother had taken great pains to share her relationship with God with him, but he hadn't heard it, wouldn't let himself hear it. As Col. Chen poured out his heart, Caleb soaked up every word. Justice and mercy, love and forgiveness, sin and pain, righteousness and hope. He'd heard it a thousand times, but this time it was new.

When he couldn't sit any longer, they paced the house, Caleb firing questions as fast as Chen could answer them. By the time Dr. Kim showed up that night, Chen's voice was hoarse, and Caleb's leg ached from the miles he'd put on. The doctor changed his bandages as they filled him in on all the details of the morning. Tears and joy mingled as Caleb asked and received forgiveness from Dr. Kim for the loss of his sister.

Caleb felt a sense of wonder as he sat surrounded by friends, brothers and sisters in Chinese clothing. They were people, not just people, they were his people. On the outside, they looked like his enemies: same eyes, same skin, same accent, but that wasn't what made them good or bad. They had hearts, good hearts, with good dreams, good intentions, better hearts than some of the people he knew who looked like him.

We're all just people. No one kind any worse or any better than another. Xiuying was not her father, and Caleb had not been living like his. Good or bad was decided in the heart. Xiuying had been right; we choose who we become. They had both suffered great loss, great injustice, but had chosen different paths. Where he had chosen hate, she chose to forgive, and the proof that her choice had made all the difference was sitting here in the room. A road less traveled by.

Dr. Kim presented Caleb with a walking cane and his washed and repaired laundry. The IV was removed and the bed lowered to a more manageable height. Col. Chen found Caleb a razor and he was finally allowed to shower with the aid of plastic wrapped around his wound. The warm water poured over him, washing his shaggy hair over his eyes. It had been months since it needed a cut. He shaved the patchy hair from his face and brushed his teeth.

It felt good to have clothes on again. Someone had taken great pains to remove the bloody stains from his pants and patch the holes. He pulled on a Chinese military t-shirt that clung to his muscular frame. Searching the drawers of the vanity, he found a small rubber band. He pulled his hair out of his face and into a small bun at the back of his head. When he was all finished, he snorted at the character looking back at him in the mirror. He was clean, and well . . . clean. He looked like some cross between an ancient warrior and a yoga instructor.

He emerged from the bathroom to a standing ovation from his new friends. With the aid of his cane, he hobbled to the center of the living room and did an awkward spin, choosing to own the embarrassment rather than retreat into the bathroom to hide for the rest of the night.

Xiuying slid over, making room for him next to her on the couch. "John Wayne?" she asked with a coy smile.

He handed her the remote. "John Wayne."

Chapter 17

For the next three days, Caleb continued to mend. His new life brought many changes, but one thing hadn't changed; his family was still heading into a trap and time was running out to warn them. It had been more than a week since Darrian had warned him of the suspicious Chinese activity.

Finding his pack in the box of his belongings, he was relieved to find the map of Tennessee inside. His pistols were nowhere to be found, but that was to be expected. He'd thought of asking for them but every time he'd gotten the chance, the question felt awkward.

It was 8:30 a.m. Saturday, and he'd already had breakfast, changed his dressings, worked his leg, and spent some time reading the Bible and praying, which was finally starting to feel normal. Col. Chen had the morning off and was currently out running errands. Caleb hoped to catch him when he returned and discuss the necessity of contacting his family before they were destroyed. A nervousness gnawed at his gut as he studied the map of Tennessee. Col. Chen was still a Chinese soldier after all, it was his countrymen the Americans were fighting out there.

Xiuying had yet to surface. Caleb had ventured to ask why she didn't go home only to discover she was in hiding. The Chinese believed she was either a captive or dead and the search for her went on. According to Dr. Kim, their family was pretty much the equivalent of Chinese royalty on her mother's side. Dr. Kim had chosen to come voluntarily when his hospital staff, mostly made up of the members of their church, were sent to America as a part of the colonization.

Major Li had considered Xiuying's mom a trophy wife, and his success in the military had more to do with her social standing than his qualifications. This explained why he'd been treated like a god. When her grandparents heard of her disappearance, they sent shockwaves through the Chinese government. Xiuying was to be found dead or alive and returned to her grandparents in China, immediately. Unfortunately for them, their granddaughter did not share their communist beliefs, or any of their beliefs for that matter, and had no intention of giving up her new life and going home.

Caleb jumped as a car door shut in the driveway. Slinking to the window, he peered outside. Col. Chen was back. Relaxing, he reaffirmed his need to get his pistols. This waiting to be discovered thing was stressful. He met Chen at the door and helped him carry in a few groceries, setting them intentionally on the map.

"What's this?" asked Chen. "Going somewhere?"

"My family's in trouble, and I have to find a way to help them," Caleb replied uneasily.

Grabbing a few items from the bag, Caleb headed for the pantry.

"I thought you said your father was dead?"

"He is, it's actually my mom and brothers who are in trouble."

"What sort of trouble?" asked Chen.

"The   you're-about-to-be-surrounded-by-the-Chinese-Army kind," Caleb replied.

Pausing, Col. Chen eyed him.

"Your family is with the American advance?" he asked, eyebrows raised.

"Leading them is more like it," Caleb grimaced.

"How do you know about the counter offensive?"

"We saw your troops redeploying on the backside of your feigned retreat."

Col. Chen nodded slowly. "My government has put a high price on your brother's head. He's as wily as a fox."

"That's Aaron, he's methodical to the point of obsession."

"And you think he'll fall for the trap?"

"He's been pushing harder than usual lately. He can smell blood in the water, we all can. He's tired of war, and he's being pressured hard by the others, our government, to get it over with. I think he's as ripe as he ever will be to make a mistake." Caleb sighed.

"At his pace, my people are calculating two weeks at the earliest." He looked Caleb dead in the eye. "This battle is China's last stand. It's all or nothing. We are throwing everything we have into this. More soldiers are arriving from China every day, more armor, aircraft, it's all coming through the docks here in Memphis. They've all but emptied the garrison, there's only the necessary soldiers left here to keep the shipments moving out to the line and fill the guard posts.

"I have to warn him."

"You can barely walk."

"It's getting better every day."

"Caleb, there are more soldiers between here and there than ever. More drones, more dogs . . . they aren't going to let this one get away from them."

"Well, it's a good thing I'm the Eagle then, isn't it?"

"An Eagle with a broken wing," he said, tapping Caleb's leg.

"What are you talking so serious about?" asked Xiuying; startling them both.

"Hey, good morning, Princess!" Caleb smiled.

Chuffing, Xiuying rolled her eyes.

"Caleb was just showing me where the Americans he was attached to are located. Trying to see if we can find him a way back," Col. Chen answered.

"You're going back? With your leg like that you wouldn't make it. Plus, there's an army out there!" Xiuying stared at him, perplexed.

"My mom is out there. Her and my brothers are walking into a trap, and I need to warn them."

"Your mom is a soldier?"

"She's more of a mother hen now than a soldier, it's complicated. What matters is all of China is about to descend on them unawares, and if that happens, I don't think they can win."

"Isn't there another way for him to warn them?" she asked Col. Chen. "You cannot be supporting his plan?"

"It's not really a plan, I haven't planned anything yet. I just know I have to warn them, that's all."

"Is there another way?" Xiuying asked.

Col. Chen furrowed his brow for a moment. "We could try and radio them," he said.

"That would be difficult, they change their frequency on a rotation twice a day, every day. I've got a handful of the frequencies memorized but, to be honest, I've never been the greatest communicator, and I wouldn't know the rotation at any rate," Caleb sighed.

"How about you give me the frequencies you do know, sometimes I have the intelligence room to myself. I could try scanning your channels and possibly get lucky. If I find them, I could let them know."

Xiuying turned to Caleb, searching his eyes.

"It's worth a shot, but we don't have much time before going on foot is our only option. And, if it comes to that, I'm going no matter what."

"Do you have a call sign I should use? Something they would trust?"

"Give them the code number 081706."

"What does that mean?" Col. Chen asked.

"It's our family code in case we ever got separated. The first numbers are my parent's anniversary, the last two numbers mean I'm the sixth member of the family. It's simple, but it's worked so far."

Caleb jotted down a list of frequencies; 26.97500, 27.03500, 27.06500, 27.16500, 27.21500. "I'm afraid that's all I can remember. There are a lot more, but like I said, I wasn't really good at the whole communication thing."

Col. Chen took the list with a nod, "I will do my best."

"I appreciate it."

The anxiety was almost tangible by the time Col. Chen left for work. In his condition, it would take Caleb a week to reach Aaron under the best circumstances, and even then, he may be too late. His leg was healing, he pushed it hard every day, but without the cane he was limited to short distances before waves of nauseating pain began drumming in his thigh.

Xiuying watched him both in admiration and concern as he completed his third lap through the house.

"If you do not slow down you are going to make it worse," she said, handing him a glass of water.

After taking a long swallow, he handed it back, "Thank you."

"Pastor Chen will find a way to warn them," she said.

"It's not that I doubt he'll try. I've been at this for a long time, one rule you can always count on is nothing ever goes according to plan."

"But sometimes that works together for good," she said, giving him a smile.

"Yeah," he agreed. "So, Dr. Kim tells me you're practically a princess," he said, changing the subject.

"China does not have princesses."

"Yeah, but your family is rich and powerful. He said they want you back."

She sighed, looking out the window. "That is not me. My mom was led to the Lord when I was only five by my English tutor, an undercover missionary from England that my uncle, Dr. Kim, had recommended. He helped her find an underground church and, with my dad working so much, we were able to attend services regularly. It changed her, made her warm and caring, even my dad noticed, but he just said she had finally "come around."

"I gave my life to the Lord when I was seven, my uncle baptized me. I think my grandparents know that he is a Christian, a black sheep, but they would never admit it openly and risk shame on the family. My mom did a better job of disguising it, and when she died, I am sure I became the last viable heir of the family."

"So, they're really hoping you're alive then?"

She nodded.

"And you're willing to give that all up for this?"

"I'm willing to give up all that to be free," she said.

"How long have you known Col. Chen?"

"He joined our church in China about a year before my dad sent for my mom and me. It was a good thing too; we were in desperate need of leadership. Our previous pastor had been arrested and imprisoned, no one has seen or heard from him since. We have lost many of our leaders since then, but they have never figured out Pastor Chen. He is more or less the only leadership we have left besides Dr. Kim."

Caleb sat back shaking his head.

"What?" Xiuying asked.

"I just always thought you guys were of one mind, you know, that all Chinese people thought the same. I never imagined that so many of you lived in fear of your own country, or that so many of you wanted the same thing we want."

"We see what we want to see. You were not looking for a reason to see us as anything different than what you believed."

"How many of you are there? Christians in Memphis, I mean?"

"Somewhere around a hundred. Most of them work at the hospital. My uncle pulls strings, as you Americans put it, to get them jobs there after they turn to the Lord. There are a handful of soldiers left who have not shipped out, and a few dock workers. Several of the families relocated to colonize this area have given their lives to the Lord. The church is far more helpful to them than the government after they arrive; it is a wide-open door."

"No one talks when they get arrested?"

"No, for a Chinese person, to give your life to the Lord is to accept that one day you may die for it. We accept both at the same time," she said softly.

"That's incredible. . . . Where do you guys, you know, have church?"

"The basement of the hospital is basically a bunker with tunnels connecting the various wings of the hospital. It is an easy place to meet and then disburse if anything suspicious happens."

"And you've lived this way all these years?"

"Yes."

"Aren't you afraid?"

"We were not given a spirit of fear, but of power, love, and a sound mind," she said with a smile. "Yes, we are afraid, but we believe that the Lord is for us, and in this is our peace."

He frowned, unsatisfied.

"When you believe that God has prepared a place for you, that this life is not the end, then you can have peace, even if today is your last day on earth, that you will wake up to the Lord forever. We all die at some point, no matter how long we live, this life is short. If I cannot have peace dying at twenty-one, I will not have peace dying at eighty-one. Dying is dying, it does not matter when, what matters is the Lord is waiting for me. This body is only our temporary home. One day, sooner or later, we will all go to our eternal home and that is a comforting thought."

"For me, it's not the dying that's frightening," Caleb replied, "it's being responsible for the death of someone else. If I cause my own death, so be it, but the weight of someone else like Darrian, or Sam, or . . . your mother . . . I have to live with that. If I don't find a way to warn my brother, I'll be adding countless names to that list."

"We will find a way, Caleb. Now, let's take another lap." She handed him his cane.

It was after 6:00 p.m. when Dr. Kim showed up to examine Caleb's leg. He poked and prodded, had Caleb walk laps around the living room, and poked and prodded again.

"What do you think, Doc?" asked Caleb.

The doctor grunted and frowned before he spoke.

"It is healing faster than he expected," Xiuying interpreted.

"Well, that's good news," Caleb said excitedly.

The doctor sighed, shaking his head before he continued.

"Not exactly. . . . The damage to your muscles and nerves was extensive and he is afraid the scar tissue—your leg is never going to fully recover." Xiuying's voice trailed off.

"What does that mean?" he asked softly.

Doctor Kim didn't wait for an interpretation before he continued.

"You will always walk with a limp, and . . . there will likely always be pain." Xiuying said.

Caleb twisted his hands on his cane processing the news. "How long before the wound is closed up?"

"A few more days. But it will be at least two weeks before it is as healed on the inside as it is going to be," Xiuying said.

"I am sorry," Dr. Kim said, placing his hand on Caleb's shoulder.

Squeaking brakes in the driveway drew their attention to the window. Xiuying peered through the blinds and gave a thumbs up.

"It is Pastor Chen," she said.

Footsteps flew up the stairs and the door swung open with a bang. The three of them stood in alarm as Chen entered the living room.

"We may have a situation," he blurted.

"Were you able to contact my family?" asked Caleb.

Chen shook his head. "Not yet, I am sorry, but my people picked up an American boy today breaking into one of the colonist's homes. My people think he is one of yours."

Col. Chen pulled out his cell phone. Opening a picture, he held it out.

Gasping, Xiuying took it. "It is Rice."

Caleb nodded. "He was with us. We rescued him from a compound a little ways from here. He's just a kid; he doesn't know anything."

"It will not matter what he knows, my superiors will want a full examination of the prisoner."

"But he's just a kid?" Caleb pleaded.

"He is an American who was traveling with the Eagle, and the Eagle has Xiuying. The truth is, General Yang is a big fan of yours," Col. Chen replied. "Well, maybe not a fan, but you have his admiration. You are the great American warrior the movies make you all out to be."

"There must be a way to get him out," Caleb said.

"He is being held in the most secure building in the entire compound," Chen said.

"Don't you work there? Think! There has to be a way to smuggle him out of there," Caleb demanded.

"I only found out about him an hour before I came home to tell you. I am on your side, Caleb; I am not giving up. We will work together and find a way to help your friend."

Caleb squeezed his head in his hands. It was all coming too fast. First his family, then his leg, now Rice. He took a deep breath and let it out.

"Ok, we have work to do."

"We will help also," Xiuying said, gesturing to Dr. Kim.

Caleb nodded. "If God be for us . . . right?"

"Right," answered Chen.

Grabbing his cane, he began pacing the floor. "We need to work on both situations simultaneously. Col. Chen, you're going to have to be our eyes and ears. I need all the information you can give me about the compound and that building. I'll get you a list of specifics when we're done. I also need to be kept up to date on the American progress into the trap so that I have an accurate timeline to work with, along with the Chinese redeployments and checkpoints between Memphis and the Americans."

Tapping his cane on the floor in frustration, he continued. "Xiuying and I can't be seen outside the house, and Dr. Kim can't be missing from the hospital. . . . How are we going to pull this off?" he groaned, looking at the ceiling.

"God can provide a way," Col. Chen assured them.

"When will his interrogation begin?" Caleb asked.

"Tomorrow. We like to give them a night in the isolation cell to soften."

Caleb clenched his teeth picturing the dark emptiness of the shipping container all those years ago. No light, no sound, just a cold unfeeling darkness.

"Can you make sure he's fed and gets water and care if he's injured?"

"I will try, but there are cameras everywhere, inside and out. Everything is monitored."

"Well, you must be able to shut them off or freeze them, right?" asked Caleb.

Col. Chen thought for a moment.

"Like you do when you're listening for my family's frequencies when no one else is there?" Caleb prompted.

"Oh, yes, I suppose I could do that," he answered.

"Good, I know you'll do your best," Caleb said. "Let me get you that list."

Caleb glanced around and caught everyone watching him with concern.

"Trust me, this is what I'm good at," he assured them.

Dr. Kim pointed to Caleb's leg and spoke.

"He says you should give it some rest," Xiuying repeated.

Caleb had hardly noticed the pain since hearing the news about Rice, but he nodded respectfully and took a seat on his bed. Grabbing a pad of paper and a pen, he began jotting notes. Xiuying headed into the kitchen, the sound of running water and a clanking carafe heralded the coming of a fresh pot of coffee. They were going to need it.

Caleb divided his list into two columns; one side was a list of intel to help Rice, and the other, intel to help his family. He already knew quite a bit from their surveillance on top of the hill, but it wasn't enough: he needed personnel counts, guard schedules and rotations, camera locations and sectors of coverage, security measures, prisoner schedules and movement routes, key personnel arrivals and departures, drone schedules, supply deliveries coming and going, base power grid, building power panels, and control room just for starters.

"Is there a map of the compound?" he asked, glancing up from his lists.

"I can pull up an overhead photo on my computer," Chen offered.

"That would be perfect."

Taking a seat next to Caleb on the bed, Col. Chen pulled his laptop out of his briefcase. He held his finger on a small pad and then punched in a five-digit code. He clicked on a folder and scrolled through its contents before selecting a file. An aerial image of the compound filled the screen. Satisfied, he slid the computer onto Caleb's lap.

"How recent is this photo?" asked Caleb.

"It was taken last week. The compound has so many moving parts it is difficult to monitor everything. We take these photos to keep track of inventory and detect anomalies. You Americans are proficient with your sabotage."

Chen showed Caleb how to work the touchscreen to zoom in and out of the image.

"The building where your friend is being kept is this one here just south of the center of the compound. It is the main headquarters building of the remaining Chinese forces in America. There are many top-ranking commanders coming and going every day," Chen concluded.

"Are prisoners ever moved outside of that building?"

"Only if they are dead."

"I'm going to need copies of that photo. One of the whole compound and surrounding area and a close up of that building. Please?"

"I'll get them for you," Chen said, patting him on the shoulder.

Chapter 18

Caleb tossed and turned in his bed. He'd quit taking Dr. Kim's pain medication because it made him dizzy. The picture of Rice sitting between two Chinese guards haunted him. The boy was suffering because of him. Throwing off his blankets, he grabbed his cane and began pacing.

"No sleep?"

Her voice startled him. He glanced towards the hallway where she stood outside her room.

"No. You?"

"No." She walked over to him. "I need to tell you something. About Rice," she whispered.

He waited while she composed her thoughts.

"Rice . . . is not a boy."

"What?!"

"Shhh!" She held her finger to his lips.

"What do you mean?" he hissed back, pulling her hand away.

"Rice is pretending to be a boy. Rice is a girl."

"That's impossible," Caleb whispered.

Xiuying looked at him sternly. "She told me while I was with you. She was trying to make me feel better by talking to me and she said she was glad to have another girl around, someone she could talk to."

Caleb thought hard, trying to remember if he could recall anything that backed up her claim. Rice had been plenty private, but Caleb had just assumed it was because he was a little guy. Rice made excuses about the water temperature when they had all gone skinny dipping to freshen up. But none of that was conclusive.

"Trust me, Caleb, Rice is a girl, a sweet girl," she whispered again.

Running his palm down his face, he looked at her.

"What do you think they will do to her when they find out?" Xiuying asked.

Caleb shook his head. "I don't know, depends on what kind of interrogators they are. Maybe when they realize he—I mean she—doesn't know anything, they'll have pity on her and put her to work on the docks or something."

"And if they do not have pity?"

"I don't know, Xiuying," he sighed. "Maybe Col. Chen can do something when they find out, but if he's not careful he'll blow his cover and then he'll be the one being interrogated."

"Have you come up with any ideas to get her out?" she asked.

He shook his head. "I've been thinking and praying and running everything we know through my head all night and I just can't see it. I know if my brother were here, he'd think of something. He's always saying where there's a will there's a way."

"What does that mean?" she asked.

"It means, if you want it bad enough, you'll find a way to get it."

"Then I believe you will find a way to get it," she said.

"Yeah. I think I'm gonna take another look at those photos. Why don't you try and get some sleep?"

"Are you sure?"

"Yeah, I'll be alright. Just need some time to work it all out."

She turned and walked away, disappearing into the shadow of her doorway.

Caleb walked over to the bed and sat down. He clicked on the end table lamp and pulled out the photos from Chen. He looked up at the hallway one last time then shook his head. The room seemed dim and lonely without her presence, and he realized, as crazy as it was, she was the closest friend he had left in the world. It was no small comfort to have her in his corner.

Tomorrow, no, today, Rice would begin the interrogation. Sunday. Chen had the day off again and wouldn't be back to work until Monday. He would have to wait until then before Col. Chen could get him the rest of the intel he needed to start breaking down the compound and forming a plan. That meant Rice would have to endure one whole day of interrogation while little to no progress towards her rescue would take place. So, this is how Aaron had felt.

He studied the photos. Between what he had gathered from past surveillance and what Chen knew off the top of his head, there was one main access on the south side with the gate divided into six lanes. Three incoming, three outgoing. A single checkpoint guard at each incoming lane. He remembered seeing both incoming and outgoing lanes equipped with pneumatic barricades deployable from almost anywhere on the compound with an emergency button. Guard shacks were built into the walls every two hundred yards equipped with machine guns and manned day and night. All night crews were equipped with night vision.

The airfield was at the far side of the compound. Not big enough for large aircraft, he could identify half a dozen attack helicopters, a dozen transport helicopters, a couple small surveillance drones, and a hangar where the drones were kept. A tall air traffic control tower sat on the east side, perpendicular to the middle of the runway, maybe one hundred yards from the wall of the compound. The motor pool was just east of the docks, straight west of the headquarters building. The picture showed several armored vehicles, two dozen convoy vehicles, a crane, and a couple of bulldozers.

An artillery auxiliary consisting of six large artillery pieces was set up just outside the east wall behind a lower secondary earth barrier. If he looked hard enough, he could barely make out six four-man teams manning the guns. Another tower stood centered at the rear of the guns, probably for observation's sake. The docks made up the entire west side of the compound. Only a ten-foot chain-link fence topped with razor wire separated the docks from the main compound. Two massive gates allowed traffic to flow between the two. According to Chen, they were never closed due to the influx of supplies and men brought on by the counter offensive.

Each dock had its own guard tower and continual K-9 patrol. Two patrol boats armed with twin 35 mm cannons were permanently docked at the north and south docks and appeared to be manned at all times. They know the river is their weak point.

Leaning back, Caleb rubbed his eyes. According to Chen, at any given time, there were at least eighty-three armed PLA soldiers actively on guard, and another fifty-plus working the docks, in transit, manning the towers, and working in the headquarters, including several top-ranking officers and their staff.

Standing stiffly, he began pacing again, the rubber tip on his cane tapping rhythmically on the laminate tile floor.

"God, show me the way."

The river seemed to be the weakest point as far as walls were concerned, but the added patrols, dogs, and gun boats made it a tossup. Another problem was the docks, like Duluth, were lit up bright as day all night long so work could continue. The constant flow of goods and men provided some distraction and opportunity, but the timing would have to be perfect, or the dog patrols would pick them up.

Getting in was only one small step. Getting to the HQ would be no easy feat. At each large gate between the docks and main compound stood a sentry. Each gate enjoyed a steady flow of trucks; some civilian, some military. After the gates, there was a well-lit motor pool and, other than the vehicles, it was wide open. Then came the HQ building. Two sentries at the doors at all times checking ID's, and a thumbprint scanner, just to get in the door. He'd have to wait for Chen's intel to fill in the blanks inside the building.

All of that just to get inside. Then, if they were somehow able to free Rice, they had to get all the way back out. Once they were out, they'd have to evade the massive search that was sure to ensue once Rice's absence was discovered.

Meanwhile, they had to find a way to warn the American forces driving towards Memphis before they were wiped out and any hope of an American rebirth with them.

One thing at a time. . . .

Aaron was sharp, really sharp. He had to be studying the Chinese retreat, he had to realize it was too easy. And his mom would surely be encouraging him to be himself and to take his time; it was one of the only reasons the American's had fared so well with so few casualties. Aaron would make even Sun Tzu proud. Yeah, focus on Rice, give Col. Chen time to contact them. Trust in Aaron.

When everyone appeared that morning, Caleb was still pouring over the photos and his note pad. He didn't even notice Xiuying standing beside him until she held out a fresh cup of coffee. He blushed as he took it.

"Thanks, and good morning." He smiled.

"Want some congee?"

"I'd love some," he said, stretching.

She disappeared into the kitchen and returned with a bowl.

"We are all going to the hospital for the church service. You should come," she said.

"Is it safe?"

"Nothing is safe, but this is what we are good at," she said, smiling.

"Yeah," he agreed. "Maybe it would be good to step away for a bit."

Caleb buried himself under a lab coat and other medical paraphernalia in the back seat of Dr. Kim's car. Xiuying rode with Col. Chen. When they arrived, they parked at different wings of the hospital. Col. Chen and a disguised Xiuying went in through the front doors, while Caleb was smuggled through the loading docks. Meeting them at the bottom of the basement stairs, Col. Chen motioned Caleb to wait. Dr. Kim nodded to Caleb then entered the central basement room through the steel door.

"It is strange for an American to be here," Chen explained. "I need to prepare the people for your presence. I will only be a moment."

Col. Chen walked through the door leaving Caleb alone in the stairwell. Holding his ear to the cold steel, he tried to listen. After a few moments, a muted murmur of a handful of voices was all that indicated there was anyone on the other side. He heard approaching footsteps and stepped back. Col. Chen pushed the door open, and with a warm smile, ushered him into the room.

Caleb nearly gasped. The room was packed with people, they were all standing, no chairs, no tables, nothing. Half of them were dressed in scrubs, a few wore military dress, some civilian clothes. He found himself standing in front of a crowd of eighty or more. The people fidgeted and nervous whispers created an uncomfortable atmosphere. Caleb searched the crowd and found Xiuying and Dr. Kim standing at the front. She gave him an encouraging smile.

Col. Chen put his arm around Caleb and spoke in Mandarin. The people quieted down and listened. From what Caleb could make out, Chen was sharing how Caleb had given his life to the Lord. Caleb leaned heavily on his cane, choking the handle with his sweaty palm. As Chen finished, the people clapped quietly, many of them came forward and shook his hand or patted him on the shoulder. All of them looked at him fondly, their uneasiness had been lifted simply by the fact that Caleb had become a Christian. He was one of them now, nothing else seemed to matter.

Their acceptance rattled him. He'd judged all Chinese the same for so long. But these people didn't see a Chinese killer, an American; they saw a brother. They didn't ask about his past, or project their past dealings with Americans on him, it was just . . . family. Col. Chen quieted everyone down, motioning for Caleb to join Xiuying and Dr. Kim.

Col. Chen preached a message by memory out of the book of Mathew. Caleb had trouble keeping up, but just being there with so many joyful people warmed his heart. They finished by singing a Chinese hymn in hushed tones. As the service wrapped up, the attendees slipped away down the tunnels, and up the various stairwells, a couple at a time. The whole process took another hour or so but allowed Kim to introduce Caleb to a handful of members fluent in English.

By the time it was their turn to leave, Caleb felt full. The new friends he'd made reminded him of his mom, full of hope, no matter their circumstances. Willing to accept people as they are with genuine excitement and love. They were simple people, but brave. Not in a rough and tough John Wayne way, but in a quiet subtle way. Everyone in that room had risked everything to be there, and they had been doing it for years. Just to get together and love on each other in celebration of their common relationship with God. In that room, at least, they were . . . free.

"Could we drive by the base?" asked Caleb from his hideout in the back seat.

Dr. Kim muttered in Mandarin, but Caleb felt the car turn. In a few minutes Kim said, "Here."

Caleb peered out the window from under the lab coat. They rolled past the main gate, only a couple of vehicles waited as the sentries conducted their inspections. As they kept driving, Caleb could make out the roof of the barracks, the mess hall, and HQ building. Guards in their towers watched them as they rolled past.

"What did you think? Dr. Kim asked in stunted English.

"Of what?" Caleb asked, peering out the window.

"Of our people."

"Oh, they're warm, like family. Kind and gentle even though they didn't know me and I'm an American," Caleb replied.

"Yes, Jesus makes us family, but we are also crafty like snakes," Kim replied. "We . . . want to fight."

"You'd be an army of lambs," Caleb scoffed.

"But you are a lion," Kim answered, raising his eyebrows enthusiastically.

Dr. Kim turned up the street paralleling the eastern wall. He drove cautiously, never accelerating above fifteen kilometers an hour.

A flash of fur and fangs slammed into the window, snarling wildly. Caleb instinctively slunk to the floor behind the seat, drawing the lab coat over his head. The car skidded to a stop. Caleb heard Dr. Kim straighten in his seat and roll down the window. The glove box clanged open followed by the rustling of papers. A Chinese voice scolded the dog who hadn't quit clawing at the door. Caleb's leg throbbed in its cramped position; adrenaline sent a heat wave through his body, causing his hands to quiver.

He could hear footsteps circling the car. The dog's collar jingled as the beast strained against the leash. The footsteps stopped, the latch on his door popped, and the door swung open. Tensing his muscles, Caleb prepared to pounce. A cold muzzle slammed through the lab coat snarling wildly before its owner pulled it away. Then . . . laughter.

Peering out from under the lab coat, Caleb saw a familiar face looking down on him. It was one of the soldiers from the service that morning. He reached in and ruffled Caleb's hair, grinning ear to ear. Then he held his finger to his lips and closed the door.

As Kim pulled away, Caleb lay gasping on the floor.

Turning up a side street, Dr. Kim turned to Caleb, still smiling. "One of us."

"Are you trying to kill me?!" Caleb gasped.

Dr. Kim furrowed his brow. "No kill, John Wayne," he said, "Fan Ming, one of us."

Caleb flung off the lab coat and lay across the back seat. He was soaked in sweat.

"We were lucky," Dr. Kim said, still chuckling as they pulled into the driveway.

Caleb staggered into the house, still recovering from the adrenaline dump. Xiuying rushed over and helped him to the bed.

"That bad, huh?" he asked.

Dr. Kim gave her a nervous smile.

"What happened?" she demanded.

Caleb laid back and closed his eyes as Dr. Kim explained. It was his turn to smile as Xiuying laid into him in the hottest fastest Mandarin he'd ever heard. When she was finished, Dr. Kim walked over to the bed and apologized for the ruse before retiring to the kitchen.

"He should not have done that," Xiuying fumed. "At first, Dr. Kim did not recognize who the patrol officer was, but after he did, they decided to play a trick on you," she sighed. "We have lived this way for so long, always under suspicion, always watching our backs, always afraid. It is rare we get the chance to have a little fun." She looked at Caleb. "He did not mean to cause harm."

Sitting up, Caleb shook his head. "I'm fine. Scared the crap outa me. I didn't think anything was more ferocious than that dog, but I think you've got it beat. I just hope the doctor will recover," he snorted.

She punched him playfully on the shoulder. "He will be fine. He has always been that way. My mother used to scold him when he would take his jokes too far. I think he likes it."

Her eyes met his and, for just a moment, they lingered.

Chapter 19

By the time Col. Chen completed his shift Monday night, Caleb's stomach was in knots. He needed to know how Rice was faring, if they'd discovered that she was a she, and if so, how that was affecting her treatment, but most of all, he needed intel. Xiuying had left that morning in disguise to collect information on the patrols outside the wire of the base. Dr. Kim was at the hospital doing surgery and was likely to be back late.

Meeting Chen at the door, Caleb immediately began firing questions until Chen held up his hand.

"Slower, Caleb, slower. I have everything you asked for right here," he said, tapping his briefcase.

Caleb cleared off the breakfast bar while Col. Chen collected his papers. Caleb waited impatiently as he laid out several sheets of paper including a printed map. Most of the information was in Mandarin with notes written in English beside them.

"How's Rice?" Caleb finally asked.

Chen pulled out his phone with a new photo of Rice. Her left cheek bore a bruise and her lip had been split. She looked afraid.

"It's not good, I'm afraid. My superiors believe he knows where you are hiding Xiuying. He spoke her name when they were questioning him and that is when things turned."

"You said he?" asked Caleb.

"Yes, the boy," Col. Chen affirmed.

"Is he hurt bad?"

"No, not bad. Mostly on the surface. Xiuying's family is insistent on her return, it is better that my superiors believe he knows where she is. If he ever gave them her whereabouts or they came to believe that he really did not know, they would likely kill him for being one of yours. Their suspicion is the only thing keeping him alive."

Caleb studied the photo. He knew exactly what she was going through.

"Hold on," he whispered, running his finger over her face.

"There is something else," Col. Chen continued. "Your brother has picked up his pace."

Laying his tablet on top of the pages of intel, he pulled up a map of Tennessee. Zooming in on Jackson, he pointed to an arched blue line stretching about five miles wide centered on the city.

"This is the American front; they have already taken half of Jackson and are not slowing down."

He pointed to two wide sweeping red arcs northeast and southeast of Memphis, a good thirty miles out of the way on either side of the Americans' route to Memphis.

"We have controlled the skies between us and the Americans. Our intelligence says that they are buying our retreat, and that all of the eastern United States military is with them. If the Americans fall into the trap, it will be the end of the war."

Caleb studied the map, his brow furrowing. "Aaron will stop once they take Jackson to assess how they're faring and scout what lies ahead. He won't want to give the PLA enough time to recover, but he won't rush ahead, even if it looks like he should. He has good people around him, if it seems too easy, he'll know. Memphis means as much to the Chinese as it does to us. He'll send out scouts wide, he always does. If the PLA are where you say they are, he may detect them. If he discovers the trap, they'll pull back to Jackson and fight from a position of strength. If I had to bet between the two in that fight, I'd bet on Aaron."

"So, if you were the PLA, you'd pull your troops back further to avoid his detection," said Chen.

"Yeah, much further, at least twice that. Aaron didn't get this far by being reckless, no one is more thorough. I honestly feel better after seeing this map; odds are, the trap will fail," he said with a satisfied sigh. "But that doesn't mean we should give up trying to contact them."

"Of course not," agreed Chen. "I only had a few moments alone today and was unable to find their signal, but I will keep trying."

"Thanks."

"I collected as much information as I could of what you requested," Col. Chen said, sliding the map out of the way. He picked up a piece of paper and began discussing the guard schedules.

Hours passed as Col. Chen laid out all the information while Caleb made notes in his notebook and on the pictures of the compound. Caleb was grateful for Chen's patience as the interrogator became the interrogated.

"What about the base hospital?" Caleb asked. "You didn't mark it out on the map."

"There is no base hospital. We have a clinic, but anyone requiring serious medical attention is brought to the hospital."

"Even prisoners?" asked Caleb.

"If they are necessary to save, but that is rare."

Caleb bounced his cane on the floor excitedly as he thought.

"You said Xiuying's absence was causing the top brass a lot of misery, right?"

"Yes. General Yang and his staff are all sheep. Spineless. They received their positions because they will do whatever China asks regardless of the strategic cost. You should be grateful; this is why we are losing this war."

"All the better for us," Caleb replied.

"Yes, yes," answered Chen.

"And those same top brass believe Rice knows where she is?"

"Yes."

"Would that make Rice valuable enough to take to the hospital if he was in dire need of care?"

"Yes, for the moment . . . I think I see where you are going, but how do we get Rice to that level of danger without risk of killing him?" Chen asked.

"I haven't gotten that far yet, but I think this is our way," he said enthusiastically.

The door creaked causing Caleb to jump.

"Don't worry," said Chen. "I'm an intelligence officer, there is no need for a random inspection of my home, if it comes through that door, it is a friend."

Xiuying walked in wearing a ball cap and sunglasses. Her hair was pulled back in a ponytail that fell just beyond the collar of her windbreaker. She tossed the cap and sunglasses on the kitchen counter and began taking out the ponytail when she caught him watching her.

"What?" she asked.

"Nothing," Caleb said sheepishly. "I think you should leave it, looks nice."

"It's just a ponytail," she chuffed.

"I know."

She smirked and looked away before pulling her hair tight.

"So, what are you guys working on?" she asked.

"I think we may have found a way to rescue Rice and it's all thanks to you," Caleb said.

"Ok . . ."

"If we can find a way to necessitate it, we can have him taken off the base and moved to the hospital, from there rescue shouldn't be too difficult."

"What does that have to do with me?" she asked.

"The only reason they're keeping Rice alive is because they believe he knows where you are," Caleb said.

"And the only reason they wouldn't just let him die was if they believed your whereabouts would die with him," finished Chen.

"Being a princess has its perks," Caleb said.

Xiuying snorted. "You mean prisoner," she whispered.

"What's that?" Caleb asked.

"Nothing. How is she—"

Caleb caught her eye, shaking his head almost imperceptibly.

"I mean, how is he doing?" she asked.

"He has been roughed up but is holding on. He is actually quite impressive for such a young person," Chen answered.

Xiuying nodded her head. "How are you going to get him to the hospital?"

"That's the tricky part," Caleb admitted. "Any ideas?"

"I could encourage the interrogators to change their methods, but I could not be sure the damage would not be permanent," Chen offered.

"Yeah, you people are good at that," Caleb said wryly.

Col. Chen looked offended.

"I meant Chinese soldiers, bad ones, are good at inflicting pain," Caleb corrected. "Sorry, I'm still getting used to the idea that you're not all like that."

"I understand," Chen said, patting him on the shoulder. "It is ok."

"I don't want to see him hurt," Caleb said. "There has to be another way."

"My uncle will know a way," Xiuying said.

Col. Chen nodded in agreement. "The doctor is best for this task."

"Alright," Caleb agreed, pacing again. "When someone is taken to the hospital from the base, how do they get there?"

"That would depend on the reason. If it is a broken leg or something like that, someone from the base would take them. If they appear to be in a trauma situation, an ambulance from the hospital would come and take them," Col. Chen answered.

"Even for a prisoner?"

"What good would taking a prisoner to the hospital be if they died on the way?" Chen answered.

"Fair enough," replied Caleb. "I'm assuming a soldier escort would ride along?"

"Of course."

"Then we need Rice to need an ambulance."

"Why?" asked Xiuying.

"Because we need our people in the ride to deal with that escort," Caleb said.

"I agree, that would be the simplest way," Chen said.

When the doctor arrived at the house, it was half past eleven. The three of them waited on the couch poised like cats ready to pounce.

"Yes?" the doctor said, entering the living room with raised eyebrows.

Xiuying was the first to speak. Her Mandarin was fast, and Caleb gave up trying to follow after the first few words. He watched Kim's facial expressions change from surprise to concern, from concern to concentration, from concentration to excitement.

As Xiuying finished, Dr. Kim turned to Caleb nodding emphatically. He began talking, moving his hands this way and that. There was a clandestine twinkle in his eye as he spoke, barely pausing to take a breath. Caleb looked to Xiuying for help, but she only held up her hand.

Left with no other choice but to study faces, Caleb watched Xiuying. Her ponytail bobbed up and down as she reacted to what the doctor was saying. Her face seemed focused and positive. Col. Chen nodded his head occasionally, also chiming in from time to time as the doctor rambled on. He seemed optimistic as well, even chuckling as the doctor finished.

At last, Xiuying turned to Caleb, "He says there are many ways to induce the kind of trauma that would require an ambulance. Most would require Rice to ingest a medication that would cause him to pass out, his heart rate to slow, or even cause seizures."

"Would Rice be harmed?"

"No. Depending on which trauma we choose, the effect would either wear off or could be reversed with a simple injection," Xiuying answered.

Caleb took his cane and began pacing. "How could we get him to ingest the medicine?"

"I could slip it into his food," Chen offered. "It would not be difficult."

"He is eating, then?" Caleb asked.

"Every day, you have my word," Chen replied.

"Ok, ok," Caleb paced again, "How long after he eats will the effect take place?"

Xiuying passed on the question to the doctor.

"He says it depends on the medication."

"How about seizures?" Caleb asked.

"He says five minutes," Xiuying replied.

"Does he eat at a regular time every day?"

"He does: 7:30 p.m." Chen replied.

"Good. Do the seizures require an injection?"

"Yes."

Caleb thought for a moment. "Can we arrange who rides in the ambulance?"

"Yes, Dr. Kim is the head of the hospital," Xiuying replied.

"How are ambulances handled at the gate during a medical emergency?"

"They are supposed to be inspected, but when the lights and sirens are used, this is not followed, they are let in without a check," Chen replied, grinning.

"Ok, this is what we're gonna do. Col. Chen, you're going to slip the seizure medicine into Rice's food. When the seizures begin, you have to be the one to make the call to get an ambulance. We can't leave that part up to chance. Dr. Kim, we need a couple of people we can trust from your staff to drive the ambulance, they have to be apprised of the situation and willing to take the risk. I trust you to choose the right people.

"After the call is made, the ambulance will pick me up at the loading docks before heading to the base. I'll hide in the back of the ambulance in medical clothing, a mask, and one of those medical hat things. Once Rice and his guard are loaded and the doors are closed, I'll deal with the guard and give Rice the injection. We'll have to dump the ambulance with the body. Wipe it down good and find another way back. Dr. Kim, you will give us an hour or so to clear the scene before calling in and reporting a stolen ambulance."

Giving Xiuying a moment to translate, he turned to Col. Chen. "The only thing I can't figure out is how to keep your superiors from figuring out they have a mole in their midst, and that the mole could be you."

Col. Chen gave him a reassuring smile. "I like your plan, do not worry about me. I've been living a double life for many years; this is what I am good at. Remember, General Yang is not a brilliant man, he is just a uniform, he will believe what I say."

Caleb gave him an appreciative bow.

"My uncle wants to know why you must be in the ambulance?" Xiuying said.

"One, because Rice will be afraid when he comes to, and he knows me. And two, because if something is off, I'll know it. Rice is my responsibility; I'm going to be there."

"The boy's time is running out," Chen said. "We need to act fast."

Caleb nodded. "Tomorrow?"

"Tomorrow."

Chapter 20

At breakfast, it was obvious no one had slept much, and by 8:30 a.m. they were already into their third pot of coffee. Caleb rehearsed the plan, covering every step in painstaking detail as he had watched Aaron do countless times. His cane bore the wear of nervous hands, its black lacquer handle worn to the wood.

"Do you have a system for alerting the church if someone believes you've been discovered?" Caleb asked.

"It is a necessity," Chen replied. "Or we would have been wiped out long ago. Why do you ask?"

"How does it work?" Caleb continued, ignoring his question.

"A code word goes out on our phones to all the group leaders. The group leaders send the message out to all their members. All the names are in code so if any member is caught, they do not reveal the names of the other members. Different code words mean different things. A new list of code words and their meanings is sent out every week."

"Who makes the list?"

"Dr. Kim. He is the oldest and most trusted member of the New China church here," Chen replied.

"So, something happens, and you get a message, then you send out another message to the congregation?" Caleb asked Col. Chen.

"I do not send out any messages," Chen replied.

"Why not?"

"I am the pastor. The Chinese government sees pastors as the real prize in their war against religion. If I were to know who the group leaders were and was able to communicate with them, I could be used to destroy the whole church. It is better if I do not know. I am treated like any other member, only knowing my group members and leader," Chen replied.

Caleb nodded his understanding. "So, Dr. Kim is the only one who knows everyone in every group?"

The doctor shook his head, and Xiuying answered, "Dr. Kim only knows who the group leaders are. Each group leader recruits members to their team as new members join the church. Leaders are only aware of the members who are on their team, and each member is only aware of their own leader and teammates."

Sitting back in awe, Caleb asked, "You all meet as one for church and no one violates this system?"

"The system means the difference between life and death. When you have lived how we have lived it is not complicated to understand," Xiuying said.

"Each member ready to die to protect the identity of their fellow members . . ." Caleb ran his fingers through his hair. "Boy, was I wrong about you people."

"What does this have to do with the rescue?" Col. Chen asked again.

"Every good strategy has an escape plan. I remember Dr. Kim saying that your people, the church people that is, are crafty as snakes. How would you get out if this rescue went south?" he asked.

"The base will be monitoring cell phone traffic, so we will need code words to communicate," Chen said.

"The church has several safe houses throughout Memphis that are indicated by code words. You will need a safe place to go if the plan is discovered," Xiuying added.

"Agreed. Does Dr. Kim know of a place?" Caleb asked.

Dr. Kim nodded reassuringly as Xiuying interpreted the question.

"And what happens if the plan does fail?" asked Xiuying.

"We come up with a plan B, and fast."

"And if that plan fails?"

"We go with Plan Z," Caleb said.

"What is Plan Z?" asked Chen.

"The one with almost zero chance of success," Caleb replied with a smirk. "Alright, we've got a lot of work to do before 7:30. We'd best get after it."

Xiuying chewed her lip nervously as they waited for the trolley to ramble past.

"Remember, after you drop me off at the loading docks, don't stick around. Go back to the house and wait for us there," Caleb said.

"I will be praying and waiting," she replied, turning into the hospital parking lot.

"We're gonna need it," he said.

Jumping out as she rolled past the docks, Caleb called over his shoulder, "I'll see you back at the house," and watched her drive away.

Pulling his mask up over his nose, and his head net down to his eyebrows, Caleb leaned against the dock. Fidgeting with his phone, he managed to get the screen to light up. A large 7:22 took up most of the screen, he shoved the device back in his pocket. His scrubs made him uncomfortable, he longed for his tactical pants and light hoodie. He flipped his phone over and over in his pocket, without his cane there was nothing else to absorb his merciless kneading. He could count his pulse in his leg, the pain was constant but bearable.

He fought the urge to dive behind the dumpster as a military transport rolled by. As it passed, he pulled out his phone, illuminating the screen again, 7:23. He grit his teeth, slamming the phone back into his pocket. How did he even know such a device kept the correct time? Xiuying claimed they were all synchronized by satellite, but he still doubted it.

Hospital staff and patients flowed constantly through the parking lot, coming and going from the hospital. Caleb watched as the majority moved with their cell phones pressed to their heads. Pulling out his phone, he held it to his head and paced back and forth moving his free hand from time to time as though he was in a passionate conversation.

A spontaneous vibration sent the phone flying from his hand and skittering across the parking lot. Glancing around nervously, Caleb scooped up the phone. A long crack cut through the words, Alarm 7:30, and the phone continued to pulse in his hand. He tapped the word stop on the screen and the vibrating ceased. It was go time. In fifteen minutes, Rice would be flopping on the floor and the call would be made.

Caleb bowed his head. Praying was a new language, and he was no expert, but if God could save him, then He must be able to save a kid like Rice.

"Father . . . she's just a kid," he began. "I don't know how involved you get in things like this, but I know my mom would say this whole thing was your idea . . . that I wouldn't even be here if it wasn't for you. If that's true, then please help us succeed tonight, and keep everyone safe. In Jesus' name. Amen."

His phone buzzed again. Pulling it out, he saw a message up on the screen. The package has been delivered, standby for call. Rice had eaten the medication. He leaned back against the hospital wall, fish swam in his stomach. He wasn't used to having so little control or having to depend on so many people. He wasn't used to caring about anyone, including himself. This anxiety was a weight he'd never carried.

Slipping his hands under his scrubs, he felt for the handle of the knife hidden in his waist band. He hated killing with a knife. It reminded him of Eddy and the thought turned his stomach. He'd always chosen pistols because they allowed him to get close, allowed him to show his enemies that they no longer scared him, no longer owned him, but made touching them unnecessary. But tonight, for Rice's sake, he was going to get really close.

The wail of an ambulance siren set his heart on fire. The Eagle was still in there. His mind shifted, focused, shutting out everything but the mission. His muscles hummed, hungry with anticipation. The ambulance whipped around the corner, screeching to a halt in front of him. Two Chinese EMT's waved frantically for him to get in. Sprinting to the back, Caleb jumped in, and the driver punched down on the gas.

Stumbling into the box, he took a seat on a bench. He recognized the codriver from the church service, he'd gone by the code name Monkey. The driver was unfamiliar, similar in age to Monkey, somewhere in his mid-twenties. He remained stoic as he raced through the streets of Memphis towards the base with the sirens blaring.

"We're going to help your friend, John Wayne," Monkey said, patting him on the arm.

Of course, Dr. Kim had given him the code name John Wayne.

"Thank you," he replied. "Who's this?"

"Ahhh, this is Iguana," Monkey said, slapping the driver on the arm.

"Seriously?" Caleb chuffed.

"There are a lot of us, and only so many animals," Monkey replied. "You should see my phone; my contacts are a zoo," he laughed.

Approaching the gate, Caleb motioned for the driver to slow down. Several vehicles waited in line in front of them at the gate, several more pulled up beside them and behind them. Gritting his teeth, Caleb punched the gurney.

"Night shift," Monkey said.

Caleb checked his phone. 7:47. "Hang in there, Rice . . ."

Then something hit him, a feeling, his senses warning him, something was out of place. He studied the traffic around them, a few vehicles made a feeble attempt to let them through, but the traffic was a crawling gridlock. No, it wasn't the traffic. Looking ahead at the gate, the feeling grew. What was it?

Then he saw it. The sentries at the gate had doubled in number since Xiuying's reconnaissance, and even more troubling, they were heavily armed. Normally, the guards only carried their sidearms, no helmets. These guards had their rifles slung over their shoulders, and helmets on their heads.

"Something's up," he said.

The driver slowed to a stop.

Caleb's phone vibrated in his pocket. Pulling it out, he checked the screen.

"Abort!" is all it read.

"We've got to go!" Caleb shouted. "They're on to us."

"Go where?" the driver demanded.

"Just start moving, they'll find a way to get out of the way," Caleb commanded.

The driver began crawling, honking his horn furiously. To Caleb's amazement the vehicles around them cleared a path six inches at a time.

Caleb went back to his phone, tapping wildly. "How do I send a message on this thing?!"

Monkey took the phone out of his hands. "Who are you trying to contact?"

"Zebra, I need to contact Zebra."

Tapping the screen twice, he asked, "What do you want to say?"

"Tell him we had to abort and need instructions," Caleb said.

"Sent," Monkey said, handing him back the phone.

"We are out, where do you want me to go?" asked the driver.

"I'm working on it!" Caleb said.

The phone vibrated and a codeword popped up on the screen.

"Head to the old east side elementary school in the dead part of town. Dr. Kim—er, Zebra said you would know where it is."

"We know it," replied Monkey.

The driver turned hard, and they were once again racing down the street.

"How could they have known?!" Caleb yelled.

"They always know . . ." Monkey replied.

"What's that supposed to mean?"

"They always find us, no matter where we hide, how good our code, they always find us. They know who our leaders are, they know when they are vulnerable, they know where to catch them," Monkey answered. "This is what we live with every day, wondering if we will be next."

As they reached the dead part of town, the contrast was breathtaking. The Chinese had moved into Memphis and began restoring it, starting along the river and working their way out. Streets in the dead part had been cleared of rubble and debris to allow traffic to flow in and out of the city, but the streetlights remained dark. Yards filled with rubble and waste lined the roads. Burned and bombed out buildings loomed in the darkness illuminated here and there by glancing headlights from the populated area.

According to Monkey, patrols were made to the dead areas during the day in an attempt to catch criminals who took refuge in the chaotic mess, but during the night not even the military dared venture beyond the lights. They rounded a corner where three silhouettes stood watching them as they rolled by.

"Should we be worried?" Caleb asked.

"No," Monkey replied. "Most of these folks are poor people who were forced to move here, they lost what little they had in China, and it broke them. Some are here for drugs, some are here because they were accused of crimes, some guilty some not. Some are here because they are rebels who no longer have a reason to serve the State. All of them are here to hide. Dr. Kim and other church members come here at night and give them food, medicine, even deliver babies, but most of all they give the love of God. They are the untouchables, and that is where Dr. Kim believes God has called him to be."

"How many are there?" Caleb asked.

"No one knows, maybe hundreds."

"We are here," the driver said, pulling the ambulance into a dilapidated bus barn.

"Alright, let's wipe it down. Dr. Kim said the police will probably find it in the morning. There will be a car waiting for us two blocks north of here in . . . about an hour."

Chapter 21

Wh", "What happened?!" Caleb asked, entering Chen's house. Meeting him at the door, Xiuying threw her arms around him. "I am sorry, Caleb."

Pulling back, he pleaded, "What happened?"

"Rice is fine. Pastor Chen said one of the other interrogators had seen the seizures trick before and knew how to cure it. He called the clinic, and the antidote was administered in minutes. The base went on high alert, and they were planning on trapping you at the gate.

"Dr. Kim did what you said and reported the stolen ambulance. Pastor Chen is at the hospital now, investigating. He said he will fill us in when they both get home later tonight."

Grabbing his cane, Caleb swung it back preparing to put it through the wall when Xiuying caught his arm.

"Caleb, don't! The important thing is that Rice is ok, everyone is ok. We will come up with another plan."

"There was nothing wrong with this plan," he said in desperation.

"But it did not work. If you do not come up with another plan, then who will rescue Rice? We cannot give up; God would not give up. He will give you another plan."

"How do you know that?!"

"There is a story in the Bible about a father, Abraham, and his son, Isaac. Do you know it?" she asked.

"Yes," Caleb nodded.

"God told Abraham to sacrifice his son, this made Abraham very sad, but he trusted God that his son would be his heir. They loaded up everything they needed and headed to the mountain for the sacrifice. When they get there, they build the altar together and put wood on it, then Abraham puts his boy on the wood and prepares to kill him. When all hope seems lost, God tells Abraham not to kill his son. Abraham sees a ram stuck by the horns in a bush, so Abraham takes the ram God supplied and sacrifices it instead, and God blesses him because of his obedience and faith through a great test," she said.

"So, you think God is testing me?" he asked.

"Life is full of tests, Caleb, it is only in the tests that God can show us who we really are. David with Goliath, Daniel and the lions, Joshua and Jericho. God knows Himself and you, but you do not know Him or yourself. You will only know what is possible once you have done it." She looked up at him warmly. "God will not abandon you in the test, Caleb, don't you abandon Him."

He let his arm hang slack and she released It. hobbling over to his maps, he picked up his pencil and started scribbling. Xiuying brought him a cup of coffee, taking a seat across from him. His mind churned with thoughts. Rice. The shadowy untouchables. What Monkey had said about the Chinese always knowing, about Abraham, and . . . Xiuying. She was so delicate, yet possessed the power to restrain his rage, quiet the storm, freeze his spinning world with a word. She was . . . incredible.

When Chen arrived, Caleb did his best not to bowl him over with questions. He waited until he'd entered the kitchen and dropped his briefcase.

"Is Rice alright?"

"Yes. Did Xiuying explain what happened?" Col. Chen asked. Caleb nodded.

"I am so sorry. I had no idea he knew about the induced seizures. I have been put in charge of the investigation so there is no need for you to worry about discovery. But I am afraid we have created a problem," he said solemnly.

"After tonight's attempt, my superiors have become nervous. With the big battle coming, they believe the boy's presence may cause more harm than good. They have decided to execute him tomorrow afternoon. I did all I could to change their minds, but they are convinced this is the best course."

"What?" Caleb said. "He's just a kid!"

"They see him as an American who is one of yours," Col. Chen said.

Xiuying turned to intercept him, but it was too late. Caleb caught the end of the coffee table and sent it cartwheeling across the room.

"Where are my guns?!" he seethed.

"Cale—"

Breaking his cane over his knee, he yelled, "Where are my guns?!"

Caleb moved through the house, rifling through drawers and overturning beds. He fought through both of them as he made his way to Chen's room and kicked in the door.

"Caleb!" Chen bear-hugged him from behind. "Stop. Your guns are not here, I have never seen them, I give you my word."

Caleb fought his grip, pulling at his fingers to get free.

"Caleb, if you attack the base by yourself, you will be killed."

"It wouldn't be my first time," he grunted.

"I have read your file. Remember, you have never gone up against a complex like this, not even close. You are a good fighter, a great fighter, but you are not the fighter you used to be, and this base is not like any you have ever encountered. If you attack like this, your sacrifice will be for nothing, and the boy will still die!"

Sacrifice . . .

Caleb stopped struggling. His muscles relaxed. His breathing slowed. Chen released his grip and lowered his arms.

Turning around, Caleb saw the two of them standing wide-eyed in the hallway. Chen panted heavily, massaging his wrists.

"I know what to do," Caleb said. "I'll trade myself for Rice."

"What?!" Xiuying asked.

"I'll be his ram," Caleb said definitively, limping slowly back to the living room.

Flipping up the coffee table, he carried it back to its place.

"You cannot surrender, Caleb," Col. Chen said.

"It's the only option we have left; Rice is out of time, and you said your superior, General Yang wants me," Caleb replied.

Stooping over, he began collecting his maps and papers, and placed them back on the table.

"Yes, but what about the Americans? Your brother is still pressing forward, and I have been unable to contact him," Chen added.

"Find a way!" Caleb said.

"Caleb, I do not make plans. I analyze data, make predictions, interrogate prisoners, but I do not make plans. If I cannot contact your brother, the Americans will be defeated, and we will all lose," Col. Chen pleaded.

"I will do it."

Both of them turned to face Xiuying.

"They want me, too," she said simply.

Caleb opened his mouth to protest, but Xiuying continued.

"If you surrender, they will kill you, and the Americans will most likely lose the war. That is not a fair trade. If you trade me, Rice will live and I will live, General Yang would not dare hurt me. Pastor Chen is right; America still needs you."

"But you'll be a slave," Caleb said.

"I have always been a slave," she said, her eyes turning to the floor.

"She is correct. The military will not harm her. She would be sent home to her grandparents," Chen added.

Caleb let the papers fall from his hand. "Rice is not even one of your people . . ." he whispered.

"You are my people," she said, lifting his chin.

Collapsing into his chair, he felt dizzy, out of control. Nothing seemed simple, nothing made sense. Why was this new life so hard? He'd finally found a home; was God really going to take it all away? What was the purpose of this test? Why was God taking it out on her? He felt sick, he was supposed to be the ram. Now, he was Abraham, only it wasn't a ram he'd be sacrificing . . . it was his heart.

His emotions mingling with the pain in his leg made him nauseous and sent him stumbling for the bathroom. When he came out, he found her waiting for him on the other side of the door.

"You ok?" she asked.

"Yeah . . . no, not really."

Reaching out, she took his hands. "You have to let me do this. I have lived this way my whole life, never really understanding why, but now, I think it was so I would be ready for this, to make this decision. When I lost my parents, I thought my world was over, that my hope of having some joy had died with my mother. But then you took me, and I did not understand why, but God would not let me hate you. Then, when you gave your life to Him, I thought, that must be what God was doing, but I was wrong again; He had even more planned. You are the only friend I have ever had. And being with you is the only freedom I have ever known. If I am only ever able to make one decision for myself, I would want it to be this one." As she spoke, a tear spilled over and rolled slowly down her cheek.

Pulling her in close, Caleb wrapped his arms around her.

"You're the best person I know," he whispered against her hair.

They held each other until a car door heralded Dr. Kim's arrival. Wiping her tears, Xiuying met him in the kitchen. Caleb watched as she sat him down and explained what had happened to Rice and what she had decided to do. Dr. Kim's hands shook as she spoke, but he didn't interrupt. He looked from Xiuying to Caleb to Chen and back again, his tired eyes pleading with them.

When she finished, Dr. Kim stood on shaky legs and walked out and sat on the back steps.

"I will stay with him," Xiuying said, following him out.

Caleb's heart and mind jockeyed for dominance in the awkward silence that followed. Col. Chen brought a chair from the kitchen, taking a seat next to Caleb at the coffee table.

"What is next?" he asked.

Shaking his head, Caleb said, "We're gonna need to buy some time."

Taking a piece of paper out of his pad, he scribbled down a note and handed it to Chen.

"I have Major Li's daughter and I understand you want her back. I am willing to trade her for the American boy you have in your possession, but you must follow my instructions to the letter, or I will kill the girl. You will answer this cell phone when I call you on Friday at 10 a.m. If you do not, the girl is dead. You will do only what I tell you, when I tell you, or the girl is dead. You know who I am, you know what I am capable of. Signed, The Eagle," Chen read aloud.

"I'm going to need three burner phones; only one phone needs to have the numbers of the other two phones, the other phones can be empty," Caleb said.

"I can get you phones," Chen said.

"Tomorrow you will 'find' this note and one of the empty phones and bring them to your superiors. Hopefully they will take the bait and buy us some time to plan the rest," Caleb said.

"I will make sure it is convincing. General Yang is under so much pressure from the government to find her, I am sure he will jump at the chance," Chen said. "It is a good start."

"So far . . ." Caleb said. "I'm gonna need Dr. Kim's help with locations, I hope he's up for it."

Caleb paced the living room nervously the following morning, waiting to hear how his ransom note had been received. Xiuying's eyes followed him playfully as he hobbled.

"Missing your cane?" she asked.

"Yes," he said, not slowing down.

"How is it?"

"Hurts, but I can ignore it."

"Caleb, your plan will work. Look at me, my face is dirty, my clothes, my hair is a mess."

"Don't forget about my jacket over your shoulders," he added.

"Exactly. General Yang will see my photo on the phone and have no choice but to believe it," she said.

Caleb stopped pacing and met her gaze.

"You should sit down, Caleb, it is going to work."

"That's what I'm afraid of . . ." he said honestly, plopping down and dropping his head into his hands.

"None of that!" she snapped. "It is my decision, and it is also my decision not to let the future steal this time I have left. I am going to enjoy it," she said with a defiant smile.

"You would say that," Caleb said, throwing up his hands.

"Teach me how to play cards," she said.

"Now?"

"Yes, I want to learn to play cards right now."

Getting back up, Caleb walked over to a drawer and pulled out a deck.

"I noticed these when I was . . . rearranging the place," he said.

Caleb laid out the cards and taught her one of the only games he knew, King's Corner.

"Can I ask you a question?" he asked, shuffling the cards.

"Yes."

"What will happen to you when you go back?"

Sighing, Xiuying answered, "I will go back to being a 'Chinese Princess.'"

"What if they find out you're a Christian?" he asked.

"Thanks to you, they won't. They will believe I was your prisoner and probably baby me for months," she said, checking her cards.

"But what if they did find out?" he pressed.

Studying him for a moment, she said, "If I were a common person, they would send me to a reconditioning camp. A place where they put people who do not worship the State to . . ." She searched for the right words. "Brainwash them?"

Caleb nodded.

"To brainwash them, so they can put them back into the State system. Those who cannot be restored, vanish," she said.

Caleb shook his head in horror.

"But I am not a common person," she continued. "My family would never admit to my being a Christian, it would bring shame on them. They would hire a private reconditioner and lock me away until I was ready to return."

"What if you resisted?"

"I would!"

"Then what?"

"Then they would lock me away forever, only bringing me out when absolutely necessary to satisfy public curiosity," she replied.

Caleb fell back in his chair. "We have to convince them you're my prisoner. I don't think I could live if I knew you were going through all that."

"Caleb," she chided.

"I mean, aren't you worried at all?"

"I said, none of that. You have to have faith, Caleb; the Lord gets the final word. This life, it is temporary, it is not the end," she said. "And I am out of cards; you lose."

"Third round in a row! You're a card shark!" he teased.

"I do not know what that means."

"It means you're really good, or just lucky!"

A vibration in his pocket set his hair on end. Xiuying heard it too and paused picking up the cards. Caleb withdrew the phone and checked the message.

Sighing in both relief and agony he said, "They bought it."

"I never had a doubt," Xiuying replied.

"Wow."

What?" she asked.

"Col. Chen says, and I quote: 'General Yang broke down in tears' when he saw your picture."

"My family can be a little overbearing," Xiuying said sheepishly.

"So that's it," he said. "We're on."

Chapter 22

Two days had flown by faster than any of them could have imagined. All that remained to plan was to set the location, and for that, Caleb needed Dr. Kim. The doctor had been avoiding Caleb since Xiuying had shared her decision with him. Reluctantly, he'd agreed to take Thursday off and come to the house.

When he arrived, Dr. Kim held out a new cane for Caleb. "Olive branch," he said.

Caleb nodded appreciatively, leading him to the living room. They sat beside each other on the couch, looking over the maps spread out on the coffee table. Xiuying, deciding it was best to give them some time alone, had jumped in the shower.

"She is all I have left," Dr. Kim began. "I have lost everyone I have loved."

"I know, Monkey told me. All your friends have been taken," Caleb said.

"I have lived my life in hiding and it has saved me nothing." His voice quivered. "And now, I will lose Xiuying." His eyes searched Caleb's.

Caleb shook his head. He didn't have the words, what's more, he felt the same way.

"She said it was a test, that the Lord would have the final say," Caleb said at last.

"She believes, even when others do not. She has lost everyone too," he said.

Dr. Kim removed his glasses, wiping a tear. "What do you need from me?"

Caleb spent the next hour explaining his plan to Dr. Kim with Xiuying's help. Dr. Kim laid out several covert locations the church had used over the years to hide members, store Bibles, and hold services. Caleb discovered that being part of the Chinese church meant constantly looking for hiding places, and Kim knew them all.

By the time they agreed on the perfect locations, Dr. Kim's reluctance had warmed to a general cooperation thanks to Xiuying's constant optimism. They covered escape routes, alternative locations, timelines, code words, and communications. The selected locations were far from the lone cell tower that Chen had informed them only had four sectors. Triangulation was impossible, the best the PLA would get would be a ninety-degree swath of the city and a rough distance. Therefore, the further from the tower, the more territory the PLA would have to search, and the more time they would have.

When they finished, Dr. Kim stood nodding his head.

"It is an impressive plan."

"If you think this is impressive, you should see me in a fight," Caleb said.

"I hope you are better at planning," Dr. Kim said, tapping him on his wounded thigh.

"Yeah . . ." Caleb chuckled, scratching his chin in embarrassment.

Caleb shook Dr. Kim's hand. "We couldn't have done it without you."

"It will work, John Wayne," he said, patting Caleb on the shoulder.

That evening, Xiuying requested a movie and ice cream. There was nothing left to plan and going over it one more time would only add to the anxiety threatening to swallow them all. Xiuying chose a movie called *Braveheart* and by midway through the film, he couldn't for the life of him figure out why. An army of unarmored men in skirts was busy attempting to hack its way through an army of well-armed oppressors.

The story was brutal, a desperate struggle for freedom fraught with betrayal, heartbreaking loss, and impossible odds. Caleb found himself riveted to the screen as the hero, William Wallace, was strapped to a cross and slowly disemboweled, his captor promising him reprieve if only he will submit. Then, the crowd goes silent, the hero summons all his remaining strength and yells, "FRRREEEEEDDDDOOOOOOOOOOOOOOMMMMMM!" And it's all over, his struggle ends, and he returns, at last, to his beloved.

But the story didn't end there. The prince who betrayed him leads the battered peasant army out onto the battlefield to finally submit itself to its oppressor. The prince rides slowly towards the opposing army, and they prepare to receive him. Then he turns, and drawing his sword, asks the peasant army who bled with the hero to bleed with him. And an army of starving peasants, without a chance in the world, charges the field and wins their freedom.

And then he understood why—why she had picked such a story to be her last. She was Wallace.

Caleb couldn't sleep, he doubted any of them could. By 4:30 a.m. he'd given up. His mind was a tangled mess of what had happened, what could happen, and William Wallace. Entering the kitchen, he noticed the back door ajar. Grabbing a glass of water, he walked over to the door. It was Xiuying, she was sitting on the steps gazing up at the stars. He watched her for a moment. Even now, with no one to impress, her face glowed.

Deciding to join her, he pushed open the door. As he did, she looked up.

"Couldn't sleep," he said.

"Me either," she replied.

"Mind if I join you?"

She shook her head, and he took a seat next to her.

"Worried?" he asked.

"No. Nervous maybe, and a little sad. I haven't seen my grandparents since we moved to America. I believe they do care about me, but they care about our family honor first. I will miss this life, and the people in it, but I also believe that God is not finished with me, my story will continue," she said.

"I wish I believed like you do, my stomach has been in knots since Wednesday."

"It takes time, you are just a baby," she teased.

"I don't know how I'm going to do this without you, maybe that's part of the reason I'm afraid," he said. "I don't want to do this without you."

"Me too," she said, leaning her head on his shoulder.

They sat together in silence until the rising sun drove them into the house. Dr. Kim met them with two cups of coffee and an understanding nod. Col. Chen joined them in his military uniform. He prayed over them before picking up his briefcase and heading for the door.

"I'll see you in a little while," he said to Xiuying.

The three of them sipped coffee in silence until it was time for Xiuying to prepare. She dawned the same dirty outfit from the photo and messed up her hair, finishing the ensemble with makeup that made it look like she'd spent a month living in a cave.

"If you were going for the Wallace look, you failed," Caleb teased.

"I would not want to scare them," she smiled.

"Here," he said. "Take this, it'll add to the drama," he said, handing her his Harley Davidson Jacket.

"Are you sure you won't miss it?"

"I think the Eagle's days are over," he said, patting his leg. "Besides, I want you to have it."

She took it, wrapping it around her shoulders with a warm smile.

"Hold that look," he said, taking out his phone. Snapping a picture, he said, "We might need it later."

"It is time," Dr. Kim's voice broke in.

Xiuying's face flushed.

"I will pull the car around," he said, and headed for the door.

Caleb walked Xiuying to the front steps, handing her a phone.

"Remember to be ready at ten o'clock for my call. You must sell it."

"I will," she said, taking the phone.

Dr. Kim pulled the car in front of the steps.

"Well, I guess this is goodbye," she said, with a courageous smile.

Caleb nodded. "Thank you, for everything."

As she turned and took a step down the stairs, Caleb reached out, catching her by the hand.

"Xiuying, I . . ."

She threw her arms around his neck, pressing her lips into his cheek. "This is not the end," she whispered.

Letting go before he could react, she trotted down the stairs and jumped into the car.

Caleb bit his knuckle to keep from screaming as they drove away. He waited until the car turned the corner, rolling out of sight, before returning to the house. His emotions raged within him; snatching a pillow from the couch, he screamed his heart into it. It was a cruel pain unlike any he'd ever felt, but there was no time, no mercy, no other options.

He had to focus; he would process all of it later, but right now, they needed the Eagle. Trotting over to his box of possessions, he pulled out his pack and double checked its contents. Flashlight, compass, a map Dr. Kim had drawn, a map of Memphis, burner cell phone, two bottles of water, and a Chinese military ration. He dug into the large pocket, taking inventory of the change of clothes for Rice when his hand hit something solid and cold.

Could it be?

Jerking the object from the bag, he felt a familiar savagery bristle beneath his skin. It was his guns, still hanging from his pistol belt just like he'd left them that night under the bridge. As he turned them over, he noticed a piece of paper protruding from one of the holsters. Pulling it out, he opened it and read, "Just in case," signed, Dr. Kim.

So, Chen had been telling the truth, the doctor had been keeping his guns.

He strapped on the belt and pulled on his light hoodie. Shouldering the pack, he headed for the door. As he passed through the kitchen, he found a pair of sunglasses. He put them on and pulled his hood over his head. Lastly, he set his cane on the counter before heading out the door.

Hitting the street, he pulled out his phone bringing up the map app. Xiuying had put a pin at his position to make it easier to navigate. He cut through several back alleys, before hitting the deserted streets of the dead part of town.

It was an hour of hard walking before he arrived outside his destination, and he'd felt every step. His clothes were damp with sweat, but he felt a sense of pride when he checked his watch. 9:09. He studied the old water treatment plant with his binoculars. A large two and a half story building stood in the center of a network of semi-buried tanks and ponds. The first story was ringed with floor to ceiling mirrored glass windows, the majority of which were still intact. A large parking lot to the north, still dotted with a handful of rusted-out utility vehicles, was flanked by a football field sized yard to the east separating the building from the first pond. To the west, a series of ponds and tanks stretched on for a good two hundred yards, the same was true on the south side.

From the building, Caleb would be able to see anything coming for over two hundred yards in every direction. A ten-foot fence topped with barbed wire surrounded the facility except for a large hole cut on the east side. Keeping low, Caleb crossed through the fence and down the path between two ponds. As he reached the yard, he stopped and scanned again. The yard was overgrown with waste high weeds and grass. The occasional buried acorn had produced several young oak trees.

Crossing the field, he made for the center of the building. Nearing the plant, his foot landed on a solid surface concealed under the matted vegetation.

"Right where Dr. Kim said it would be, ten meters from the center of the building," he said out loud.

Reaching down, he grasped the cold rusted handle. As he pulled, a two-foot steel door tore free of the weeds revealing a concrete tube and ladder.

"So far so good," he said, dropping his pack into the hole.

Climbing into the tube, he lowered the hatch, propping it open slightly with a stick. Reaching the bottom, he pulled out his flashlight and switched it on. He found himself in a four-foot tall tunnel system running north, south, and west. Pipes and wires ran overhead in each direction. Ten meters down the tunnel heading west was another door. He scooped up his pack and crawled to the door.

Pulling the lever handle, the door swung open into a small room with a vaulted ceiling. Tall blue tanks lined one wall connected to a series of pipes that disappeared into the block wall. A short flight of stairs led to an open first story, well illuminated by the mirrored windows. A handful of small birds flitted here and there, eyeing him curiously. A thick layer of dust and bird dung covered the receptionist's desk, brown plastic chairs were strewn around the room. Graffiti decorated the majority of the walls, most of it he'd rather not read. Dr. Kim had been right, it was perfect.

He checked his phone, 9:36. Pulling out his binoculars, he scanned the fence to the east, he could clearly make out the hole and the road beyond. He scanned the parking lot and the ponds to the west and south. Satisfied, he set up a chair in the center of the room and waited.

His knee bounced rhythmically as he kneaded the cell phone in his pocket. He dreaded the demons of the wait. The inquisitors of everything that was about to unfold. They fed on the silence, slowed every minute, mocked every detail.

His phone buzzed in his hand, freeing him for the moment. Checking the screen, he read her message.

"In position."

He checked the time. 9:43. *Almost there . . .*

He checked his gear again, checked his guns, pulled up the map app on his phone, rubbed his leg, and scanned his surroundings again.

His phone buzzed again, setting his hair on end. He flipped it over. Alarm 9:59.

"God help us . . ."

Chapter 23

Picking up the burner phone, Caleb tapped the contact labeled Xiuying. The phone rang twice on the other end before a video appeared. Xiuying sat huddled in the corner of a burned-out trolley car. Her mouth was gagged; trembling, she glanced about nervously.

Tapping the second contact, he whispered, "There's no turning back now."

In a matter of seconds, a second video popped up on the screen. General Yang sat center camera flanked on either side by staff members, including Col. Chen. The general wore a stern and confident face, but his fingers dancing at the edge of his desk betrayed his nerves.

"General Yang!" Caleb gushed, as though they were long lost friends. "I understand I have someone you want, as you can see, she is alive and well at the moment. Now, before I get ahead of myself let me make one thing clear, just to avoid confusion. If you do not follow my instructions, and only my instructions, to the letter, I will blow the bomb I've placed with the girl, and you will be responsible. The bomb is on a one-hour timer that only I can disable, so let's not waste time."

He waited as the interpreter translated and General Yang had a moment to process his message before continuing.

"If I sense any of your people near me or the transfer site, I will blow the bomb. If I hear a drone or a helicopter, I will blow the bomb. If I see anything that leads me to believe you are deviating from my instructions, I will blow the bomb. If you refuse my instructions, I will blow the bomb. If this communication is severed for any reason, I will blow the bomb. Do you understand? Oh, and you should probably know, the bomb is in her stomach."

He waited, watching Yang's staff eye each other nervously as his words were translated. General Yang nodded and Caleb continued.

"You will bring the boy, in the manner I tell you, to a location that I will disclose as we go along. You will deliver him to me in the manner that I tell you, and you will allow us to leave. If I find a tracker on the boy, I will blow the bomb. Only when I believe we haven't been followed and are safe will I disarm the bomb and allow you to collect Major Li's daughter. Do you understand?"

Caleb waited for the interpretation, chewing on the inside of his cheek in order to hide his own tell. General Yang's staff swayed and whispered nervously. Then Yang spoke.

"We cannot give you the boy while you still hold Li Xiuying," the interpreter said. "What is to prevent you from killing her after you have received the boy?"

"Nothing," Caleb replied coldly.

"Then we do not accept these terms," replied the interpreter.

"Fine, then keep the boy and watch her die," Caleb said, slamming his hand into his pocket."

"Wait!" cried the interpreter.

General Yang's face turned pale, sweat rolled down the crease between is wide eyes. His hands were folded together in front of him. He mumbled something in Mandarin that caused his staff to murmur, but he held up his hand to quiet them. At last, the interpreter answered.

"We agree to your terms."

"Great," said Caleb, withdrawing his hand from his pocket. "You will take the boy from his cell and place him in a silver four door car with a single English-speaking driver. The phone I've provided for you will stay with whoever is handling the boy at all times. I'm sure you're listening on other devices so don't bother acting surprised. If I see anyone tailing the car, I will blow the bomb. Remember, do not deviate from my instructions; I'll be watching you. You know who I am, and you know what I'm capable of."

He waited for the interpretation.

"What are you waiting for, General Yang, let's get the show on the road," Caleb chided.

The room sprang into action, the phone was on the move and Caleb drank in every detail. A hallway lined with photos, a wide room filled with monitors and soldiers in headsets, an elevator, another hallway, three cells, and Rice. Caleb watched as Rice was pulled to her feet and cuffed behind her back. She was marched back down the hall by three soldiers and the phone holder. At the end of the hall, they entered the elevator and rose one floor to the open room with the monitors. The outer walls of the building were solid block, narrow slit like windows provided natural light every ten feet or so. Another short hallway led to a double steel door guarded by two sentries. Outside the door stood two more sentries and then the motor pool.

Caleb caught a glimpse of Chen in the corner of the frame tossing his keys to a young soldier who opened the door to Chen's silver sedan. Rice was placed in the back and the young soldier climbed into the driver's seat.

"Very good," said Caleb. "Now, set the phone in the window so I can see what the driver sees."

The phone jostled side to side before coming to rest pointing out the windshield.

"Good. Now remember, no following, no helicopters, no drones, no soldiers, nothing. If I even feel something is off, you can kiss your princess goodbye."

He waited, allowing his words to sink in.

"Driver, can you hear me?"

"Yes."

"Good. Drive."

"Drive where?"

"Just drive, I will instruct you as you go. This is your last warning, never question my instructions."

The car pulled forward out of the motor pool.

"Head out the main gate," Caleb said.

The car turned and Caleb watched the gate come into view. Having a terrifying reputation had its benefits.

"Rice, are you ok?"

"He is gagged," the driver replied.

"You'd better fix that, driver!" Caleb barked.

The car swerved for a moment and then Rice spoke.

"Caleb?"

"Yeah, it's me. Hey, we're going to get you back today, but you have to do exactly what I say, ok?"

"Ok . . ."

"Are you hurt anywhere? Are you able to walk and run?" Caleb asked.

"I'm ok, they only beat me a little bit."

"Humph," the driver grunted.

"Driver," Caleb said, "You'd better pray that I don't find you in your bed one night and skin you alive. Now, take the next left."

The car turned and began moving towards the dead part of town. The driver hesitated as they reached the border.

"Keep driving," Caleb commanded.

The car rolled forward past the rubble filled yards, bombed out houses, and graffiti until Caleb could just make out the water treatment building. Three blocks to go, two, one.

"Driver, take the next left."

Pulling up the binoculars, Caleb watched the silver car make its way up the long fence.

"Driver, slow down . . . stop."

The car stopped. Caleb's pulse pounded. He scanned the sky; nothing. He scanned the road, the ponds, the yard; nothing. He listened for the telltale sounds of rotors; nothing.

So far so good.

"General Yang, I know you're listening. You've followed my instructions so far, let's not trip at the finish line. If you do what I say, you will have Major Li's daughter back before you know it, you have my word."

"Driver, exit the car with your hands in the air, and bring the phone with you."

Caleb watched the driver's door open, and the solder stand up in the street with his hands in the air.

"Driver, walk to the back door and open it. Good. Now, take the boy out of the car. Remove all restraints. Good."

The soldier looked around nervously, obviously aware Caleb had eyes on him.

"Driver, I need you to listen to me carefully. Are you listening?"

"Yes," the driver replied in an annoyed tone.

"Easy, you're not out of the woods yet. Let's have a little respect," Caleb said.

"Yes," the driver replied humbly.

"That's better. You are about to hand the phone over to the boy, so I need you to pay attention. You will dive away, all the way back to the base. You will not deviate from a direct course back to the base, if you do, I think you understand the consequences. Now, hand the phone to the boy, get in the car, and slowly drive away."

Caleb watched the driver follow through and drive away, leaving Rice standing alone outside the fence.

"Rice, can you hear me?"

"Yes," she said, her face filling the screen.

"We're on a bit of a time crunch, so I need to you to follow what I say without hesitation, ok?"

"Ok."

"Good, we're almost free. Do you see the hole in the fence?"

"Yes."

"Go through it. Good. Now, do you see that path between the two ponds? The one that lines up with the center of the building?"

"Yes."

"Great, I need you to follow that path all the way to that overgrown yard."

"Ok."

Caleb's knee began to bounce as she picked her way through the vegetation towards him. Everything was going according to plan.

"Caleb!" Rice shrieked.

"What?!"

"Is that Xiuying? What's happening to her?"

"Uhhh yes, it is, but it's going to be fine, she's going to be fine. You have to trust me; for her to be fine, you have to do what I tell you, ok?"

"What's happening?!" Rice asked.

"Rice, I promise I will explain it to you, but right now we don't have time, if you don't keep moving, she will die."

"Ok," she said, her voice quivering.

"Very good, keep coming. Just keep coming."

As she hit the yard, Caleb scanned the area again. Still nothing. No helicopters in the air, no vehicles driving by.

"Alright, pick a point in the center of the building and don't take your eyes off it until I tell you. Start walking forward, I'll tell you when to stop. Go."

Rice marched forward across the field never dropping her gaze. Caleb dropped the binoculars in his pack; she was close now.

"A little further, ok, stop. Look down. Do you see it?"

"Yes."

"Do you know what to do with it?"

"Yes."

"Good. Now, take your phone and throw it into the pond behind you, and do what's next."

Caleb watched her toss the phone into the water. Opening the hatch, she disappeared into the tube.

"General Yang, there is nineteen minutes left on the bomb's timer. You have my word that I will disarm it in seventeen minutes. If you interfere before that time, her blood will be on your hands. Remember that I still have a remote detonator that will still be able to detonate the bomb until we are out of range. Unless you interfere, you will be able to safely collect your princess in an hour and a half. This will be our last communication. Don't mess it up."

Smashing the phone on the floor, he shouldered his pack and made for the door to the tunnels. Inside, he found Rice nearly to the bottom rung of the ladder.

"Rice!" he shouted.

Crawling to her side, he threw his arms around her.

"Are you alright?"

"Yeah. I didn't think anyone would come for me," she said, clinging to him.

"Well, you were wrong. Here, change into these, Col. Chen said they'd probably hide a tracking device in your clothes."

Biting her lip, she reluctantly took the clothes.

"It's ok, Xiuying told me your secret, I won't look," he said, turning around.

"You said Col. Chen told you?"

"Yeah, he helped with the plan. We tried to rescue you a few days ago, but they figured it out, so we had to come up with a new one. The seizures, that was us. I'm sorry you had to go through that."

"Caleb, he's tricking you! They caught me the day we got separated. He interrogated me for a few days trying to locate you, but I told him I didn't know anything. Then one day he just stopped. I overheard him telling another officer that he'd found you and you were feeding him information on how to beat the Americans. He was worried because General Yang was demanding he find Xiuying and he thought arresting her would jeopardize his position with you, and possibly cost them the war. But General Yang was getting desperate, so he had to find a way," she said.

"He's just putting on an act, like I said, he helped me plan the whole thing."

"Caleb, I don't know anything about seizures, I've never had any. I've just been sitting in my cell doin' nothing for over a week. It's a trap, I'm telling you!"

Caleb's mind spun. He said he put in the medication himself—why would he lie to us?

"You're sure you heard him right?" Caleb asked, already shaking.

"Yeah, I was raised by one of them," she chuffed. "Finished."

She stepped in front of him, studying him in the beam of the flashlight.

"Caleb?"

"Oh no . . ." he gasped, dropping to his knees.

Like a thousand tiny pictures, he saw it all. The disappearing church members, the failed rescue plan, the strategy talks. Chen knew Xiuying would offer herself for Rice; knew he could manipulate everyone into believing it was the only way by threatening to execute Rice the day the rescue failed. He had been playing all of them, for years. He knew Caleb would know how to beat Aaron, and if it wasn't for Rice, he'd be heading back home right now to seal his fate. Chen knew Xiuying was a Christian, he'd no doubt plan to bribe her grandparents for his own gain with that information, and Xiuying would be headed home to reconditioning. Because of him, Chen was now able to rescue Xiuying, defeat the Americans, wipe out the Christians in Memphis, and make a fool of the Eagle. He'd be a Chinese hero, recorded in the history books, immortal.

"I've killed them all . . ." Caleb choked.

Burning pain filled his chest and his vision blurred. He clawed at the ground trying to maintain control, gasping for air. He could see all their faces, staring, silent. Xiuying's light gone from her eyes; her cries drowned out by Chen's echoing laughter. He saw himself, chained like an animal in an open square, mocked and jeered, the mighty Eagle now fallen.

"Caleb. Caleb!"

A sharp pain brought him back.

"Caleb!" Rice screamed, shaking her reddening hand.

"I've killed them all," he repeated.

"Caleb!" She shook him. "We are not dead!"

He stopped gasping as her words sunk in.

"What are we going to do?!" she asked.

Caleb shook his head, clearing his mind. *I'm not dead . . . Dr. Kim!*

Chapter 24

We need to move," Caleb said, shouldering the pack.
They crawled down the north tunnel for a hundred yards before coming to another tunnel headed west. Pulling out Dr. Kim's map, he looked at Rice.

"Time to change the plan."

The west tunnel was tight, the concrete floor tore at their knees and palms. Caleb's leg had long since gone numb, but he refused to stop.

"How—much—further," gasped Rice.

"Two hundred yards, maybe."

"Maybe?"

A dim light grew in the distance. Cool fresh air swirled past them.

"Almost there."

At last, he reached a steel grate, the lock had been cut by Kim's people long ago. The muddy water of the Mississippi flowed lazily just outside.

Caleb opened the grate, calling behind him, "Come on, Rice, you can make it!"

Pulling out his phone, he found his contacts and tapped Zebra.

Chen is the wolf. Send. Armageddon. Send. He waited for the confirmation, then, smashing the phone, he tossed it in the river.

"Now what?" Rice asked, as she reached him.

"Now, we jump."

The water, cool but not cold, was only knee deep. It felt good on their exhausted muscles but burned their ravaged knees. Walking again felt foreign as Caleb led them north keeping them under the shelter of the overhanging bank.

"We thought Chen was one of us," Caleb said.

"One of who?"

"Believe it or not, Xiuying saved me and brought me to her uncle who is a doctor. That's Dr. Kim. They took care of me and introduced me to Col. Chen, who we thought was the pastor of their underground church. There are actually lots of Chinese Christians here. But now . . . he's probably going to hurt them all looking for me."

"They took care of you? Didn't you kill her parents?"

"Yeah, I did . . . it confused me too. She . . . she forgave me and said her mom would have too. They loved me . . ."

"That's crazy!"

"That's why we have to find Dr. Kim."

"So he can help us?"

"No, so I can help them."

After twenty minutes of slogging, they reached the remnants of a bridge. Caleb led them up under the overhang and dropped the pack.

"Here," he said, handing her a water. "Catch your breath, I have to figure something out."

Pulling out his map of Memphis, he began measuring distances. Taking a sip of water, he looked over at Rice.

"I hope you still have some energy left. We've got about ten more miles to go."

Choking on her water, Rice answered, "Ten miles?! You've tortured me more in the last hour than the PLA have all week! It's a good thing this Kim guy is a doctor 'cause I'm going to need one."

"You're young, you'll live. Let's get going."

Leaving the river, Caleb led them along the side of the road watching for a storm drain. Finding one, he pulled away the grate and motioned for Rice to climb in.

"You're kidding. More tunnels?" she said, reluctantly climbing in.

Checking the surroundings, Caleb climbed in behind her and closed the grate. Hitting the floor, he was relieved to find the drain tall enough to walk in. Pulling out his map, he checked his distances again.

"This way," he said.

The Memphis traffic rumbling overhead echoed up and down the corridor. Here and there, piles of belongings and blankets dotted the walls, remnants of those who, for a time, had called the drain home. An earthy smell of organic decay and stagnant water hung heavy in the air. They walked for more than two hours before Rice found her tongue again.

"How do you know where we are?" she asked.

"I'm counting."

"Counting what?"

"My steps."

"How's that tell you where we are?"

Sighing, Caleb put down his pack and pulled out a pen. Writing a number on the wall, he turned to Rice.

"I used my compass to determine that these drains run north and south, and east and west. I used the bridge we were under to figure out where we were on the map before we started. I measured the distance from that bridge to where we're going, roughly ten miles or sixteen kilometers almost straight east. You following so far?"

Rice nodded.

"I know my stride is around one meter. So, every time I take a hundred steps I place a pebble from this pocket into this pocket, until all ten pebbles are in this pocket. When that happens, I know I've gone one kilometer. Still following?"

She nodded again.

"Every time we pass under a crossroad, I am able to cross check my count with the map so that I keep our current location as accurate as possible. It's pretty simple really."

"That's amazing. Where'd you learn something like that?" Rice asked.

"My brother taught me."

"So, how much further?"

"About five more miles," he sighed.

They continued on for another two hours until at last they reached the final crossroad. If Caleb was right, they were deep into the dead part of town under a road flanking a large cemetery. An odd place, he thought, to find a man you hoped wasn't dead.

"We'll wait here," he said, checking his watch. "It'll be dark in about four hours." Dropping the pack, he dug out a Chinese ration. "You hungry?"

"Starving," Rice replied.

"It isn't much, doesn't taste like much for that matter, but it should take the edge off," he said.

Sitting beside her, he opened the package and distributed the contents. "Looks like we'll be having a little rehydrated rice, and some sort of chicken with Mandarin oranges." Handing Rice the fork, he said, "Ladies first."

"What makes you think Chen hasn't already arrested your friend?" Rice asked, scooping out a forkful of rice.

"According to what you overheard, Chen is still hoping to fool me into giving him more information. The prisoner swap only took place a few hours ago, they had to find Xiuying based on a cell tower sector and a distance, which would have taken some time. Then it would have taken time for you and me to execute the original evasion strategy and eventually end up back at Chen's house. Truth is, we probably wouldn't even be there yet. Not only that, but we had talked about the possibility of needing a contingency plan during the final phase of the planning.

"I can't imagine Chen wanting to jeopardize his ruse with the church, nor add rounding up all the church members to his already lengthy list of important things to do. Meaning, he would only go after Dr. Kim and the church if he absolutely had to, and he would only absolutely have to if and when he realizes that he's lost me. My hope is that he won't realize he's lost me until tomorrow morning, when I don't turn up dead or at the house, giving Dr. Kim and the other church members the rest of today and tonight to escape."

"Wow."

"I've had a little time to think," Caleb said.

"And you're sure he'll be here?"

"Yeah . . . I'm sure," Caleb said, taking the fork.

"You said you'd tell me what happened to Xiuying."

Caleb swallowed his bite of rice, washing it down with water.

"She traded herself for you," he said.

"Is she going to die?"

"No. Something worse. Here, you finish it. I'm going to take a look around. I won't go far."

Getting up, Caleb limped slowly down the tunnel. How had he been so blind? How had he not put the pieces together? It was so obvious! They had counted on him, and he'd failed. God? I can't see a way, help me see a way.

Returning to Rice thirty minutes later, he found her asleep, lying against the pack. He took a seat next to her, leaning against the wall. He closed his eyes. Everything was tired, his body, his mind, his heart. Everything begged for rest, and he gave it, allowing Rice's rhythmic breathing to rock him to sleep.

A flash of light followed by a distant rumble woke him. Catching his breath, he relaxed his grip on his pistol. The tunnel was dark, no, it was black. Caleb's eyes fought to distinguish any detail of their surroundings when lightning flickered again. Caleb counted to thirteen before the thunder followed. Checking the glowing hands of his watch he was relieved to find it was only a few minutes past eight.

"Rice. Rice!" he whispered, shaking her gently.

"Wha—" she replied.

"We've got to go."

The lightning flashed again. He heard her sit bolt upright.

"It's ok, a storm must be coming in."

Groaning, Rice stretched and stood up. "It's night?" she asked, rubbing her backside.

"Yeah, we need to get out of this drain before the rain comes or we'll be swimming," Caleb replied.

Attempting to stand sent bolts of pain up and down his leg, leaving him nauseous and weak.

"I think I'm gonna need a little help," he panted.

Flicking on the flashlight, he held out his hand. Rice took it and, digging in both heels, she pulled. Caleb lifted with his arms and good leg and together they got him to his feet. The scabs on his knees burned as they tore free from his pants, and he knew Rice must have experienced the same thing. He really had put her through the gauntlet. Shouldering the pack, he limped painfully towards the ladder leading to the manhole cover.

As they hit the street, Caleb saw the storm moving in from the west. Towering, dense clouds flickered and rumbled menacingly.

"Where are we going?" asked Rice.

"In there," Caleb said, motioning to the cemetery.

"Why?" Rice moaned beside him.

"Come on," Caleb said, giving her a gentle push.

They picked their way through the overgrowth by the light of the storm. Everywhere, pale stones flashed and disappeared only to reappear a moment later. Rice clung to Caleb as the winds began to pick up, causing the trees to quake and shudder.

Arriving at a pond near the center of the cemetery, Caleb paused, scanning the area, listening, feeling. A chorus of frogs sang joyfully around the pond, the trees swayed, and shadows danced. If someone was there, he couldn't sense it.

"Let's go," he said.

Circling the pond, they came to an oddly out of place rocky structure with an ancient looking wooden door. A bronze placard near the door read, The Crystal Shrine Grotto.

"I'm not gonna lie, this is much creepier than I imagined," Caleb said.

"You think your friend is in there?!" Rice whispered.

"Yeah," Caleb said, taking out a pistol and the flashlight.

Standing in front of the door, he extended the pistol forward, and nodded to Rice.

"What? I'm not opening that thing!" she hissed.

"I'll go in first and make sure it's safe, you'll stay out here, ok?"

"I thought you said your friend was in there!"

"I do think he's in there."

"Then why do you need a gun?!"

"In case he's not in there!"

"You said you were sure!"

"I am sure! Mostly."

"Give me a gun!"

"Rice, I'm not giving you a gun, now open the door!"

"Open it yourself!"

"I can't, my hands are full!"

"Then give me the flashlight!" she said, with her hands on her hips.

"Rice, I'm begging you. If we stay out here much longer that storm is going to hit or a drone is going to fly over and blow us both to bits, ok? Please, open the door and stand out of the way."

Reluctantly, Rice grabbed the handle.

"3, 2, 1, pull!"

The door flew open, flinging Rice to the ground. Charging in, Caleb clicked on the flashlight.

"John Wayne!" came a delighted cry.

"Wait, who's John Wayne?" asked Rice, peering around Caleb.

A room full of sighs went up as recognition washed away fear. Dr. Kim threw his arms around Caleb, and even in the dim light Caleb could see his tears. The cavern hummed with murmuring conversation, a mixture of joy and anxiety. Within minutes, dozens of candles sent light glistening off thousands of crystals cast into the walls and ceiling. The effect was magical.

"I knew you'd be here," Caleb said, giving the doctor a final squeeze before separating their embrace. "I could tell this place was special to you."

"Yes, John Wayne," the doctor said.

"Xiuying?" Caleb asked.

"They have her," Dr. Kim said, looking at the floor. Then he spoke in Mandarin, but it was too fast for Caleb to keep up.

Looking around the room, Caleb saw Rice marveling at a column of crystals.

"Rice!" he called.

Leaving the crystals, she joined him. "This place is amazing!"

"Rice, this is Dr. Kim, Xiuying's uncle. His English is as bad as my Mandarin, could you help us?" Caleb asked.

"Sure," she said with a smile. She spoke in Mandarin and, bowing, held out her hand. Dr. Kim nodded and shook it.

"Ask him to repeat what he just said," Caleb said.

Rice did and repeated the translation back.

"He said he got your message and tried to get to Xiuying, but by the time he arrived, they had already taken her. He fears that Chen will use the knowledge that she is a Christian to bribe her grandparents for anything he wants," Rice interpreted.

"Tell him I thought the same thing."

"He says he can't believe that Chen would do this to them, he's been a part of their church for many, many years."

"I'm sorry I didn't catch it sooner," Caleb said.

"He says it's his fault, it was his job to protect the sheep. He fears there's no way out this time."

"That's why I wanted to find you. I think our only option left is a Plan Z. I've got an idea that's desperate, possibly impossible, but if we pulled it off, there's a slim chance we'd be able to save Xiuying and the Americans. The odds are high that people will get hurt, likely killed. Maybe all of us, and in the end, we may accomplish nothing. I've been looking at it from every angle today and I'm afraid it's the only option we have left apart from surrender," Caleb said somberly.

The doctor nodded his head thoughtfully as Rice interpreted.

"He says, at this point, to do nothing would end the same."

Chapter 25

By the time Caleb turned himself in, Dr. Kim had already confirmed his suspicions; Chen and a small detachment of soldiers were at the hospital interrogating staff members. As they led him through the main gate, the K-9 officer's shepherd nuzzled his cuffed hands. The gate guards took a step back as he limped through, eyeing him apprehensively. Apparently, his reputation proceeded him.

Inside the gate, a second soldier joined the K-9 officer marching him at rifle point to the HQ building. At the first door a sentry patted him down, it was his third time in the last fifteen minutes. He'd never surrendered since the train, never had a reason to, until now. Chen changed things, and if there was even a slim chance of saving Xiuying, it was worth it.

They marched him through the second door into the open room with the front desk. The two soldiers running the desk stood as he entered, checking him out from head to toe. Another soldier to the left of the desk pouring a cup of coffee, gawked at him until the scalding liquid escaped his cup.

To his right, he heard an elevator door ding down a short hall. In moments, a pudgy General Yang appeared followed by four of his staff. Grinning ear to ear, the general walked up to the K-9 officer and shook his hand, apparently praising him for Caleb's capture.

"I turned myself in, actually," Caleb said, leaning in.

General Yang chuckled, shaking his finger in Caleb's face. Then he spoke in Mandarin.

"The general says your plan to save the girl was impressive. He was most intrigued by your bluff about the bomb in her stomach, you showed great creativity, and proved to be the warrior he has heard so much about."

"I have to admit, I was amazed myself with how you ordered Chen to use me to defeat my own county. I mean, claiming to be an underground Christian for over ten years, that's beyond impressive," Caleb said.

The general's smile faded.

"Speaking of which, I don't see Chen here. Was he not invited?" asked Caleb.

"The general says Col. Chen is currently searching for you at the hospital where your friends work, he will be very surprised when he returns to find you already here," the interpreter said.

"You didn't tell him about my capture?" Caleb asked in shock.

The general chuckled.

"He says Col. Chen can get a little high on his horse, it is good for him to remember his place."

"I completely understand," said Caleb. "I mean, Chen used to gloat about how it was his strategy and wit that was going to win the war. What was it he called you . . . a puppet? Yeah, I think that was the word he used. Hardly appropriate for a general like yourself who has expertly maintained the largest operational base this side of the Mississippi, and no doubt has played a large role in strategizing the upcoming battle with the Americans."

The general had everyone take a step back except for the K-9 officer who held firmly to Caleb's arm. Slowly, he walked around Caleb, inspecting him from top to bottom as he went.

"You know . . ." Caleb said as General Yang returned in front of him. "I've got a secret way of dealing with folks that get too high on their horses."

As he heard the interpretation, General Yang's face lit up.

"He asks you to share it with him," the interpreter said.

"Do you really want them to know?" Caleb said, motioning towards the general's staff with his head. "I'll tell it to you in Mandarin," Caleb said in his best Mandarin, gesturing for the general to come close.

The general's smile grew as he leaned in. In a flash, Caleb broke the half-cut link on his handcuffs and drew the pistol from Fan Ming's holster, holding it to a squirming General Yang's head. Fan Ming swung up his rifle, ordering everyone face down on the floor.

Panicking, General Yang squawked orders and everyone in the room hit the floor. Fan Ming got on his radio and in minutes, the two front door sentries entered and began disarming their fellow soldiers, zip tying their hands behind their backs.

"I'm the Eagle!" Caleb said. "And unless you do exactly what I say, I will butcher you all. Starting with . . . you," he said, pointing to the trembling soldier with the coffee burns.

Fan Ming translated and the soldier with the burns whimpered where he lay.

Caleb checked his watch.

"Tell him to order the gate guards to allow the ambulances through," Caleb said to Fan Ming.

Fan Ming barked orders to General Yang, handing him his radio. The general shook violently as he gave the command.

Caleb watched through the slit window as four ambulances came rolling into the motor pool with lights and sirens blaring. They pulled up to the front door and unloaded, seven persons to a vehicle. Caleb nodded as Dr. Kim entered the room, followed by a small army of young Chinese in scrubs and street clothes.

"He says they all have military experience," Fan Ming said.

Zip-tying General Yang to a chair, Caleb left him with Fan Ming. Together, with help from the door sentries, he armed the hospital staff with the weapons they had taken from their prisoners. He took a moment to connect with Monkey and lay out the plan for clearing the rest of the HQ.

Breaking into two teams, they cleared the building without incident, bringing their total number of prisoners to seventeen. Caleb ordered them out of their uniforms, having them trade with the church members. Then he had General Yang call in the main gate guards, sending out church members as their replacements. When the gate guards arrived, they were disarmed and had their uniforms traded for scrubs.

Using his phone, Dr. Kim showed his ambulance drivers two more of his safe house locations. After confirming their assignments, they drove out the main gate.

One by one, Caleb had General Yang call in the guard towers, the patrol boat crews, the dock patrol crews, the dock tower guards, the heavy equipment operators, clinic staff, airfield, artillery, and the barracks. Each time replacing them with members of Kim's church. Chen had been telling the truth, the base had been running on a skeleton crew; even so, Caleb was only able to man it with half the strength.

We need more time . . .

Caleb had Fan Ming order General Yang to tell Chen to come back with the Eagle or not to come back at all. Maybe it would work, but he got the feeling Chen followed his own orders.

Within three hours, the entire base was under Caleb's control. Dr. Kim was still busily tracking down all his people; they were up to sixty-five. Caleb had raised the pneumatic barriers at the main gate, and Fan Ming was on the radio turning back cargo ships coming into the docks, while the guards at the gates turned back vehicles, declaring the base on lockdown under General Yang's orders.

Dr. Kim rolled up to the gate and was allowed access through the barriers. He'd found six more church members, including Rice. Dr. Kim handed him his cane with a queer smile.

"You went back to Chen's house?!" Caleb asked.

"He said he still had a key," Rice said. "He also said I could keep these," she said, trying to put on Caleb's gun belt.

"I doubt it," he said, taking the belt. "So . . . did you burn it down?" Caleb asked the doctor.

Chuckling, Dr. Kim shook his head.

"He says the house didn't do anything wrong," Rice said.

"I've never really thought about that . . ." Caleb admitted. "I've just always been a big fan of house fires."

"He wants to know how things are going?" Rice said.

"The base is ours, for the moment. We've got people on the radios turning back everything headed this way from the river, air, and land. We've cut the artery feeding the PLA waiting to ambush the Americans. I haven't had time to ask about Xiuying yet, but she's not in the holding cells," Caleb said.

The doctor nodded his head.

"Without this port, the Chinese army won't be able to survive for long. If we can hold it, and we have to hold it, eventually they will have to return and take it back. It's the only way to save my family," Caleb said. "To be honest, Doc, I didn't expect us to get this far, but if we're going to survive, we're going to need a lot more people."

"Have faith, John Wayne," Kim said, patting him on the arm. *Have faith . . .*

"Fan to John Wayne, come in. Over," Caleb's radio barked.

"This is . . . John Wayne." Caleb rolled his eyes.

"Chen is on his way. Over."

"Understood; hold him at the gate, I'll be right out," Caleb said, grabbing body armor and a helmet.

Arriving at the gate, Caleb could see the heavy guns in the towers trained on Chen's two vehicle convoy, stopped just outside the barrier. The sentries on the ground had their weapons trained on the lead vehicle. Caleb walked up to the gate between the sentries. Chen sat facing him in the passenger seat of his silver sedan with a troop truck behind him. His expression was menacing but given his poor taste in vehicles, he was at Caleb's mercy.

Waving him over, Caleb waited as he exited the car with his hands in the air and walked between the barriers. His driver wrung the steering wheel behind him, his eyes wide with fear.

"Impressive, you truly are a hero." Chen clapped slowly.

"Surprise," Caleb answered.

"How did you know?" Chen asked.

"The kid," Caleb answered.

Chen nodded his head. "Things are never what they appear. A pastor is not a pastor, and a kid is not just a kid," Chen said.

"How could you do it?" Caleb asked.

"For power," Chen said. "Do you really think I wanted to live my life cowering like these Christian sheep? In my world, power, not God, gives freedom."

"You should look around, this isn't your world," Caleb answered.

"We will see," Chen said greedily.

"Where's Xiuying?" asked Caleb.

Laughing, the colonel replied, "She is on her way back to her family, though I am not sure how they will feel about her being a Christian."

Caleb flushed. "What do you mean, on her way?"

"She left in a plane an hour after we found her. Just enough time to clean the princess up, you'd made such an awful mess of her. Oh, I allowed her to keep your precious jacket—she wouldn't let go of it, plus, it will help me prove my case," he sneered.

Caleb pulled a pistol, holding it to Chen's head. The colonel looked coldly into his eyes, his sneer never fading.

"Tut, tut, tut," he said. "You are a Christian now, Caleb, you have to set a good example for the sheep." Turning, Chen walked back to his car.

Caleb followed him through his sights until Chen stopped at his door.

"I am going to go now, and when I come back, it will be with the shearers," he said, getting into his car.

The troop truck backed out followed by Chen, and turning, they drove towards the highway leading out of Memphis.

Caleb stood shaking with rage. He'd missed her. She was on her way home to a life of imprisonment; if the public got wind, possibly banishment, or worse. One hour, they'd only had one hour. Caleb looked to the sky. Holstering his pistol, he returned to the HQ. The clock was ticking.

"Why'd you let him leave?" asked Rice.

"We need someone to call back the wolves," Caleb replied.

Chapter 26

Alright everyone," Caleb said, standing in front of a group of around thirty Chinese Christians, now wearing full military gear. "First, Dr. Kim and I would like to thank all of you who participated today. I don't think Chen, General Yang, or even the State government ever imagined they could lose their most strategic base to a handful of common folks. That's exactly what happened; you won today, you came out of hiding today, you brought down the giant today. And we here are all witnesses along with God above, whether history ever records this victory or not, so long as there is breath in our lungs, we will remember."

Fan Ming interpreted, adding lifted arms in his own passionate flair.

"If you look here," Caleb said, pointing to four-foot wide TV screen with a map of southwest Tennessee on it, "the red lines are the various People's Liberation Army units set up northeast and southeast of the American and Canadian advance, indicated by the blue dashes. Not only do the PLA have almost double the manpower, but they're also set up in a strategic trap that would decimate the American flanks in minutes, and the army in hours, leading to the end of the war for the eastern United States."

He waited for Fan Ming to interpret.

"If the Americans lose, there will be nowhere left for us to run. Chen and the State will never stop hunting us. But, if the

Americans win, that's our chance to all be free. I don't know how
the new American government would treat you, but I do know
there are good people in their ranks that believe in the freedom of
everyone who wants to be part of it, myself included. And I give
you my word that, if we survive, I will continue to fight for each
and every one of you no matter the cost."

Several heads nodded amidst the murmuring.

"Before you commit, I feel I need to explain the situation, our
position, and the odds so you can decide for yourselves. We now
control the main supply artery of the PLA. Without this port, their
army will only last a matter of days. That fact is going to require
them to retake it, and they will need to take it intact. They will no
doubt underestimate us and send as small a force as possible:
helicopters, light vehicles, and troops. We must defeat them. They
will send more, and we will hold, and still more, until they're given
no choice but to redirect their army back here in force, leaving us
to face the full wrath of the PLA for as long as we can endure.
When that happens, the trap will crumble, and the Americans will
be able to break free.

"As you can see on the map, the situation is desperate; without
our help they'll be destroyed. The odds of our success are slim,
and I can't promise any of us will survive. That's the truth of it.
So, the choice is yours to make, and there will be no judgment if
you choose to go. What you all did here today was impossible, and
I will forever be grateful to you."

A heavy silence filled the room as Fan Ming finished
interpreting. After a few moments, Dr. Kim walked to the front
of the room and spoke in Mandarin. When he fell silent, a wave
of Christian soldiers came forward to stand beside him, not one
remaining behind.

"What did he say?" Caleb asked Fan.

"He said, 'Alexander the Great once said, "I am not afraid of
an army of lions led by a lamb, but I am afraid of an army of lambs

led by a lion." If God has seen fit to send us a lion, then by His grace, we will be his lambs.""

Caleb felt his throat tighten, his eyes blurred, and for a moment he was overwhelmed by the courage shown by such a gentle people. All of them ready to lay down their lives for people they'd never known.

With the help of Dr. Kim and Fan Ming, Caleb broke their little army into teams. Everyone with military experience was assigned to their area of expertise; the civilians were assigned the same. A team of construction workers and heavy equipment operators went to work fortifying all critical structures, especially the HQ and the clinic. Bunkers were built flanking the river. A team of nurses and doctors turned the clinic into a hospital. Another team filled the airfield with debris.

Armorers took turns training everyone in all weapons systems including shoulder fire rockets. A bulldozer filled the gates with mounds of earth. Cooks took over meals and supply inventory. Communications were set up both for the base and to monitor PLA traffic. Those who knew how to operate the artillery were paired with civilians to train, and the antiair systems were brought online. Anyone not actively assigned a task, filled sandbags.

One thing they had going for them was that the base, being a port, had well supplied warehouse bunkers stocked with ammunition, body armor, night vision goggles, communications equipment, fuel, medical supplies, rations, bedding, toiletries, and more; enough to keep an army going for a month. What they didn't have was an army, an air force, or a navy.

It was nearly dusk when the first Chinese helicopter hovered towards the base at high altitude. A scout. Caleb decided not to show his hand, commanding the antiair team to stand down. No reason to reveal these lambs had teeth just yet. It stuck around watching them work for twenty minutes before flying back south.

Working by the freight yard lights, the teams continued through the night in shifts, building fighting positions, distributing munitions, medical supplies, rations, and gearing up their soldiers. By dawn, the base had three rings of defense. The outer walls with their guard towers, an inner ring of newly built-up bunkers looking out over the first ring, and an innermost ring of bunkers encircling the HQ and clinic.

Dr. Kim had led the last team of the night and had somehow managed to go AWOL. Worse yet, he wasn't answering his phone or radio.

Caleb's radio cackled as he paced uneasily on the HQ rooftop.

"John Wayne, this is Fan, do you read me? Over."

"Go ahead, Fan."

"Caleb, the air traffic control tower reports a large group of civilians headed this way coming from the east."

"On my way to the wall, keep me posted. Caleb out.

"All units, this is John Wayne. Battle stations, I repeat, battle stations; large force moving in from the east!"

Caleb raced out to the wall, climbing up the guard tower.

"What have you got?" he asked the soldier manning the tower.

The soldier put down his binoculars and stared blankly at Caleb.

"Are you kidding me?!" Grabbing his radio, he called out, "Rice, Rice this is Caleb, do to read me?!"

"Yeah, what?"

"I need you at northeast guard tower now!" Caleb replied.

"Which way is east?"

"Argh, the tower to the left of the gate!"

"Ok, ok, stop yelling!"

In thirty seconds, Rice was running up the stairs.

"What?" she asked.

"Ask this guy what he's seen out there?" Caleb said.

"He says he hasn't seen anything yet," Rice answered. "Are we fixin' to be in a fight?"

"I don't know, the tower reported a large force heading towards the base from the east. Wait there," Caleb said, snatching the soldier's binoculars. That's odd, they're not in uniform, but there certainly are a lot of 'em."

Handing the binoculars back, he turned to Rice.

"Ask him to look and see if he knows who they are or what they are," Caleb said.

The soldier took the binoculars and studied the incoming horde. Suddenly, he turned to Caleb and spoke.

"He says they're the untouchables, and they have Dr. Kim."

"What?!"

Caleb snatched the binoculars away again, searching.

"That is Kim, I can't tell what they're doing with him. He doesn't seem injured," Caleb said, grabbing his radio. "All stations, this is Caleb, hold your fire until I say otherwise. Kim is with them." Then he held the radio down by Rice.

"What?"

"I need you to repeat it for the ones who don't speak English."

When she finished, Caleb said, "From now on you stick with me. Wherever I go, you go, understand? This is never going to work if I can only communicate with twenty-five percent of the team."

"John Wayne, this is Monkey, come in. Over."

"Go ahead, Monkey."

"I do not think they've taken Kim; I think he's leading them."

Caleb grabbed the binoculars again.

"Caleb, this is Fan, the tower is seeing the same thing. They also say there are over a hundred of them."

"I understand, Fan. Over. All stations, looks like we're going to have guests; let them pass. Keep on the lookout, trouble is out there somewhere," Caleb said. "Rice, repeat it and follow me."

Caleb left the guard shack and trotted over to the mound of earth filling the gate. Climbing to the top, he watched Kim and his mob coming down the block. As Kim crested the mound, he stopped, waving his friends through the gate.

"Is your radio not working?" Caleb chided.

"I wanted you to see it," Kim said.

"He says he went to tell them that he wouldn't be able to help them anymore, and when he explained why, they all volunteered to help," Rice said.

Tears rolled down the doctor's cheeks.

"They told him he's the only one who's ever fought for them, and if he's fighting with you, then that's good enough."

Caleb watched in awe as an army of rag tag drug addicts, prostitutes, rebels, and castoffs, men women and children climbed confidently up and over the berm and into the base.

"We needed an army and God has found us one, John Wayne," Kim said proudly.

"It doesn't seem possible," Caleb said.

"Believe," Kim replied, patting him on the arm.

Over the next two hours, the new recruits were showered, clothed, and fed. Those needing medical care were sent to the hospital, women with small children were set up in a bunker tuned barracks, men and women able to fight were processed through the armory to get equipped and assigned to the various teams based on experience and need.

Training began immediately. The makeshift shooting range was popping constantly, a couple of Kim's new recruits taught improvised fighting techniques in the yard. After what had happened with the untouchables, ambassadors were sent into Memphis to recruit from the more fortunate colonists with limited success. By noon their numbers had swelled to two hundred and sixty-three fighting persons, and half as many dependent noncombatants.

At 12:45 p.m., Caleb's radio squawked.

"John Wayne, this is Fan, do you read me? Over."

"Go ahead, Fan."

"Caleb, the tower reports three incoming choppers, they'll be here in fifteen minutes."

"Roger that."

"All units, all units, we have incoming helicopters, I repeat, we have incoming; everyone to your stations. Antiair Team stand by for my order. Over!"

Caleb looked at Rice, who repeated the command proudly, and the base flew into action. Everyone ran to their posts, children and mothers fled to the barracks, and Caleb and Rice moved to the HQ.

By the time the helicopters hit the eastern edge of the city, everyone was in position. Caleb wrung his cane to keep his stomach from churning. They flew low over Memphis, their rotors thundering through the atmosphere. One transport flanked by two attack helicopters.

"All units, this is Caleb, get small in your positions; we're going to let the fighters pass. Antiair Team, once they've passed, light up that transport. Over."

Without hesitation, Rice repeated the command.

Caleb had seen it so many times. Tensing, he watched as the attack helicopters broke off from the transport, strafing the base fighting positions with Gatlin guns and rockets. He'd missed this. The struggle. The great contest of wits and metal.

"Hold."

Rockets slammed into the HQ sandbags with little affect.

"Hold."

The choppers continued their attack through to the river before banking. The transport was swinging low towards the street in front of the main gate.

"Engage!"

An antiair missile sailed across the base, punching through the transport's cockpit, sending its occupants spraying out the other side. The helicopter spun once before slamming to the ground, its rotors shredding the powerlines as it ground to a halt.

"Nice hit, nice hit! Stay sharp, everyone, those fighters are coming around. Antiair, fire at will, all gun crews give fire support. Let 'em have it!" Caleb ordered.

The base erupted in gunfire as the attack helicopters came in for a second pass. The lead pilot, unable to bank in time, went down hard in the firing range, the second banked in time while taking rounds from the heavy guns. With smoke trailing from its rotor the second pilot was forced to limp home alone.

"That's the way!" Caleb shouted, slamming his cane on the floor, as a cheer rose up all across the base.

"We won!" Rice said.

"We won," Caleb replied, ruffling her hair. "Tell everyone I need a status report, and . . . good job."

"Yes, sir!" she said, giving him a salute.

Chapter 27

Victories, no matter how small, should be celebrated, and this one was no different. Their tiny army had downed two helicopters, recovered three prisoners, and only sustained minor injuries to the base and personnel. What's more, they had upped the ante. The PLA now knew the rebels would require a greater level of persuasion if they wanted the port back.

Dr. Kim lead everyone in a prayer of thanksgiving for their success and God's protection, praying also for their enemies; for the salvation of their souls, and that if, by some means, their goals could be met without bloodshed, that the Lord would make it so.

Training continued in shifts around the clock. No one went anywhere without their weapon, armor, and radio. When they weren't training, they took turns at the fighting positions or sleeping; most of them choosing to sleep where they fought. Meals were delivered to each position three times a day by the dedicated mess team.

Communications had been cleaned up by adding an English-speaking radio operator to each team. Rice was Caleb's shadow, allowing him to watch over her, and ensuring he was never without a translator.

Their relationship was changing. He slowed down to teach her things, to listen to her, to take notice and praise her efforts, and worked hard to keep her smiling. He made sure she had good hygiene and took care of herself, went to bed on time, and woke up each day knowing she'd never be alone again; he would always be there watching over her.

Caleb got the construction crew together with the antiair unit to create a plan to play hide the pea with the antiair battery. If they were to succeed, they had to force the PLA to fight them on the ground. They designed and built several bunkers from one end of the base to the other, able to conceal the entire battery, enabling them to move the battery to a host of different locations between battles, only needing to expose it briefly to take a shot.

They were only a day into the supply disruption and already the intelligence team was picking up chatter of impending shortages. This was good news. Good news that meant bad things were on their way. But that wasn't the most interesting news. The intelligence team, working their magic, had also picked up some traffic from across the river. Apparently, the Russians had observed the helicopters attacking Memphis and were beginning to wonder how the battle was faring with their eastern neighbors.

"Do you think they would go to the Russians for help?" Fan Ming asked.

"I don't think they could live with the humiliation," Caleb replied. "Besides, we're only sheep."

Fan Ming grinned.

"Keep listening anyway, they've got good reason to take interest. According to the Canadians I fought with, the western Americans aren't just laying down either," Caleb said.

"John Wayne, this Monkey, do you read me? Over."

"Go ahead."

"The artillery spotters at the edge of town say we have about a dozen armored personnel vehicles coming this way from the east. They're about five kilometers outside the city."

"Roger that, Monkey, good work."

"Artillery, this John Wayne, you are clear to engage the APCs headed this way. How copy, over?"

"John Wayne, this is Artillery, good copy. Engaging APCs east of town. Over."

The three cannon crews opened up with a deafening volley.

"All teams, all teams, this is John Wayne, man your fighting positions, I repeat, man your fighting positions. We have enemy armored vehicles approaching from the east. Prepare to engage. Over!"

The radio squawked adjustments from the team of spotters and a second volley erupted.

Wringing his cane, Caleb watched out the HQ upper windows. He'd always been on the field, in the fray, his adrenaline had always had an outlet, a purpose. This was different, the added responsibility of the lives depending on him increased the surge. He watched the base like a hawk, his eyes never still, his ears filtering the chatter, painting a picture of the battlefield in his mind, the grand chess board.

"Fan, get some people down there clearing the first block of houses to the east. Go door to door if you have to. If we turn the people of Memphis against us, they'll aid the enemy, and we can't afford that. We have to minimize damage to the town as best we can! GO!"

Fan Ming called over the radio and in less than two minutes, a team raced over the berm and into the street.

"Artillery, this is Caleb, do you read me? Over."

"Go ahead, Caleb."

"Artillery, if those APCs reach the city, disengage. I repeat, if they reach the city, disengage. We cannot harm civilians. Over."

"John Wayne, this is Artillery, roger that. Artillery out."

Another volley shook the base.

"Caleb, this is Monkey, we have a hit. One APC has been destroyed. The other APCs are breaking formation and fanning out. Four kilometers from the city."

"Monkey, this is Caleb, good work. Stay after them."

"John Wayne, this is Tower, we picked up a drone coming in from the southeast."

"Antiair, this is John Wayne, we've got a drone incoming from the southeast. You guys have to pick that thing off or the artillery will pay the price. Over."

"John Wayne, this is Antiair, we are on it! Over."

Grabbing the binoculars, Caleb watched the antiair unit roll out from one of the bunkers.

The artillery team busily laid down fire as fast as they could load the guns.

"John Wayne, this is Dock Tower! We have two enemy PT boats approaching from the south! Over."

Spinning, Caleb looked towards the river. He could see the boats closing fast.

"All dock teams, all dock teams! Prepare for contact, you are free to engage on sight! Mortar Team, Mortar Team! Turn your tubes to the river and take your orders from Dock Tower now! And for the love of us all, don't hit anything Russian! Over!"

"John Wayne, this is Mortar Team, understood. Over!"

"John Wayne, this is Antiair, we have a lock, firing missiles now! Over!"

Two missiles streaked over the base as the mortar team began shelling the river.

The HQ rumbled under the concussive force of their indirect fire. Lights flashed as mortar tubes and artillery guns poured out their ordinance. Caleb closed his eyes, allowing the drums of war to feed up his body; he was born for this.

"Caleb, this is Monkey, the artillery has taken out two more APCs; the remaining APCs are three kilometers from the city. Over."

"John Wayne, this is Tower, the drone was destroyed, redeploying the antiair battery now. Over!"

Pacing from window to window, Caleb watched the battle unfold.

"Artillery, this is John Wayne, great work, keep after them! Tower, keep your eyes peeled, there could be more; great job on that drone!"

"John Wayne, this is Dock Tower, we are holding the river. Boat Team One is reporting three casualties: two wounded in need of aid and one KIA. Over!"

Caleb froze. He knew they were coming; the losses, he'd been around them for years, but they'd never felt close. In fact, since Sam, he'd not let himself feel a single one. The pain shocked him, cut into him. He'd lost someone, one of his lambs.

"Uhhh Med Team, Med Team, this is John Wayne. Over."

"Go ahead."

"Med Team, I need you to get to Boat Team One and get those casualties out of there now! And be safe about it! Over.

"All teams, all teams, this is John Wayne. We can hold them! Keep up the fight! Over!"

The drumming of artillery and mortars continued as he unsteadily leaned back against the table.

"Are you alright?" asked Rice.

He shook his head. "It's all different this time. I fought for hate for so long, hiding from the pain, I'd forgotten what it feels like to lose someone you care about. It hurts," he said.

"Then, please . . . don't let anything happen to you," Rice said, biting her lip.

"Caleb, this is Monkey, the six remaining APCs are one kilometer from the city. Over."

"Monkey, this is Caleb, don't stop hitting them until they reach the city."

"John Wayne, this is Dock Tower. Med Team arrived and secured the casualties, they are enroute to the hospital now. The enemy PT boats sustained heavy damage and are retreating. Over."

"All dock teams, this is John Wayne, good work! Mortar Team, cease fire and reset your tubes to the east.

"All teams, this is John Wayne. The APCs are still on their way, if they don't turn back, we need to be ready. If you don't have shoulder fire rockets at your fighting positions, contact the armory now. Mortar and all dock teams, make sure you resupply ammo. Over."

Caleb," Fan Ming said. "It's Dr. Kim, he says we lost one of the casualties, but he was able to stabilize the other."

"Tell him I'm sorry, and to keep up the good work," Caleb replied.

"That's two," Rice said.

"There will be a lot more before we're done."

"Caleb, this is Monkey. The APCs have turned and are retreating to the east. Over."

"Monkey, have those scouts watch them until they're out of sight. Give them my congratulations. Over. Artillery, this is John Wayne, cease fire, I repeat cease fire. The enemy is retreating, well done. Over."

"John Wayne, this is Artillery, ceasing fire. Over."

"Thank God . . ." Caleb said, running his hand through his hair. "Fan, you stay on top of things here, I'm going to the hospital. Let's go, Rice."

Pulling up to the hospital, Caleb turned to Rice. "If you want to stay out here, that's ok."

"I've seen lots of dead and hurt people already, it isn't going to hurt me to see these. Besides, you need me," she said, jumping out of the truck.

When they entered the hospital, they were directed down a hallway to a large room divided into smaller compartments by curtains. A nurse led them to a compartment and lifted the curtain. Inside, Dr. Kim was busily performing surgery on the third casualty. He nodded at Caleb before continuing his work.

"He says the soldier took three rounds: one to his calf, one grazed his hip, and the other caught him in the lungs. He was able to stabilize the patient in time, he'll survive," Rice said.

"Tell him good work. And I want him to contact me the moment he's conscious."

The doctor nodded.

"Where are the others?"

Dr. Kim motioned to the curtain beside them.

"Thanks," said Caleb.

Entering the second compartment, he saw two gurneys with bodies draped in sheets. Pulling back the sheet on the first, he recognized the young man from the church service. He'd been one of the first to follow Kim the night they took the base. Replacing the sheet over his face, he lifted the second sheet. It was a woman, one of the untouchables, she'd been eager to learn, a good shot, a former prostitute who'd fought for a better life. He pulled the sheet back over her face.

He closed his eyes. Where was Xiuying to tell him it wasn't the end, to assure him there was a bigger plan, that God was for them and not against them. Where was she to tell him it was worth it, that the cost was right, that he was right.

"It's hurting again, isn't it?" Rice asked.

"Yeah . . ." he said. "Come on."

Returning to the HQ, Fan Ming gave them a situation report. One of the docked PT boats was badly damaged but the construction crew and engineers were already working on it. All the rest of the damage was only cosmetic. Ammunition had been replenished and weapons maintenance was underway.

"How's everyone's morale?" Caleb asked.

"Spirits are high. Do not worry about that. We have always lived with the senseless loss of our people, but today, they died with purpose," Fan said. "When you believe what we believe, you know it's not the end."

Caleb shook his head.

"What?" Fan Ming asked.

"That's exactly what Xiuying would've said."

That evening, Dr. Kim led a service, and they buried their dead. It was the most hope filled funeral Caleb had ever attended. They honored the dead as living. This is not the end . . . if he'd heard it once, he'd heard it a hundred times. They believed it, lived it, died for it. It was their honor to suffer for doing right, they'd lived it all their lives.

The service was wrapping up when the air traffic control tower came over Caleb's radio.

"John Wayne, this is Tower, do you read me? Over."

"Go ahead, Tower."

"We've got a large aerial force heading our way from the southeast. Over."

"How large? Over."

"At least twenty; possibly mixed attack and transport. Over."

"ETA?"

"Thirty minutes. Over."

Chapter 28

All teams, all teams, this is Caleb—er, John Wayne—you know who I am! Man your fighting positions!" Caleb yelled, running for the HQ.

Racing into the elevator, he held the door for Rice.

"Let's go, Rice!"

Reaching the third floor, Caleb trotted over to the windows.

"What have we got, Fan?" he asked.

"All teams are in position and in night vision."

"Good."

"What do you think?" Fan asked.

"Twenty is too many for our lone antiair battery. If we bring it out of hiding, it'll be exposed, and they'll destroy it. I don't think they'd try and deploy inside the base; they've learned the hard way we can bring the fight. They'll probably air assault into the city and hit us that way. We need to keep an eye on the river in case they try and hit us from both sides again, though they have as much to risk as we do if they accidently hit the Russians," Caleb replied.

"So . . ."

"So, I think we'll have to leave the antiair battery out of this one. Hit them the best we can with the heavy guns; there's more than enough there to take down a bird. The choppers can't stay for the fight, they'll have to return and refuel. Then we prepare for their ground assault. I want those artillery guns buried in sandbags; they won't do us any good this time around."

Fan relayed Caleb's orders. The lights of the base were turned off, the artillery sandbagged, everyone was on high alert. The tower called out the new ETA every five minutes: an ominous countdown to the unknown. Everyone listened, their ears grasping at silence as time seemed to have ground to a halt.

"Cale—" Rice began to say, but he held up his hand to stop her.

There it was, the distant thunder of rotor blades, the harbinger of the reaper.

"All teams, this is Caleb. As Fan put out, we can't afford to lose the antiair battery so we're going to have to do the best we can with the heavy guns. We've fortified this base well, and they don't want to damage it any more than they have to. That means most, if not all, of their fire is going to target the fighting positions and the HQ.

"I'm not going to lie to you, this is going to hurt, but the attack helicopters are only a screen to protect the troop deployment. Once that's done, they'll have to return and refuel. We must weather that storm and come out ready to fight troops on the ground. That being said, don't do anything foolish, take your shots at the birds and then find some cover. If God be for us . . . Caleb out."

"Three miles out," Fan relayed.

"You hear anything about the Americans yet?" Caleb asked, watching out the windows.

"Nothing. Maybe we are too late?" Fan asked.

"I don't think so," Caleb said. "If we were, the whole PLA would be knocking at our door already."

"All teams, this is Caleb, you are clear to engage."

Erupting with fire, the base fighting positions lashed out at their attackers. Thousands of tracer rounds lit up the night as the two deck-mounted Gatlin guns aboard the PT boats joined the fray. A wall of rockets poured out of the night sky as the helos screamed over the base. Explosions shook the guard towers and elevated bunkers. The radio room filled with situation reports as the helos prepared to make a second run.

"All teams, this is Caleb, calm down! Save it till we're out of this fight, they're coming around again, keep on them!"

"Scout Team, Scout Team, this is Caleb. Do you have eyes on those transports? Over."

"John Wayne, this is Scout Team, they are deploying troops on the field of the sports stadium to your southeast. Over"

"Caleb, the attack helos are pulling out," Fan reported.

"Antiair, Antiair, this is Caleb. Hit those helos now! Over."

Hobbling from window to window, Caleb directed his army. Twenty-five separate teams working independently yet completely dependent on the faithfulness and success of every other team; all of them depending on the Eagle.

"Artillery, Artillery, this is Caleb. Can you dig those guns out and hit that stadium without tearing the city apart? Over."

"John Wayne, this is Artillery, I can put a round through Chen's front door if you need me to! Over."

"Roger that, Artillery, turn that stadium into a crater. Over."

"John Wayne, this is Tower, we took a direct hit. Most of the equipment was protected by the sandbags, but we sustained one KIA. Over."

"Tower, this is Caleb. I understand. You're our eyes, stay in the fight. I'll find you a replacement. Over."

"Fan, I need you to get me a full sitrep. You need to filter them for me, I have to stay in the fight, only what you can't manage report to me. Get the medical crews moving, have the armorers resupply ammo; we're only halfway through this one. Understand?"

Fan nodded. "All teams, all teams, this is Fan Ming . . ."

Caleb jumped as the artillery guns opened up on the stadium. Looking for Rice, he found her climbing out from under the table.

"They startled me too," he said, giving her a sympathetic smile. "Are you ok?"

She nodded to him. "I'm scared," she confessed.

Kneeling, Caleb put his hands on her shoulders. "So long as I'm here, no one is going to harm you. You'll see, when the sun rises tomorrow, we'll still be here."

"Caleb, the scout team is reporting the artillery has driven the infantry from the stadium. Casualties unknown, strength estimated around a hundred, approaching the base from the southeast," Fan said. "Also, we have four KIA, and another seven wounded. One of the artillery guns is damaged. I have deployed the engineers to the tower to see what they can do to get it all back online. Reinforcements are enroute to the teams who have casualties, medical teams are on their way, ammo is being resupplied."

"I don't know what I'd do without you, Fan," Caleb said, patting him on the back and grabbing his radio. "All teams, all teams, this is Caleb. You did well. We have incoming infantry only a few blocks out approaching from the southeast—a lot of infantry. Team leaders, we need to know when you're at half ammo so we can get everyone resupplied. Use your cover, we're in the position of advantage, and they still haven't figured out how many we are. Remember to reload behind cover, calm yourself down and take well aimed shots. Machine gun crews, communicate with each other, keep them pinned down; I don't want them to have a moment when they're not under suppressive fire. Over."

Switching radios, Caleb continued. "Tower, this is Caleb. Are you able to fight? Over."

"Caleb, this is Tower, to the end. Over."

"Roger that, Tower Team! God bless you! Mortar Team, this is Caleb, take your orders from Tower Team. There's nothing we can do about that first block of houses; they've all been cleared of civilians; you are clear to engage as the tower directs. Over."

From the city, hundreds of tiny lights flashed, followed by the unmistakable crackling of rifle fire. Tracers zipped back and forth between the base and the first block of houses as the base fighting positions returned fire. The display was beyond words. He'd never seen the fight from this vantage before, not like this. Shoulder-fired rockets blew holes in houses as mortars turned garden sheds and garages to rubble. In his night vision, tiny soldiers ran from house to house as his machine gun crews left little place to hide.

It was clear in minutes the PLA was outgunned and overwhelmed by the base's fire superiority. The base had access to almost unlimited ammo and supplies, reinforcements, medical teams. They held the high fortified ground, had mortar support, and fought with awe inspiring poise. It was as if they'd been waiting for this chance to rise up all their lives.

Tossing a radio to Rice, Caleb said, "Turn it to channel four, I need you to be my direct link to the scout team, it's getting too confusing with everyone on the same channel."

"Scout Team, Scout Team, this is Caleb. Switch coms to channel four, Rice will be your contact. Over."

"John Wayne, this is Scout Team, switching to channel four."

"Rice, tell them to spread out and attack the rear of the infantry, I think we can convince them they're surrounded.

"Scout Team, Scout Team . . ." Rice hesitated.

Giving her a confident nod, Caleb said, "Spread out to the rear of the enemy position and engage. Convince them they're surrounded. Over."

"Scout Team, Scout Team, this is Rice," she started again. "Spread out behind the enemy and engage. Make them think they're surrounded. Over."

She looked at him with an apologetic wince.

"Sounded good to me," he said, turning back to the window.

"Rice, this is Scout Team. Understood, moving to flank the enemy now. Over."

Turning, Caleb gave her a thumbs up.

"Sniper Team Two, Sniper Team Two, this is Caleb. Report to the roof of the HQ. Over."

"John Wayne, this is Sniper Team Two, on the move. Over."

"Sniper Team Two, no one gets to that wall, do you understand? Nothing. Over."

"Understood John Wayne, no one will reach the wall. Over."

In two minutes, the sniper team was in the stairwell on its way to the roof.

"What have you got for me, Fan?" Caleb asked.

They'd been fighting for over five hours. Caleb watched with pride as his rebels pushed the PLA back into what was left of the houses all across the front. Their resolve was unbreakable. The PLA had surged several times attempting to breach the walls and had been driven back by an impenetrable wall of lead. A handful of PLA light armored vehicles burned in the streets where rebel mortars and rockets had met them.

"All teams are holding strong. Armorers are working on a heavy machinegun malfunction in the second elevated bunker. We have twenty-three casualties, seven KIA," Fan said.

"Thanks," Caleb said. "Keep me posted."

"The scout team is in position," Rice said.

"Tell them to engage, but carefully. If the enemy doesn't buy that they're surrounded, the scout team is going to be outgunned."

Rice got on her radio, more confidently this time, and gave the order.

"All teams, this is Caleb, pour it on them, everything we've got! Now! Over. Mortar Team, I don't want to hear a break in your barrage, you hear me? Keep that fire constant, don't let them come up for air! Over."

Houses exploded and fires raged as the base poured every weapon at its disposal into the frantic ranks of the helplessly outgunned PLA infantry.

"John Wayne, this is Tower, we have two helos approaching from the south, possibly attack, fifteen miles out."

"Understood, Tower. Antiair, Antiair, this is Caleb, it's time to rise and shine. Bring those birds down or turn them around. Over."

"Caleb, this is Antiair, understood. Over."

Hobbling over to the south window, Caleb watched four missiles race into the night sky. In the distance, a spray of flairs from one of the helos was followed by an explosion. Two more missiles streaked past the windows, another spray of flairs. Caleb punished his cane as two more missiles flew to intercept the helos, no flairs, then a ball of flame momentarily lit up southern Memphis.

"John Wayne, this is Tower, targets destroyed."

"Antiair, this is Caleb, nice shooting."

"Caleb, the southeast guard tower is reporting a white flag waving in the upper window of a house across the street," Fan said.

"Check with all teams and see if the enemy has ceased firing on us. We don't quit until they quit," Caleb said.

"Understood," Fan said, getting on the radio.

"Tower, this is Caleb, we've got a white flag, do you have eyes on any active enemy? Over." Taking in a deep breath, Caleb let it out, tapping his cane anxiously.

"John Wayne, this is Tower, that is a negative, I do not see any enemy return fire. Over."

"Thank you, Tower. Over."

"All teams, all teams, this Caleb. Cease fire, I repeat, cease fire. Keep your eyes on the enemy, do not fire unless fired upon. Over."

"Rice, tell the scout team to hold their positions and to watch for escapees."

"Yes, sir."

"Fan, get a bull horn down to Monkey and get these guys to come out of hiding and lay down their arms."

"On it," Fan said.

"All teams, all teams, this is Caleb. We're almost through this one, good job everyone. Do not become complacent, keep your eyes on these guys until they've been patted down and processed through to the prisoner bunker. Tower, as always, keep your eyes peeled for incoming enemy. Over."

For the first time since the funeral, Memphis was quiet. Caleb felt a nudge at his side.

Without saying a word, Rice slipped her arm around his waist, snuggling under his arm. Wrapping his arm around her, he gave her a squeeze. "You did good, Lieutenant."

Returning his squeeze, she said, "You did good too."

Chapter 29

By morning the Memphis civilian fire department, with the aid of several base teams, had all the fires under control. There wasn't an intact house along the whole length of the base wall. The pocked street paralleling the base was a graveyard of destroyed vehicles. Two teams worked tirelessly to remove the fallen PLA in order to prepare them for burial. Tattered sandbags, bullet holes, and rocket bursts adorned the wall and fighting positions. The airfield tower bore the scar of the helo rocket that had killed two of their team members.

A backhoe busily dug a long single gave for the fallen, both PLA and rebels. Combined, they would be burying over sixty. The rebels had captured forty-three PLA and killed or injured another sixty plus. It was their third engagement in the past two days and all total they had lost twenty-one, with twice as many wounded.

Limping from fighting position to fighting position, Caleb had to admire their resolve. They were tired, dirty, had fought and killed the enemy, lost friends, and knew worse was coming. And yet, they didn't want any pity, didn't look for excuses to skip the next one, they just went back to work. Training, sleeping, building, repairing, and preparing.

Walking into the hospital, Caleb found Dr. Kim sewing up a wounded PLA soldier.

"I heard we won, John Wayne," the doctor said lightly.

"We did," Caleb replied. "How are things here?"

"He says they will win too," Rice replied.

"That's good. Do you need anything?" Caleb asked.

"Rest."

"Yeah . . ." Caleb said, looking around the room full of casualties.

Patting Dr. Kim on the back, he said, "Keep up the good work, my friend; hopefully we will all get some rest."

On their way to speak with their new prisoners, Monkey met them escorting three PLA soldiers in cuffs.

"These men were with the church; they were deployed with the army as part of the trap. I checked their weapons and extra magazines; they never fired a shot during the attack," Monkey said.

Eyeing them, Caleb leaned on his cane. "How long have you known them?"

"Three, maybe four years," Monkey said.

"And you trust them with your life?"

"I would not have brought them to you if I didn't," Monkey answered.

"Run them by Fan Ming and the doctor, if they give them a pass, then they're in, if not, they go with the others. Understand?"

"Understood," Monkey said.

Caleb limped to where the prisoners sat in formation in the motor pool.

Nodding to the rebel in charge, he moved to the front of the formation.

"Last night was horrible for all of us," he began, giving Rice time to interpret. "But that's often the price of freedom. We don't hate you; we don't wish to kill you. The Chinese State Government would have us all be slaves; you and me. Our fight is with them. You're not our enemy unless you fight with them, even so, we will do you no more harm."

He paused, watching his words sink in.

"This free country we wish to rebuild may have a place for you, but your freedom must be earned. If you're willing to put in with us, though the odds are against us, then we'll put in with you when this conflict is over. If there's anyone who longs for freedom and is willing to fight and die to have it, stand up now."

He waited, and then one by one, a third of the prisoners stood.

Caleb nodded and the rebels guarding the prisoners got the rest of them up and marched them to the prison bunker. Those who had stood were formed into a platoon, three rows of five, where they awaited instruction.

"You will be broken into teams filling sandbags, pulling carts, and resupplying ammo. You will be under heavy guard; trust is earned, but if you work faithfully under these conditions I will work faithfully for your freedom when this war is over. Do you understand?" he finished.

The prisoners nodded, some thanking him for the opportunity. Caleb got on the radio and called their new team leaders over. Once assignments were given, they were marched over to the showers.

"We need all the help we can get," Caleb said to Rice as they walked back to the HQ.

When they arrived in the main room, Fan looked up, a worried expression spread across his face.

"What is it?" Caleb asked.

"I just picked up traffic from the PLA near Jackson. They are springing the trap today," Fan answered.

"You haven't been able to reach the Americans?" Caleb asked.

"No, I am sorry."

"They're springing it early," Caleb said, looking at the large monitor. "My brother isn't deep enough to trap his flanks. They'll suffer some losses, but he'll retreat to Jackson, his position is much stronger there. See," he said, showing with his hands the flaw in the attack. "He must retreat back into Jackson. The numbers are still against him, but he'll last much longer there.

"We forced their hand," he said, tossing his cane slightly and catching it. "If we continue to hold, and choke the life out of their supply line, they'll have to come for us. When they do, we must be ready for them. Every day we survive, the Americans gain advantage; enough advantage, and they'll break through. We must hold, Fan. Freedom is counting on us to hold."

"The next time they come will be the last. If we hold, we survive, if we fail . . ."

He caught Rice watching him wide-eyed.

"We won't fail," he said. "Fan, call all team leaders, including Dr. Kim, for a briefing."

By the time everyone was assembled, Caleb already had a map up on the large monitor. His palms were sweating, and his leg throbbed. They'd been fighting all night, there had been little rest for anyone in the past couple of days. But to be honest, he'd rather be on a battlefield anywhere than speaking in front of a crowd. That was Aaron's thing. Lord, tell me what to say.

Clearing his throat, the room quieted down, and all eyes were on him.

"I'd like to start by saying that you've all done a great job. Three times you've defied one of the most powerful armies in the world, not only defied: you won. You didn't start out soldiers, but now there's no one I'd rather fight with. I've never seen such a display of selfless courage against such an enemy by so many in all my years of fighting. You've learned quick, become proficient, and continue to challenge yourselves. You should be proud of the things you've accomplished.

"Today, Fan got word that the PLA trap has been sprung early, and you did that. The time isn't strategic, so it must be out of necessity. They're running out of supplies and couldn't afford to call the attack off. If you look on the map, you can see that, as the trap closes, the PLA won't be able to encircle the Americans, which will allow them to retreat to Jackson. From Jackson, the Americans will be able to hold out much longer, putting stress on the PLA who are running desperately short of supplies, thanks to you all.

"The Americans will hold out longer than the PLA hope they can, I know their grit. They didn't come this far to lose this way. They'll be outgunned, and if the PLA is able to resupply, I do believe they would gain the upper hand. If that happens, eventually the Americans would be forced to retreat or possibly surrender.

"That's where we come in. The fate of the war rests in our hands. The PLA will come for us again. They will first work their trap hard, it will probably take two, maybe three days for them to realize the Americans aren't going to surrender. They cannot afford to fail again, or they'll lose the war, and America. They will come hard, there will be thousands, they will hope to win quickly before the Americans in Jackson take advantage of their situation. It may be as many as half the PLA currently engaged up there. That's what I'd do."

Caleb nodded to Fan who brought up a map of Memphis.

"This is us," Caleb said, following the outline of the base on the map. "The base is long and narrow with access from both land and the river. As we learned last night, it's difficult to cover that much wall effectively even against a hundred of the enemy. We did it, but it took hours, and we took a beating in the process. If we use the same defense next time, we'll be wiped out in an hour."

The team leaders glanced at one another nervously.

"What if we moved the base?" Monkey asked.

"Move it where?" Caleb replied.

Getting up from his chair, Monkey walked up to the monitor and pointed to a large island labeled President's Island, southwest of Memphis.

"Here," he said. "The only connection to the city is narrow, and it would be easy to defend against boats. Their armor would have no choice but to come over that narrow bridge."

Rising from his chair, Dr. Kim walked to the front and began talking excitedly.

"He says there was a battle like this in history where a small number of warriors from Greece were able to hold off an army of a million Persians," Rice said. "They funneled the Persians down a narrow corridor where their numbers made no difference."

"How would we move the whole base in two or three days?" Caleb asked. "We'd get caught somewhere in the middle and be destroyed."

"He says it wouldn't be the first time God built walls in an impossible amount of time," Rice interpreted.

"Nehemiah, I know," Caleb said. "But this . . ."

"You said we would not stand a chance if we fought here again. If we could move the base, would we stand a chance?" Monkey asked.

Caleb looked at the map and then back at Monkey, a feeling of helplessness washing over him.

"Yes, but—"

"Then we will move the base," Monkey said.

Several heads nodded amongst the team leaders.

Moving to protest, Caleb felt someone grab his arm. Turning, he saw Dr. Kim with that familiar mischievous look in his eye.

"Have faith, John Wayne. We will move mountains."

"Aargh," Caleb groaned, running his hand down his face. "My mom would really like you."

"He says lots of ladies have liked him," Rice said, shrugging her shoulders.

Caleb nearly choked as the old man grinned.

"Ok, let's put it to a vote. Everyone in favor of moving the base by faith, in record time, knowing there's a horde of thousands of PLA who could show up at any time on any day, raise your hand."

Without hesitation, every hand shot up.

"Unbelievable . . ." Caleb said. Dr. Kim's smile spread ear to ear.

Giving it a moment to sink in, he felt a strange peace; if they were going to be the ones to die, why shouldn't they have the right to choose where?

"Alright, if we're going to move the base, we need to start now. Here's what we're going to do. Tower Team, you're going to have to be our eyes, and Fan, our ears. We need to know if trouble is coming as far in advance as possible. Construction team and engineers, we'll draw up a new base as soon as we're finished here. Monkey, I want you to break the teams into three shifts; we'll work around the clock, each shift will be eight hours. We need to get all the empty Hesco barriers moved to the island. Get the dozer, crane, and loader over there too. Dr. Kim, I need you to keep an eye on everyone, rove from team to team; we have to remain fit to fight. If Dr. Kim gives an order, it must be followed.

"Once the new base is drawn up, the engineers will take over until the base is complete. Each team will take orders from the engineers and work on the section they're assigned. Anyone who can drive trucks will be moving supplies; anything we can't move in time, we blow.

"Go prepare your teams, we'll have the plans in an hour," Caleb said.

A spirit of optimism mixed with urgency permeated the rebels as they began loading trucks with materials headed for the island. The new base was a long rectangle with the east wall right up on McKellar Lake. The north wall faced the narrow strip of land connecting the island to the mainland. The southern wall ended a quarter of the way down the island, with the west all facing into the island itself.

Given the island had been completely logged off sometime before the civil war, the landscape had become an overgrown pasture with only a few young trees dotting the otherwise flat terrain. The only cover on the whole island would be what they created for themselves, leaving the enemy at a severe disadvantage.

Any boats targeting the base directly would be squeezed between the island and the mainland for a good mile before reaching the base, allowing rocket teams access to either side of the boat long before it reached the rebels. Amphibious vehicles would have to deploy south of the base to have a chance of a successful landing on the island and then work their way north across open ground. Heavy armor would be forced to take the narrow approach from the mainland, making them easy targets for the artillery and mortars. Infantry could either cross the narrow lake or follow the armor; neither were good options.

The more Caleb thought about it, the more he realized the island wasn't just a good idea, it was their only chance. They made an old chemical factory into the new headquarters building and, with a little engineering magic, was running on generator power. The prisoners were broken into crews and put to work harvesting materials from old buildings, filling sandbags, unloading trucks, and cleaning out both the HQ and new hospital.

The bulldozer cleared old buildings and piles of materials, followed by a survey team who laid out the lines of the outer walls of the new base. Following the survey team, another team unfolded and tied the empty barriers together. Once a barrier was in place, the loader filled it. At miraculous speed, a new wall crawled its way down the eastern shoreline of McKellar Lake.

As the day ended, the engineering team set up lights they'd scavenged from the docks so the work could go on. Several shipping containers were buried creating new bunkers that were rapidly filled with ammunition, supplies, food, and fuel. Other container bunkers became barracks, mess facilities, and civilian shelters.

Looking up from his battle strategies, Caleb watched the work out his new HQ window. Fan played operator on the radio behind him, directing and connecting teams with tireless professionalism. Rice lay sleeping on a pile of blankets Miss Wen, one of the supply team, had brought over.

He got up, stretching. At the current pace, the walls of the new base would be completed by morning. Hold on, Aaron. You're not alone.

"Still nothing from the Americans?" he asked Fan.

"Nothing, I have these three radios on at all times scanning the frequencies you gave me. If they were to say anything on those channels, we'd hear it, given we are in range," Fan said.

"How about the PLA?"

"Sounds like you were right; the Americans are retreating towards Jackson, but they suffered heavy casualties on their flanks."

"They haven't surrendered yet."

Chapter 30

I wish Xiuying could see this," Caleb said to Dr. Kim as they took a break in the HQ the next morning.

"She would be proud of you," Dr. Kim replied.

"Me? This is your doing."

"So it is," the doctor chuckled.

"Will she be alright?" Caleb asked.

"Chen would have told her grandparents all of it. If China loses the war, it will be even worse. They will look to pin their failure on someone. She is a Christian and a traitor. She may be worth more to Chen if he turned her over to the State," Kim replied heavily.

"So, if we win, she dies?"

The old man nodded his head. "A public trial, and then . . ."

"You've known that all along?"

The old man nodded again.

Pushing himself up from the table, Caleb staggered over to the window. He couldn't breathe. Below him, the loader rolled by with another bucket of sand. Engineers crafted fighting positions into the walls. Prisoners carried sandbags to the hospital. It was all killing her. How? How could there be no way out?

"God . . ." his voice trembled.

"Caleb, the engineers need you to clarify something on the base plans. They are waiting for you downstairs," Fan said.

Leaning heavily against the window, Caleb wrestled against such a reality.

"Caleb, in this war there are many who die, how is it right for us to place those we hold dear above the rest?" the doctor said softly.

"Because she isn't like the rest of us, Doc!" Caleb said, storming out of the room.

After satisfying the engineers, Caleb limped over to a pile of gravel in the corner of the wall. Picking up a broken 2x4 he stabbed it into the middle of the mound. Taking fifteen steps back he drew his pistol and proceeded to punish the wood. He hated Chen, hated himself for being fooled.

The Eagle could do it again; climb over that wall and disappear. It might take him a lifetime, but he'd hunt him down, hunt them all down, every last one of them. Dropping the magazine, he slammed in another without looking and continued, turning the unfortunate timber into splinters.

A tug on his shirt made his heart jump.

"He wants to know if you'd teach him to do that," Rice said.

He'd forgotten she was there. Turning, he saw a bright-eyed kid, probably fifteen or sixteen, drooling over his pistols.

"They don't bring happiness," Caleb said.

"Then what are you hoping to do with them?" Rice asked.

She was quick.

"You wouldn't understand."

"What? About Xiuying?" she asked.

Again, he'd forgotten she was there, in the moment. She had truly taken the shadow thing to heart.

"Shooting a bit of wood isn't going to change anything. You can't help her anymore, but you could help save him," she said, nodding to the boy.

Looking past the boy, Caleb noticed almost everyone around them was watching him. Before he knew it, a chant began.

"John Wayne, John Wayne, John Wayne . . ."

"They believe in you," Rice said.

"Yeah . . ." Caleb chuffed, relenting. "Here." He handed a pistol to the boy. Pulling out the other, he handed it to Rice.

"Are you serious?!" she asked.

"Only for practice."

***

That evening, before heading out on his shift, Caleb stopped by the new hospital where Dr. Kim had just delivered an untouchables' baby. Finding him near a sink washing up, Caleb waited. When Kim had finished, he directed Caleb to a separate room full of supplies.

"I wanted to apologize," Caleb said. "Caring about people isn't something I've done in a long time. . . . It seems that every time I get close to someone, they die, or I guess you could say the PLA kills them. And I don't want to lose anyone else," Caleb said. "But it's more than that, I've never really loved anyone before either, but I think I do now, and there's nothing I can do."

"Then fight, John Wayne. And trust God to fight for what you cannot," Kim said, patting him on the back.

Caleb nodded. "I'm not quite used to doing that either."

Getting up, he headed out to find the engineer on duty for his shift. He walked past fighting positions already complete with weapons systems. The wall was double thick on the bottom with a secondary layer dotted with sandbagged positions for small arms soldiers. The bulldozer was busy on the opposite bank of the lake clearing trees and other cover, leaving nothing for the enemy to hide behind. In the morning, two teams would place mines all over the back side of the island, the far bank, and the small island on Lake McKellar.

A large dump truck rolled past pulling one of the artillery cannons, followed by a second doing the same. He found the engineer near the south wall and reported for duty. He was promptly assigned to a team that would be creating a fortified alleyway, allowing the antiair battery to move under cover from the north end of the base to the south, behind shipping containers filled with sand.

Since he possessed no real engineering skills, Caleb's job was to work with the welder cutting holes in the tops of the containers so the loader could fill them with dirt. As the crane lowered a fresh container, Caleb and the welder rolled the cutting torch from the previous container onto the new one and cut two loader bucket sized holes in the top. The work was hot and slow. All the kneeling made his leg ache, but he was grateful for the experience. The welder took the time to teach him how to cut and by the time they started on the second column, he was getting fairly proficient.

By the end of their shift, they had two columns of containers stretching from one end of the base to the other with enough room in between for the antiair unit to drive back and forth. It would take a hit from directly above the unit to destroy it. At four places along its track, there were gaps to allow personnel through and store additional missiles for quick reloading.

On his way back to the HQ to get food and some sleep, Caleb inspected the artillery positions. Each gun was surrounded by a double high barrier except for a personnel-sized opening. A small internal bunker held a few dozen rounds, with additional rounds kept in a buried container directly behind the battery. The container was accessible by a series of trenches that tied the entire battery together, allowing the container to not only supply ammo but also provide protection for the crews during bombardment.

The various bunkers, including the HQ and hospital, were being tied together by a network of concrete culverts running the length of the base, allowing the rebels to move almost anywhere within the base underground: an idea one of the church members had come up with to reduce casualties.

Everywhere he looked, progress was being made at a seemingly impossible rate. Trucks continued to roll through the gates, emptying the PLA warehouses of their stores. The heavy equipment never ceased moving, clearing, and filling. As he entered the HQ, exhausted and filthy, he was satisfied. The sun was just beginning to glow in the east to begin their third day. They had moved mountains, just as Kim had said. Any additional time from here on was grace.

He nodded to Fan who was just beginning his shift on the radio.

"Wake me up in four hours unless something happens," he said, slipping onto a couch from the old HQ. Before Fan could answer, he was already asleep.

Caleb sat up, checking his watch. "Fan! I said wake me up in four hours. It's been almost six!"

Holding up his hands, Fan said, "I am following orders. You said we have to follow whatever Dr. Kim says. He told me to let you sleep."

Sighing, Caleb replied, "I did say that. Anything to report?"

"Believe it or not, the antiair crew shot down a drone and you slept right through it," Fan said.

"When?" Caleb asked, standing up.

"About thirty minutes ago."

"Did Tower say whether or not they think it got close enough to figure out what we're doing?" Caleb asked.

"It was about eight kilometers out when they brought it down," Fan replied.

"We might be ok. Better safe than sorry; I think it's time we move the tower equipment to this base. I don't want them getting caught out there alone. Tell the engineers to get them up as high as they can and call it good," Caleb said.

Fan jumped on the radio relaying his orders.

"Also, I got an idea from my dream. I want us to fill the channel where Lake McKellar empties into the river with all these piles of old steel. It'll prevent boats from entering and will also make it impossible for the PLA soldiers to use it as a bridge," Caleb said.

"I like it," Fan said.

"We need to make sure we place charges in the tunnels. If the PLA make it into the base, we need to be able to retreat to the HQ and bury whoever follows," Caleb said.

"You have scary dreams," Fan replied.

"Oh, I don't know, I always manage to make it out of them," Caleb smiled.

"I'll let the engineers know about the charges," Fan said.

"Where's Rice?" Caleb asked.

"She said to tell you she's at the hospital helping Dr. Kim, and that she took a radio so you could contact her and not be completely helpless."

"Completely helpless?"

"Her words, not mine," Fan said. "Coffee?"

"Yeah . . ."

"I picked up some more bits from Jackson. Your Americans are making the PLA pay for every block. They are holding out so far," Fan said.

"That explains the drone . . ." he said, thoughtfully. "We need to have a scout down river. They aren't going to rely on the supplies they believe we have; they will send new shipments upriver. If it were me, I'd want those boats waiting just out of sight when I got there, so as soon as the battle was over, the supplies could be delivered. That may be our best warning."

Caleb limped to the stairs; he was already missing the elevator of the old HQ. While he'd been asleep, barriers had been placed around the HQ, sandbags framed the windows, and steps led down into a short trench that opened up into a tunnel entrance.

Looking down the tunnel, he could see several shafts of light from the various fighting positions.

Hunching over, he entered the tunnel and followed it to its first exit. He found himself in the mortar pits where a team of prisoners were busily filling sandbags under guard. He thanked them for their work only to be met with blank stares. He tried again in his best Mandarin, only making things worse. He looked at the guard who shook his head and shrugged his shoulders.

Reluctantly, he reached for his radio.

"Rice, this is Caleb. Over."

"What is it?" came Rice's reply.

"I need you over at the mortar pits. Please," Caleb said.

There was a moment's hesitation.

"Alright, give me a sec."

"Thank you."

Rice arrived, shaking her head.

"I can't leave you alone for five minutes," she teased.

"Tell them I appreciate their work."

The prisoners looked at him suspiciously.

"They think you're trying to trick them."

"Tell them, no tricks, we couldn't have done this without them."

One of the prisoners nodded.

"Ask them if they need anything," Caleb said.

The prisoners all shook their heads emphatically.

"Alright," Caleb said. "Be safe." He turned and headed back into the tunnel.

"Why are you being so nice to those guys?" Rice asked.

"Because I don't want them to feel the way you and I did. Someday, hopefully soon, this will all be over, and they'll go back to being just people. Dr. Kim told me the best way to defeat an enemy is to make them a friend," Caleb replied.

"You really have changed," Rice said.

"Better or worse?"

"Better," Rice said. "Still helpless, but better."

Their next stop was the mess bunker. Two containers had been buried end to end with a door connecting them. Caleb shook hands with the rebels who were between shifts getting some much-needed rest and fellowship. Their joy was infectious, if it weren't for the surroundings, you would have thought a church service had just let out. No one was thinking about the impending battle, no one except Caleb.

From the mess, they moved on to the supply bunkers where a team of ladies tirelessly organized supplies on metal shelving. Caleb and Rice joined in and helped sort hygiene items and toiletries, while making conversation with the members of the team. After an hour, they moved on to the artillery battery and helped stack ammunition. Next, they arrived at the new tower build.

The engineers were busily creating a tower of barriers with a shed on top that was being sandbagged to oblivion. Power wires were being run out of the tunnels up a thick conduit in the middle of the structure and into the floor of the shed. An interior ladder running inside a narrow culvert leading to a trapdoor in the floor and was the only access. The radio and radar equipment had been set up before the shed was put into place. One team ran wires, another placed sandbags, while a third set up the equipment in the shed.

Rice and Caleb joined the sandbag crew hefting the bags into the loader. It was humbling; not the work, the faith they all put in him. At every stop they made, the rebels cheered his presence, shared their ideas, and allowed him to share in their work.

The base had grown beyond anything he could have imagined. It was truly the fruit of a community of brilliant minds. Each project was led by those with the most experience, rank didn't matter. The artillery team designed the artillery battery, the mortar team the mortar battery, heavy gun positions by those who used them, and so on.

The weapons systems were also stripped from the docked PT boats and mounted to fighting positions at the north and south ends of the base, covering their flanks with the Gatlin guns. Claymore mines, ringing the outer walls, were run to switches inside the fighting positions, with a master switch in the HQ. The narrow road leading onto the island was mined with antitank mines. The only thing left to do was destroy the old base.

Caleb and Rice climbed up to the tower as the sun dropped behind the horizon.

"Demo team, this is Caleb. Blow it."

Booming explosions echoed down the river as fireballs leapt into the sky. The old docks flew into the air amidst geysers of water. The air traffic control tower twisted and fell, smashing onto the airfield. Flames billowed out of the supply bunkers, followed by multiple explosions as the remaining ammunition and rockets gave in to the heat. The tremors shattered glass in the city, setting off car alarms. They rippled down the river and shook the base, carrying the vibrations through their bodies.

"I've got a feeling they felt that in Jackson," Caleb said, looking down at a wide-eyed Rice.

"When do you think they'll come?" she asked.

"If the Americans last the night, they'll come for us tomorrow," Caleb said.

"How do you know?"

"I can feel it, they're already on their way."

Chapter 31

That night Dr. Kim held a church service. Why he hadn't taken over the pastoral position sooner was a mystery. He was passionate, challenging, kind, and even funny. The scouts who had explored down river had discovered two heavily loaded Chinese barges anchored only ten miles away, waiting for a PLA victory in Memphis. Fan had picked up more radio traffic and between the two, it was certain the enemy was coming.

As Kim concluded, he had an altar call and over forty people came forward to accept Christ as their Savior: soldiers, untouchables, and even prisoners. There was no time like the present, especially when the future was so uncertain. A spirit of joy and forgiveness descended on them as enemies rejoiced together over a common salvation. Even Rice went forward, and Caleb watched with gratefulness as tears of joy at the love and forgiveness of God rolled over her cheeks.

"Thank you," Caleb said, his eyes to the sky. She would forever be his.

Dr. Kim found no reason to hesitate and marched the whole congregation down to the river. After a brief explanation, the new converts, including Caleb, were baptized one by one. Coming up out of the water, Caleb knew that Xiuying would be proud. All of this was because she chose to love her enemy as herself. This was her reward. And when he met her on the other side, he promised himself he would tell her all about it.

Wiping a tear, he threw his arms around a shivering Rice, picking her up.

"I'm proud of you," he said.

Burying her head in his neck, she whispered, "I love you."

Caleb swallowed hard. "Me too," he choked.

"Congratulations, John Wayne," Dr. Kim said, throwing him a towel.

"You crushed it, Doc."

"The harvest was ripe," the doctor chuckled.

Before everyone went their separate ways, Caleb divided the rebels into two shifts. From now on, all positions would be staffed around the clock. No one complained. Dr. Kim moved several gurneys along with boxes of medical supplies to the lower level of the HQ to be used as a backup hospital. Caleb sent a team into Memphis to warn the civilians of the impending battle, urging them to stay inside and those with basements to use them.

Caleb bounced his cane softly as he watched Rice sleep. He wished he could send her away some place. She deserved to grow up, to be loved and have a family.

"War." He shook his head.

She'd never known a day in her life without it.

"I believe we will win," Fan Ming said behind him.

"Why's that?" Caleb asked, without turning around.

"Because love never fails. And the way you watch over that little girl; that is love," he answered.

"My sister used to tell me that all the time," Caleb chuffed. "I never took the time to understand what she was trying to say. What are you going to do if we win?"

"I don't know, that will be up to America I guess," Fan replied.

"I promise I'll fight for all of you; you're as American as anyone," Caleb said. "You've earned the right to be here. Have

Dr. Kim write up a list of everyone on the base, I don't want to miss anyone. We're going to need good people like you."

Fan nodded. "You'd better get some sleep; we are going to need the Eagle."

"Caleb."

He sat up in the dim red light of the HQ.

"Here is some coffee. Our scouts at the edge of town say they see headlights heading this way down the highway. They say it is a lot of lights," Fan said.

"How far out?"

"Five kilometers."

"What time is it?"

"5:14."

"Any air support?" he asked, taking the cup.

"Not yet."

"They must be tied up in Jackson, or they're tired of us shooting them down . . . or maybe they have a trick up their sleeve," Caleb replied.

Fan looked at the floor solemnly.

"What is it?"

"I picked up some traffic about an hour ago. I was not sure how to tell you. It said the Americans have surrendered."

Caleb's skin tingled, causing his hair to stand on end.

"They know we're listening; it's a bluff," he said.

"How can you be sure?" Fan asked.

"We've been fighting this war for ten years, never in all that time have I ever heard the word surrender unless it was coming from the PLA. My brother would die first."

"Maybe he is dead."

His words cut like a knife.

"Maybe. But if we surrender, we're all dead anyway."

"It would be better to die fighting," Fan agreed.

Caleb looked at Rice still sleeping peacefully on her cot. "Forget about dying, it'll take care of itself. Let's concentrate on living."

He shook Rice gently. "Time to go to work," he said.

Picking up a radio, he hobbled to the window.

"All teams, all teams, this is Caleb; We've got enemy inbound from the east, currently five kilometers out and closing. Everyone strap in, this is it. Over.

"Artillery Team, this is Caleb; the enemy is well within your rage, you are clear to engage. Take your orders from Scout Team. Over."

Caleb watched as a dozen tiny lights danced about the artillery battery. In moments, the base was trembling with blasts from the big guns. Handing Rice a radio, he switched it to channel four.

"I want you to tell me every time the scouts report a hit," he said. "Fan, we need to keep those guns supplied with ammo."

"Armorers are already on it," Fan replied.

"Tower, this is Caleb; are you able to make anything out from up there? Over."

"John Wayne, this is Tower; it's difficult to make anything out, they have switched off their headlights. Over."

Caleb paced in front of the windows as the guns continued firing.

"Have the scouts reported a strength estimate?" Caleb asked.

"They said they haven't seen the end of the column yet."

"Tell the artillery to shoot a flare over them; give the scouts a chance to give us some real intel."

Watching intently, Caleb saw the tiny light appear to the east. It flickered for several moments before going out.

"Well?" Caleb said.

"They said there are a lot of armored vehicles, tanks, APCs, trucks, all still heading down the highway three and a half kilometers out," Fan said.

"Scouts reported a hit," Rice said, "and another!"

"Tower is reporting several drones approaching from the southeast," Fan said.

"They're going for the artillery."

"Antiair, Antiair this is Caleb, you've got drones approaching from the southeast. Fire that thing up and clear them out! Over.

"Artillery, Artillery, this is the Caleb; we have inbound air support, stand by for command. If they get through, you get small. Over."

In rapid succession, eight missiles streaked across the sky, followed by distant explosions.

"John Wayne, this is Tower; one got through and is maintaining course. Over."

"South Gun Team, this is Caleb; are you ready to intercept if that thing fires on us? Over."

"John Wayne, this is South Gun Team; our gun is online and waiting. Over."

"Antiair, this is Caleb; you've got to hit that thing. Over." Caleb leaned into his cane.

"John Wayne, this is Tower; enemy drone is firing missiles."

"Artillery get small now!!!" Caleb yelled into the radio as the antiair battery returned fire.

At the south end of the base, the Gatlin gun opened up, spraying the air with tracers and hitting one of the incoming missiles. A second missile slammed into one of the artillery guns, erupting in a fireball. Caleb turned in time to see the antiair missiles destroy the drone just over the edge of the city.

"Artillery, this is Caleb; all clear! Is everyone alright? Over."

"This is Artillery; the gun is gone but we are all ok. Over."

"Roger that, Artillery; move to assist the other crews. Thank God you're alright. Over.

"Antiair, this is Caleb; good hustle. You're keeping us alive. Keep up the good work. Over."

Turning, Caleb looked at Fan, who gave him a thumbs up. Behind him the artillery picked up their barrage.

"The scouts are reporting several hits, but they believe the PLA has over one hundred armored vehicles, and double that in transports, with innumerable infantry on foot," Rice said.

"That's too few . . ." Caleb said.

"Too few?!" Rice exclaimed.

"If the Americans have surrendered, they should've brought twice that, maybe more. We know they're hurting for supplies; Jackson isn't that far away, why not just bring the whole army here to resupply? It would be much more efficient," he said, leaning over his map. "It's a hopeful theory at any rate."

Picking up a pencil, he scribbled notes on the map.

"We're looking at roughly two to three thousand infantry," he sighed. "Good thing the PLA left us plenty of bullets."

Rice looked at him in shock.

"Numbers aren't everything," he said, turning back to the window.

Just before 6:00 a.m., the front of the PLA column entered Memphis. The artillery continued to hammer away at the rest of the traffic which had fanned out, racing for the cover of the city. As the sun appeared on the horizon, the scout team reported thirty-three vehicles destroyed, and a seemingly endless sea of new targets arriving every minute. As the personnel carriers reached the city, their troops deployed, working their way down the streets towards the island.

"Tell the scouts to pull back. The artillery already knows what it needs to know, there's no reason for them to risk getting caught," Caleb said.

"Do you want the mortar team to engage as they move through the city?" Fan asked.

"No. We won't put the civilians at risk."

"But it's war?" Fan replied.

"We cleared all the shoreline around us for a couple hundred yards on both sides of the lake, there's not so much as a tree's stump for cover. When they come for us, there will be no civilians, no place to hide, and no mercy. We wait," Caleb said.

At 6:30 a.m., Caleb ordered the artillery to cease fire. In the stillness that followed, the sound of hundreds of diesel engines echoed through the city. The earth trembled as the PLA approached. Tiny men leapfrogged each other down the streets towards the clearing and the lake, ducking behind cars and buildings only to appear again seconds later.

The artillery adjusted their positions, now targeting the narrow land bridge. The mortars prepared to bombard the opposite shoreline. Gun crews readied their weapons as rebels fidgeted in their fighting positions on the wall.

Caleb was in the middle of final radio checks when he heard it. Singing. Faint at first, the chorus swelled, rising from the fighting positions until it drowned out the sound of the engines. A song proud and strong, from every corner of the base.

"What are they singing?" Caleb asked.

"We will walk with each other; we will walk hand in hand. We will walk with each other; we will walk hand in hand. And together we'll spread the news that God is in our land. And they'll know we are Christians by our love, by our love. Yes, they'll know we are Christians by our love," Rice sang along.

Caleb sank into his chair.

"We will work with each other; we will work side by side. We will work with each other; we will work side by side. And we'll guard each man's dignity and save each man's pride. And they'll know we are Christians by our love, by our love. Yes, they'll know we are Christians by our love."

Caleb let the tears fall as she translated the final verse.

"What is it?' Rice asked, as she finished.

"They're not hiding anymore," Caleb replied.

Then he saw them. Tanks, light and heavy, pulling onto the old expressway. APCs and amphibious assault vehicles outnumbering the heavies three to one as they exited towards the land bridge. Endless swarms of infantry trotted beside the armor as the column slithered out of the city, winding its way towards them.

Caleb was about to give the artillery the order to engage when the column stopped a hundred yards from the bridge and the lead tanker held up a sign.

"What does it say?" Caleb asked.

"The tower says it's a radio frequency," Fan said.

Caleb picked up a spare radio, handing it to Fan. "Let's see what they have to say."

Fan tuned the radio and spoke in Mandarin.

Caleb watched the column through his binoculars.

"They say the Americans have surrendered and if we do the same, they promise fair treatment," Fan said.

Caleb thought for a moment. "Tell them that's not the word we've received from the Americans," Caleb said.

Without questioning, Fan relayed the message.

There was a long pause before the PLA replied.

"He says the Americans are lying, they are defeated."

"Ask him, if they have surrendered, how are they able to radio lies to us?"

There was another long pause.

"He says the Americans are surrounded and will be defeated by the end of the day, and assures us if we surrender, we will be given better treatment," Fan said with a grin.

"He may be telling the truth this time, even so, surrounded is not surrender," Caleb said. "Tell him it's a kind offer, but we'll have to get back to him after the battle."

Smirking, Fan relayed the message.

Picking up his radio, Caleb said, "Artillery this is Caleb; prepare to engage. Over."

Chapter 32

The tanks divided into two columns. The heavies, knowing the silty shoreline wouldn't hold their weight, rolled towards the land bridge, while the lighter armored vehicles peeled off and moved towards the shoreline opposite the base. The infantry also divided, two thirds following the light armor while the rest went with the heavies.

The heavy tanks paused to fire on the base momentarily as they pressed on towards the bridge. The rebel artillery, down to only three guns, punished them as they funneled together. The mortars had begun to work on the light armor bogging down in the freshly tilled shoreline. In the wide open, they were sitting ducks as the spotters called in adjustments from the tower.

Caleb strangled his cane as he pivoted from window to window calling out corrections and encouragement. The heavies were being slowed by destroyed tanks filling the choke point but continued to advance. Caleb watched armorers appear like gophers out of the tunnel delivering rounds from the buried munitions bunker to the gunners.

Tensing, Caleb watched as the first heavy tank reached the buried mines at the beginning of the bridge. With a flash, the mines exploded, disabling the tank. In seconds, another came up behind, pushing it off the road and down the steep bank. When the second tank hit the middle of the bridge, Caleb gave Fan the

254 Rise of the Eagle

signal and a stockpile of munitions carefully placed in the culvert detonated, sending the tank rolling end over end into the river, and leaving a chasm between the mainland and the island.

The explosion rocked the base, sending up a spray of mud and concrete several meters into the air. The shockwave sent glass spraying out of the HQ windows, nearly knocking Fan out of his chair. Dusting Rice off, Caleb returned to the window with his binoculars. The tanks were frozen in place as the artillery continued to hammer them. Then, in unison, they turned and retreated towards the city, the infantry on their heels.

"Call a cease fire," Caleb ordered Fan. "We have a lot of munitions, but we've also got a lot more fighting to do."

A cheer rose up over the base as the PLA raced for the protection of the city. Over twenty armored vehicles lay smoldering on the other side of the lake and near the bridge. The base had suffered no casualties or significant damage so far.

"All teams, this is Caleb; great job, I repeat, great job. I wish I could say that was the end, but they can't afford to lose any more than we can. They will regroup and try again. Meal teams this may be your only chance for a while; let's get some food out there. Resupply ammo and stand by. Over and out.

"Rice, how about getting us something to eat."

"Yes, sir!" she replied, heading for the stairs.

Caleb grabbed a broom and began sweeping up the broken glass.

"What do you think?" he asked Fan.

"I think the big tanks are going to need a bridge, and they are going to try and find a way to deal with our artillery. I agree, they must be desperate, or they would not have funneled into the choke point so foolishly. They would have taken their time and found another way," Fan said.

"I was thinking the same thing. They know they have numbers, they thought perhaps that would be enough, and we would just fold. Now they'll take their time, this next assault will be more strategic," Caleb said, looking at the map.

"We know they are divided, most of their air support must be heading to Jackson. Anything we can draw away from there increases the Americans' chance of survival."

Sitting back, Caleb chuckled, "Are we mad men, Fan? Who, in this circumstance, wishes air support was added to the challenge?"

"Someone who loves not his own life," Fan replied.

"How many lives do you think these guys are willing to give?"

"In the PLA, failure is not an option. For the officers, it would be better to die here than to return home defeated. In China, the worst possible crime is to dishonor the State," Fan replied.

"So, they're as desperate as we are . . ." Caleb said, running his hand through his hair. "War is madness. Xiuying is right, what can possibly survive in a world where peace is not an option. What kind of logic is there when fighting to the death is the only hope of survival—what survival? What remains at the end of all that? What other option do the people have but rebellion against such an irrational system?" Caleb said.

Fan handed him another cup of coffee.

"So, what you are telling me is, we'll have to kill them all if we want to survive?"

Fan didn't answer.

"Hand me that radio, the one they called us on," Caleb said.

Turning it back on, he said, "Hey, do you speak English? Over."

There was a long pause, Fan eyed him curiously.

Finally, the radio crackled, and an interpreter introduced himself.

"Great," Caleb said. "This is the Eagle, I'm sure you all know of me. Here's the deal, we know the Americans are giving it to you up in Jackson, and this attack on us is in hopes of reestablishing your supply chain to your army. As you have no doubt noticed, we are well established here and despite your numbers, you are at a disadvantage. My executive officer, Fan Ming, one of yours, has informed me you're required to fight to the death or risk dishonoring your country."

Caleb paused, allowing the interpreter to catch up.

"Now, you made us a pretty good offer earlier and I appreciate that, but now that I understand your position, I'd like to make you a counteroffer. If you surrender to us, and call off this attack, I give my word as the Eagle, that I will do everything in my power to see that you're given the opportunity to stay in this country. I know that's a lot to take on faith, but I mean every word, and no more folks need to die here today."

He waited nervously for the interpreter to translate, Fan watching him in shock.

The radio crackled followed by a response.

"I appreciate your generous offer, but the odds are in our favor. Given that fact, I must do what I must. My offer to you still stands."

Sighing, Caleb set down the radio.

"It was worth a try. Have everyone send a status report, let's get ready," Caleb said.

At 2:30 p.m. that afternoon, the armor showed up again just off the clearing on the far side of the lake and opened up on the base. Cannons and machine guns punished the barriers and sandbags surrounding the fighting positions. The base artillery and mortars returned fire simultaneously, creating a dizzying din of concussive blasts. The rebels manning the wall fighting positions hunkered behind the berms as dirt and debris rained down on them.

Heavy machine gun rounds pelted the HQ, several rounds sailing through the window, hitting the wall above Fan's desk. Caleb poked his head up with his binoculars watching the far side. The occasional plume of thick black smoke indicated a successful hit on enemy armor.

All at once, the cleared no man's land on the far shore swarmed with infantry. Some carried boats while others ran, firing their weapons beside them.

Land mines exploded all across the strip, sending bodies flying into the air. Fan relayed the engage message to the gun teams, and a horrific swarm of lead and steel poured through the ranks of PLA. Hundreds of bodies jerked, spun, flopped, and fell in the dirt. Gatlin guns rattled off thousands of rounds a minute into the sand and bodies piling up across the river. As they crawled further and further across the clearing, more mines exploded, more bodies fell.

For the first time in his life, the battle sickened him, more than that, it angered him; but rather than let it deter him, it fueled him. The common people of the world needed a place where they could live freely, the way they saw fit, where their lives were valuable simply because they were human beings. If such a place didn't already exist, maybe they could build it together.

"Caleb, the tanks are pulling back, but the infantry has almost made it to the water," Fan said.

"Have the artillery stay on those tanks until they're gone, have the mortar team switch to that infantry. Remind the tower to keep their corrections separate," Caleb said.

"Wall teams, wall teams, this is Caleb; the tanks are pulling back, it's time to stand tall and pour it on 'em. Do not let that infantry reach the water. Over."

Caleb watched as rebels popped up from behind the barriers and returned fire, doubling their suppressing fire. Mortars sent up sprays of mud and dirt all across the clearing, cutting down swaths of enemy soldiers. The number of PLA was beyond counting as they continued to pour out of the trees. Small arms and rockets continued to pelt the base as thousands of PLA fought for their lives across the narrow lake. Medical teams raced in and out of the tunnels providing care for wounded rebels, while reserves climbed into fighting positions vacated by their fallen friends.

"Call down to Dr. Kim and get me a status report," Caleb said.

"On it," Fan replied. "Tower reports that the armor has returned to the city, they want to know if you want the artillery to fire on the infantry?"

"No. Have them pivot back to the bridge and cease fire. We need to conserve ammunition; they're the only defense we have against those tanks," Caleb replied.

"Dr. Kim says we have fifteen casualties, six will return to duty, five are stable but unable to return, two are critical, and two KIA," Fan reported.

"That's incredible," Caleb said, looking at the rows of dead across the lake. "How do we get them to stop?"

A sudden boom thundered over the HQ.

"What was that?" Caleb asked.

"Thunder, I think," Rice replied.

She was right; in seconds, large drops of water began to spatter the sandbags outside the window. Another clap of thunder and Caleb watched as a wall of rain swallowed the base, then the lake, the clearing, and all of Memphis. In minutes, the clearing became a soupy mess of silty mud and blood. The PLA soldiers sank up to their shins, slipping, tripping, weapons plunged into the mire as soldiers fought to steady themselves.

The rebels continued relentlessly hammering the clearing until Caleb saw the PLA remaining on the field turn and slop their way back into the trees.

"All teams, all teams, this is Caleb; cease fire, I repeat, cease fire. Over. Supply team, get tarps out to all positions, once they're up, deliver towels and blankets. Over. Armorers, resupply ammo to all positions. Over."

"Caleb, the supply team is reporting flooding in the tunnels and bunkers," Fan cut in.

"Engineers and construction team, we have an urgent situation. There's flooding in the tunnels and bunkers, we need a solution now. Over."

"How did we not think of that?" Caleb said, palming himself in the forehead.

"The engineers will solve it. Believe in them," Fan said.

"Yeah. . . . Have Dr. Kim send up another status report. I need to know how we're doing."

"We are doing better than they are," Fan said, motioning across the river.

"Toss me that radio again."

"Interpreter, this is the Eagle, do you read me? Over."

"We hear you, Eagle."

"How about a two-hour cease fire. Get your dead and wounded out of the mud. No soldier deserves to be left like that, especially when he has given so much. Over."

"It would take more than two hours, Eagle. Over."

"How much time do you need?"

"Three hours."

"You've got it. Three hours without engagement. Do not, I repeat, do not betray this trust. Over."

"You have my word and thank you. Over."

"Hey, before you go, what's your name?"

"I am Sergeant Ho, I serve General Fang."

"Your people fought bravely, take care of them. Out."

Caleb looked out over the lake. There had to be several hundred if not a thousand PLA laying in the mud. A handful had made it within fifty yards of the water's edge before a mortar hit the boat they were carrying, killing them all. Stretcher crews appeared by the dozens slopping about the mud, rolling bodies onto their stretchers and then attempting to trudge back.

"Engineers are digging pump pits and installing pumps in the tunnels. They expect to have the situation under control in the next hour. Kim says there are forty-seven casualties, fifteen KIA, leaving us with two hundred eleven fighters. The armorer also reported we are down to half of our artillery and mortar rounds," Fan reported.

"Don't fret about the ammo, they're running out too, remember. With every conflict we endure, their position grows weaker both here and in Jackson. Weaker and more desperate," Caleb said. "This storm might last for several hours, maybe even until morning. The ground is getting softer by the minute, the PLA have to be taking refuge in the city somewhere, commandeering Kim's old hospital for their wounded. They may try hitting us during the storm but that would limit them to the bridge which would have to be repaired. Have we heard anything new from the scouts down river?"

"Nothing new from the PLA, but they did mention the Russians seem to have stepped up their traffic of both military and supply vessels," Fan replied.

"I'm sure they're very interested in what's going on over here. Like watching two dogs fight, waiting to pounce on the winner as soon as the fight's over," Caleb said.

"You think they are planning to invade this side?" Fan asked.

"Only if it was worth the risk, time will tell; and I can only focus on one fight at a time."

Caleb looked out over the base. Camouflage tarps were stretched tightly by any means possible over the fighting positions. Dozer tracks created little rivers throughout the base. Raindrops drummed on buckets hung over the barrels of the artillery guns.

"We have three hours, Fan. Tell the team leaders to send half their team to bed. And when you're done, you get some rest too. I'll man the radios."

Caleb squinted through the driving rain. The island shore was just a hazy blur, what was left of the bridge was impossible to make out. He checked his watch; 6:04. A little over an hour left of the ceasefire, and two hours until sunset. The thought of them working on the bridge, using the rain for cover, ate at him, and again, it was his cane that took the beating. His leg was throbbing and between the two, he felt sick.

He endured for another twenty minutes before picking up a radio. He couldn't do anything about his leg, but for his anxiety he could find a cure.

"Monkey, this is Caleb. Over."

"Caleb, this is Monkey; go ahead."

"I hate to ask it, but I need you to select someone dependable with a radio to keep an eye on that bridge. They've got to stay out of sight, we can't afford anyone getting caught out there, so choose wisely. Give them the designation Bridge Scout and have them radio HQ when they're in position. Over."

"I read you, Caleb. I will get someone out there. Monkey out."

Caleb sent up a prayer for whoever drew the short straw.

Hearing footsteps on the metal stairs, Caleb turned to see Dr. Kim. He looked tired but smiled warmly when he saw Caleb. Taking a seat, he let out a sigh; it must have been the first time he'd sat since the battle began.

"How you doing, Doc?" Caleb asked.

"Better than most of my patients," Kim replied.

"I'm sorry you have to get the ugly end of this."

"It is all ugly, man killing man," Kim said.

"Yeah . . ."

"We are the Alamo, John Wayne. We are buying your country time."

"Hey, you're right," Caleb chuffed. "You're living it, Doc, and thanks to you, I can't get anyone to call me anything but John Wayne."

"Unfortunately, they all died, as did the Greeks . . ."

"The Greeks were defeated? You didn't say that when you said we should move the base out here!" Caleb whispered trying not to wake Rice.

"Do you think the other base was better?" the old man frowned.

"Well, no. We'd probably all be dead already," Caleb answered.

"Then I was right."

"Sorry, I was so glad to see a friendly face I forgot to ask you what you came for?" Caleb said.

"To see a friendly face," Kim replied. "I see her spirit in you. So, sometimes, when I feel alone or troubled, it does me good to see you."

"I know what you mean," Caleb sighed.

The radio chattered as the Bridge Scout reported in. Dr. Kim stood, turning to Caleb.

"I will go now. Stay safe, John Wayne."

"Stay safe, Doc."

At 7:00 p.m., Sgt. Ho reported that the dead had been removed and thanked Caleb for the cease fire.

The diplomacy seemed so out of place given the fierce conflict that had raged only a few hours before. He'd watched Aaron do similar things in the past; he'd been so blinded by hate back then it had driven him mad. Now, he'd give almost anything to see an end to the conflict that didn't involve everyone dead on one side or the other.

"John Wayne, this is Tower; we have incoming. Over," Caleb's radio cackled.

Chapter 33

"Roger that, Tower; what are we looking at? Over," Caleb replied.

"John Wayne, this is Tower; three drones approaching from the southeast. Approximately fifteen kilometers out and closing fast. Over."

"Fan, time to wake up that air defense!" Caleb shouted.

"John Wayne, this is Tower; drones have launched missiles, I repeat incoming missiles."

"North and south guns, target incoming missiles! Over. Fan! Where's that antiair!"

At the south end of the base, the Gatlin gun sprang to life spraying tracers into the storm. A blast rocked the HQ, flinging Caleb to the floor. The red light flickered as sand and debris settled. His ears rang, through groggy eyes he saw blood running down his arm. Coughing, he pulled himself to his feet. The room spun. He saw a ragged chunk of wall laying across her cot.

"Rice . . ." he groaned, dropping to his knees.

Sliding his back under the wall he lifted with all his might. His legs trembled as the load began to rise. Locking his knees, he roared as he heaved the wall and muddy sand out through the opening, letting it fall to the level below.

The spinning slowed as he picked off the last few chunks of debris.

"Rice!" he shook her.

Missiles screeched by outside, friendly this time. He covered his ears involuntarily until they were away.

His mind fought to grasp the situation. What do I do?

He held the back of his hand in front of her nose and mouth but felt nothing. Rolling her over, he slapped her back hard. She jerked in his arms, coughing. Standing, he held her in a sitting position and rocked her back and forth.

"Are you alright?" he choked.

Collecting herself, she nodded.

"Anything hurt, can you move everything?"

One by one she tested her joints. Everything moved as it should.

Another explosion shook the base outside.

"Here," he said. Placing a pillow behind her and leaning her up against the wall. "Take it slow, I've got to get back to work."

She nodded her head, wrapping herself in her blanket."

"Ok," Caleb said, ruffling her hair.

"Fan, Fan! Are you still with me?" Caleb said, rolling him over.

He opened his eyes and nodded.

"Hold on," Caleb said, shaking out a towel and tying it over a large gash in Fan's head.

"Can you still work?"

"Yes, I think so."

Caleb helped lift him into his chair. "I need you to figure out what's going on."

Caleb picked up his radio off the floor. "Tower, this is Caleb; come in. Over."

"John Wayne, this is Tower; glad to hear your voice. Over."

Caleb coughed. "Tower, what's the situation? Over."

"The drones turned back, they launched six missiles, we were able to shoot down three of them. One hit the HQ, one took out another artillery gun, and one hit outside the wall. We haven't heard of any casualties so far. Over."

"Thank you, Tower, keep up the good work. Over."

"One of the artillery members took a few bits of shrapnel but they are alright, we are down to two guns," Fan said.

"Good, have Dr. Kim send one of his people up here to sort us out. We need to stay ready," Caleb said. "And tell the air defense team they had better be sleeping in that truck from now on, that response time could have cost us a lot more," Caleb barked.

Fan nodded, relaying the orders.

In a few minutes, Dr. Kim arrived at the HQ.

"I told them to send someone from your team," Caleb apologized.

"I am someone on my team, John Wayne," the doctor replied.

Caleb nodded his head. "Start with the kid and Fan; I'm doing alright," Caleb said.

The doctor looked at Caleb's arm. Frowning, he turned to Rice.

"You should not sit so close to the window," the doctor chided.

Rice had quite a few bruises and minor cuts but she had fared well, considering. Fan received thirteen stitches in his head, the rest of him had been shielded by his desk. Caleb was spattered with shrapnel, he winced as the doctor removed over twenty metal slivers from his face, neck, and arms. Lastly, he removed a piece the size of a popsicle stick that had lodged itself in Caleb's tricep.

After he completed wrapping Caleb's arm, he handed him two white pills from a plastic bottle.

"For your headache," the doctor said.

Caleb nodded his appreciation and took the pills.

"Thanks, Doc."

After Kim left, Caleb sat up with Rice on her cot and watched the lightning flash out the hole in the wall. He held her until she fell asleep.

"Don't you ever leave me like that again," he whispered.

"You are clay in her hands," Fan mused.

"Yeah," Caleb agreed, combing his fingers through her hair. "I'm glad you're ok."

"You too," Fan replied.

Caleb checked his watch, 2:30 a.m.

"The storm is dying out, but after all this it's going to take at least a day to dry out enough for armor. Whatever they throw at us tomorrow is sure to be interesting. Tell the teams to be ready for anything, especially with the storm letting up."

Fan relayed the message while Caleb carefully slipped out from under Rice, laying her head on a pillow.

"John Wayne, this is Bridge Scout; come in. Over," chirped Caleb's radio.

"Go ahead, Bridge Scout."

"I've got movement at the bridge, an APC and about a dozen soldiers. Over."

"Roger that, Scout. I'm going to patch you through to artillery, do you think you can direct their fire? Over."

"Yes. Over."

"Stand by."

"Artillery, this is Caleb; we've got movement at the bridge. I want you to drop some incendiary rounds on them. We've got to put that bridge out of their minds. Take your corrections from Bridge Scout. Over."

Like ants pouring from their nest, the artillery team raced out of the tunnels and went to work. In a couple of minutes, the guns were unleashing their fury.

"Caleb, the scout down river just reported two PT boats and several transports just passed his position at a high rate of speed," Fan said.

"They'll never make it into the lake because of the barrier; they may come around the top or deploy on the back side of the island. Alert all teams; if they come from behind, the mines will warn us. Tell Tower Team to watch our six," Caleb ordered.

Fan relayed the message, barely finishing before Tower Team called in with more incoming aircraft.

"Tell that air defense team they better impress me this time. How many did they report?" Caleb asked.

"Looks like three drones, with a couple trailing helos," Fan replied. "Bridge Scout reports the APC and troops were destroyed; I'll call in the cease fire."

"Do it."

The rain had died to a fine mist. The lightning had moved further east, leaving the night as black as could be. Caleb set his binoculars down in disgust. He hated defending in the dark, waiting for his enemies to sneak up on them, letting them call all the shots. It dawned on him this was his first defensive action ever. He made a mental note that if he survived, he would not make a habit of it.

Missiles from the air defense rocketed into the darkness, too fast to count. The enemy aircraft fired off several missiles before they were in range, most of them never reached the walls and those that did were shot down. The helos broke off the attack before they could suffer any losses and headed back the way they'd come.

Fan was delivering the report about the helos when mines began to explode on the backside of the island, revealing the river transports had deployed behind them. Moments later, Bridge Scout reported that PT boats had arrived and were holding position just north of the bridge.

Looking out the back window of the HQ, Caleb could see the debris sprays of exploding mines still a mile out. He checked his watch, 4:05. The dawn was taking its sweet time.

"All teams, this is Caleb. We have enemy approaching from the west, strength unknown. I want the mortar team and the heavy machinegun teams to direct your fire to the west. I also want Wall Teams Two and Four to move to the west wall and prepare to make a stand. Until we have a better idea of what we're dealing with, all other teams remain in your current fighting positions. Mortar Team, start firing as soon as you get the word from the tower. Hold fast everyone, and God bless you. Caleb Out."

Without warning, random small explosions began rocking the outside of the west wall.

"Mortars!" Fan said. "Small ones!"

"All teams, all teams, this is Caleb. We've got incoming mortars, everyone get small. Mortar team how about a little return fire! Over."

"John Wayne, this is Mortar team; our tubes are in position, returning fire. Over."

"They're going to have as rough a time as us spotting the fall of their rounds by night vision. Keep your eyes peeled for scouts, let's not make it easy for them. Over," Caleb said.

Slowly the enemy mortars crawled closer to the base walls. They were little more than grenades, a minimal threat, but their presence was unnerving. Then the east wall began taking fire from the woods across the lake from several armored units. A high rate of fire made for poor accuracy. Caleb ordered everyone to hunker down, allowing the fortifications to take the barrage.

"Artillery, this is Caleb, put some heat on that armor! Over."

The base was a blaze with fire from both artillery and mortars, the ground quaked under a relentless thunder of warfare. Across the lake, muzzle flashes twinkled like Christmas lights amongst the trees. Caleb pulled Rice into a corner as rounds hammered the barriers outside the HQ.

"Stay here!" he said, getting back to his feet.

"The bridge scout is reporting armor and infantry at the bridge!" Fan relayed over the chaos.

"Tell the artillery to put a gun on that bridge and let Tower Team know to direct their fire!" Caleb shouted.

"Infantry is fording the gap in the bridge. The scout doesn't know how many, but he can hear them!" Fan relayed.

"North Gun Team, this is Caleb; you've got infantry coming your way. I repeat, infantry have crossed the bridge and are heading your way. You are clear to engage, nothing reaches the walls! Over."

"John Wayne, this is North Gun Team, no one will reach the wall. Over."

Caleb checked the time. 4:47. One more hour.

A fireball erupted in the woods across the lake as the artillery scored another hit. The incoming mortars were now landing inside the walls but at half the rate they had previously fallen. The north Gatlin gun sprayed rounds towards the bridge as the infantry advanced. To the west, tiny flashes of small arms and light armor fire were now only a kilometer out. The base was being engaged from three sides dividing their numbers.

"Caleb, Tower reports incoming air support. Four attack helos; they have already alerted air defense!" Fan yelled.

"Keep pouring it on!" Caleb yelled into the radio. "We're holding them!"

The rebels intensified their return fire as both sides traded tracers.

"Mortar Team, give me some light. Over!"

"Understood. Over."

A flare lit up the night, illuminating two APCs and about fifty infantry approaching from the west. To the north, an endless stream of infantry waded across the gap in the bridge, artillery rounds wiping holes as they went. Those fortunate enough to survive the artillery surged forward only to be decimated by the Gatlin gun once they reached the clearing. To the east, nothing crossed the clearing, only the armor's relentless barrage posed a threat, most of it being absorbed by their fortifications.

Missiles raced to intercept the incoming attack helos approaching from the south. Everyone was engaged. The armorers resupplied ammo as it was depleted. The medical team treated the wounded who could still fight on site, while ferrying the critical and dead to the hospital. Fan worked feverishly to fill vacancies with reinforcements.

The PLA pressed the attack to the north, taking advantage of the divided focus of the artillery. The APCs to the west had been disabled but were now providing cover for the infantry and mortars as more boats arrived deploying additional troops. The attack helos had been forced to launch early and turn back. The armorers reported the base was down to its last forty antiair missiles.

At last, the dawn broke and with it the tower was better able to direct the fall of the artillery rounds. The base began to push the PLA back as several more armored vehicles were destroyed. At the north end, the rebels were able to pick their targets crossing the clearing and the price of advance went up significantly.

By 9:00 a.m. the PLA abandoned the attack from the north and retreated back across the bridge. This time Caleb did not let them go quietly; the rebel artillery dogged them all the way back to the city. Likewise, the armor in the trees across the river retreated to the city, leaving behind the smoking remains of their comrades. To the west, the infantry had dug in behind the disabled APCs and were establishing a small, fortified position. Mortars continued to fall sporadically inside the base.

The rebels had fought for over five hours, suffering their heaviest losses so far. They were down to one hundred and twenty-eight fighters, most wounded to some degree. They were on their third day without proper sleep, wet, and cold, but they had once again repelled the enemy.

The fallen bodies of PLA soldiers dotted the clearing to the north, covered both sides of the bridge, floated in the water of the lake, and left a trail all the way back to the city. Sgt. Ho called about another cease fire, but Caleb refused, telling him the best the rebels could do was accept the PLA surrender. He couldn't allow the PLA free access across the bridge, not even for the dead. Sgt. Ho had understood.

Caleb and Rice toured the base encouraging the rebels. They all knew they had far outlasted the PLA's expectations, there was no reason for him to say it. The horrific loss of life on both sides affected them all differently, it hurt the heart to know that none of them would ever be the same. They had experienced things and knew things that no one should ever have to know. The cost of war was always innocence.

Lastly, they visited the hospital. Caleb held the hands of the living and the dying. All of them wishing him the best, some breaking down in tears at their inability to return to the fight, all of them believing it was not the end. Dr. Kim continued joking with patients as he stitched them up, praying with those he couldn't save, encouraging his staff to keep up their vital work. Doing an impossible job with impossible grace.

When they arrived back at the HQ, it was nearly noon, and other than the occasional mortar, things were quiet. The base was in shambles, the barrier walls were more or less berms of sand and silt now. The tunnels were wet with mud and blood. Sandbags leaked their contents from dozens of holes. Fighting positions drooped, the brand-new tarps from the night before hung in tatters over rebels who looked much the same.

"Something is up," Fan said. "The river scout just reported that the resupply barges have pulled up anchor and are on their way upriver. Not only that, they have been joined by two empty barges."

"The only reason to send the barges is if they believe they're going to win," Caleb said, looking out the window towards the city. "The Alamo," he whispered.

Chapter 34

If it had been any other day, in any other place, it would have been glorious. The sun was warm, drying the muddy landscape. A gentle breeze carried dandelion seeds over the walls and across the base. Birds flitted here and there seemingly unaware of the conflict around them. A pair of butterflies floated through the air along the lake where a family of ducks swam, the parents calling out in frustration at every mortar blast.

Caleb tightened his boots and adjusted his vest. Dusting off the sight on his QBZ-95 he pointed it out the window, testing the feel.

"Fan, have the dozer and loader pile dirt all around the hospital as high as they can. From now on the only access will be the tunnels. Tell the engineers to check the explosives in the tunnels, I want everything rigged but the tunnel between the HQ and the hospital. When the loader's finished with the hospital, have it do the same with the HQ," Caleb said.

"All teams, all teams, this is Caleb. Prepare for engagement. This is going to be the fight of all fights. The battle of our lives. No one needs to tell you the amazing feats you've accomplished, you've lived them and will go on reliving them as long as you live. We have one last mission to carry out. Today we fight for hope, we fight for love, side by side, hand in hand. Today we fight as a free people, here by choice, to breathe our last breath into the lungs of a nation reborn, made up of free people no matter what they look like, where they come from, or what they believe. Today we will stand and bring down this Philistine."

A roaring cheer rose from the rebels as Caleb reached for the other radio.

"Sgt. Ho, this is the Eagle. You should've accepted my offer. Eagle out!"

Caleb locked eyes with Fan and nodded his head. "Raise the black flag."

Fan radioed the mortar team, and they opened up on the entrenched soldiers on the west side of the base. Incendiary rounds rained into the trenches. Rebels on the wall laid down heavy fire on the fleeing soldiers.

The tower reported armor moving towards the bridge, sending the artillery into action.

"Tower, this is Caleb, we need to make every round count now; tighten up those adjustments! Over."

A roar rose across the lake as hundreds of PLA raced across the tacky ground towards the water. The rebels laid into them as soon as they reached the clearing, cutting them down as fast as they could, but their numbers were painfully depleted and now divided. The north Gatlin gun was busy mopping up infantry fording the bridge gap, leaving only the south gun to aid the rebels on the wall.

"Have the mortars switch to the east, we have to thin them out!" Caleb ordered.

No sooner had the mortars switched to the east, than the PLA on the west pressed the attack. More armor appeared in the woods above the clearing to the east and began pounding the base, forcing the rebels on the wall to take cover. As they did, the hordes in the clearing pressed forward with their boats. The mortar team couldn't miss but it made little difference.

"Tower says we have incoming aircraft from the southeast; at least a dozen," Fan said.

"Get that air defense up!"

"Caleb, this is Monkey, we have boats in the water! Over."

Caleb looked up and saw a half dozen boats making their way across the lake.

"East side wall teams, you're going to have to engage those boats, do the best you can! Over."

"Artillery, this is Caleb; forget about the armor at the bridge! Clear that wood line to the east! Over!"

"Air defense reports it hit nine targets but the other three are pressing the attack, and they cannot rearm that fast!" Fan reported.

"South Gun, South Gun, this is Caleb. We have three incoming attack helos from the southeast, you are all we've got! Over."

"Roger that!"

Gritting his teeth, Caleb watched the helos roll in. The lead bird took heavy fire from the Gatlin gun and spiraled towards the ground, the second unleashed a storm of rockets and the south gun went quiet. The third followed the second over the base, hammering the tower with its rockets. As they banked over the river, they were met with missiles from the rearmed air defense.

"Tower, this is Caleb; come in. Over."

Static.

"Tower, come in!"

"John Wayne, this is Tower," came a coughing reply. "I am all that is left. Everyone is gone."

"Can you move? Over."

"Yes. Enough."

"Grab whatever you can and come to the HQ; we still need you! Over."

"The south gun team is gone," Fan said.

Caleb paused, mind spinning. "Do you hear that?" he said, grabbing his binoculars.

Scanning the wood line across the river, he studied the enemy armor.

"Hear what?" Fan asked.

"Their rate of fire; it's slowed. There are only a few of them still firing on us . . ." Then it hit him. "They're out of munitions! Tell Artillery to switch to that infantry; get everyone back up on that wall! Now!" Caleb ordered.

When the Tower team leader arrived, battered and a little shell shocked, Caleb threw him a radio.

"I need you to call the shots for the artillery; hammer that infantry," Caleb said, patting him on the back. "Fan, get those mortars back on the west side."

"Artillery is reporting they only have a few rounds left," the tower operator said.

"Mortars are running low as well," Fan added.

"We can't beat them divided like this," he said, slamming his cane down on the table. "Has the river scout reported any more troops coming upriver?"

"No, just the barges," Fan replied.

"That means there's only a few handfuls of them left on the west side. Have all artillery and mortars concentrate their fire on the west side until they're gone. Then we'll move everyone back to the east side and have a fighting chance! Tell them to fire every round. The PLA are running out of ammo too!" Caleb said. "We have to make them believe we can beat them!" Caleb swung up his rifle, firing rounds into the boats crossing the lake.

As the armor across the lake ceased firing entirely, they drove out into the mud as far as the ground would allow them, creating cover for the infantry. The PLA on the west side were annihilated under intense indirect fire, allowing Caleb to move the wall teams back to the east wall where they began to gain the upper hand.

"We're gonna beat them," Caleb said, looking to Fan. "That infantry has to be running on empty."

Loading another magazine, he continued taking shots at the infantry floundering across the lake in sinking boats.

"They've stopped coming out of the woods," Fan said.

Caleb looked where he was pointing.

"I think they are out," Fan said.

He was right, the seemingly endless streams of infantry had stopped. There were still several hundred stretched from the bridge all the way across the clearing, but there weren't any more being added.

"Do we have any mortars or artillery left?" Caleb asked.

"The mortars are all used up, I had them fill holes in the wall teams. The artillery must be down to their last couple rounds," Fan replied.

"Have them hold them, just in case," Caleb said. "And find out how we're doing on small arms ammo."

"Armorers report there are over ten thousand rounds of small arms remaining, but it's going fast," Fan said.

"Tell the teams to pick their targets, no spray and pray," Caleb said.

"Caleb, the river scout just had four more empty barges heading this way with a PT boat escort," Fan said.

Walking over to the map, Caleb studied it. "What are they up to? Fan, you served in the PLA, ever see them do anything like this?"

"We never fought anything like you before." He shrugged.

"What would they need a half dozen empty barges for? You don't think they'd be using them for troop transports, do you?" Caleb asked.

"They would not be able to fit very many without just putting them on the decks. We have done that before, but the river scout said they are empty."

"They're up to something. I don't like it."

"John Wayne, I think they are retreating," the tower team leader interrupted.

Walking to the window, Caleb picked up his binoculars, studying the opposite shoreline. "I think you're right."

All across the clearing, the remaining PLA fled for the woods, boats paddled for the far shore while other soldiers swam. Hundreds of tiny men slogging their way to safety. What armor could still move, pulled back into the woods and out of sight.

"Should I call a cease fire?" Fan asked.

"Yeah, do it," Caleb said.

The sound that followed was the most defining silence he could ever remember. He felt numb in his mind, but his body hurt everywhere.

"Have—Have the teams send up a sitrep and find out from Dr. Kim how we're doing. Please," he said softly.

He sat at the window. Looking down, he saw his map; in the corner was a handwritten note: The barges don't make sense.

Empty barges?

"Caleb," Fan said, wide-eyed, his face turning pale. "Air Defense picked up a high-altitude stealth bomber already dropping its ordinance."

Antiair missiles flew to intercept, as the first bombs hit the nearside shoreline with devastating impact, walking their way towards the base.

"Everyone get down!" Caleb screamed into the radio.

Grabbing Rice, he dove under the table, covering her with his body.

Caleb huddled over Rice, screaming in rage at the injustice, as each bomb exploded nearer and nearer. The radios cried out with undiscernible reports as the roof of the HQ collapsed halfway into the room. Shrapnel and debris perforated the remaining walls, as the bombs continued their march up the base. Caleb choked on the dust, his eyes burning, his body humming.

Shaking Rice, he confirmed she was ok. Crawling out from under the table he could hear the last few bombs detonate. Digging in the rubble he found a squawking radio.

"All te—" he coughed. "All teams, this is Caleb; status report. Over."

"Fan," Caleb groaned. "Fan! Are you there?"

Caleb crawled over to where Fan's desk had been, his arm slipping over the precipice of a gaping hole in the floor. In the swirling dust he could make out Fan's body lying below in the rubble half covered by his overturned desk, a pool of blood forming beside him.

"John Wayne, this is Artillery. The guns are gone, my team was in the bunker we are ok. Over."

"Artillery team, spread out and find whoever you can and bring them to the HQ. Over."

"John Wayne, this is Wall Team One, there are four of us left. Over."

"Wall Team collect weapons and ammo and meat at the HQ. Over," Caleb said, coughing again.

"John Wayne, this is Supply Team," came a woman's voice, "We are all good."

"Supply Team, gather water and bandages and meet at the HQ. Over."

"John Wayne, this is the med team. We took a direct hit, most of the hospital is gone . . ."

Caleb braced himself.

"Dr. Kim, I, and three nurses are still good. We have too many casualties to count. Over."

Caleb breathed a sigh of relief, he couldn't help himself, he loved the old man.

"Med Team, I know this is difficult, but we have to treat the ones who can still fight. I need you to grab whatever equipment you can find and meet at the HQ. Over."

"All teams, anyone who's left, report to the HQ. Bring all the ammunition you can carry. Over." He tossed the radio to Rice. "Tell them in Mandarin, please."

Caleb hobbled to the window, or what was left of it. The fresh air felt good on his lungs, the sun was warm on his face. He glanced up and down the base, the damage was hard to comprehend. What a hundred and fifty armored vehicles had failed to do in over three days one bomber had done in three minutes.

A hole in the east wall large enough to drive a truck through. An overturned dozer, a sandy mound that used to be the south gun position. The tower shack had been peeled off its structure and lay shattered on the ground. The sand filled containers around the air defense were caved in but had at least protected the unit itself. The hospital had taken a direct hit, three quarters of the building was smoldering debris.

He watched as rebels rose from the dilapidated ramparts, some walking, some limping, some being carried to the HQ. Across the lake, the body strewn clearing was quiet. They'd known about the bomber; they hadn't been retreating, they were fleeing. He turned to the west; at the far side of the island, the barges had arrived and anchored just off the sandbar. Groping in the mess below the window, he found his binoculars. He focused them on the river, studying the barges. They had placed ramps from the sandbar to the decks, but no one disembarked, they just . . . waited.

"Rice, could you ask any of the remaining team leaders and Dr. Kim to join me up here. Please," Caleb asked.

"Where's Fan?" she asked.

"He's gone . . ." Caleb answered.

Rice's eyes widened, then she nodded her head, inhaling deeply.

"Thanks," Caleb said.

Soon there were thirteen of them gathered in what was left of the command center.

"I need a sitrep," Caleb said.

"There are fifty-two of us left who can still fight, including you. The air defense survived but is down to its last two missiles. All we have left is small arms, a machine gun, a dozen shoulder fire rockets, and several cases of grenades," Monkey said.

"Thanks," Caleb replied. "Doc?"

"He says they moved everyone who could possibly be saved to the HQ, the rest they left at the hospital. They're running low on IV's but are well stocked on everything else. He lost over a hundred people in the hospital," Rice interpreted.

The doctor's tired eyes were wet with tears as he finished his report. Caleb put his arm around him.

"I'm sorry Doc," Caleb said, fighting back his own tears.

Distant small arms fire drew their attention to the window. Caleb watched the tree line through his binoculars, but he saw nothing.

"Is it just my ears, or does it seem like that's coming from the city?" Caleb asked.

"It sounds distant," Monkey said.

"There!" Rice pointed to the road leading into the city where swarms of infantry were pouring onto the road heading towards them.

"Where did they come from?" Caleb gasped.

There were thousands of them, running disorganized amongst armored vehicles, too many to count.

"Have everyone take up positions between here and the hospital, now! Distribute that ammo evenly, tell supply we need them to reload magazines as we empty them. Doc, you have to keep as many of us in the fight as you can, whatever it takes. We are the Alamo!"

As Dr. Kim turned to leave, Caleb stopped him. "You need to find yourself a weapon."

Turning to Rice, he said, "You stay behind me, when I hand you a magazine, I need you to reload it and hand it back, ok?"

Rice nodded.

"Put this on," Caleb said, handing her Fan's body armor.

Tromping down the stairs, Caleb rummaged through Fan's desk looking for the remote switchboard. Flipping the desk over, he turned the body of his friend. Carefully cradled under his body was the board.

"Thank you," Caleb said, squeezing Fan's hand.

Racing back upstairs, he rolled several sandbags into position in front of the hole in the wall, creating himself a prone fighting position.

"Caleb, this is Monkey; everyone is in position. Over."

"No one fires until they come over those walls. Over," Caleb said, switching his safety off.

Reaching behind him he slipped one of his pistols out of the holster and held it up.

"Here," he said to Rice. "Take it."

Reaching for it, she hesitated. "No." She took her hand back. "You said as long as you're here, I won't need it."

With an affirming smile, he slid it back into its holster.

Outside the window, Caleb watched countless PLA throw themselves into the lake and begin swimming for the island, others clung to the few remaining rubber boats. The armor had bogged down at the choke point on the bridge, there many of the crews abandoned their vehicles and joined the infantry fording the gap.

"What's going on?" Caleb asked.

As the first wave reached the eastern wall and began to climb over it, Caleb hit the switch on the board and a hundred claymore mines exploded simultaneously. Millions of ball bearings peeling the flesh off of hundreds of soldiers sprayed fifty meters out into the lake. The blast threw bodies from the wall into the reddening water. The effect was horrifying; still the PLA kept coming.

Hitting the switch for the north wall, Caleb watched as steel balls swept through another wave.

"Everyone, engage at will," Caleb said as more PLA climbed the wall.

As soon as the first soldier crested the wall, the HQ opened up.

"Doc! Doc!" Caleb screamed into the radio. "Get your people some weapons and get up here. Over."

The PLA scrambled through the hole in the east wall while the soldiers crossing the bridge moved around the base to the west.

"We're about to be surrounded, Doc," Caleb said as the doctor took up position beside him.

"So was Elisha," the doctor said. "He asked the Lord to open his servant's eyes so he could see that there were more with them than there were with the enemy."

"Let me guess," Caleb said, slamming in a new magazine. "They all died too."

"No. John Wayne. God sent an army of angles to fight for them," Kim said.

Caleb looked around the room as rounds chipped chunks out of the walls, sending up sprays of sand as they crashed into the bags. All around him voices cried out in pain. Rice huddled under the table with her hands over her head, her eyes clinched shut. Dr. Kim jerked beside him as shrapnel peppered his arm.

"God, help me see . . ." he whispered.

"Blu—eam, Arch—el—ver." Somewhere in the debris, a radio crackled.

Caleb froze.

"Arch—gel, th—s is Blue Tea—, over."

Could it be?!

"Blue Team, this is Archangel, push southwest. Over," the radio called again.

Crawling to the corner, Caleb dug frantically through the pile of rubble, throwing chunks of concrete and metal out the window until he found it.

"Archangel, this is Blue Six, pushing southwest," the radio spoke again.

Trembling, he picked up the radio and held down the transmit switch. "Mom?" his voice cracked.

Chapter 35

This is Archangel, who is this? Over," the voice on the other end quivered.

"Mom—" Caleb choked. "It's me, Caleb; we need help."

"Caleb?! Where are you?!"

"We're on the island southwest of the city. We're surrounded, they're killing us," he replied.

"Caleb, hold on!" she gasped. "We're coming!"

"Keep fighting!" Caleb screamed into the room. "Help is coming!"

Diving back behind his fighting position, Caleb unloaded on the incoming PLA.

"Who?" Dr. Kim asked.

"An Angel."

"Caleb, Air Defense is reporting incoming fighter jets!" Monkey yelled.

"Tell them to hold their fire, I think they're friendly!" he shouted back.

In less than a minute, three Canadian fighter jets screamed down the river, firing rockets into the PLA climbing over the walls.

"Caleb, the soldiers to the west are fleeing towards the barges."

He turned in time to see Russians across the river open up on the barges and fleeing troops sending them diving for the ground.

The Canadian fighters made another gun run, driving the PLA back to the far side of the lake as American forces pushed through the city, pinching them between the rebels. Caleb and the remaining rebels watched in numbed silence as thousands of PLA with nowhere left to go laid down their weapons and raised their hands.

They won.

At first, no one moved, no one could believe it. Minutes ago, they were a breath away from annihilation and now—now it was over. Looking behind him, Caleb noticed everyone looking to him for direction. Standing, he dusted himself off . . . he'd never won a war before. He felt like he should say something, but words failed him.

"We won," he choked.

He looked around at each one, filthy, bloodied faces, eyes filled with exhaustion, having endured incomparable horrors. He saw deep sadness mixed with pride as each one nodded humbly at his gaze.

"You're all lions in my book," he said, nodding to each one of them, struggling to hold himself together. Then he looked at Dr. Kim. "I'm so sorry; I lost all your people." His tears bubbled over, burning their way down his wounded cheeks.

Dr. Kim shook his head, his own tears mingling with the blood on his face.

Caleb drew a deep breath, letting it out slowly. "I'm not gonna lie; I don't know what happens next. The Americans will have good medical staff, I'll make sure you're all taken care of. I don't know where we go from here, but you'll always be my family, and I swear I'll fight for you. You saved my life. Thank you."

Reaching down, Caleb helped Dr. Kim to his feet, being careful of his arm.

"You know, it hurts crazy bad getting those things pulled out," Caleb said.

Dr. Kim smiled. "They will use pain killers."

Sliding the table out of the way, Caleb picked up Rice with his good arm and carried her down the stairs, the rest following behind. Climbing up the berm, he stopped to survey the scene. The base looked like a colossal third grader had played army in the sandbox. Nothing was left intact, and the bodies were beyond comprehension. Rice buried her face in his neck, he couldn't blame her. Gently he carried her from fighting position to fighting position looking for survivors. They were all gone. All the smiling faces filled with hope, the gentle love that had welcomed him home, all the precious lambs who had fought with a lion . . . were gone.

"This is not the end," he whispered.

A helicopter circled the base overhead as American soldiers worked their way across the landscape taking in the prisoners. Satisfied, the pilot landed near where the south gun had been. A woman in a sniper's cloak hopped out, her feet already running as they hit the ground.

"Caleb!" she called. "Caleb!"

She hit him full force, throwing her arms around them both. Sobbing, she clung to them, kissing his cheek.

"I thought you were dead," she said, gasping. "We heard on the radio about a group of rebels holding out in Memphis, but I never dreamed it could be you." She held his face in her hands. "When I heard your voice on the radio I couldn't breathe. It felt like you were back on that awful train, and I was going to lose you again."

"You saved us, Mom," Caleb choked through his tears.

"You saved us, Caleb. I saw from the air what you did, and all I could think was, how is that possible? Where did you find soldiers?"

"They weren't soldiers, they were lambs," Caleb said, shaking his head. "They're all dead, Mom. All my lambs."

"Not all of us," Dr. Kim said behind him.

The doctor walked up beside him and held out his good hand.

"I have been told you would like me," he said. "I am Dr. Kim."

An American medical team set up a temporary hospital in the middle of the base. Several patients were rescued from the hospital building, and the children and elderly were dug out of the bunkers, bringing their total number of survivors to one hundred forty-seven. Caleb had been treated for his many wounds and sat outside the medical tent getting some air. Rice sat beside him quietly picking the petals off a dandelion.

A team of Americans marching a row of prisoners by stopped in front of Caleb.

"This guy wanted a word with you," one of the soldiers said.

"I am Sgt. Ho, I wanted to apologize for not accepting your offer, it was not my call to make," the man said.

"Would you have?" Caleb asked.

"It is difficult to choose between the honor of your country and the lives of your men. To live without honor is worse than death, and to give your life for honor is honor without life," Sgt. Ho said.

"But what is the honor of a country sending so many to die for so little? What was gained?" Caleb asked.

"You can ask that because you won. If you had lost, I would be the one asking you if it was worth so many," Sgt. Ho answered.

Sighing, Caleb nodded.

"It was my honor to fight such a warrior," Sgt. Ho said, bowing.

Caleb nodded in return, and they marched the prisoners away.

Cringing at the sound of more approaching boots, Caleb looked up.

"We're looking for the Eagle?" Aaron said.

"Aaron!" Caleb said, jumping up, then he paused. "I'm . . . I'm sorr—"

Aaron threw his arms around him. "Forget it. I'm just glad to have you back."

"Me too," said Seth, hugging them both.

"You're late again," Caleb jested.

Aaron nodded. "Only the Eagle could make this big of a mess."

"Who's this?" Seth asked, gesturing to Rice who'd tucked herself into their hug, her arms wrapped around Caleb's waist.

Taking a step back, Caleb put his arm around her shoulder. "This is Rice, she's . . . my daughter."

He felt her embrace tighten as he said the word.

"Seems a little old," Seth said as Aaron elbowed him. "But if you say she is, then she is."

"Welcome to the family, Rice," Aaron said, holding out his hand.

Rice took it, shaking it limply.

"She's had a hard few days," Caleb said.

"I can't imagine," Aaron replied.

"So," Caleb said. "Those guys are friendlies now?" He gestured to the Russians.

"I think they're just buying time while they figure out what to do; best to throw in with the winning team," Aaron said.

"If they meant it, I think they would've helped us days ago, they just watched us take a beating until you showed up," Caleb said with contempt.

"I agree," Seth said. "They're only here looking out for themselves."

"What's next?" Caleb asked.

"We've been working on putting together a government using the old constitution, it's more of a parliamentary situation right now. We need to consolidate our military, figure out what equipment we have at our disposal, and figure out how to defend what we've won," Aaron said.

"Another objective is to round up as many Chinese as we can before they can escape. The Chinese State Government is going to want its army back, and the more of it we have, the higher the price will be when the official surrender is brokered," Seth added.

"Makes sense," Caleb said. "I'm assuming they don't want these back?" he said gesturing to the clearing still filled with dead."

"No. I think they're satisfied to let us deal with them," Aaron said.

"It's a pity, we should send them back. Those people need to understand the cost they asked these soldiers to pay. So many wasted lives."

"I know exactly how you feel," agreed Aaron.

"I heard you offered them a chance to surrender. Ha! You are a lion," Seth said.

"Hey, could you guys find a way for us to have a funeral service for my people? They deserve more than just being thrown in that big hole over there," Caleb asked.

"Sure thing," Aaron said. "I've never seen anything like what you guys did, no one could refuse giving them the honor."

"Thanks," Caleb replied. "And there's one more thing."

"Shoot."

"Are you keeping prisoner records?" Caleb asked.

"Sure, why?"

"I need to find a Col. Chen before he gets back to China," Caleb replied.

"Why?" Aaron asked.

"Because it's my last chance to help someone I love."

That night they held a funeral in the base. Several thousand Americans and Canadians were in attendance. Dr. Kim spoke while Monkey interpreted. They were dubbed the heroes of Memphis, and Sara Redding vowed there would be a monument placed on the island to honor them. The service concluded with the remaining rebels singing They will know we are Christians by our love, hand in hand, side by side, followed by a twenty-one-gun salute. One hundred ninety-four bodies were laid to rest.

Later, while Sara ran a comb through Rice's hair, Caleb sat next to the fire and told her all about Xiuying, his changed life, and the rebels who'd become his family.

Chapter 36

If everything you've told me is true, then we've got to help her any way we can," Sara said, as Caleb finished telling her about Xiuying.

"I need to find Chen before he leaves; he can never go back to China or have contact with them. He's a crafty guy, he likes to hold his cards close to the vest, I doubt he's divulged everything. Xiuying is his golden goose. If he turns her in, and she's killed as a traitor, that's the end of it for him," Caleb said.

"So, the best-case scenario for her is she lives her life a princess prisoner?" Seth asked.

"Yeah, that's what she risked for me," Caleb said.

"I still can't wrap my mind around what happened between you two and, well, what happened to you," Aaron said.

"Join the club," Caleb said.

"We've got a prisoner database set up that I can access," Sara said. "I'll start digging today and see what I can find, but remember there are a lot of prisoners, and not everyone logs them as they should."

"I understand," Caleb said. "If it helps, the earliest he could've been captured is a few days ago."

"It's possible he may not even be in the database yet," Aaron said.

"Part of the problem is that if he hasn't been captured, there are still planes and ships leaving our coast for China from the lower states that haven't been completely mopped up yet. We don't have a navy or an air force, the Canadians are doing what they can, but we all know that it's going to come with a price tag," Sara said.

"Then I'll go south and help," Caleb said.

"We're boating soldiers down to the coast as we speak, the remaining Chinese seem to have gotten the message; we've had very little resistance," Aaron said. "You need to recover Caleb. We'll have all our people looking. I'll dig through the Chinese servers and find a picture we can send out to all the units and have him put at the top of our wanted list."

"He's a snake. He won't be easy to catch, in fact he'll probably pose as a good guy. He's really good at it," Caleb warned. "Be sure to have them check the civilians too."

"We'll find him, Caleb," Aaron said.

Rice entered the room rubbing her eyes. "Morning . . . Dad," she said, blushing.

Grinning, Caleb held out his arms.

"Morning, kid," he said, lifting her onto his lap. "You sleep good?"

"Mm hmm," she said.

"I'll make you some eggs," Sara said, getting up from the table.

"Real eggs?!" Rice gasped. Hopping down, she rushed to the stove to watch.

"Yes, real eggs," Sara smiled.

"Unfortunately, I have to get some work done. I'll keep you posted on what I find," Aaron said, patting Caleb on the shoulder.

"Yeah, thanks," Caleb replied, watching him leave.

"What are we going to do today?" asked Rice from the stove.

"After you finish breakfast, you're going to brush your teeth, and then I guess we'll see if there's any way we can help Grandma get things done," Caleb said.

"Why? Did you?" Rice asked, then her eyes lit up. "Ohhh, that's right, if she's your mom, then . . . I have a grandma!"

Blushing, Caleb took another sip of coffee.

"So, how's the whole fatherhood thing going?" Seth asked.

"Heh, I'm still getting the hang of it," Caleb answered.

"Well, don't be too hard on yourself; not everyone can juggle an adoption, defeating a world superpower, and hunting down the man threatening the love of their life," Seth said.

"Thanks, I think," Caleb said. "Hey, can she stay with you for a bit? I'd like to go see how Dr. Kim is doing; maybe he has more information that could help Xiuying. He knows his family and he's known Chen for over ten years."

"I'll come with you," Rice said.

"The hospital is a mess right now, and you've seen enough. It's time for you to just be a kid, time to let your heart and mind begin to heal," Caleb said kneeling in front of her. "I told you I'd always protect you, and I always will. Dr. Kim will be up in no time, and when he is, I know he's going to want to come visit you," he said, brushing her cheek with his finger.

"Of course, she'll be a big help to me," Sara said.

"Thank you," he said. "Don't listen to a thing Uncle Seth says, he's a bad influence," Caleb called over his shoulder.

Seth feigned innocence, then winked at her.

Reaching the medical tent, Caleb took his time working through the wounded rebels. He talked with them, encouraged them, and prayed with them.

It had only been a day since the battle and yet the base and its surroundings already seemed foreign. The bodies were all gone, the destroyed armor was being loaded onto trains to be repaired or melted down. The smoldering fires had been put out. Helicopters flew fresh supplies into the jaws of waiting forklifts.

Everywhere people rushed about getting things done and heavy machinery beeped as the base was rebuilt around them.

"Hello," Dr. Kim said, as Caleb approached.

"How long are they gonna keep you in that bed? Rice is dying to see you," Caleb asked.

"The bed is soft, John Wayne," smiled the doctor, but his eyes looked worried.

"What is it?" Caleb asked, not falling for the cheerful face.

"My arm is infected; they tell me I might lose it," the old man sighed.

"Naw, you know us Americans, we're dramatic," Caleb said. "You'll be fine."

"You forget, John Wayne, I am also a doctor."

Caleb nodded. "I came here for two reasons: to see you, and I think there's still a way we can help Xiuying."

The doctor pushed himself up with his good arm. "How?"

"The way I figure it, Chen is a smart guy, he's going to get everything out of this situation he can. If he turns her over to the government right away, he'll get a reward, sure, but that will be the end of it. But there's an old saying, 'You don't kill the golden goose.' He'll want to blackmail your family for as long as he can. Only after they've reached their limit would he turn her over to the State. I agree he's probably already told your family, but I don't believe he'd be foolish enough to tell the government. If we can find him and keep him from talking, maybe Xiuying could live," Caleb said, already fighting back emotions.

The doctor pondered his words for a moment.

"Yes, you are right, John Wayne." The old man searched his mind. "If we can stop him, I will return to China and look after her. My family cannot reveal my shame either."

Caleb took Kim's hand. "We can still save her," he said.

The old man squeezed hard, nodding his head defiantly.

"I need to know everything you know about Chen. We have to find him before he escapes, and he's crafty. My brother is checking the prisoner registry, but my gut knows he won't find him there. They're going to try to find a picture of him in the Chinese servers they've collected and get it out to all the units rounding up the remaining PLA and civilians," Caleb said.

"He enjoys being alone," the doctor said. "He never lives close to his neighbors, even in China. He likes quiet places," the doctor said.

"What about his habits, or a way he does things that would make him unique?" Caleb asked.

"Hmm. I remember him mentioning that he will not fly. He had a brother killed in a plane crash," Kim said.

"Do you believe him?"

"There was no reason for him to lie about it, his emotions were real."

"That's what I needed," Caleb said, patting him on the arm.

"There are far fewer shipping ports than airports! I need to get this back to my family," Caleb said.

The old man nodded. "Go, John Wayne."

"I'll be back to check on you later," Caleb said. "And don't you give up on that arm!"

When Caleb returned to the house, Leah and Wu were there. After all the greetings, Leah took Rice on a car ride, her first as a free person, while Caleb, Sara, and Wu discussed catching Chen.

"According to Kim, he won't fly," Caleb said.

"That will complicate his escape," Wu said. "According to our intel, there are only two ports that are still docking ships for China, and they are both gulf ports. Once we have closed off the gulf, that will be the end of it."

"How long will that take?" Caleb asked.

"We are already working on it. We have seized over a hundred PT boats and are outfitting them with crews. Part of the trouble is not many of our army want to spend any more time away from family than they already have. They won the war, and now they want a break. To make matters worse, we do not really have our finance system set up yet so paying soldiers to stay on is not possible," Wu said.

"They aren't just planning on letting the Russians stay, are they?" Caleb fumed.

"I said break, not quit," Wu said. "It has been a long war, and they have done what no one in the world thought was possible; they have earned it," Wu said. "We are going to help Xiuying, she has also earned it. Have faith, Caleb."

"That's what she would say," Caleb sighed.

"How was Dr. Kim?" asked Sara. "He's kinda charming."

"I knew you'd like him. They're saying he might lose his arm, but I think you could take everything from him, and he'd still be more worried about everyone else," Caleb said. "These people, Mom, we don't deserve them."

"They probably feel the same way about you," she said.

"Archangel, this is Command," Sara's radio said.

"Go ahead, Aaron," she replied.

"Tell Caleb I got a hit on the photo I sent out. A prisoner one of our teams took in Georgia said that Chen and a small team of staff stopped at their firebase for the night and pushed on for the coast this morning. The only active port in that area is Tampa, I've made a request to the Canadians to secure the port from the air until we can land troops there by boat sometime this afternoon. If the prisoner was telling the truth about Chen's departure, we'll beat him to the port. Over."

"Caleb is right here, thanks for letting us know. Archangel out."

"I need a map," Caleb said.

"You boys and your maps," Sara said, getting up.

"It's how I cope."

She handed him her tablet with a map of the United States pulled up on it.

"I like the paper kind."

"It's the best I can do," she said.

"Once that port is locked down, Chen won't go anywhere near it. He's not a survivalist so he won't go hiding in the sticks, he'll be in town somewhere, probably on the outskirts. Can you make this thing just show me Tampa?"

Sara spread her fingers on the screen, zooming in on the city.

"Thanks. With the whole country locked down, his only chance of getting back to China would be—"

"After the official surrender is brokered," Sara finished his sentence.

"Exactly. He'll try to blend in with everyone else headed home. Any idea when that will be?" Caleb asked.

"We've tried multiple times to discuss it with the government, but China is still in denial on the world stage," Sara said.

"How long can they keep that up?" he asked.

"Not long; Canada is already propagandizing our victory," she said.

"Can you get me down there?"

"Caleb . . ."

"Mom, I'll go crazy if I stay here. I have to be doing something until he's caught. Come on, you understand, I have to do everything I can," he pleaded.

"What about Rice? She needs you too," Sara said.

"I know, but she cares about Xiuying too, she'll understand. Besides, she has you, she's never had a grandma before."

Sara looked at Wu.

"I can get him there," he said.

"Caleb . . ." she tried again.

"I'll be careful, Mom. I promise, you won't have to rescue me this time," he said.

"Don't forget your cane," Sara sighed.

A large transport helicopter landed at the base, loading up men and supplies for Florida. Caleb knelt down and gave Rice a hug.

"I'll find Chen and be back in a few days. I know you'll be good, so I won't ask you. You're the greatest thing to ever happen to me, and I miss you already."

Getting up, he checked his body armor rack and pistol belt one more time.

Shaking Aaron's hand he said, "Keep me posted." With his pack over his shoulder, he boarded the helicopter, and it lifted off.

They had been flying for an hour when he realized he hadn't eaten in a while. Digging in the snack pocket of his pack, his fingers brushed something unfamiliar. Hooking the object, he pulled it out. Dangling from his fingers was Xiuying's locket. He turned it over and opened it. On the right side she had put a picture of herself, on the left side was a piece of paper with a tiny note.

"This is not the end," he read out loud.

His whole body tingled as he read it. He'd lost his only picture of her when he threw his phone in the river, seeing her now—his heart burned.

He closed the locket, holding it firmly in his fist.

"I'll get him, Xiuying," he said through clinched teeth.

When he landed in Tampa, a security force had already set up a fire base in the port to work from and was busily processing PLA and civilians who had been trying to flee. The port was a zoo. Piles of weapons guarded by soldiers lined one of the docks. People and belongings lay everywhere awaiting their fate. An admin team sat at a long table with computers and cameras as folks were processed through.

Walking up to the admin table, Caleb asked, "Where are you housing all these people?"

"At the moment, we're using the ships, once they've cleared processing, that is," the man said without looking up.

"Everyone gets photographed?"

"Yup, allows us to keep 'em straight in the data base. If it finds any two faces that are the same, we know somethings up," he said.

"And it checks for wanted individuals and war criminals?"

"That's right."

"Thanks," Caleb said.

He walked along checking the security near the docks and ships; it wasn't great. A trained individual could easily slip on board without going through the checkpoints. He watched the masses of people moving like molasses towards the table. It was a nightmare. He dug in his pocket and pulled out the picture of Chen, walking over to the lines of Chinese he held it up.

"Has anyone seen this man?" he asked.

No one even looked at him, they just kept trudging forward, their long faces unflinching.

"Hey!" he yelled. "Has anyone seen this guy?"

One man looked over and shook his head.

Sighing, he stuffed the picture back into his pocket.

Walking back over to the admin table, he asked, "What is it these people want?"

"To have won the war I imagine," the man at the table answered, annoyed.

"No. Right now, what do they want?"

The man sighed. "Most of them want to stay. For the soldiers, they would be going home disgraced, and for the commoners, they never had it so good," the man said.

"Thank you," Caleb said, stepping away from the table.

Drawing his pistol, he held it in the air and pulled the trigger.

The man at the table jumped to his feet. Everyone turned to look at him.

"Thank you!" Caleb yelled. "Now, if any of you can provide me with the location of this man," he said, pulling out the picture and holding it up. "I will see to it you get to stay in America."

A murmur rose from the crowd.

"You can't promise that!" the admin officer grunted.

"This is a tier one target. I am authorized to find him at all costs, and according to this order, you and anyone else I deem necessary will aid me in that endeavor in every way you can," Caleb said, handing the man his orders.

The man read the order and handed it back. "I'm sorry, I didn't recognize who you were. I heard about what you guys did, it's just a little crazy right now."

"Nothing to be sorry for," Caleb said. "I'm a little on edge myself."

Turning to the crowd, he said, "So, how about it? Who knows where this guy is?"

Caleb walked along the crowd holding up the photo.

"They don't believe you," a man in the crowd said, pushing his way to the outside. "I am Lt. Lee, an interpreter."

"And you want to help me?" Caleb said.

"If you will help me," he replied.

"You think you can make them believe me?" Caleb said.

"Give me a moment," he said, taking the photo.

Caleb's satellite phone rang, and he answered it.

"Hey, Aaron . . ."

"How goes the hunt?"

"Oh, you know, making friends."

"Yeah, hey, we got some more information on Chen. My team chased down an email he sent this morning, to a firebase on the north side of Tampa. In the email he mentions having to find another way home, leading us to believe he's still in the area and hasn't escaped on one of the ships," Aaron said.

"Did he mention anything about Xiuying?"

"Nothing."

"Ok, I appreciate it," Caleb said.

"Love you, brother."

"Yeah . . . you too."

Running up, Lee pulled a man in front of Caleb.

"He says he saw Chen this morning."

"Where?" Caleb asked.

"North of the city," Lee said.

"Tell him to take me there."

Grabbing a couple guys who had flown in with him from Memphis, Caleb followed Lee and his informant north through Tampa. Driving through the city was like being in the wild west. The Americans may have beaten the army, but that didn't mean everyone was ready to go just yet. With so few American soldiers in the area, it was difficult to tell exactly who was running the show.

The scene was third world, Chinese civilians wandered the streets in a defeated stupor hardly avoiding their vehicle as it drove by. Looting, rape, suicides, and murder were commonplace in the vacuum created by the fleeing Chinese officials who had been the first to ship out. The old Caleb would have rolled on by without feeling a thing, but he couldn't anymore, he had felt their helplessness, he knew their stories and what awaited them back home.

It's always the common people who pay the highest price, they give their sons and daughters, and in the end are left with nothing. The Americans were not equipped with the people or supplies to deal with so many. And the situation was still too unstable without the official surrender for the rest of the world to send humanitarian aid.

Reaching the north end of the city, the man directed them east. After another fifteen minutes he told them to stop and pointed to a small, sandbagged compound two blocks ahead, at the top of a small hill.

"This is the spot?" Caleb asked.

"He says Chen was in the HQ building a few hours ago and did not leave with the others when the base was evacuated," Lee said.

"Ok." Caleb pointed to one of his guys. "You stay here and watch these two, anything fishy, use whatever force is necessary. You come with me," he said to his driver.

Getting out, they checked their gear.

"Name?" Caleb asked.

"Eli."

"You ready for this, Eli?"

"Not my first rodeo," Eli said, charging his rifle.

Together they worked their way up the hill, leapfrogging behind cover. Caleb's leg was steadily improving, and his limp was more annoying than debilitating.

Reaching the outer fence, Caleb scanned the compound. It looked deserted, the gates were left wide open, trash and equipment flanked the buildings, a few empty vehicles were parked in front of the largest building.

Nodding to Eli, Caleb rounded the fence into the compound, stopping behind a sandbagged guard position. Pausing, he let himself feel his environment, his senses probing beyond what his eyes could see, his instincts deciphering the elements. His adrenaline, like a thoroughbred clawing at the gate, begged for its release.

He waved Eli forward. Bounding past Caleb, he reached a smaller building next to the HQ. Bracing himself, Caleb ran for the first vehicle as shots rang out from the HQ, ricocheting off the vehicles.

Diving to the ground, Caleb rolled under a troop transport. Eli opened fire on the windows of the HQ, drawing their fire.

Crawling to the edge of the transport, Caleb drew his pistols and returned fire, allowing his partner to reach the building.

Caleb continued to engage as Eli crept to the window and tossed in a grenade. As it detonated, Caleb jumped to his feet and ran for the door, hitting it in stride. The door tore from its hinges and slammed to the floor with Caleb landing on top of it. Swinging his pistol left and right, he saw three PLA soldiers lying on the floor. Two were obviously dead, while the third writhed where he had fallen.

Getting to his feet, Caleb inspected their faces. They were not Chen, but he recognized two of them from the video of General Yang's office.

"Chen's staff," he said.

"Someone's running out the back!" called Eli.

Sprinting through the building, Caleb caught a glimpse of a soldier diving into an SUV. Caleb emptied both pistols into the bulletproof rear window as the vehicle tore out of the gate.

"Call our guy and get the vehicle up here!" Caleb yelled, reloading his pistols.

In less than a minute, their vehicle rolled through the base, and they jumped in.

"That way!" Caleb yelled. "Go! GO!"

They tore out the back gate and into the suburban neighborhood. In front of them, the SUV took a hard right. Caleb braced himself for the follow. The driver rounded the corner and slammed on the pedal. Houses and cars flew by as they gained on the fleeing soldier. The car banked around another corner, and Lee gasped as Caleb's weight was thrown into him.

The SUV turned down a cul-de-sac. As Caleb's team rounded the corner, it plowed into a yard and the soldier jumped out, running to a house and slamming through the front door.

Caleb's driver stopped behind the SUV and, without being asked, Eli jumped out and ran to the back yard. Hopping the fence, he disappeared around the corner.

"I've got the back door secured," Eli panted over the radio.

"Roger that," Caleb said.

He moved towards the front of the house; pistols drawn. Reaching the steps, he saw drips of blood leading through the front door.

Reaching the door he hollered, "You are surrounded, lay down your weapons and come out with your hands in the air!"

"Caleb?" a voice called out. It sent shivers down his spine.

"That's right, Chen; it's me."

"It wasn't personal, I am a son of my country," Chen called out.

"Don't kid yourself, you were always in this for you!" Caleb replied. "How could you do this to Xiuying?"

"She is a traitor to her nation! She is shameful, how could she do this to China?!" he replied.

"She just wanted to be free, isn't that what we all want? What you want?" Caleb asked.

"Don't be foolish, Caleb, there is no freedom, only power!" Chen replied.

"Give yourself up, Chen. It's over. I know you're wounded, let me get you patched up."

"Hah," Chen scoffed. "You and Xiuying are two of a kind: naïve. The world will never work the way you want it to."

Caleb moved into the house, following the trail of blood up the stairs.

"I've got no reason to kill you," Caleb said. "I just want to know what you told China about Xiuying."

"You think you can save her?" Chen laughed. "Her family knows everything!"

"And the State?"

Reaching the top, Caleb crept down the hallway towards a partially cracked door. Stopping just outside, he prepared to enter.

"You were just sheep," came a mournful whisper.

A gun went off, sending Caleb diving for the floor, then silence. Caleb lay on the tile, his heart racing, pistols trained on the door. Then he sensed it, the emptiness. He was alone in the house. Getting to his feet, he pushed the door open with his pistol. Stepping inside the room, he saw Chen lying on the bed, a white bedspread soaking up his blood.

"All clear," he said into his radio.

He felt an emptiness as he looked at the lifeless body. It felt as though his last connection to her had been severed, there was nothing more he could do for her. He hadn't expected the loneliness this situation brought, a tragic finality in the midst of victory. From here she would drift on without him, a princess prisoner, and the thought of drifting on without her was more painful than anything thing he'd had to bear.

Walking over to Chen, he leaned over and closed the staring eyes. Taking the pistol out of his hand, he placed one hand on the other across his chest. For all his evil, Caleb only felt pity that he had lived such a lonely desperate life.

"Eli, could you come up here and help me with something?"

"On my way."

Together they carried Chen's body out of the house wrapped in the bedspread and placed it in the trunk of their vehicle before driving back to the base.

Chapter 37

On the helicopter ride back to Memphis, Caleb sat across from Lee and the man who had helped them find Chen. Chen's body lay on the floor between them still wrapped in the blanket.

Caleb fished out Xiuying's locket and held it in his fist. She was as safe now as she was going to be.

"I guess this is the end," he whispered.

When they arrived, Sara, Aaron, and Rice met him. Chen's body was removed and Caleb requested that it be buried properly.

"He killed himself," Caleb said, looking at Sara.

"Are you alright?" Sara asked.

Caleb shook his head. "I don't know, I can't feel her anymore. It's like Chen was the last thing that tied us together."

"Love never ends," Sara said. "It will always tie you together."

Swallowing hard, he nodded.

Rice walked over, throwing her arms around him. "I missed you."

Bending over, he held her close. "I missed you too."

"Aaron, these two guys helped me track down Chen. I promised them they could stay in the country; I hope that doesn't cause a problem," Caleb said.

"Since when did you start caring if you caused me a problem?" Aaron jested.

"Yeah," Caleb chuffed. "You've got big shoulders."

"Let's go back to the house," Sara said. "You look exhausted."

"I wanted to ask you something, Caleb," Sara said later that evening. "When all this is wrapped up, I'm retiring. I want to return home, to the farm and John, but I can't rebuild or take care of it all by myself. Aaron's getting pressured to take a government position, and he should. Seth's leadership is needed in the army, but I was thinking that you might want to take Rice and come back with me?"

Caleb sat picking at the table, pondering her words.

"Rice needs a stable life, to know she's safe, and that you're safe. You've both been through enough, this would be a chance to have a little peace. Not that it would be easy, but we'd have each other," she said.

"I trained my whole life for war, to become an unstoppable storm, the Eagle, and when I achieved it, I was shocked to find that my greatest enemy was me," he scoffed. "Then Xiuying happened, and then Jesus happened, and I couldn't see the world the same anymore.

"The Eagle couldn't have won that battle. Only love could have put up that kind of a fight. I've learned that love doesn't go looking for a fight, but it doesn't run from one either. It doesn't look for excuses or permissions, and only a fool would want to tangle with it. I guess what I'm trying to say is, I don't need to fight anymore. If Seth needs me, I'll come running, or hobbling anyway, but if not, I think I'm ready to go home too."

Sara smiled wide, at a loss for words.

"Can't waste a gift like that little girl. Even with everything that's gone on, God didn't leave me empty," Caleb said.

"You make a good dad," Sara said.

"I have a good mom," Caleb replied.

The following morning, Seth called Sara and Caleb to the island base. When they arrived, Seth met them in the motor pool. Popping the back hatch of a convoy vehicle, he turned to Caleb.

"The Canadians downed a commercial jet trying to flee the country a week ago, when they inspected it, they found this," he said, pulling out Caleb's Harley jacket. "Someone on the team recognized it from a picture of you he'd seen and called me asking if you'd want it. So, I had them send it over and it just arrived."

Caleb choked, searching for air. Sara put her hand on his shoulder covering her mouth with the other. Holding out a trembling hand, he took the jacket and turned it over and over. It was his.

"They also found this," Seth said, opening the door. "She insists she's one of yours."

Caleb lifted his eyes as a pair of white shoes, followed by the hem of a white dress, fine bare arms, long dark hair, slender neck, soft lips, and tear-filled eyes floated out of the seat.

Falling to his knees, he held his hands over his face and wept.

Dropping down in front of him she put her arms around his neck and whispered, "I told you; it was not the end."

She stayed with him there, in the dirt, rocking him back and forth, letting the tears wash away all the pain, all the fear, all the loneliness. He was afraid to open his eyes, afraid to breathe, afraid to wake up from the dream. He didn't speak, afraid she wouldn't answer. He just wanted to stay there forever, and she never let go of him even for a moment.

Opening his eyes slowly he gasped as he saw her though the tears.

"It's you . . ." he whispered.

Nodding her head, she said, "It's me."

Reaching out his hand, he paused beside her face. She took it and placed it on her cheek.

"You're real?" he said. "How can you be here?"

"I am real."

"Then there's something I have to tell you," he choked. "Li Xiuying, I love you. I love you; I love you. I should've told you before. There hasn't been a day that's gone by where I haven't spent the lion's share of it thinking about you, praying for you, worrying about you. I've hardly slept, my heart's—"

Leaning in, she kissed him.

"I know you love me," she said. "When it is real, you hear it without words."

Caleb got to his feet. Lifting her up, he dusted off her dress.

He saw Sara still wiping away tears.

"Mom, this is Xiuying," he said.

Sara walked over and hugged her. "I've heard so much about you."

"Dad!" Rice shouted from across the motor pool. "Is that . . .?"

Running with all her might, Rice threw her arms wide open. "Xiuying!"

Xiuying closed her eyes, smiling as they hugged. "Dad?" she asked, looking up at Caleb.

"Yeah," Caleb chuckled. "Hope you don't mind a guy with kids."

Xiuying shook her head. "I do not mind this kid."

"Wait. What are you guys talkin' about?" Rice asked.

That evening, Xiuying and Caleb walked hand in hand along the lake. He told her all about the battle, what her church had done, and the friends she'd lost. He told her about Dr. Kim's bravery and undying optimism that kept him in the fight, of his mother's voice over the radio just in time. He told her about Chen, the emptiness he'd felt when it was all over, and how he'd lost his taste for war.

Then he told her about Sara's plan to move back to Minnesota and that he'd volunteered to go with her.

Dropping to a knee at the water's edge, with the sound of waves lapping at the shore and a star filled sky overhead, he said, "I've had to let you go so many times in my heart, each time carving deeper than the last. I didn't know how empty I was, or what it felt like to be full before you loved me when no one ought to. I know this whole thing is crazy, you and me, and our relationship has been brief, unspoken, and well, separate most the time, but I've never been more sure of anything in my life. I don't want to be without you anymore, I want you to come back with us, I know my heart will never feel at home without you. Li Xiuying, would you marry me?"

"Did you ask my uncle?" she asked. "It is customary in my culture for the young man to seek permission from the young lady's father or guardian."

Caleb felt all the blood drain from his face.

"It's ok," she laughed. "I asked him for you. Yes, I will marry you."

Grabbing his heart with both hands he fell back into the sand. Dropping down beside him, Xiuying leaned over him.

"You are your uncle's niece," he said, still holding his heart.

"I love you," she said, grinning. And leaning in, she kissed him.

The following morning, Caleb met the rest of the family for breakfast. Xiuying had stayed with Dr. Kim and would be coming over later. When he entered the room, Seth and Aaron were having a deep discussion at the table, while Sara cooked omelets at the stove.

"Morning, Mom," Caleb said, still grinning from the night before.

"Good morning," she said, "Do I detect a hint of matrimony in your tone?" she teased.

"She said yes," Caleb beamed.

"Congratulations!" Aaron said, standing up and giving him a hug.

"Yeah, congratulations," Seth said, walking over to hug him. "Look, I've been thinking about it, and I shouldn't have led you on with your jacket, especially knowing what you were—"

Out of nowhere Caleb drilled him with a right hook, knocking him over a couple of chairs and onto his back.

"Now you know how I was feeling," Caleb said, shaking his sore hand.

"Caleb!" Sara gasped.

"No. It's alright, Mom. I had that one coming," Seth said from the floor, adjusting his jaw. "Are we good?"

"We're good," Caleb said.

"Yup, that's Caleb alright," Aaron said.

"So, what were you guys talking about when I came in?" Caleb asked.

"The Russians," Aaron replied.

Caleb helped Seth off the floor.

"They want to stay . . . peacefully," Seth said.

"And?" Caleb asked.

"That's not an option," Aaron said.

Epilogue

It was a humid day in late August as Xiuying and Caleb fought the last of the timber joists in place. It had taken them the better part of a month to get the farm cleaned up enough to be usable. The charred remains of the old house were torn down and cleaned off the foundation. Aaron had secured a generator for them, some power tools, and a chainsaw. An army tent with a cook stove proved to be a satisfactory temporary home.

Sara and Rice had finished planting flowers on the mound of earth under the old oak tree and were busy weeding their new garden. A few chickens scratched for bugs here and there. While dairy goats chewed their cud in the overgrown pasture.

Xiuying handed Caleb a bottle of water.

"It's so quiet," Caleb said.

"I have heard that peace disturbs men of war."

"I wonder if it's because we don't trust it," Caleb said.

"Peace is a condition; it is humanity that you do not trust," she said.

"I trust some of it," Caleb said. "Just not your uncle."

"I heard that," Dr. Kim said, standing below him. "I do not trust you, John Wayne, which is why I came with Xiuying," he said indignantly.

"Missing your movies yet, Doc?"

"Who needs movies when I have you!" the doctor fired back.

"I'm gonna take that as a compliment," Caleb said.

When they finished setting the joists, they decided to call it a day. Caleb built a small campfire to help keep the bugs off everyone while he and Rice went swimming in the pond. She gave him back his childhood; when they were together, it was all goofing off. Sara and Xiuying had their hands full trying to keep the two of them out of trouble. That evening, when they got out of the water they chased their respective moms around the yard with their soaking wet bodies, as Dr. Kim sat back near the fire slapping his knee with one hand and holding his teacup in the other.

A ringing satellite phone brought the mayhem to a close.

Rushing over, Sara picked up the phone, holding up her hand for everyone to be quiet.

"Hello," she said.

"Mom, it's Aaron. I just wanted to give you a heads up. We've been negotiating with the Russians almost every day until two days ago when they cut off all communication. We haven't been able to reach them since, which gives us reason to believe something's about to happen. This line isn't secure, so all I can tell you is, be praying for Seth and his team; America depends on it."

What did you think?

I'd love to help other readers enjoy this book as much as you have. If you'd just take a minute and let them know your favorite scene, how the story impacted you, or what book or author you'd compare it to, it will help other readers find it. It's your best way to show your support for us and we greatly appreciate it!

Just scan this QR code to get to the Amazon review page and leave your review!

(Even if you purchased or received this copy from somewhere else, you're still eligible to leave a review on Amazon if you have an active account.)

Sneak Peek of Book 4!

Operation Gray Owl

Sometimes it takes a ghost to catch a ghost.

A lone.
With stars twinkling above and billowing clouds below, icy wind tore at the exposed skin on his wrists as he plummeted towards the ground from thirty–five thousand feet. Somewhere below him, in the murky chaos of the Western United States, was his target, Yuriy Mykolayovych Shpilka, the most powerful Russian agent operating in the United States and the keyholder of all remaining US nuclear options in the west. First objective; "Just find out where he is."

Just.

The truth was, he'd rather be here than home. Things weren't all that great in the new Eastern United States (EUS). The end of the war with China had created an implosion of all remaining infrastructure. Nearly half a million Chinese POWs and civilians were crammed onto floating prisons awaiting a trip home to China. The EUS had no means to meet even the most basic needs of its own remaining citizens, creating a humanitarian crisis of an impossible magnitude.

The simplest thing would be to send all the Chinese back home, but the problem was Russia and China were still at war with Europe, Southeast Asia, and Australia. A new power had risen, called the New World Alliance (NWA). Born out of NATO's collapse, the NWA demanded that the Americans hold their prisoners stateside, rather than send them home, only to be put back into the war on the other side of the globe.

The Eastern United States had requested aid but were told none would be coming until the Russians were defeated in the western states, and the entire US pledged its support for the NWA fighting the war on the other side. A notion which did not sit well with the remaining Americans who hadn't forgotten how those very same countries had abandoned them to their fate when the wars began.

It was truly a mess, a mess costing thousands of lives a day. The most recent catastrophe was the reason he was currently blasting through clouds at over a hundred miles per hour. After a little over three months of negotiations, the Russians had dropped a bomb on the Eastern United States, or at least they threatened to. According to the NWA, the Russians were planning to nuke the Eastern United States with its own missiles unless the Chinese prisoners were sent home, and the EUS consented to Russia maintaining control of the western states.

The Eastern States were trapped. Everyone was exhausted after a decade of war, their supplies were running thin, and now they were running out of time. Sara Redding, symbol of the American resistance for the last ten years, ever the optimist, and his mother, had pulled everyone together believing God had not brought them this far to abandon them now. That's when his older brother, Aaron, now the Secretary of Defense of the Eastern United States, had come up with a risky plan, and Seth volunteered to be the spearhead.

The mission was simple. Or suicide. Seth wouldn't know which until he arrived at the outcome. He'd volunteered to go in alone, drop from thirty–five thousand feet, become a gray man, locate Shpilka, who was affectionately known as "the Ghost," and radio his location to a team who would remain on standby for as long as it took to find him. The team would deploy via HALO jump to assist Seth in grabbing the target, move to the extraction point, and be airlifted out. Swoop in, swoop out. Operation Gray Owl.

Snatching Shpilka would take the Russian's queen off the chessboard and hopefully tip the odds back in their favor, or at least give them some options.

As the ground approached, Seth checked his altimeter. This was only his second solo jump—his fourth overall. He'd been trained by an NWA jump team who'd seized the opportunity to stick a thorn in the enemy's paw. Twice Seth had jumped strapped to an instructor, and once he'd jumped solo with an instructor. This was his first *solo* solo jump, first night jump, first jump into enemy territory—nothing to it.

At eight hundred feet, he pulled the ripcord and gasped as his decent slammed to a near halt. He'd never get used to that part. Checking the GPS attached to his wrist, he guided his shoot towards a river to his left. Switching on his night vision, he caught sight of the silvery serpent carving its way along the Texas–Mexico border. Aligning himself with a sandbar, he glided not so gracefully to the ground, allowing himself to be partially drug into the river.

When he finally came to a halt, he froze, listening in the darkness for any sign of enemy contact. Hearing none, he shimmied out of his harness and stripped out of his jump suit, revealing a faded blue t-shirt pulled taut across broad shoulders and a worn pair of jeans. Repacking his parachute, he crammed in his helmet and oxygen apparatus, before adding a couple of stones. Satisfied, he tossed the chute into the middle of the river.

He shouldered a weathered backpack with a gray hoodie strapped to it and donned his sweat–bleached navy–blue ball cap. Time to go.

He would head north by northwest, there was a small, abandoned town there called Shafter, and beyond that, Marfa. If he was lucky, he could find a place in Shafter to sleep for the day, and then make Marfa by the following morning. There he'd bump into his first Russians and the hunt would be on.

He'd missed this. Since the peace in the east, everything had gotten political and complicated. He was a soldier, missions were simple, objectives clear, obstacles eliminated, goals achieved. What Aaron was dealing with had no simple solutions. If he'd stayed, he'd likely have gone mad or shot someone. No, this is where he belonged, where he could make a difference.

The coarse desert landscape ground under his boots. He'd never been to Texas before the wars, though he remembered his dad talked about being stationed there. By the looks of it, it was the armpit of the earth. Even in the dark he could sense he wasn't missing anything; the only solace was the clouds were moving off, revealing a bigger sky than he'd ever seen before.

The spectacle was breathtaking; a billion stars looked down on him, here and there one streaked overhead before vanishing as suddenly as it had appeared. He wondered how far away that world must be, and if anyone had ever traveled up there among the stars. How far did it go? Were there other worlds? He supposed God could make as many worlds as He wanted, though he'd never heard of any. Maybe theirs was the only one, a special world.

He'd hiked for over two hours by the time his watch read 00:00 hours. Stopping atop a rocky ledge, he dug into his pack, his hand brushing past a red tab connected to the back pad. He pulled out the radio antenna and pointed it towards the eastern skyline. Switching on the radio, he held the switch.

"Owl Nest, this is Owl One; over." He flicked a pebble off the ledge as he waited.

"Owl One, this is Owl Nest, it's good to hear your voice, we read you Lima Charlie," Soraya replied.

"Roger that, Owl Nest, I'm making good time, roughly ten kilometers from checkpoint one, I'm all greens; over."

"Good copy, Owl One, proceed to checkpoint one; over."

"Roger, Owl Nest. Owl One, out." Switching off the radio, he folded up the antenna and placed it back into the pack.

Soraya was also a Redding, though by marriage. She and his brother, Aaron, had been married since the resistance first began over ten years ago. She was good for him; lightened him up a little. She'd lost her brother around five years ago, it'd knocked her down, but she'd rolled right back onto her feet. She was sharp, and determined, not someone to be trifled with, and as much his sister as Leah.

Leah—the fight against the Chinese had been extra hard on her. Once the typical older sister, she'd come through tragic loss and a crippling breakdown, and become indispensable to the intelligence branch of the resistance efforts. It was going to be her job to help him make sense of all the information he'd gather.

Taking a couple deep gulps from the two–liter water blader built into his pack, he stuffed the straw back into the shoulder strap. Those two liters were all he had to get him to Marfa, and tomorrow's forecast called for 105 degrees and sunny.

The night was expectantly quiet. They'd purposely dropped him in a wasteland to avoid Russian detection and further exasperate an already delicate situation. The only dangers out here were the critters. Mulling over the extensive list of poisonous creepy crawlies sent a shiver down his spine.

He hated creepy crawlies, especially after one of his guys had gotten bitten by some sort of nasty spider during a mission in Tennessee. His flesh had started eating itself, the medic had to cut out a chunk the size of a chestnut to stop its spread. Poor guy spent the next two weeks packing his butt cheek full of gauze as the wound healed.

He shook the unknown from his mind and focused on the mission. His goal was to catch the Ghost, but to do that he needed intel. The Russians had successfully prevented the eastern Americans from contacting anyone resisting their occupation in the west, but enough rumors had crossed the river for them to know resistance fighters were present and active somewhere in the west. If he could manage to make contact with the right group, hopefully they could point him in the right direction and possibly aid him in that endeavor.

Where better to look for resistance fighters than Texas, home of the proudest, most patriotic folks in the states, right? At least, they'd have to be to live in a place like this.

After seven and a half hours of hiking, staggering into Shafter was a little underwhelming. The pale grays of dawn were already glowing in the east, the omen of a brutal day ahead. Barren, half-covered cement slabs marked the last remnants of the majority of the buildings in town. The only accommodation seemed to be a partially collapsed steel pole building near the northeast corner of town.

Stepping inside through a loose flap of steel siding, he was pleasantly surprised to find an old pickup truck with a topper over the bed. Other than some rodent damage and a layer of dust, the truck appeared to be in mint condition. Lifting the topper, he was relieved to find the bed in good shape and, apart from a few empty feed sacks, was empty.

Dropping the tailgate, he threw his pack inside and climbed in. Kicking off his boots and socks, he laid them on the tailgate to dry. Lastly, he wolfed down a food bar before rolling up one of the feed sacks into a pillow and closing his eyes. In the darkness he let the sound of windblown sand tinkling on steel lull him to sleep.

Quiet.

As he cracked his eyes, he felt it. A thick, lonely, quiet. The wind outside had subsided, dim shafts of light filtered in through the cracks in the steel around him; it was still day. Checking his watch, he read 15:47; still five hours before he'd leave for Marfa. He was stiff everywhere. His stomach gurgled and he decided now was as good a time as any to answer the call.

Slipping out through the flap of steel, he made his way around to the back of the building. Why? It just felt right, not that there was anyone in town to see him, but still, it made him more comfortable to take it out back. Unbuckling his belt, he slid his drawers down and was mid squat when a sharp rattling to his right froze him in place.

Instinctively he raised his hands in surrender. A tongue flicked out from a bit of steel just eighteen inches from his boot. His legs began shaking under his weight, frantically trying to hold him still in the awkward position.

"H-hey, buddy," he stammered. "I can see you're upset—and I would be too if I caught someone about to do his business on my front porch. I see we both prefer the same type of hotel; best place in town, am I right?"

The tongue flickered again, and the rattle intensified.

"I appreciate your patience, seeing as you haven't bitten me yet. How about you let me take my business elsewhere and we both just laugh about this later?"

The sun's rays bouncing off the steel began to bake his hind parts as negotiations continued.

"Lord," Seth choked as his knees began to buckle. "Don't let me die like this. . . ." Gently, he began to slide his offending foot away from the flickering tongue.

At once, the agitated reptile withdrew its head from the edge of the steel and Seth was sure it was about to strike. He closed his eyes, awaiting the excruciating pain which was sure to follow, but nothing happened.

He shuffled his foot a bit further, and still further, until it met up with his other foot. Collecting his remaining strength, he bolted away from the building still clinging to his pants. He hated being alone on this mission, but at the moment, he was grateful. If any of his siblings had witnessed this event, death would be the only escape.

By the time he arrived back at the truck, it dawned on him; he'd nearly had the crap scared right out of him! He had to laugh at himself, he'd always figured it was just an expression. His down south survival crash course taught him rattlesnakes were edible, though the idea of tangling with one made him question the cost–benefit ratio. That and he reckoned the critter had more of a right to be there than he did.

War had changed him; life—in any form—was more precious than anything, and he'd only take it if he had to. Many of the blessings in his life had come from the lives they'd chosen not to take rather than those they'd taken. Once you pull the trigger, there's no taking it back. Besides, he doubted there was a person alive who could convince him to eat a snake.

Time ticked slowly by as the sun beat down on the metal of his dwelling, turning it into an oven. Sweat seeped from his pores, running down his face and neck, soaking into his shirt. The environment was killing him. He found laying on the cool concrete floor offered some respite but added a new environmental hazard; the local wildlife knew the trick as well.

He spent the remaining hours in a waking nightmare with only a two–foot length of stiff wire standing between him and a seemingly endless horde of brown tarantulas and scorpions, snakes and mice, emerging and then disappearing from bits of rubble and trash strewn about the room. Their little feet scratched on the concrete as they scurried around him vying for the coolest corners of the pad; a bit of cardboard shuffling here and there, a shifting pop can, the grinding of tiny teeth, their menacing movements echoing off the walls.

The effect was maddening.

"Hey!" he yelled, flicking a scorpion back over a crack in the cement. "Stay on your side."

At this point he was sure there was an eighty–five percent chance someone would find his corpse twenty years from now still clinging to the bit of wire. A young man, gone before his time, forced to choose between death by heatstroke and bugs.

He checked his watch, three hours till dark.

Find *Operation Gray Owl* and learn more at JERibbey.com

About the Author

J.E. Ribbey, a husband & wife team, deploys a compelling writing style, combining a fast-paced action thriller with deep character immersion, giving readers an edge-of-your-seat adventure they will feel in the morning. A combat veteran, outdoorsman, and survival enthusiast, Joel enjoys mingling his unique experiences and expertise with his passion for homesteading and the self-sufficient lifestyle in his writing. A homeschooling mom, homesteader, and digital designer, Esther brings the technical, editorial, and design skills to the author team. Together with their four kids they manage a small farmstead in Minnesota, where, besides taking care of the animals and gardens, they also run an event venue and small campground. If you'd like to know more, you can find the Ribbeys on Instagram @j.e.ribbey or at their website JERibbey.com.

Made in the USA
Columbia, SC
22 December 2024

50385612R00183